ALSO BY JANICE ELLIOTT

The Godmother
Angels Falling
The Kindling

A STATE
OF PEACE

A STATE OF PEACE

JANICE ELLIOTT

ALFRED · A · KNOPF

NEW YORK 1971

THIS IS A BORZOI BOOK
PUBLISHED BY ALFRED A. KNOPF, INC.

Copyright © 1971 by Janice Elliott
All rights reserved under International and Pan-American Copyright Conventions.
Published in the United States by Alfred A. Knopf, Inc., New York,
and distributed by Random House, Inc., New York.
Originally published in Great Britain by Hodder and Stoughton, London.

ISBN: 0-394-46919-4
Library of Congress Catalog Card Number: 79-154908
Manufactured in the United States of America

First American Edition

for Robert

Contents

A STATE
OF PEACE

Part One

"PEACE," said Mrs Armitage. She raised her glass of water.
She, if anyone, could transform it to wine. The young people
round the table acknowledged her power. Even the modest
dinner she invested with the properties of a feast. A candle
glowed by each place. Only Catherine, the younger
daughter, knew how her mother had run around after the
makings of this party, charming and bullying the ingredi-
ents from shopkeepers, presenting it now with the ease of a
goddess to whom miracles come naturally.

Catherine's stepsister, Olive, alone refused to fall under
the spell. She seemed tired and her nails were dirty. Crum-
bling bread, she looked round the table and saw that Christopher, her brother, was talking to Diana, the beautiful girl.
There was always a beauty at Mrs Armitage's parties.
Maurice, the civil servant, was explaining something about
the Ministry to Mrs Armitage, who nodded and smiled while
her eyes flashed around casting spears. Intended for me,
thought Olive, and saw that the American beside her, in
uniform, was looking at a peach, wondering how one ate
them in England. He had been responsible, apparently, for
the peaches and the butter. He was obviously amiable, ad-
justable, willing to learn to eat his meat with a knife and
fork, though he was rich enough, Olive guessed, to eat with
his fingers if he liked. He was one of Mrs Armitage's young
men, a succession of courteous, pliant creatures who turned
up at the door with parcels of butter, coffee, tinned meat and
chocolate. Christopher said they were spirits Mrs Armitage
summoned from the air and they would vanish the day war
ended. Harold looked solid enough.

Olive saw that Catherine's lids were drooping. She was

drowsy, just as though the water had indeed been wine.

Christopher said, "Wake up, Cat."

They looked at her. She flushed. Poor Cat, Olive thought, poor Cat, to live with our mother and to be sixteen, suddenly in the last two years so tall that she seemed among her family a big-breasted giantess, a fairground figure. No wonder when she entered the house she dipped her shoulders, ducked her head as if to be stoned.

They had been talking about the peace. Maurice was laying down the law, holding forth about the next, the Russian threat. Berlin, he said, would be the flashpoint, it was a matter of time, five, ten years if we were lucky. Delivered of this prophecy, he sank his long teeth into an apple. Olive imagined his stomach beneath the parliamentary waistcoat squeezing out digestive juices. Catherine was speaking:

"That's awful. We must have learned. There *can't* be another war."

Mrs Armitage smiled and stirred the beads at her throat.

Christopher said to the American, "My stepsister, Harold, is a romantic. The last of the few."

"I wonder," said someone, "if all we cynics are not repressed romantics?"

The American decided to peel his peach. Catherine was saved. They got from romanticism on to love, courtly and carnal, passion, love for partners, parents, children. Self-love. The American, who had not spoken, smiled at Catherine. Suddenly brave, she spoke up for love. Olive saw the courage this took, and thought, one day Cat will be hurt. Love was outvoted.

Olive, silent till now, was curious. She turned to the American. "What about you? You haven't said."

Now they looked at Harold. A moth fluttered among the candles. Lorries churned outside in the square. It was a September evening. There was no sign in the quiet streets of a peace having been won. Harold looked politely at his peach. Having peeled it, whether to slice it or not? They awaited his verdict.

4

"I think," he uttered in his soft voice, "that love is possible."

After dinner they drank Harold's coffee. Christopher put on some Schubert. Mrs Armitage passed coffee and seemed to bless them all. She willed them to agree, or to disagree only a little, to make her party a success. Her parties were mostly a matter of will. She wished Olive would pull herself together. It had been quite unnecessary for her to come in uniform. Her daughters puzzled her. She sighed.

The record ended. The silence was drawn out too long: in the distance an angel approached. Mrs Armitage shivered. Abruptly Christopher snapped on the lights. They were all caught out. Maurice, his long striped legs crossed above the knee, looked as though he were roosting. The beautiful girl had put her feet up on the sofa. Only Olive was sitting exactly as she had been before the light faded: hunched and smoking on the window-seat, turning the pages of a magazine she could not see in the dark. Yet not relaxed. Olive always looked, even in the moments when she made some effort to please, as if she were waiting to be attacked. Chris said she was pigheaded. He said one day she'd meet something she couldn't fight, and she'd crack her head. Catherine, who found that nowadays her attitudes to everyone were ambivalent, perpetually shifting between poles, mostly loved Olive, sometimes feared her.

Catherine took the tray downstairs. Olive followed her to get a drink of water. In the kitchen she found Catherine eating chocolate cake (Harold again) and talking to the cats. The cat was in the basket with its kittens. Olive smiled as Catherine bent over them, and the mother raised a warning paw and watched, wide-eyed with alarm as Catherine picked up one of the ratty scraps of fur. It was only a day old and still blind. She gave it a finger and it nosed and sucked.

Olive drank the water, washed the glass and put it to drain. She flung open a window. She was tired yet tense, both thankful for the peace and inwardly raging, desperate

5

like someone running in a dream again and again against a high, unscalable brick wall. She groaned. "Oh God, those people!"

"They scare me," said Catherine. "I wish we could just stay here in the kitchen."

"They make me angry."

Upstairs again, Mrs Armitage was talking. "It is quite appalling but if it was the only way I suppose we must accept it. In the end lives will have been saved."

"But if we could simply have shown them we had it?"

"Not enough. It had to be *used*. Imagine, if you were fighting a war with bows and arrows and someone came along with a gun who would believe you if you didn't fire it? And kill with it?" Maurice explained patiently. The beautiful girl watched him, nodding as he made each point. She was clearly impressed. Christopher yawned. Olive thought, in a moment Maurice will say, you can't make an omelette without breaking eggs. Maurice said, "You can't make an omelette without breaking eggs. It was a political necessity." Christopher winked at Olive.

Mrs Armitage shook her head, not in contradiction but with grave sadness, as if she were in church.

"Like the Russians, I suppose. One doesn't care for them, but one had to put up. And now we have these reds in Parliament. Those funny dull little men actually singing The Red Flag in the House. They'll sell us out. You see."

Christopher said mildly, "They're Socialists, mother, not Communists."

"What's the difference?" Her sombre mood, though still theatrical, was deepening. "I don't think I shall care very much to live in this world."

Olive spoke abruptly from the place she had taken up again in the window-seat. They were startled to be reminded of her presence.

"And what was so marvellous, mother, about yours? What was so fine about suffering so that you could live in power and privilege? Everything you've said has been foul." Now

6

she turned on them all. She could hear her own voice, running on, pleading, see their astonished faces turned to her. Even while she was speaking she saw herself behaving in a way that was utterly boorish and unforgivable, and worst of all, futile. "Don't you see, it's the first chance we've had? At last we might create something sane, a society in which this could never happen again. Don't you see the danger? That awful bomb. Do you *know* how many it killed? And it doesn't just kill, it poisons. Twenty years from now people will be dying of it, like medieval lepers. No one will know how to treat them. They may be sterile. They may have deformed children, monsters." There was an awkward silence in which Olive smoked, broken by Christopher, the peacemaker.

"But, Olly love, what do we *do*? Crawl on our knees to Hiroshima?"

"Something like that. That would be a start." Her hand was shaking.

"Sooner you than me."

Mrs Armitage began to speak to Maurice, telling in her clear, pleasant voice, a long, quite amusing story about a lost ration book and the rudeness of the authorities and the forms and forms it would be impossible ever to fill in. She was covering up, hoping to bury Olive's little scene. Maurice Leverett said he had a friend in the M.O.F. and something could surely be arranged. Diana said she must go and Maurice offered a little too promptly to drive her home. She looked at Christopher, who had brought her.

"You go," he said, but amiably, "I'm only a sailor. I don't get Ministry petrol."

Maurice looked stuffy. "Can I give anyone else a lift? Olive?"

"No," she said, then, "thanks, I'm staying the night."

Diana swept Maurice off. Mrs Armitage came back into the room. "There was no need, Christopher, to be rude to Maurice. I'm sure he gets no more petrol than anyone else."

7

"He's a pompous ass."

"Well." She moved around the room, touching cushions, emptying ashtrays. She was pleased with the way the party had gone, but it had been a strain. "My children are speaking their minds tonight. You would never believe it, Harold, but they can be quite nice."

"I think they're charming."

"Dear Harold. And now if you'll forgive me I'll go to bed. Don't go. You children stay. There's half a bottle of rum, somewhere, Christopher, I was saving. It wasn't enough to go round. But that at least we owe to Harold, the patron of the feast. Catherine, don't stay up too late."

It was Harold who opened the door for her. Olive thought he looked younger than she had imagined. He and Christopher looked at their glasses. Olive drank quickly.

Christopher said, "How's the lady's army?"

Olive pulled down her mouth. "The same."

Christopher explained to Harold, "My sister doesn't care for her national duty."

"I'm a rotten soldier."

"I think," said Harold, "we'll all be glad to get out."

Olive yawned. "I'm deadly tired." But she walked not to the door but the window. "It's funny, not having to pull the curtains. It's been a queer day, rather awful. It doesn't feel like peace. What does peace feel like?"

"Peaches," said Catherine, and smiled at Harold.

"Out of the mouths of babes." Christopher stretched. "Not being killed. Not being hungry. Being bawled out by someone different, not in uniform, who is kind enough to give one a job. With luck."

Harold said quietly, "I'll be sorry to leave Europe."

"You're mad. It's finished. Mother was right about that, even if she'd got the values wrong. Maurice Leverett's our master now. A world of Leveretts." Christopher groaned.

Olive said, "I thought he was a civil servant."

"He is. But that's what I mean. The world of the grey men. If I were you, Harold, I'd pack up and get out as fast as

8

you can. All the same, Olly, you went for mother."

"She deserved it."

"Not altogether. It's worse for her than us."

"I can't see that."

Harold said, "Then you think people are responsible for the times in which they live? In that case, are we proportionately guiltier than you because we dropped the bomb? How do you parcel out the guilt between those who made it, decided it should be dropped, condoned it, dropped it?"

Olive mumbled, "I wasn't blaming the Americans. We're all to blame. That's what I meant. We can't just shrug it off like mother."

Harold persisted gently, not arguing, but trying, apparently, to understand. "So we must all live in guilt? Isn't that asking too much?"

Olive shook her head. "I don't know. I'm tired. That was why I made that stupid scene, I suppose. It was pointless."

"On the contrary," said Harold, "I found it very interesting. I can't believe things will be so bad. But I should like to be here, to see how it turns out."

Olive smiled for the first time that evening. The rum had brought the colour to her cheeks. Just for the moment she looked handsome, the long hair humped into an untidy bun at the back of her head, but some brightness about her face. "Then you'd better come back," she said, "or you'll never know."

Christopher became busy, collecting glasses. "Time the children were in bed." Catherine felt sorry. She wanted this evening drawn out. It was the first time she had been admitted without teasing into an adult conversation.

Harold took his leave. The room seemed dull without him, though within it he had hardly disturbed the air. They watched him walk across the square, then Christopher turned off the lights. They were lost. It seemed like Christmas without a greeting. It was sad to part for the night as if this were any day in the year, just the end of another party.

9

"Look!" said Catherine. Christopher was asleep on the sofa. So it was Catherine and Olive who saw the children file around the square with candles, to show that the blackout had ended and, in this respect at least, the peace had begun.

OLIVE had to get back the next morning. She said she expected her demob quite soon. She imagined they'd be glad to get rid of her. Catherine sat at the foot of the bed while her stepsister pushed her night clothes into a khaki grip. When Olive was home they shared a room. The top floor and the basement had been let—better, Mrs Armitage said, than being requisitioned. Mrs Armitage had an ambivalent attitude to the authorities: serfs, she believed when she needed them, to spring to her will; malicious zombies when they interfered with her life. By taking tenants, at however ludicrous a rent, she had, she felt, cheated the forces of a world of which she strongly disapproved. In this fashion, by such small victories, she had in her way enjoyed the war, blotted out with trivia the true horror of summary extinction.

Catherine watched, fascinated, while Olive crammed her dark hair into its bun, sticking in grips vaguely, like pins in a cushion.

"You're a good driver."

"Anyone can drive a car." Olive screwed up her face at the mirror, a pin in her teeth. The bun collapsed. "Damn. I wanted to escape before Mother got up. I made a fool of myself last night."

"It was that sort of night. Mother will forget. She always does. I liked Harold."

"He's all right, I suppose." Olive groaned and sat down, her hair half fixed. Half up and half down, she looked like a mad gipsy. She lay back on the bed and groped for a cigarette. "Honestly, Cat, I don't think I can bear to go back."

"It won't be long."

Olive sighed, sat up and touched Catherine's knee. "Poor Cat. You're only a child, and we talk to you like an old woman. You'll have to watch out later. You're the sort of person people batten on to."

"I don't think I'd mind that. I like people. And I'm not a child."

"Sorry, I'm sure." Olive's second of tenderness passed. She swung off the bed, finished her hair and was ready to go. "Cheer up. It's not the end of the world, whatever I said last night."

"I'm all right." Catherine looked down glumly at her sensible lisle legs. She was getting the curse. She felt like an elephant. She wanted to be old enough to talk properly to Olive, Christopher, anyone who would listen. She was like someone stuck in a door. She loved Olive. If she could live with Olive, and listen to her, she would be happy. Since that was unlikely she dreamed, in fanciful moments of which she was later ashamed, of bestowing blessings upon her loved ones: to Christopher, a marvellous job, to Olive a husband (which surely she wanted however much she pretended otherwise); and in a surge of saintly benevolence, riches upon her mother. She truly wanted them content, but she longed also for gratitude, to be loved as she loved them, to be marvellously, brilliantly loved for the generosity which she recognised to be her single and sometimes shaky asset. She meant well. That much even Mrs Armitage gave her. What an epitaph. She must have sighed because Olive paused, smiling, in the door.

"You *are* down."

Catherine mused, chin propped on her knuckles, "Harold did seem nice."

Olive grunted. "I can't think where mother digs up these leprechauns."

"He's too tall for a leprechaun. He's very young to be a captain. He's frightfully rich and his uncle grows peaches. Harold can't decide whether to grow peaches, or stay in England or be a tycoon, mother said."

12

"Poor Harold. Hard luck." Olive shrugged. "I'm off before Madam catches me."

The stepsisters did not kiss. Catherine saw her off, stood for a while on the pavement regarding a world that was not after all transformed by peace, then like a conspirator, slipped back into the house. Christopher came down rubbing his eyes and grumbling about shaving water. They heard Mrs Armitage stir above.

"Don't you know there's a war on," said Catherine, then remembered, and they laughed.

Mrs Armitage decided after all to take peace by the horns. Failing the easing of restrictions they had all hoped for, she improvised. Catherine was to leave school at once, and, since it was clear she would never get into a university, she must learn shorthand typing, flower arrangement, French or cookery. Maurice Leverett must find a job for Christopher. Olive must pull herself together. This meant, of course, marriage, but meanwhile a nice job where she could meet men and look her best.

Her children always said Mrs Armitage would have made a good crook. In her fiddling, her daring excursions into the black market there was a childish pleasure, an innocence and an odd moral code of her own making. She would take eggs, stockings and cigarettes, but never petrol, because petrol was needed for the war effort. She would take anything from the Americans, because the Americans, she said, grew fat while Europe starved. All this she did with the greatest charm, graciously cowing infatuated shopkeepers, haggling like a fishwife with marketeers, accepting, goddess-like, her due from those who had to give.

Mrs Armitage liked to be in control of her world and to a large degree succeeded. Only her daughters escaped her: Olive grown shabby and sullen in these last years of the war; Catherine difficult in a more practical way—shooting up so fast no amount of make do and mend could keep pace. As if to compensate for a lack of direction in her temperament,

13

she grew, upwards and outwards. Watching her daughter embattled against the physical world, awkward with her hands, clumsy among her mother's furniture, Mrs Armitage wondered if she had created a monster. Had forty been too old to bear a child? One heard things. One was sometimes afraid and rose, aching from the night's fears which could not, unlike the bombs, the war, Teddy's death, be named and therefore could not be faced. Unchallenged, they lived, like spirits in trees, in the fabric of Mrs Armitage's life. They could not be exorcised, only stilled, the cracks stuffed through which they might speak. Mrs Armitage was afraid to be still. She was admired for her vitality. She held the plum velvet up against Catherine. It was like dressing a rock. Her mouth bristled with pins. She took them out and sighed.

Catherine was afraid of her mother. She loved her and feared that the velvet would be a failure. Her mother was sitting back, eyes narrowed, shaping the velvet in her mind. She decided. High neck. Long, narrow sleeves. Full skirt. The velvet had been curtains. It was marvellous it hadn't faded.

"There."

Catherine wanted a beautiful dress so much she dared not look. She knew her mother thought her ugly, believed the velvet would be wasted on her.

"Don't you want to look?"

"No. Not till it's finished."

"I don't believe you care how you look. I don't understand you. I wonder, sometimes, Catherine, what will become of you."

This was familiar. Catherine could seem to listen, head bowed. Sometimes she used to cry, afterwards, but she never quite despaired. Something would happen. It might be the dress.

When Olive heard about these scenes, never told but guessed, she was angry. One summer afternoon at Aunt Cat's in the country, Olive on leave quarrelling with Mrs Armi-

14

tage on the lawn. Sound travelled on waves of heat to Catherine under the tree with a book.

"Selfish . . . entirely selfish . . . nothing of her."

"For her own good . . ."

". . . her good qualities. A child. You expect a child to be pretty and clever, to live your life for you, just because . . ."

". . . lonely. I can't expect my children to understand my life. Least of all . . . You at least. You and Christopher . . . so much."

Catherine huddled back close against the tree. She could neither show herself nor cover her ears. She was aware, as if this were something she must write down and remember for ever, of the startling greenness of the lawn, the shaking light which broke the quarrelling women into fragments of yellow linen, Olive's sea-green dress. Mrs Armitage almost invisible beneath the canopy, Olive raging in the full heat of the sun:

"You didn't love him. You take it out on her."

Aunt Cat came across the lawn carrying a tray. Olive ran indoors. Catherine stayed under the tree. She was twelve.

Edith Armitage was first married, when she was Edith Drury, to Edward Asher because he stole her glove. He stole it in 1914 at a dance, and carried it through the war like a knight his lady's token. Edith was already twenty-five, handsome, unmarried because easily bored. Teddy Asher, of the high coloured cheeks, pale moustache and blue eyes, left before he could bore her. Like the last person seen before sleep, they remembered one another through the war. She was his talisman. If he had been the praying type he would have prayed to her picture, if he had had a picture. While he was away Edith Drury remarked that Teddy Asher wasn't bad. Then she said she hoped he'd get through. Even before he returned she supposed she might marry Teddy. When she saw him she was seized for the first and last time in her life, at the age of thirty, by love.

Passion survived the births of Olive and Christopher.

15

Would boredom have set in? The war had suited Teddy Asher. Peace dulled his features. He might have grown heavy but died first, under a bus. A dark night, a wet pavement; a friend, Charles Armitage, a bit of a wag with a face like a split orange, called out to warn him, but had to tell Edith. She scared him, as much in her grief as her former content. He felt bound to call, grew attached to the children. As Edith's spirits improved he clowned for her and wagged like a dog when she laughed. He enjoyed pleasing her. She missed him when he was not there. It seemed obvious they should marry.

IN the icy room in South Molton Street Miss Wilson dipped her blue nose into her utility handkerchief, sniffed and regarded with watery and disenchanted eye a dozen young females, heads bent over their pads. She pounced:

"Catherine Armitage, transcribe."

Catherine looked hopelessly at the half page of meaningless squiggles. They danced and swam. One wild loop she had decorated with ears and whiskers. Her fingers were blue. Miss Wilson wore purple mittens. Outside in the street people toppled against the February wind. A slim girl in grey seemed to be blown into the arms of a tall man in uniform. They kissed and walked away, sloping against one another. Rosalie Todd is in love with her cousin. She is writing to him in her shorthand notebook. Barbara Blake has a moustache. Rebecca Davies is nice and pretty. She has curling brown hair and a cheerful chin. She had the curse when she was twelve. No one looks at Catherine, scenting one of Willy's ritual sacrifices to the god of shorthand typing. Rebecca looks sorry.

Catherine has written in the back of her notebook:

Rebecca Davies is nice and pretty
Rosalie Todd is in love with her cousin
I wish Olive would come home
I don't mind not being beautiful. I DON'T MIND
Every day in every way I get better and better. Not true
Willy is silly

Catherine stood. She looked at the ears and whiskers. Rebecca had scribbled a query at the bottom: Rabbit? Cat?

Dear Sir,
   We are in receipt of yours of the . . . We are in receipt
. . . We have received your letter of the . . . We . . .

Willy waited, a killing half smile on her face.
"I'm sorry, Miss Wilson. I can't read it back."
"Perhaps, Catherine, I can help you if you care to bring your book."
Horror. An expression of gruesome sympathy from Rebecca. Under the cover of her arm Rosalie Todd pulled two pages out of her pad and pushed them in her pocket. Catherine knew a girl who had fits. You could faint if you held your breath the right way. Chris used to do it in chapel at school.
Miss Wilson, still smiling, took the pad. She glanced through the letter to be transcribed. Her smile grew radiant. She began to turn the pages. Strike me dead, oh Lord, let the world end, Catherine prayed. She held her breath. Nothing happened except that her ears buzzed. Then suddenly, just as Miss Wilson must have reached that hideous last page, everything happened.
There was a moan, then a chair crashed. Catherine hardly dared to turn, fearing what her prayer might have brought down. The bossy Barbara Blake, Greek messenger to calamity, announced, "It's Rebecca, Miss Wilson. She seems to be ill."
"Put her head between her knees."
"She's going to be sick."
"She's a frightful colour."
Rebecca reclined, broken apparently, her head tipped oddly sideways. Rosalie Todd whimpered and patted her hands. Someone flapped paper in her face. Everyone was concerned, excited, warm for the first time that day. Anarchy was possible.
Miss Wilson spoke. "Everyone will leave the room. You may take your luncheon early." Rebecca was removed to the sickroom. Barbara Blake looked put out.
"Coming?"

18

"No," said Catherine. "I'll have sandwiches here."

"You were lucky. In the knickers of time."

"Yes."

The Blake snorted. She looked suspicious and left unwillingly. Catherine ate her Spam sandwiches. She was shocked by her appetite. There seemed no end to childhood. You felt grown and then you said something stupid, or ate like a pig or someone laughed at you. You had so many thoughts but no one, even Olive, really listened. Would her father have listened? He slapped his pockets: well, old lady, I'm off. Under orders. He smelled nice. He had nice hands. He made her laugh. She was ten.

A door slammed. Feet were coming along the corridor. What if Rebecca died? Oh God, father in heaven, let Rebecca live, let me be struck down if Rebecca lives and Olive is happy and my mother does not die. Let my father be all right.

It was Miss Wilson's step in the corridor. Let Willy find my notebook if Rebecca will not die.

"Ah, Catherine. Since you are here you had better take Rebecca home."

"Is she all right, Miss Wilson?"

"Of course she's all right. She's been sick and she's sorry for herself."

Rebecca didn't look right at all. She smiled bravely at Catherine and Miss Wilson, helping her down the narrow stairs. Miss Wilson sniffed. She did not like young females. She had never been one. Youth, like illness and fear, was a state of mind to which one did not give way. Miss Wilson had stayed in London right through the buzz bombs. She had refused to go to the shelter. She had lain each night in her small room and looked fear in the face. She had kept watch. Towards morning she had slept and dreamed she was a child.

Rebecca walked hunched, as if she had a spike in her middle. Her soft hair was plastered in damp whorls to her forehead. She held a handkerchief to her mouth.

In the taxi going to St John's Wood she suddenly gasped, flung herself on her side and made a strange choking noise. Catherine was terrified. She liked Rebecca but hardly knew her. She was rich, pretty, exotic; she wore rings and lipstick; she was a soft animal with padded paws. Should Catherine stop the taxi and take her to a hospital? What if she died on the way home?

Finally Rebecca sat up, still choking. Her face was pink and tears were running down her cheeks. She was laughing.

"How did it go? Did I do it all right?"

"You mean you were putting it on? You scared us to death and all the time you weren't ill at all?"

"Of course."

"But *why*?"

"For you, you goose! I couldn't just sit there and let Willy eat you alive."

"But how did you do it? You looked frightful."

"I felt frightful. I pushed my finger down my throat. It's quite easy but foul. I wouldn't do it for anyone."

Catherine was awed and intensely happy.

The Davies family lived in a flat in a modern block built just before the war. There was a carpet in the hall and a porter. There was even a carpet in the lift which carried Catherine regularly once a week after that first visit, up to heaven. Her mother, she guessed, would have called Mrs Davies common, though Mrs Armitage would not have used the word any more than she would have said that Sara Davies was fat, vulgar and Jewish. She would simply have looked vague when she was mentioned, if she had known her. Sara Davies wore satin in the afternoons and a frilly apron. She was in contact, in a way Catherine had never seen before, with the physical. When she spoke to her children she touched them. Love to her was something quite ordinary, immediately accessible, to be expressed in this touching, in food, in kissing on meeting and parting. Her children laughed at her, kindly. Her dark husband remained obstin-

20

ately thin. Ah, my Moshe, she sighed, how can we then fatten you up? Yet she was proud of his perverse, handsome thinness, as if it were a gift. They were not orthodox, but they kept Fridays. Catherine basked, astonished by the ease with which they accepted her. The family opened, like a circle around a fire, to let her in.

The two girls spent many Saturday afternoons and some evenings in Rebecca's room. Catherine had no illusions about her new friend. There was no question of worship. Rebecca was a warm, kind cat, pretty, composed, wilful but too lazy to scratch. She lay back on her bed, hair in curlers (Rebecca was always going somewhere). Catherine prowled the room.

"That's a new lipstick."

"Try it."

Catherine sat on the padded stool, outlined her mouth and pressed her lips together.

"Ugh."

Rebecca propped herself on her elbow.

"Mmm. You do look a bit odd. Sort of mad. Interesting."

"I wish I were."

Catherine wiped her mouth. Her whole face looked smudged. The mirror gave back a white blur. Who was she? Rebecca talked about her family which was enormous and spread all over Europe. She had German cousins, Polish cousins, a Russian uncle, a whole American branch. They were mostly English or American now, because of the war. They had marvellous names: Solomon, Samuel, Ruth and Isaac. Benjamin, her father's brother, settled in Palestine before the war. Isaac's father died in Warsaw.

Rebecca asked, "What happened to your father?"

"I don't know. He went away."

"Did you like him?"

"Yes."

"Then why don't you find him?"

"Mother wouldn't like it. And I don't know where he lives." This was not true. There was an address, five years old. Catherine knew it by heart: 5 Arnold Row, Battersea. Rebecca's sharp eyes glinted. Catherine began to talk about Olive coming home, Christopher's row with Mrs Armitage about Maurice Leverett's job. She told Rebecca, it was awful at home at the moment, they only stopped fighting when Harold was there.

"Who's Harold?"

"An American, though you'd hardly know he was."

"What does he look like?"

Catherine pondered. "Tall, fair. Rather serious. He's like those knights you see on tombs."

"Have you got a crush on him?"

"Harold? Good heavens no."

"Why not?"

Catherine lay on her stomach on the floor. She felt ashamed of her inexperience. She had never had a crush on anyone, not a man at least. She liked Rebecca's brother, Sam. She thought Mr Davies was rather splendid. Ronald Colman in *Kismet* was all right. But passion had passed her by, certainly had no place in her feelings for Harold. Yet he was important.

"I just don't see him like that. And I doubt if he sees me at all."

Rebecca nodded, already bored. She hopped like a bee from one topic to another; there was no honey in Harold. She was madly, desperately in love with the most marvellous boy, but he wouldn't look at her. Catherine didn't believe a word of it.

Mrs Davies called from below, "And do I cook all this food and no one will eat it?"

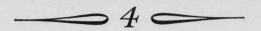

IT was a bleak spring. Rations were cut. Mrs Armitage complained. Olive and Christopher came home, cross as dogs; though Christopher was very cheerful the first week of his demob. He brought back presents, teased his mother and did jobs around the house, the sailor home from the sea. Time for a job, no hurry, he said, leave a chap alone. The second week he began to meet friends, old shipmates presumably, in pubs. In the daytime he skulked in his room reading newspapers and magazines. Catherine, dusting his bedroom, found a comic under a cushion.

Mrs Armitage said dried egg was bad enough but no dried egg was worse.

Christopher yawned. It was a cold evening, for spring. Harold had brought daffodils and they sat round them, like a fire. Harold sat next to Mrs Armitage on a pouffe at her feet, but his gaze was on Olive and she was aware of it, shared with him for a brief, faintly embarrassed flash, the picture of herself on the rug: the high cutting bones of her face, the chin a shade too emphatic, thick dark hair released now from its army bun in a coil at the back of her neck. "I must have it off, I must *cut* it," she had said frantically that morning. Now she pushed back with her fists the wings that fell each side of her parting, white as a scar. They had been talking again about the black market, fiddling.

"Everyone does it. You'd be hungry, not to mention thirsty, without it."

"I'd rather be hungry." Olive yawned. How easily, she thought, one falls into allotted roles. She did not really care so much where Mrs Armitage got her eggs or her whisky, and she enjoyed them herself cheerfully enough; yet because she was expected to care she protested and then found that she really did care.

Christopher responded idly, "Come off it, Olly. Who does it hurt if we get a dozen eggs or a bottle of booze over the odds?"

"I don't know." Olive spoke with her head averted, tracing with her finger the pattern of the rug. Having thrown out her challenge she had lost interest already in defending it. "I think, in a way, it hurts us all."

"I think," said Mrs Armitage, "that it's time you found a job. I can't imagine what's the matter with the pair of you. The war's over. We're all alive. Thanks to what you call fiddling we live, compared to most people, in comfort."

Harold surprised them. "I agree with Olive. The only thing is, I'm not sure I'm strong enough to act on it. One can see how one ought to behave in an ideal world. But you compromise, acknowledge your weakness . . ."

"Of course!" said Mrs Armitage. "We've spent so long surviving, just holding on, ethics are a luxury we simply can't afford."

"And without them?" Olive was looking at Harold. They might have been alone. Mrs Armitage felt herself excluded. "Where does that end? Who can live by the easy way out?"

"I don't know," said Harold, and he smiled because Olive looked so fierce. "I really don't know."

"Anyway," said Olive. "I've got a job."

Olive astonished them all. Not only had she found a job—working as an orderly in the local hospital—but she enjoyed it. The pay was poor but then if you had the money, there was nothing to buy. The hospital provided overalls, which saved clothes. Night work left her the afternoon free, after a morning's sleep. Later, some time, something more permanent would turn up. Meanwhile this was not only a job but one she liked.

"You forget yourself," she explained vaguely to Catherine. "It makes everything you worry about seem silly. Not because you're doing good—you don't think much about that over bedpans—but because you're just too *busy* to think. You're tired all the time, but even that's all right, being tired. Do you see?"

Catherine thought. "Yes. But I couldn't do it."

They were having lunch in a small restaurant near the typing school. Olive had come up to the West End to buy some shoes. Normally careless about her appearance, she would make a sudden slapdash effort about twice a year which left her, exhausted, in possession of new clothes that might be frightful or marvellous. At these times she shopped (as far as her coupons permitted) like a drunkard, apparently with her eyes closed. Mrs Armitage groaned. Olive yawned and said clothes were boring. She had never met a man she cared about enough to dress for his pleasure. And no man she could respect would consider clothes important. That was what she said when she was twenty. Now, when she might feel differently, the habit stuck and became part of the odd, seemingly motiveless defiance which was her nature.

Most of the other lunchers were women, assistants from the department stores in Oxford Street, typists and shoppers. Catherine was still eating. Olive smoked.

"You could. And you'd do it for the right reasons. You're the good one in the family."

"How awful. I don't feel good. I'd rather be pretty." She didn't mean pretty, she meant beautiful, like Olive. As well as the shoes, Olive had bought, on an impulse, a queer, burnt-orange scarf, very long and thin. Grinning, she wrapped it round and round her throat. The only man in the restaurant stared. Olive had already forgotten it.

"Pretty! What good is that? It's a disadvantage, really. The better looking you are, the less inclined people are to take you seriously."

"But if you're plain no one even notices you."

"Cat! Stop running yourself down. It's boring."

"Sorry."

"And don't creep. Look at these shoes." Olive fished in her carrier bag and plonked them down on the table. They were awful. The sisters laughed. The waitress looked shocked. "But you must admit they're frightfully *good*."

Catherine gasped. Giggling was one thing, like eating, that caught you out. "It's bad luck to put new shoes on the table."

"I don't believe in luck."

They paid the bill and walked out into the street. It was one of those hallucinatory, windy, sunny days of spring when this seemed a good time after all. A barrow at the corner was laden with lilac and daffodils. Catherine sniffed at the warm air.

"What do you believe in, then?"

"Sticking it out."

"It must be better than that?"

"Perhaps it is. Yes, it must be. We're not dead, we can still change things. It could be marvellous."

"Marvellous!" echoed Catherine, and the two girls walked off quickly towards Grosvenor Square, where rooks whirled in the higher trees, sign of a good summer.

Life for a few weeks was comparatively peaceful. Olive, busy with her job, found it easier than usual to be forebearing with Mrs Armitage. Vaguely, she worried about Catherine, who seemed alternately depressed and elated, but Catherine spoke of a friend she had made at the typing school, she was often out and surely, if she were really unhappy, she would ask for help? It never occurred to Olive that her stepsister might find her alarming.

Olive herself had been out once or twice with Harold Peterson, who was now permanently in London, seconded to the Embassy. She had met someone at the hospital, a patient now discharged, who had been in with psoriasis, a nervous skin complaint. When Olive first encountered him he was nearly cured and had talked to Olive about some kind of welfare group he ran in the East End. At first Olive was merely curious about Dennis Rawston. He seemed so little her idea of a social worker—more a wild, half-starved young prophet. Yet extraordinarily methodical: he was always working, reading, writing messages. Rather to her astonishment, Olive found herself acting, off-duty, as an unofficial secretary, looking up references in libraries, making telephone calls on his behalf. He made no attempt to convert her either to his cause or to his left-wing politics, but his intensity served to kindle further the shapeless discontent which had led to her outburst at Mrs Armitage's party. She said nothing to him of her own feelings—he would find them naïve, but she began to regret, increasingly, the day he would be discharged. She told herself this was simply because she would be unlikely to see him again and she would miss their talks. He was a kind of person she had never met before, living a life she could envisage only vaguely and never for herself.

She was wrong in thinking he would not seek her out again. He was waiting one day at the hospital gates, a pale young man in a shabby raincoat. He came straight to the point, brushing aside her questions about his health. There was to be an important meeting, something to do with the housing situation. Did she want to come?

While they were talking Catherine approached. She had taken the long way round from the bus to meet Olive at the hospital. Dennis seemed anxious to be off.

"Can you make it, then?"

"I'll do my best."

"That's good." He nodded abruptly, as if a debating point had been settled satisfactorily, then suddenly he smiled and touched her hand. She saw how he got people to do things for him. "See you, then."

Catherine joined her. "Who was that? Someone to do with the hospital?"

Olive shrugged and thrust her hands deep in her pockets. "In a way." They walked on, then she said suddenly, as if Catherine had pressed the question, "Dennis Rawston. He

27

was a patient. He runs a sort of group. I said I might go to a meeting."

"He didn't look well."

"He's not strong. He does too much."

The chestnuts were out in the square. Pigeons whirred and settled on the roofs. After a showery day the sky was swept. It was a beautiful, distracting evening. Catherine wished she had something to do. She felt, with prescience, that what Olive had to say was important, she should listen. She waited. Olive went on, answering some dialogue, question and answer sustained in her own mind, "He wears me out. I couldn't put up with him for long. God help the silly girl who falls for him. But I've never met anyone like him."

"In what way?"

"I don't know." Olive pulled a face. "I suppose he's good. That sounds so frightful and worthy. I mean—it's all mixed up with politics and, whatever he thinks, he's out of his depth there—but while the rest of us moan about the state of things, he tries to do something. He really cares about people."

"Will you go to the meeting?"

"I might."

Catherine would have liked to ask more, but now they were in and Harold was waiting to take Olive to the theatre. She was always vague about these evenings. Catherine lay awake until Olive came in and went straight to bed. She slept at once. Catherine turned in bed, quietly, not to disturb her sister.

Oh God, let Olive marry Harold Peterson and have breakfast in bed for the rest of her life and be happy even if she goes to America and I never see her again. Let her not be hurt or disappointed.

Catherine said to Rebecca Davies, "Everyone says nothing will ever be the same again, but if you don't remember how it used to be, what are you supposed to feel?"

Rebecca said, "You think too much."

Harold said, "You ought to be bothering about yourself."

28

Rebecca said, "If I wanted to see my father so much, I'd go and find him. Nothing would stop me."

One night when Catherine got home from Rebecca's Mrs Armitage was having a flaming row with Christopher.

"You'll do as you like, whatever I say."

"Yes."

"Maurice Leverett has found you a job."

"I prefer, mother, to find my own."

"This Toby Tait . . ."

"He's all right. He's a friend."

When Mrs Armitage had gone to bed Christopher sat on. The light had gone out of the sky. Christopher was drinking but not drunk.

"Cat?"

"Yes?"

"What's a chap to do?"

"I don't know what you want to do."

"Something of my own, for a change, that's all. Something I've settled, no one else. Build boats in Hampshire with my friend Toby Tait. Madam doesn't like Toby Tait, or boats or Hampshire, or anything she hasn't fixed herself." He walked to the window. "I'm no good at rows." He turned. "Is it too much to ask? The only thing I've ever wanted. Not much."

"No. If you really want it."

He had been talking to himself. Now he seemed to notice her.

"What do *you* want, Cat?"

Catherine decided that night to find her father. Like Christopher, she would have something of her own. It was so obvious, she wondered why she had not thought of it before. It was all very well asking God, but there were some things you had to do yourself.

5

In May Mrs Armitage went to stay with Aunt Cat. She did not like the country. It disturbed her, she felt doubts, draughts, resented the relentless application of nature to its own concerns, the self-renewing, self-destructive cycle of growth and decay. "Man," she said, "was made for towns or he would go on all fours." But she went, for bridge and food and a change.

While she was away Christopher brought Toby Tait to the house. He was a lean, brown-looking man with a crooked, secret smile and pointed ears. He had the air of a gipsy or a gentleman jockey. They sat for hours over plans, drinking the thin beer which was all you could get. They had served together. Tait had been torpedoed in the North Atlantic and walked with a limp. Christopher, the younger by five years, clearly admired him.

"He's got drive. He gets things done. There's no one else I'd go in with on a thing like this."

While her mother was away Catherine had been experimenting. She had let out an old black dress of Olive's, borrowed a lipstick from Rebecca and done her hair in a new way. Olive didn't notice. Rebecca said it made her look marvellous, like the whore of Babylon. Catherine spent hours before the mirror, transfixed and horrified.

Christopher finally looked up from his plans. He was the first man she had tried her new self on.

"My God, what have you done to yourself?"

"Don't you like it?"

"You look like a tart."

"I'd rather look like that than . . ."

"What?"

"Me." She peered again in the sitting-room mirror. He was right.

"Isn't it awful!" She began to laugh. She pulled the pins out of her hair and kicked off the shoes. Olive was out with Harold. It was nice to have Christopher to herself. While Mrs Armitage was away they led a wonderful, picnic life, eating vague meals at odd times. "Are you hungry?"

She made some sandwiches and tea. The cats, normally banned from the sitting room, followed her up.

"Where will you get the money?"

"Gratuity. And Madam."

"She won't like Toby. She'll say his eyes are too close together."

"She'll pay up."

Catherine thought how nice it would be to be Christopher, to be someone for whom in the end, in spite of everything, people paid up, pledged themselves. She could imagine girls dying for him. The cats crawled all over him, even the scratchy mother. Mrs Armitage would pay, regardless of the distance between Toby Tait's eyes. Chris had charm, a charmed life.

"You're lucky."

"I suppose I am. It scares me. I do nothing for it."

"Olive's not."

"No."

"What was my father like?"

Christopher pushed away his plate and lit a cigarette. Catherine thought he was quite astonishingly, brilliantly good-looking. He looked content. He was like a cat who settles where it is fed. He flattered by accepting the tribute the world gives to the amiable and beautiful. He pondered Catherine's question.

"I liked him. I was only a kid when I really knew him, but he was good with children. He never seemed to be bored by us, or if he was, he didn't show it, and we weren't even his. He was great on treats, not obvious things, or expensive, but things kids like, Madam would never think of. It's funny, but I used to think he was lucky."

"Wasn't he?"

"Depends what you mean. Mother kicked him out. Perhaps that was luck. There was a woman, you know about that. You were too young, but it was quite a scene, Madam going on and Charlie couldn't finish packing his bags. She threw them after him downstairs. Poor old Charlie."

Christopher was expansive tonight. He was happy about Toby Tait and the boatyard. It had been fantastic luck to land the right job. Life had a way of sorting itself out. Catherine took advantage of his mood. She was greedy.

"Why poor?"

"I don't know. It's the sort of thing you say about Charlie, silly I suppose. There were chaps in the war like that. They were always the ones who got left out of the lifeboat, lost an arm or a leg or a wife." The light was fading. It was a struggle for Christopher to understand another person, but he was interested. "They don't get killed. They survive. Someone gets up a benefit and you think: poor sod."

"But if he really cared for this woman . . . ."

"He did. I saw her once, she was a stunner."

"Then he *must* be happy?"

"Yes. Perhaps he is. I hope so. He was all right."

Olive came in. She looked pretty, smarter than usual. Harold always put her in a good temper.

"I must say, money is nice. Who's all right?"

"Charlie."

In the bedroom Catherine was in bed first watching Olive undress.

"Where did you go?"

"A new place. Standard courses, but very good. Black market."

"Your principles?"

Olive grinned. "I rested them." She brushed her hair. "I'm human. And Harold is very—persuasive."

Catherine hoped. "You do like him, then?"

"Enough to go to dinner with, nosey." She turned off the

33

light and climbed into bed. "What about Charlie?"

"I was asking Chris. Did he really love that woman terribly?"

"I don't think so. When mother chucked him out, she was there. He wasn't the sort of person to live alone. He was a bit like Chris in a way, or how Chris might be in a few years, though he wasn't his father."

For Catherine, the picture was still blurred, incomplete. There was so much she wanted to ask, but Olive's breathing was shallow and measured. She was falling asleep.

"Then he did mind going?"

"Oh yes."

"For mother? Because he liked the family, children?"

"Partly, yes. He was *in* love with her. He was fond of us. But you were the only one he really loved. In the end, for Charlie, there was only you."

Catherine was so happy she thought she might die in her sleep. But in the morning she woke and it was her secret that this was not just another day. Her life was changed and glorified. Before, she had seemed the only one without a purpose. Now, in her own way, like Olive and Chris, she had somewhere to go.

6

CATHERINE did not go at once to find her father in Battersea, because in June Rebecca asked her, or rather commanded her, to join the Davies family on holiday in Bournemouth. The school was closed for six weeks.

"What will you do?"

"Nothing." Catherine knew perfectly well what she meant to do. Once or twice she had almost told Rebecca, but instinctively, with an effort like holding your breath, kept her secret. She thought Rebecca was adorable but amoral. She would not change her, but neither would she trust her. If she went on holiday with her the effort might be too much. She could burst. In a way, she wanted to burst.

"Then you'd better come with us."

"I can't afford it."

"Don't be stuffy. Daddy will pay."

"My mother might not let me."

"Ask her."

"Of course," said Mrs Armitage, "it would do you good. When I was your age I went everywhere."

"Where?"

"Where?" said Harold Peterson.

"The Elephant and Castle."

"I'll take you."

"No," said Olive, "you wouldn't like it."

"I wouldn't mind. Unless," he said, "you don't want me to come?"

"I don't. I'm sorry. I don't know why." They were walking in the park. It was a fine, late afternoon in summer and Olive saw with a pang of regret the couples twined on the grass. It might have been nice. Harold had guessed, as usual, what she was thinking.

"It seems a pity on an evening like this." He added, "I'm selfish, of course, I want you to stay with me. But you do miss something . . ."

"I know."

"You don't mind?"

"I don't stop to think."

That was not true. She thought, I'm happy with him, mindless. To marry him would be the happy, vacant, easy choice. *Too* easy. She touched his hand.

"I can go right through, from here, on the northern line."

He looked doubtful. "What's the Elephant and Castle?"

"A place. A pub. A Spanish princess, though you wouldn't know it."

"Oh."

She went into the Underground. Harold walked back to the park and sat for a while until he grew cold.

When Olive arrived the meeting had already started. She slipped in beside Dennis Rawston.

"Who's that?"

"Larry Towers. London District Committee."

"Oh."

Dennis sat with his hands clenched on his knees, leaning forward. Larry Towers was a skinny, terrier man with a pale moustache. He was a dull speaker but clearly, from the reception he was given, a star. Olive wondered why. The atmosphere in the hall made her sleepy, and for a second she actually slept, dreaming in a bright green flash of the brilliant park, Harold sloping beside her, shining water, and rich children running with expensive toys. The hall was dark. She shivered and blinked. The meeting was over. Dennis was stuffing papers in his pockets. They were to meet Larry Towers in the pub.

Crossing the road, he took her elbow.

"Sorry I dropped off. I was on at the hospital last night."

36

"I'm glad you came." It was a beautiful evening but Olive guessed that Dennis would never notice if the sun fell out of the heavens or the earth opened at his feet. Even his attention to her was, she imagined, perfunctory; anyone who listened would do. And yet, mercurial by nature and shifting in his moods, in her company he did seem at his most hopeful. Now as they stepped back for a tram to rattle past she could feel his impatience even at this small delay. His mind was running on. She wondered if he had eaten that day and told herself this was none of her business.

"What were they talking about while I was asleep?"

"Housing. But you missed nothing. What Larry has to say isn't for public consumption. I hope he'll tell us now."

"He's a Communist, isn't he?"

"Yes."

"Are you?"

They were in the pub now, waiting for Larry Towers. Dennis knew the barmaid and got Olive a gin. He did not drink himself, but he lit a cigarette and seemed to relax a little, though he kept his eye on the door.

"No." He grinned. "But I don't mind who I run with if I get what I want."

"The ends justify the means?"

"Most of the time, if it's the only way to get things done. You don't agree?"

She smiled. Larry Towers was coming towards them. "In theory. In practice I'm a coward or a Puritan. I can't stand cheating, devious methods. I suppose I'm simple. I . . ."

"But don't you *see* . . ."

Larry Towers sat down. Olive was puzzled by the way Dennis jumped like a lackey to serve him, yet there was something about him, as there is about all single-minded people. Dennis, for all his passion, was vulnerable. Nothing would break Larry Towers, because doubt was beyond him. She listened. Larry explained that London District was forming squatters' committees to take over empty flats and houses. There were many such places, unlettable because of

37

high rents, or requisitioned in the war and now abandoned. They talked for half an hour about ways and means, then Olive asked, "What about the police? I'm sure it's a brilliant idea, but the fact remains, it's illegal."

Dennis looked at Larry.

"She's right. What's the point if someone's going to chuck them out the morning after?"

"We've thought about that. Don't worry. Leave the details to us."

Dennis looked doubtful. "I don't like violence."

"There'll be none." Towers had a grating voice. He was very neat, almost dapper in a drab way. He smelled of soap. Olive could not place him.

"Are you with us? That's all I need to know. If you want to find your friends some decent sort of life. If you're with us or against us?"

"I'm with you, of course."

"Right. Don't spread it around, that's all. I'll be in touch."

Larry left. Dennis turned in triumph to Olive. "What did you think of him?"

"I thought he looked like a hungry dog."

"He's our only hope."

"He could be using you."

"I don't care if he is."

They were walking to the tube station. On the tram lines Dennis stumbled.

"Talking of hunger, when did you last eat?"

"This morning."

"Have you got a job?"

He looked sheepish.

"I could find something for you, I think." Olive thought of Maurice Leverett and smiled to imagine what he would make of Dennis. "If you weren't fussy."

"I don't mind what I do."

"You'd have to behave."

"I'll do my best." She had not expected him to thank her.

He took what was offered not from apathy, but because his mind was elsewhere. There were times when she wanted to slap him. He wore her out. She was thankful not to be in love with him, to do what she did for him out of admiration, which had bounds. Then, suddenly, he charmed her. He took her hands in his. "I don't know what I'd do without you."

"You'd manage. You may have to."

"I hope not."

Then he went on to talk about Larry Towers. He said he had tried everything; this was their last chance.

Christopher got the money for the boatyard. He was, when you came down to it, amazingly practical. Olive thought he was sly. Somehow he got round Mrs Armitage. She did not like Toby Tait (whose eyes were too close together), or Hampshire, or boats, but she paid up. Chris dazzled her with figures. He bored her into submission until she yawned and paid and began to believe that it had all been her idea, from the start.

Catherine was enchanted by Bournemouth. She was convinced this must be what her mother meant by everywhere. The hotel was not in the town but above Studland Bay, among pines. At first she was alarmed.

"I've got nothing to wear."

Rebecca scoffed.

"No one dresses since the war."

"What will we do tomorrow?"

"Sam's got a dinghy."

"I've never been in a boat."

"Then it's time you did."

"How do you *know* so much?"

"I don't," said Rebecca, powdering her chest from her mother's puff. "I make it up as I go along."

They were in the parents' bedroom where Rebecca had gone to hunt among her mother's jewellery. Catherine was

39

impressed by the way her friend made free with Mrs Davies's property, flinging open cupboard doors, pulling dresses off hangers, bouncing on the deep, soft bed. The room altogether fascinated her, made her shiver at this invasion—licensed yet somehow daring—of a privacy and intimacy so intense it hung like a presence in the air. She sniffed Sara Davies's sweetness, Moshe's lime and said, "Do hurry up."

Mr Davies was, in a quiet way, a bit of a dandy. The lime was something he put on his face. His brushes were silver-backed. What would it be like, Catherine wondered, to live with a man? Not your father or your brother, but an alien and mysterious male invading with his own scents, habits and demands, everything private, personal, special to you. As long as Catherine could remember Mrs Armitage had her own room, even in the Charlie days. One did not enter Mrs Armitage's room except by invitation, which rarely came. Having burned to enter one was finally inside and longed at once to leave.

Rebecca chose a crystal necklace. Catherine refused pearls. She felt sad.

"What's the matter, Hog?"

"Nothing."

Dinner was best, for it supplied Catherine's two principal delights: food—enormous, incredible, undreamed-of quantities of food—and the chance to observe. Rebecca chattered. Mrs Davies sparkled, literally, with diamonds. She had a gold tooth. She liked puddings. Her bright eyes ran around her children's faces, picked off for Moshe a favourite morsel.

"Mother!" Sam protested. Mr Davies, the only member of the family who was a poor eater, read his book propped against the water jug. "In a minute you'll want to see the kitchens."

"And so if I have?"

There was a family joke, something about Uncle Abraham and kosher cooking. Rebecca yawned. Catherine realised that she too was sleepy, stunned by experience, pines, sea, sun and everything that had happened since she arrived. The world seemed suddenly boundless. She shared a room with Rebecca. Although she was tired she could not sleep.

"Who's Uncle Abraham?"

"A rabbi in New York. He was once in the most awful fix, in the war somewhere. There was nothing to eat but pork. He was starving."

"What did he do?"

"He ate his boots."

In the morning they went sailing in Sam's dinghy. Sam had his father's good looks but he was plumper—not fat but cushioned. He was twenty-four, looked older, and combined with a sunny temper an ease with girls unusual at his age: the ways of a male genuinely, compassionately, lethargically (for he made little effort in that direction), interested in all females of any age, rank or disposition. Puberty had not disturbed him. Men bored him and presented, accordingly, no challenge to stir him to sexual adventure or to sulk. He smiled, nodded and looked round for a woman. His ease inspired women to frankness, his laziness reassured them. He might finish fat, unmarried, buying pictures; or a gross, heavy-lidded sultan in a silken tent. Within him struggled mildly English upbringing and Armenian ancestry, buttered toast and Turkish delight.

Catherine hardly noticed him.

Rebecca said he was uxorious.

"But he's not married?"

"Oh, Hog, you are dim!"

Catherine was intrigued by the formation of rocks at the corner of the bay.

"It looks like a door. Can we sail through?"

It was a rising tide so they could. They pulled the dinghy up to the beach and Rebecca said she was going to swim, at once, immediately. Sam yawned and pulled his linen hat over his eyes. The girls went into the water. At last Sam followed them, paddling out and back like a stolid dog look-

41

ing for a stick. They ate their sandwiches and he went to sleep.

Catherine and Rebecca walked along the beach.

"You are lucky, having such a marvellous family."

"Am I? I'd never thought."

"That's what I mean."

The cliffs here, beyond the door of rock—as if it really were a door to another world—were fabulous, carved like temples. The sea too was a deeper, more interesting blue. Charlie seemed a very small dot, a diminished (though not quite extinguished) secret in this wide, enthralling universe.

Catherine wondered, "Everyone says it's going to be awful, from now on."

"Look!" said Rebecca. She had found some seaweed, a silky, fragile green. "Wouldn't that make a super dress!"

"Olive, my sister, says the bomb changed everything."

"Don't be a bore, Hog. Just make up your mind what you want to do and do it."

"What do you want?"

"A husband, children, a lot of money. A *lot*." Rebecca threw the seaweed away. "It's slimy. What about you? You must want something? You've been looking sly. Have you fallen for handsome Harold?"

"Don't be silly."

"My father says you're deep. That's funny because he hardly notices people, except us. Have you got a Plan?"

"I might have. But there's no hurry. It can wait." The two girls were walking back along the fringe of the tide. Out to sea a little boat was becalmed, sails slack. Effortlessly Catherine resisted the urge to confide in Rebecca. "I don't want this to finish. It's the best holiday I've ever had."

The wind came up from the south-west and the sail back was quite exciting.

42

7

WHEN Catherine got home Olive told her that at the price of a dinner with Maurice Leverett she had found Dennis Rawston a job.

"I didn't want to ask him in front of mother," she said, "so I had to go to him. You can imagine how it was."

"Awful?"

"He was in his element. There's nothing he likes so much as being asked a favour. It suits his St Peter complex. He doesn't actually want to be God, but he loves holding the keys." She shuddered. "If your idea of heaven happens to be the Ministry of Works."

"Where did you go?"

"His flat. You know he lives with his mother in West Kensington. *West* Kensington! She's a sort of Eleanor of Aquitaine with very pink cheeks and very blue eyes. She explains a lot about our Maurice. She actually served junket."

"I like junket."

Olive did not hear. She still remembered vividly the horrors of the dinner. Maurice Leverett was her *bête noire* and there were few people on whose behalf she would have approached him as a beggar. Did this mean that she was interested in Dennis Rawston? She believed not, aware that while she liked to think her life was based on reason, she was frequently irrational. She talked about the survival of the fittest and spent half her time helping lame dogs over, or under stiles. She fumed at incompetence, woolly-mindedness, quixotic yearnings. Yet she admitted herself to be qualified for nothing, confused in her aspirations, susceptible to causes. Grudgingly she admired her mother because, as she said, Mrs Armitage was impossible but in her own way she had never compromised, she was misguided, hideously bigoted, but alive.

Catherine prompted her. "Well, what else did you have to eat?"

They were in the bathroom. Olive had been washing her hair. She wrapped a towel round her head and groped for a cigarette. "Some sinister kind of steak. Whale, I should think. Ma Leverett won't go in for the black market. She obviously sees herself as Caesar's wife, *sans reproche*. I know I've fussed about Madam fiddling but that awful sort of virtuous parsimony ... I begin to see what Chris meant about the world of the grey men. I'll never agree that anyone has the right to anything on the side, because the fact remains that you're inflating the market, stealing from those who can't pay, whether it's eggs or homes or whatever. Our only hope is some kind of equal chance and you can't legislate for that, it's a frame of mind ... But that *woman*!" Olive snorted. Olive had been seething since that evening at the Leveretts and there had been no one till now to whom she could speak of it. It was an aspect of her odd, sometimes aggressive shyness that she was painfully fastidious in her confidences. She concluded, "The worst thing was not having to crawl, I didn't really mind that. But that someone as admirable as Dennis should depend on an ass like Maurice Leverett." She frowned, speaking to herself. "I wonder if I've done the wrong thing."

"But you got him the job?"

"Oh yes. Yes, if he can at least pretend to look grateful and if he behaves, I can stop worrying about Dennis Rawston. I can put him out of my mind."

"You won't though."

"Oh yes I will."

Later Olive felt ashamed.

"Poor Cat, I haven't even asked you about the holiday."

Catherine thought. "It was rather good. The food was terrific."

"It's time you grew out of food."

"I know," said Catherine, "I wish I could."

"Rice. Tinned fruit! And bread!"

"Stuff yourself, child," said Olive, "it may be your last chance."

It seemed certain now that bread would be rationed. Catherine was unpacking one of Harold's parcels. His mother sent them and normally he brought them round unopened to the Armitages'. The bread he had smuggled from the Embassy stores. He watched, smiling. Mrs Armitage sighed, "What we'll do when you're gone, I can't think."

Olive glanced up sharply from her sewing. "Are you going?"

"I'll have to decide soon." Harold's answer sounded like a question. Olive pushed aside her sewing. Restlessly, as if she were hardly aware of it, she walked to the window and tapped her fingers against the pane. It was raining, a thin summer drizzle.

"I'd better lie down for a bit. I'm due on at ten."

Mrs Armitage complained, "That awful job. I wish you'd do something else."

"I've told you, mother, I like it. It suits me."

"It makes you tired, shabby." Some strange, inner rage had been smouldering, apparently, beneath Mrs Armitage's calm exterior. Olive wondered, does she really care or does our muddle scare her because of some failure of her own? It struck her suddenly that her mother was afraid, frightened to death. "It will make you a hag."

"Unlike you, mother, I'm not so interested in preserving myself. I don't think I'm so precious."

Olive had spoken quietly, but the silence that followed was impressive. Harold looked not shocked but unhappy. Catherine seemed to be holding her breath. Olive, having flung the unspeakable in her mother's face, did not at once leave the room. She stood, drooping and exhausted by the door.

45

Mrs Armitage did it rather well. She could have hood-winked the gods.

"And if I had, as you say, considered myself precious, you think all those years I could have managed? When you were still children and I was quite alone? The money coming from heaven knows where. Your father dead and a husband . . ."

"Who would have died for you. It's funny," Olive added in a flat voice, as if this were a normal conversation, "how you always get people to do things for you in the end."

"I . . ."

"Shut up!" Catherine had noticed first that her hand was shaking. This was interesting. She was alarmed only when she found the trembling to be uncontrollable and was inspired, obliged if she were not to collapse, to run from the room. "Shut up, shut up, shut up!"

Olive came into the bedroom. She studied Catherine solemnly, as if her stepsister might be ill. She had a strange, unreasonable feeling that Catherine might be in danger, though how she might help her, or what the peril was, Olive could not have said. She walked to the dressing-table and began, pointlessly, to rearrange pots and brushes. She tried to remember herself at Catherine's age but the war, that dark wall, blocked recollection, and the times had been so different.

"Sorry. I was a bit spiky."

"It's all right. But . . ."

"What?"

"Families. You can't get outside, can you?" Catherine couldn't explain: the shared nerves screaming in a way an outsider, even one as sympathetic as Harold, could never understand. However apart you kept yourself, you were torn, just as Rebecca, however little she pretended to care or to notice, could not help but be infected by the love between her parents, the happiness, legends and affection of her family. It made Rebecca careless. If you were happy you

46

never noticed it in the way you did if something was deeply wrong. That was the rotten thing.

Olive turned and sat down on the stool. "It's not the end of the world. She'll be a lamb tomorrow. They don't mean anything, these scenes, not to her at least."

"I know. But . . ."

"But what?"

Catherine shook her head. "It's not just that I don't like you rowing. I know you're right about her, in a way. She likes drama, she's always much nicer afterwards." Unable to express herself and feeling if she could explain she would not be understood, she went on all the same, "I suppose I thought when things were normal again, when that beastly war was finished, everything would be different. Instead everyone seems just as miserable, worse because now they don't know what they want."

"Are you miserable?"

"Only a bit. But then I don't know what normal is. I can hardly remember. All I remember from before the war is food. Not even my father going away or if I was happy or unhappy. I don't know what people are talking about when they say everything was marvellous before the war."

Olive pondered. "Look, Cat. You mustn't take too much notice of mother. She's old and tough and because of those things she can't bend. I know she drives me mad and I show it, but I do see, when I can squeeze out an ounce of charity, that she can't help wanting what she's lost, to have things as they used to be. Heaven knows, that's not what I want, what anyone wants who cares about the world."

"I wasn't really thinking of the world."

"Then you should."

"I can only see people."

"Isn't that the same thing?"

The door slammed. Harold was leaving.

Olive said, "She wants me to marry Harold. You'd realised that?"

"No."

"The joke is"—Olive put her head between her knees and began to brush her hair, still long, then looked up—"if she hadn't thought of it, I might have done."

"You won't?"

"I never said that." Olive grinned. She scooped up her hair and peered into the mirror. "Now I've got Dennis Rawston off my hands I might do anything. I feel irresponsible."

"You ought to get some sleep."

Just before she fell asleep Olive said suddenly, "You're not planning to dig up Charlie Armitage, are you?"

"Why?"

"Nothing. But it might be a bad idea."

The next day, in fact for several days, Mrs Armitage was, as Olive had predicted, a lamb. Hardly meek—that would have been entirely out of character—but rejuvenated, busy, full of schemes. While her sun shone the family basked. It might be a good summer, after all. Bread rationing was a joke. There was plenty in the shops and units left over could be exchanged for points. Chris came home for the weekend, full of the boatyard, which was going well, and Toby Tait.

Olive said, "He seems to be going through some belated sort of adolescence. He worships the man. It's the war, I suppose. It either stops people at the age they were when it began, or turns them into old men."

Mrs Armitage frowned. "His eyes are too close together."

"Toby Tait's?"

"Neville Heath's." She spoke of Heath with a cheerful venom, as she had held forth about Hitler as someone of no account. "He's mad, of course."

Catherine looked at the paper. He was good-looking, in a film-star way.

"You think he did it?"

"You're far too young to think about such things, either way."

"But I do."

48

Olive snorted. In another mood she would have argued: who was her mother to say who was sane and who was not? But she too had been cheerful lately. Dennis seemed to be behaving. She had the day off and she was going to the country with Harold. Dennis might let her down. Harold might go, but for the moment she lived in the present. It was self-indulgent, unfamiliar but delightful. And was it so wrong to take what you could, enjoy yourself, if the alternative was Larry Towers, Maurice Leverett, dreariness, or concern, guilty and unassuageable, for people you simply could not help? Whose tragedy was none of your making. Who resented help and wanted nothing but an ear into which to pour their complaints about a world that had, in the muddle of war, let them down.

8

WHEN Mrs Armitage was in a good temper she grew careless
and forgot to be watchful of her children. She had heard of a
little man in the East End who had a bale of silk. She had no
purpose for it but she was seduced simply by the idea of silk,
which she connected with her first husband. Had Teddy
Asher given her silk? Had he approved of her in something
silk (unlikely—he never noticed clothes)? She could not remember. All she knew was, this must be a prelapsarian
association, from before the fall. She had to have it. She went
off early. So did Olive with Harold. Catherine was left alone.

Olive tried to explain to Harold about her mother. "We
live in different worlds. Literally. She might have been
pickled in 1939. No, 1935. I love her, I suppose. Yes, I do.
But I don't like her much." She shrugged and stared at her
lap. They had parked on the fringes of a wood to eat their
lunch. "I can't explain."
"You explain very well."
She looked up. Harold leaned back, smoking. He had pale
lashes. She had never seen him untidy or hot or cross. He had
a capacity for stillness she had observed in no one else. She
couldn't think how they had come to discuss Mrs Armitage.
"It's queer. She makes you so angry all you want to do is
forget all about her. Then here I am going on about her. I
expect you admire her. You're rather like her, in a way."
"I can't see that."
"I don't mean you behave like her. And your motives may
be quite different. But you're both, as I see you, like statues.
Cut off from the times. Of course, she couldn't stand the
world as it is for a moment, if she really looked at it—then I

try to *make* her see, rub her nose in it, and feel much worse afterwards than she does, because you can't make her, she's so sublimely, invincibly blind, self-blinded. But anyway . . ."

"Then I'm blind?"

"No. I think while she's just turned her back, you're trying to make up your mind. You can't decide whether to jump in at the deep end, you're not even sure where the deep end is, unless it's America. And Europe, as you see it, in spite of everything, is the warm shallows where people will still have time to talk and paint pictures and cultivate themselves. Your trouble is, the Americans are Romans and you're a Greek. You don't know, any more than mother, that the kind of life you want is finished. The war doesn't seem to have touched either of you. I often wonder, what would have happened to her if someone really close, Chris or myself, had been killed or hurt, if she'd been obliged to acknowledge . . ."

"I'd say she's not as pickled as you imagine. She's nearer than you think to the roots of life."

"The roots of life." Olive grinned. "How on earth did we get on to that?"

A little later, driving through the hop fields of Kent, Harold asked her to marry him. Olive had expected this, but was still surprised. This afternoon the thought of marrying Harold was pleasant and simplifying. She said she would need to think about it, but she knew, unless something extraordinary happened to change her mind, she would marry him and she would probably be very happy. She asked all the same for time to think.

"There's someone else? Rawston?"

"Dennis! What an extraordinary idea. I admire him, of course. He's one of the few people who are really trying to do something. Everyone else seems so apathetic, self-engrossed, as if the war had worn them out. But . . ." She shook her head.

"You've done a lot for him."

"That was nothing. Though if I did feel like that for him, I must admit the responsibility would frighten me. But

52

mostly, I know I just couldn't live up to him. Is that offensive to you?"

He smiled. "No. I'm well aware I don't come up to you. It's yourself you're not being fair to. I don't think you realise how remarkable you are."

"Don't say that." Olive looked scared, almost angry. "There's nothing special about me. I'm no heroine."

"I hope not. In a way I hope very much that I'm wrong. I'd rather you were happy."

"Which means marry you?"

"Not necessarily." Harold seemed to have settled something in his mind. He refused to be drawn and talked lightly about his father, the pressure the family was bringing to bear for him to return to America. Olive began to relax and watched him, wondering how much, in spite of his composure, he could be hurt, if he were in his own way more ambitious, less malleable than she allowed for.

She must have gone to sleep because she woke and found they had stopped in a narrow road by an army camp or airfield, their way blocked by an open lorry full of women and children, packed tight between blankets, boxes, rolls of carpet, kettles, saucepans, family pets and even birds in cages. Sleepily, Olive was reminded of pictures of refugees in the war, nameless multitudes fleeing down an endless road which seemed in newsreel pictures and newspapers always the same road, not unlike this. If you go with as much as you can carry, she used to think, and thought now, how little you can take. Catherine always cried at these pictures in the cinema, or seemed as if she wanted to cry. Olive watched, dry-eyed, and wondered.

"Who are they? Where are they going?"

"Squatters. The camp's empty I suppose. They're taking it over. Good luck to them."

"What will happen to them?"

Harold shrugged. "From what I've heard, the police will make some sort of effort to turn them out. But they'll stay."

"You mean they'll live in those awful huts?"

53

"I've lived in one. It wasn't so bad. It's amazing what you can put up with when there's no choice."

"Don't you *care*?" The lorry had turned into the camp and they could drive on. A child waved and a dog began to bark. Someone was singing. A thin cheer went up. "Don't you realise for the English to behave like this, actually to break the law, how desperate they must be? Doesn't it make you angry?"

"If I could change it, yes. If what I thought or said or did could put anything right."

"But it would be something to try?"

"I believe in the attainable."

Later, Olive told Catherine, who was not listening, "I'm very fond of Harold, of course, but he thinks Europe is a picture gallery." She did not believe this but it was one of those simplifications, unkind and consoling, which reduce the mystery of another person to manageable proportions. She did not mention the squatters and imagined by the time she got home that she had forgotten them.

Catherine, normally a good listener, was not attending because she had gone that day to Battersea. She had spent the morning looking for omens and found them. This was the last week of the holiday. She was alone. She telephoned Rebecca, and Sam answered saying his sister had gone out. Even the cats had disappeared on business of their own. After lunch she got the bus to Chelsea and walked over the bridge, upon which columns of marching soldiers were required to break step. If Battersea were the promised land it seemed very drab. She lingered on the bridge. The river flashed no message. She nearly turned back.

Arnold Row, when she found it, which was more difficult than she expected, was a street of small semi-detached villas. In front of each there was a narrow patch of garden. Railings had gone to armaments like ploughshares to swords, and there was about the whole street an air of desolation, of decency narrowly preserved long after the reason for it was

54

forgotten, against all odds. If it had not been decent still, it would not have been desolate. All around in the surrounding streets women stood murmuring and yelling, baking in the sun at their doorways; children, grubby and curious, played grandmother's footsteps behind Catherine, stopping when she stopped, moving in leaps when she moved. They left her at Arnold Row and she walked on, painfully aware of her large body in the sun, dazzled by the yellow faces of the houses. The children were pests but she missed them from a distance, as if she had met them in another world. For the first time it occurred to her that there might be something to fear in her father's house.

She clung to the thought of Rebecca who would have gone on.

She heard her own voice, prim as a sliced pear, "Mr Charles Armitage?"

"Charlie? He's out. You'd better come in." The woman seemed incurious. She was clean but wore exhausted slippers and a shapeless dress, smudged with drooping, overblown flowers. Her face, in contrast to the rest, was perfectly painted, her brows into amazing arches, her lips even more astonishing Cupid's bows. Could this be the stunner?

Catherine thought of coming back or going away altogether, decided to go in. The house was small and spotless. There was a scent of soap and wax. Cushions were pink, curtains blue. Catherine thought of a doll's house. The woman poured tea into small cups. Catherine felt like Gulliver.

"He'll be back soon?"

"I should think so." The stunner sipped her tea, nibbled a cake and lit an exceptionally short cigarette. She cocked her head. "I know who you are. You're the little girl."

Catherine smiled. She had been smiling ever since she sat down. She felt her grin would get stuck, somewhere up by her ears. She wondered, if she ate a cake, might she get smaller or larger?

"Not so little, I'm afraid."

"That's how he thinks about you. He thinks about you a

55

lot. I tell him it's no use. She'd never let you come."

"Well, I'm here."

"I said as long as she was alive he'd never see you. If he'd settle, resign himself to the fact." Her face creased, her mouth turned down. She talked as if she were starving and talk were food. "But you know Charlie."

"As a matter of fact, I don't."

The door banged. The stunner said suddenly as feet came down the passage, paused and approached, "You won't hurt him? You'll be careful? You won't upset him? He's been happy. People don't understand him. She never understood, he's not as easy as he seems. He can be hurt."

"Puss?" A voice called outside the door. "Where's my puss?"

The stunner answered, "Here, Charlie. We're in here."

Charles Armitage came in. Catherine realised she had not thought as far as this—the moment of meeting. Her imagination had leapt over awkwardness, possible disappointment, to rapture. Had she made a mistake? Did she know this man? Did she *want* to know him?

He was smallish, plump, with a light step. He looked as if any moment he might break into a music-hall tap dance. He was terribly ordinary.

Catherine did not know whether to stay sitting or to stand, to kiss him (she decided not) or to shake hands. In the end they did not touch.

Charlie said, "I'd never have believed it!" He kept saying this, repeated this in the awkward silences, of which there were several. What it was he could not believe Catherine was not clear. That she had come? That she had wanted to come? That she had grown—this surely, he would have expected but not perhaps to such dimensions? The stunner, whose name was Mrs Riley, left them. She went upstairs. Charlie said she had a rest every day about this time. She was not strong. Catherine thought she looked well enough. He spoke of Mrs Riley, who seemed to Catherine unexceptional, in tones of mingled pride and anxiety as if he were not in the

56

presence of his daughter by his lawful wife. He said she made him comfortable, it had not been easy, he rambled, then added simply, apparently not asking for pity, "I'd never have managed without her. When I got my cards she pretty well saved my life."

Catherine was embarrassed. "I don't remember much about that. I remember you going."

"That was a bad time." He shook his head, then seemed to cheer up. He slapped his pockets as if he might produce a bag of sweets, but instead he brought out a pipe. "The main thing is you've come," he said, "I'm very glad."

Catherine realised he was as shy as she was herself. She felt easier, almost in command, "I've wanted to come for ages."

He did not ask how she had come, where she had found the address. They smiled at each other. Suddenly busy, he trotted round like a child bringing out its favourite toys, offering a battered envelope of old photographs from a locked cupboard, a drawing Catherine had done for him as an infant, a school report (a good one for once) he must have pinched from Mrs Armitage's desk. She was overwhelmed, appalled and delighted. She laughed at the drawing. "Isn't it awful. And these pictures! I thought there must be some, but I've never found them. Olive said there must be some of us all together, but she'd no idea what happened to them."

"Your mother threw them after me down the stairs."

"So that really happened?"

They were laughing when they heard Mrs Riley moving around upstairs. Each photograph seemed more absurd than the one before. The hats, the clothes, Olive a skinny schoolgirl, Chris scowling, Mrs Armitage and Charlie arm in arm, Catherine caught on a beach, by a pool, holding a rubber giraffe, in circular, implacable rage.

"You'd been eating sand."

"What a frightful child."

"You were lovely. You were beautiful. You still are."

"I'm too tall and too fat."

Quite suddenly, without knowing why, she burst into

57

tears. Charlie held her, then Mrs Riley came in and Catherine said she would have to go. Charlie walked with her to the bus.

"You mustn't think," he said, "that we were never happy. But she was out of my class. It wasn't her fault, or mine." Now he seemed detached, untroubled. The bus arrived. Catherine promised that she would come again to see her father.

9

CATHERINE told no one about her meeting with her father. Or rather, she told no one but Rebecca who, vague as she was about other people, had a sharp nose for drama and was not to be put off.

"You've been up to something."

They were in Rebecca's bedroom, deep in book-keeping primers. Neither was much good at the subject but Rebecca did her exercises so neatly, in such beautiful columns, that although they were never finished even Willy was sometimes beguiled. They had agreed not to talk for half an hour and as the clock struck Rebecca spoke.

"Well, if you haven't, you're ill. You look queer." Catherine did not answer. There was a time when Rebecca would have pounced, tickled and pulled hair till she broke down her victim, but she was practising now to be a young lady. It was a phase, she would get over it, and even now Catherine knew her friend's dignity was precarious. Before her vital urges—to know something, to eat, to argue, to run—pride wavered and settled as often as not for indulgence, never regretted but, with the spontaneous amnesia of which Rebecca was capable, wiped out. When you thought about it Rebecca in most ways had the best of every world, or if she hadn't she thought she had. She was an actress, she could project herself in a flash into any role—as she had the day she saved Catherine from Miss Wilson—and just as soon abandon it. There was somewhere, Catherine hazarded, a core of truth, the true Rebecca whom she felt rather than knew to be warm, courageous, frivolous, lazy, intuitive and possibly (or was this a romance inspired by her family history?) tragic. "You might as well tell me. I'll find out, anyway."

"How?"

"I'll guess. And when I've guessed right, I'll know."

Catherine gave up. Rebecca was a force. There was almost pleasure in breaking before her.

"I've been to see my father."

"Ah! What was he like?"

What was he like? He was her father. One's parents were like no one, they were themselves.

"I don't know. He was pleased. He was a bit scared and then he was pleased. He thought at first I was grown up and that worried him. He was always marvellous with children. I think he really wanted to explain what happened with my mother but he couldn't. We had tea and he showed me some photographs. He lives in Battersea."

Rebecca protested, "I still don't know what he's *like*."

In August Olive became engaged to Harold. There were several reasons behind her decision, which was sudden. The idea she had had on the day in the country, that it would be pleasant and simplifying to marry him, had grown from frivolous, fanciful dimensions to an astonishingly sizeable conviction. As she said to Catherine, she liked him more than any man she had known, she could even imagine living with him, which was more than she could say of anyone else who had asked her to marry. There had been someone in the war, but he was dead. Olive being Olive she suffered still quite acutely from the memory but never pretended for a moment that they could have been happy—he had been weak, impossibly weak, and she had been an idiot—and felt guilty for admitting it. As Rebecca had the best of all worlds, it seemed to Catherine that Olive had the worst. She suffered from the end of an old romance and castigated herself for the fact that it could never have come to anything. Catherine was scared for her, often, afraid that she would invent some impeccably rational motive for doing something suicidal. And having run her head into a noose, would accept no comfort, because she believed in both the passionate and reason-

60

able parts of her being, that one had to put up with the consequences of a decision, however awful. With Harold she felt quite certain Olive would be all right. Catherine realised, with surprise, that this was the first time in living memory she had seen eye to eye with her mother. She suspected her mother's motives, but the end was the same. And she was thankful that Mrs Armitage, however much she had schemed, or thought she had schemed, for this marriage, had the sense to keep quiet.

But things were really settled by the fact that Harold was returning to America at the end of the month. He was to be demobilised and was taking this chance to see his family. He said little about it, but clearly the pressures were great for him to stay in the States, on the peach farm or in his father's business.

Olive asked him, "Won't you come back for a while, anyway? You said you'd always wanted to see Europe." She didn't say he could well afford to. For some reason his money embarrassed her.

"No," he said, and then repeated more firmly, as if this decision had been hardening in his mind and by saying it he might make it not only true but right, "No. If I settle there I shan't come back." Deprecating the drama of his statement, he added, smiling, "Not for ten, twenty years, anyway."

"So we may not see you again." At the prospect she felt bleak.

"Unless you marry me, come with me."

"And if I did?"

"Then it would be for you to say. We could live well in the States." He was trying to be fair. "Not so well in Europe. You know I've got money, but it's tied up there. Alone, I could manage well enough over here but it wouldn't be the life I want for you. So you see, you have to choose."

Quite suddenly she made up her mind.

"I will marry you. And I'd like to go to America. I *want* to. I mean I really want to marry you but if we do it must be something final." It seemed very important, honourable to

61

explain. "I thought this summer, peace, would be marvellous. We'd expected so much . . . I'm talking like Catherine, like a child. But I've begun to think lately that Chris was right. There's a terrible feeling in England at the moment."

Harold went to fetch another drink. They had been to an exhibition in a new gallery off Hanover Square: Harold was quietly knowledgeable about painting, a fact that never ceased to surprise Mrs Armitage who held to a conviction that Americans were too busy making money to think about anything else. For her the gates of culture slammed shut at Southampton, the moment one left British shores, going west. The pictures had been good but the drinks so unpleasant and inadequate Olive and Harold had gone on to a pub.

Harold had been thinking. "Isn't that just the let-down everyone feels after the war? A lot of people like us, who didn't suffer too much, are ashamed to admit it, but it's natural. When you've given your whole energy to something and suddenly it's finished . . .'

Olive grinned painfully. "You'll be telling me soon I ought to be grateful, that plenty are starving. Those people we saw outside that camp . . . And much worse than that abroad." She sighed as if she were physically wrung out. "It's not just the let-down—you're right of course—or that we're all just slightly more uncomfortable than we were in the war. It's an attitude of everyone out for themselves. Even my mother's fiddling is a small part of the same thing. No one condemns her for it because she treats it like a game but really she takes it terribly seriously, she'd be quite lost without it."

"If it weren't for the fiddling a lot of people would be dead. There are parts of the world where it's the only means of survival. No one stops to think if he's degrading himself when he's got a family to keep alive."

"I know," she said, "and I don't blame them, I'm not that much of an ethical prig and just lately I've begun to think I'm as bad as anyone." She had been sitting, not drinking,

shoulders hunched, talking in a low voice; now she flung
back her head in a characteristic gesture. If Harold had not
known her better he would have said she was being theatrical, but by now he was aware that these touches of drama
which in Mrs Armitage were often contrived were for Olive
quite unconscious expressions of her attitude to the world: a
mixture of defiance, bravado and painful honesty. Then, she
seemed much younger than she was and so totally unpro-
tected Harold wanted to take her in his arms. Yet the irony
was that in these moments she made herself untouchable.
She was going on about the hospital, how, since she was un-
qualified even as a nurse, it all seemed frustrating, pointless,
useless. "If only one could *do* something."

"I'd have thought you were doing more than most."

"But don't you see, it's not enough? If only I could find
something . . ." She trailed off. Olive was always the first to
see herself as absurd. "I sound like Joan of Arc out of a job.
What about you? What do you want?"

"To marry you."

"But for heaven's sake, that's not a job. For a woman, perhaps, but a man can't make his life out of marriage."

"I could."

"It's not reasonable."

"I've never thought much of reason."

She shook her head. "I think you're mad. No one could be
as patient as you."

"I'm not. You've said you'll marry me and I'm going to
see you do it if I have to beat you to the altar."

"Do we have to tell people now?"

"One or two, yes."

She gulped her drink, smiled, and said lightly, "All right.
Why not?"

Mrs Armitage behaved like a Ceres who had reversed the
legend. Not only had Olive been snatched from behind the
iron gates of the hospital, saved from lurking Plutos, but
she was making a marriage at once sensible and romantic.

63

Sensible because Harold was rich, kind and nice to Mrs Armitage. Romantic because Americans were, like the Goths, rather beyond the pale.

She would have liked a large party but Olive insisted on a small affair, drinks for the family and a couple of Harold's friends. Mrs Armitage was determined to be generous, but baffled. "But why? Are you ashamed of him?"

"On the contrary," Olive answered steadily, "it is precisely because I am not ashamed of Harold that I don't want him treated like a stud bull at a fair."

"I can't think where you learned to be so coarse. Not from me. It must be the war."

"I suppose it must," said Olive cheerfully.

In spite of her attitude to the party Olive seemed, once the decision was made, ready enough to join in, even to initiate preparations for the marriage; this was to be in October when Harold came back from the States. They were to honeymoon briefly in Paris and go on from there to New York. Olive refused a church wedding and insisted on keeping her job at the hospital till Harold's return, but she followed Mrs Armitage round shops and dressmakers like a sardonic lamb, bored to death but not actually hostile. She watched with vague amusement while her mother shuffled clothing coupons and dressed her daughter, very well it had to be admitted, in a way she considered suitable for a new life in a new world. She lost her temper only once or twice and appeared, most of the time, buoyed up by a kind of triumph at having made a decision. Catherine watched her, delighted but puzzled. Olive seemed charmed, pliant in a way she could not remember. Was it love? Sometimes when her sister was tired there was a glimpse of a different feeling, a slanting shadow, when she snapped at Mrs Armitage that really it was all absurd, everything would be easier to buy in New York, and besides she was worn out.

The night of the party Catherine found her on the bed.

"Shouldn't you get dressed?"

Olive groped for a cigarette, sighed and lay back.

64

"In a minute."

"Are you all right?"

"I'll live. I've been sick. I wish . . ."

"What?"

"Nothing. We could do it without this circus. It should be possible to put two people to bed without trumpets." Normally Olive would never have spoken like this to her sister. Catherine was embarrassed and cross to be so. She saw Olive, draped in a yellow dressing-gown across the bed, not as her sister but a sexual object. There was such a distance between theory, with which she was well acquainted, and fact. Had Olive? She did not care to think, would never ask. Olive sat up and began abruptly to slap cream on her face. "Well, at least Madam will be pleased. I suppose it's not much to give her."

Catherine ran her finger across the dress, laid out ready, the same silk Mrs Armitage had borne home in triumph from the East End. It would suit Olive. Against her will perhaps, she would be beautiful. The silk was not smooth but scratchy, when you came to feel it closely, textured all over with lifted threads. She thought how much nicer the dress would have been without the shoulder pads, but it was fashionable still for women to look square, faintly masculine, as if they could not quite abandon the mental attitudes of war.

There were all kinds of questions Catherine wanted to ask but the one she put she had not expected. She was scared sometimes by these odd corners within herself. Out of this darkness, she feared, she might some day do something mad.

"Why don't you like her?"

She wished at once she had not spoken. She had touched the most prickly area of Olive's experience: her feeling for their mother, that strange mixture of passion, anger, scorn and self-disgusted pity which Catherine found painful to observe. Normally Olive would have drily rejected the question but tonight it seemed to strike her, to crystallise something dangerous and sharp in her mood. She frowned, appar-

65

ently turning her answer in her mind, then shrugged and replied as if this were quite obvious, there was no point in putting it into words. Her face was as white as Catherine remembered from those times in her childhood when Olive defied Mrs Armitage and the thunder rolled, obscure and mysterious in origin but terrifying in its power, like a crack in nature itself.

"She doesn't tell the truth."

By the time the party began Olive had got over her mood or thrust it down. She seemed truly happy, not febrile. She had never been demonstrative in public, or in private so far as Catherine knew, but the moment Harold arrived she went to his side. Before they had seemed two people who got on very well, would be happily married, but now, standing together they were powerful, invulnerable. Catherine was awed. So was Rebecca, for once.

"I see what you mean."

They ate cheese straws. Mrs Armitage swept up.

"So this is Rebecca."

Catherine glanced nervously at her friend. She had feared this meeting and avoided it as long as possible for reasons she could not quite understand; perhaps because she was not yet ready to acknowledge her mother's power, to test her strength against her should Mrs Armitage disapprove of Rebecca. It was a matter of chance: there was a touch of the goddess, of Olympian whims in both of them. It was all right. Mrs Armitage was gracious, Rebecca decided to be charming, wide-eyed, respectful, so demure in a *jeune fille* way that Catherine wanted to applaud. She relaxed and looked round.

Olive felt something was wrong with the party. It had split into knots and failed to spark. There were too many for a single, coherent conversation, too few to set up the buzz, however meaningless, which indicates success. Maurice Leverett was talking to an American woman wearing a shrill blue dress; she looked as if she had captured a mythical

66

creature. Olive went to fetch more cheese straws and when she came back the atmosphere had changed. Two couples had left. Chris had arrived and everyone was looking out of the window. Even Maurice Leverett had unwound his long legs and stood, looking down his yellow nose at a small, absurd, red car parked by the kerb.

Chris turned in triumph.

"Isn't she a beauty? And she's all mine."

At this time it was almost impossible to buy a car. Chris, brown, and more cheerful than Olive had seen him for months, was congratulated as if he'd had a baby. After the sensation the party broke into groups again but Chris had brought in some magic. He gave Olive a smacking kiss on the cheek, and pumped Harold's hand. He had clearly been drinking before he came.

"Where did you get it?" Catherine asked.

"Ask no questions and you'll be told no lies."

"Where's Toby?"

"Minding the shop."

They had collapsed, side by side, on the sofa.

"What are you up to, Chris?"

Olive joined them, with Harold. Harold began to ask Christopher technical questions about the car. Olive yawned happily.

"It's all right, isn't it? After all."

"It's a marvellous party."

"I think I'm a bit drunk." Olive grinned like a cat. "Happy drunk." She added, quite soberly, "I've been an idiot, Cat. You were right all the time. There's no one like him."

Just then the telephone rang. Mrs Armitage went to answer it. She turned her back on the room and put a hand over her ear. Olive watched at first idly, then with a strained attention, as her mother nodded twice, then replaced the receiver. Mrs Armitage paused, then walked across to Maurice Leverett. They talked, heads dipped.

"Who was that, mother?"

67

"Oh, no one of any importance."

Olive wondered. She had no reason to think the call had been from Dennis Rawston, or intended for her at all. Yet she shivered.

She rejoined Catherine.

"What's the matter?"

"Nothing. A goose walked over my grave."

Chris offered to take them all, Harold and Olive, Catherine and Rebecca, for a ride in his car. They accepted. They drove very fast to Richmond. By the time they got back it was dark, Chris had run out of petrol, Mrs Armitage had gone out for dinner with Maurice Leverett and the party was over.

10

THE party marked a turning-point. Harold went off to America and Olive admitted, with a mild and not displeased surprise, that she missed him. When she was not with Rebecca Catherine met Olive out of the hospital and they walked home together. Olive had put on a little weight, which suited her, and it was hard to recognise in her the angry girl of the peace celebration.

"I suppose," she said, "I've learned what's good for me. It's funny, I'd never thought of marrying anyone like Harold—of marrying at all. I just couldn't see myself like that. Whenever some girl I knew got married I used to think, poor idiot. And now here I am."

It was a hot afternoon and they were walking on the shady side of the street under plane trees grey with late summer. It hurt the eyes to look at the glaring street or the flashing windows of passing cars. The city shivered in pools of heat like a mirage which might dissolve.

"What about the rest? You don't mind?"

"Not too much. I've realised how ridiculous I was, thinking I could do something. Impertinent too. I don't know enough and I'm too lazy to learn to do anything but deliver a few platitudes on the state of the world and carry round the bedpans. I'm not much good even at that. You know I used to be sick every time I emptied one?" She glanced sideways at Catherine. "D'you think I've sold out?"

"I think you've done the right thing. I was terrified you wouldn't."

"You're extraordinary, Cat. You really do want everyone to be happy, don't you? Do you never think of yourself?"

"Oh yes, quite often."

For Catherine too, things had gone well. She had been back to Battersea and found her second visit much easier than her first. Mrs Riley seemed to have accepted her and, with a rather heavy tact, left Catherine alone with her father.

"It does him good," she said, "to see someone. He doesn't get out enough. We're home bodies really."

Catherine was puzzled at first by her father's apparent lack of occupation. Often when she arrived he was cleaning the house or working in the small garden. Once she caught him making a cake and shyly he offered her a taste of the mixture on a spoon.

"Not bad, eh?"

"It's very good."

"Marjorie likes a cake. And I daresay so do you?" With a practised gesture he tipped the mixture in a baking tin and put it in the oven.

"I'm trying to slim."

"What for?"

"I don't know. I hadn't thought. Everyone slims."

"You're all right," he said. "You stay as you are." At tea-time, she noticed, he ate none of the cake, but his pleasure in her eating she found at once irresistible and curiously painful as if she could, by stuffing herself, make up for the years of her he had lost. She thought then, pity can be ugly, I don't like it. Purposely, almost vindictively, she turned down the next slice and began to talk in too bright a voice about Olive's wedding. They were interested, even Mrs Riley who wanted to know every detail of Olive's wardrobe, where they would go, how they would live. Weddings were, apparently, her special interest and as she listened, nodded and made impressed comments, she seemed younger, innocent, a child listening to a story. When Catherine had finished, Mrs Riley sighed with pleasure. Catherine decided she liked her after all, she liked them both, in this small garden inside the high fence, sweet-smelling, tidy as a drawing room, she felt safe and happy. Even Rebecca could not follow her here. This

70

was something of her own. She thought of it often when she was not there.

She realised she was growing to depend upon them. As yet she hardly understood that she also worried about them as if they had somehow become her responsibility.

Charles Armitage had been a chartered accountant before the war. That was as much as Catherine knew. She asked a little, listened a lot and discovered that some mysterious ill-health had cut short his career and kept him out of the war (though he would have been, in any case, nearly fifty when Mrs Armitage threw him down the stairs). It had been something to do with the nerves. He worked still as an accountant, from home. Catherine gathered this was not entirely satisfactory but neither was it a disaster. They managed. Catherine suspected some deep-buried suburban instinct in herself. Each time she went to Arnold Row she found it harder to leave, to return to the real world. Yet who was to say which was 'real' of the lives she led, each separate from the other like rooms to which she alone held the key? Questioned, she would have said she lived at home with her mother, but this was only a fraction of the truth, almost a lie, when she only felt herself truly alive in St John's Wood with Rebecca, or in Battersea. How did one settle for the truth? Did Olive become more real by marrying Harold? Which was Catherine: Olive's sister, Rebecca's friend, Mrs Armitage's awkward child or Charlie's daughter? Or the girl in the boat with Sam at Bournemouth? And was Charlie who lived with Mrs Riley the same husband Mrs Armitage had flung downstairs? It was all very confusing, the more so as she seemed surrounded by people who knew who they were and from the certainty of their own identities told Catherine to stand up, eat up, speak up. "Cheer up, Cat, I didn't steal it."

That was Chris grinning by the sea in Hampshire. Mrs Armitage and Catherine had gone down for the day. Catherine was quite surprised to find that the boatyard actually existed, then wondered why she had ever doubted it. Chris

71

was talking about the little red car. At the corner of her vision Catherine saw Mrs Armitage drinking tea in the office with Toby Tait. He limped around fetching sugar and biscuits. Mrs Armitage was charmed. Catherine thought, for the first time, that her mother might be stupid. It was a shock.

Chris explained, "Toby got it from a man who wanted to sell. It was quite simple. Toby's a marvel. He can get anything."

So that was all right.

Catherine said to Olive in their bedroom that night, "Mother's gone on Toby Tait."

"Well, he is rather attractive. In a gipsy sort of way." Olive had some news of her own. "I heard from Maurice Leverett today. He wants to see me. It sounded like an order. That man is one of the reasons I'll be glad to leave the country." Her voice was light, but she seemed quite serious. "I believe I hate that man."

"You don't have to go."

"I think I do."

"What trouble?"

When Maurice telephoned Olive had suggested meeting at his office but this was apparently unsuitable and he had named a new vegetarian restaurant off Victoria Street. Olive remembered it as a pub she had visited once or twice in the war, cheerful, noisy and dirty, the kind of place Maurice Leverett would have crossed the road to avoid. It had been bombed (as it happened, she heard later, only an hour after she had been drinking there) and out of the shell had sprung this shrine to patriotism, good health, economy and utter gloom. She arrived ten minutes late. One ate at a counter. Maurice rose, tried to adjust her stool, found it was screwed to the floor and looked at his watch. She pretended not to notice. He fussed about the menu, written up in chalk on a blackboard. She lit a cigarette, knowing this would annoy him.

"I've been here before." He raised his eyebrows. "When it was a pub."

"You're looking well, Olive." She knew she was. She knew she was looking splendid. Harold would be back in ten days. She had chosen from her trousseau (a word she would not admit) to wear today a simple, orange dress with a black coat. She thought she had thrown it on, but intended, perhaps, to be flagrant, to shock Maurice. Why? If she despised him why bother to torment him? It was the nature of women to offer an invitation whether or not they proposed to fulfil it. She had contempt for women like that. Sometimes Olive was appalled by her own feminine instincts. She shuddered and pulled the black coat together at the neck. Maurice's measuring eye flickered away. He ordered carrot cutlets. Olive wondered why vegetarians always looked hungry.

"Are you a vegetarian?"

"No. It's near the office, and I daresay there may be something in it."

"What?"

"Vegetables."

"What did you want, Maurice?"

He laid down his knife and fork and looked in front of them, into the reflecting mirror. Olive saw herself given back, a sarcastic female eating carrots. She pushed the plate aside. Maurice looked at his hands.

"Your friend is in trouble."

"What trouble? What friend?" she added, knowing she had been caught out.

"Dennis Rawston."

"What has he done? Pinched the petty cash?"

"It might be simpler if he had." He gave her his yellow look. She knew he would spin this out, if she wanted to know she would have to choke this contempt, anger, desire to break, spoil, kick he inspired in her. She realised she loathed Maurice Leverett because he made her hate herself; and she did fear him, at a level as frantic and mysterious as sexual horror. Yet surely not sexual? In that way she felt nothing,

73

for or against him though she would not have cared for him to touch her. "I thought he might have told you?"

"I don't see him. I just tried to help him, that's all."

"What do you know about him?"

"Nothing much. What I told you before. He was in the R.A.F., a sergeant or something. He turned down a commission. Then he got this thing that put him in hospital. Psoriasis. It's a rather foul kind of skin disease. They don't know much about it, but they pumped stuff into him and he's more or less right. Fit enough to work. Why? Is he ill again?"

"No." Maurice stirred his coffee. He carried saccharine in a silver pill-box. Olive bit her lip. "What do you know about his politics?"

"Nothing." She was both angry and scared. She panicked. "He has none. And if he had I can't see it would be your business or mine." In the mirror she looked flushed as if she had been running. She had a queer feeling Maurice wanted to rattle her; she could imagine him going home to Eleanor of Aquitaine and saying: Olive Asher is so headstrong.

"I thought you had something to tell me. If you haven't I'll go."

"I don't think that is a helpful attitude, Olive, to anyone, least of all to Rawston."

"I'm not his keeper."

"Indeed not. But in these troubled times, you must agree, we should help each other. I should like to help him. I should like to warn him—but you would do it better—to keep away from Lawrence Towers."

"Do you mean Dennis is going to lose his job because he's had a drink with a Communist? I've told you, he doesn't believe that, any of it."

"You may be right. It hardly matters. What matters is that he should be seen, positively, to have nothing to do with people like that."

Olive felt tired. She closed her eyes, and opened them to her own reflection, a frightened woman in a shrill dress. Yet nothing had changed. She would marry Harold. The world

74

would go on. One could not live like Dennis listening for the thin cry of suffering. When you thought of it like that, as a sound, the noise was deafening and if you listened you might go mad.

"If you want me to talk to him, I will."

Maurice sighed. "I knew you would see it like that."

They walked out into Victoria Street. There had been an accident. At the corner there was a police car and an ambulance. A man in a dirty grey coat lay, quite peacefully it seemed, in the gutter, with his knees drawn up in an attitude of sleep, his face cradled in his hands. An ambulance man looked down at him. A small crowd had gathered. No one touched him. All this had happened while they were in the restaurant. They had heard nothing. Olive shivered. Maurice was watching her. She said, idiotically. "It's colder since this morning."

"A stroke, I should think." Maurice jerked his chin at the body being carried now on a stretcher into the ambulance.

"It's queer." She forgot she was talking to Maurice. She walked automatically, quickly away from the accident. "You see so much of that in the war and after a while you don't see it, it's nothing. Then something like this . . ." And I'm not thinking about that wretched man at all, I'm thinking how it affects me, Olive Asher. She stopped abruptly, took her bearings. "I'll talk to him, but that's all." She added stiffly as he touched her fingers, "Thank you for telling me. Though I don't see why you should bother."

"One does what one can," said Maurice, looked as though he might say more, then tipped his hat. Watching him walk away Olive frowned. If she went home she would be caught up by Mrs Armitage in wedding arrangements; she was not due at the hospital for three hours. Yet she was restless. The air was humming, vibrant with the first snap of autumn which made her look forward to a clean, frosty winter. But of course she would not be in England this winter. Until now she had held out against this fact as if she and Harold were to have a holiday, not a life, together. She had behaved like a

75

moving statue, propelled by the general will towards a resting place of which she knew nothing except that it would be comfortable. Yet surely she had willed it, she did wish it. Certainly there was nothing else in the world she wanted. If you never went with the tide, you must spend the whole of your life in struggle, possibly waste, all in the faint hope that will alone (and how useless that was if it were directionless) might bring its own rewards, bestow a place, an identity, engender, through sheer energy, its own purpose. At this moment Olive could think of nothing she wanted to do, nowhere she wanted to be. She found herself outside a hairdresser: Alphonse, late of Paris. On an impulse she went in and had her hair cut off.

11

CATHERINE spent more time at Rebecca's or in Battersea than she did at home. Ever since Olive's interview with Maurice Leverett and the terrible scene that followed the house had been mined. She felt that something fearful was going to happen, something so appalling she could speak of it to no one, least of all to Olive who seemed, in her anger and confusion, cut off from them all as if she were ill. What Catherine felt most of all was that to talk of it to anyone, even to Rebecca, particularly to Rebecca, would be to name and therefore perhaps precipitate the unspeakable. When Rebecca asked her what was up she shrugged. To her relief neither her father nor Mrs Riley appeared to notice that she came more often and had less to say than usual. There were times when she half suspected—and was shocked by the coolness of the thought—that this couple were like self-engrossed children who would turn blank, uncomprehending faces to trouble from outside. Catherine wondered if this was what life did to you and if she would finish like that, deaf to unwelcome news, blind to all but the trivial and harmless. Without knowing quite what she was resisting she found herself saying aloud, with fists clenched: it couldn't happen to me, I won't be like that.

Olive realised that she did not know where Dennis Rawston lived. This must be a sign which meant that she need do nothing. Then she thought of the hospital file and looked up his card. There was no telephone number and none listed in the directory. She was busy. One of the orderlies was away. It would be an awkward journey. Then it seemed that the absent orderly, an older woman, was ill and alone. Olive felt obliged to visit her. The woman, for reasons of her own Olive was too tired to puzzle, resented this attention. Olive stayed only twenty minutes. When she came out she walked through the unfamiliar district looking for a bus. Normally she enjoyed walking in London. The noisy, dusty city could be oddly soothing if you had nowhere to go. Today she was exhausted: she had been tired ever since she saw Maurice Leverett; without the weight of hair she felt unbalanced, too light, insecurely anchored to the earth. She found herself gazing blankly at a street name. Dennis lived here.

There were half a dozen bells, but no names. The upper, glazed portion of the door was smashed. She had a momentary crazy vision of the people within, many people, holding the house up with their hands. Inside, the hall soared, was lost in dirt and darkness. She turned to go, she wanted to be out in the street in the bright evening strolling among easy cheerful crowds. Above, someone spoke from a half-landing.

"You looking for someone?" It was a thin, pale girl with a baby in her arms. Both looked drained of colour as though they had been shut off for a long time from the light.

"Dennis Rawston."

"He's at the top."

"Thank you."

The girl stood back against the wall to let Olive pass. She was younger than she had seemed from below. She stared at Olive with frank curiosity, neither friendly nor hostile, then someone, a man, called from inside the room. She waited till Olive had climbed the next flight, then went in. Olive could hear raised voices. As she arrived on what appeared to be the upper landing, windowless, the light went out. In the darkness she groped for a switch, could find none and fighting panic felt her way around the wall till her hand met a door-knob. There was the noise of typing from within. She knocked, the typing paused and started up again. She was tired. She was scared. There would be other doors. This might not be Dennis at all. She was afraid of this

78

house. Something warm touched her leg and she must have cried out because the door was opened at once.

"What are you doing in the dark?"

"The light went out."

Dennis smiled. "It's a time switch." He pointed to a button on the wall. "You see, you press it. Someone must have put it on as you came up. But it's not timed for this landing, it always goes out unless you set it again halfway up. Come into my attic."

"There was something . . ."

"Dulcie's cat, I expect. She's on the first floor."

"I saw her."

He nodded. He seemed quite unsurprised to see her, made no effort to play the host, ask how she had found him or why she had come but said at once, "Can you type?"

"No."

"Pity. I'm strictly two-fingered," He scowled at the typewriter, a small cranky-looking portable. "The trouble is, I've got to get these done by tomorrow." He pondered. "You don't know anyone with a roneo machine?"

Olive shook her head.

"Or a typist?"

"Not at this hour."

"I suppose not." He sat and began glumly to peck at the keys. Olive walked to the small window. To see out you had to sit or to bend. The room was so right for Dennis, like an office in which the bare necessities of private life gave away nothing about him. There was a divan bed covered with a grey blanket, a gas ring, no curtains. Suddenly she began to laugh.

"You're fantastic." He looked up, astonished. "I haven't seen you for weeks. I've never been here. You hear me screaming my head off on the landing. Don't you want to know why I've come?"

"Of course. I'm sorry." He rubbed his hand up his face, puzzled, put out. "People are always coming in, wanting something, bringing something, talking. Sometimes they

79

stay. I've been to sleep with people still talking round the bed. So you see . . ."

"People?"

"Dulcie. Tim. That's her husband . . . others. Anyone. I thought you were Dulcie."

"Larry Towers? Does he come?"

"I suppose. I really am sorry. I'm truly pleased you're here. In fact I wanted to see you." Now he had decided to give her his attention he found beer, cigarettes and a packet of smashed digestive biscuits. "You didn't ring me back."

"I didn't know you'd rung."

"Several times."

"When? When exactly?"

"Does it matter?" He told her. She explained she had had no message. That was another problem; it would keep. He had telephoned to say that someone was checking on him, Maurice Leverett had been hounding him, he even had an idea he was followed. A man in a pub had asked him about Larry Towers and London District. To Olive it was all a terrifying muddle of the probable and the fantastic. If Maurice had not warned her she would have dismissed it all as absurd. "Well," he concluded, "what do I do? What *can* I do?"

"Give up your job. Or drop the other thing."

"I need the job. And I can't give up the other." He was standing over her, hands clenched, as if she actually had the power or the wisdom to reconcile the impossible. He behaved (but then he probably behaved like this with everyone) as though he had some right to her time, her thoughts, her anxiety. She guessed most people gave way to him as she was doing now or was about to do. The prospect was a blank to her like running against a wall.

"I promised him I'd talk to you. That may keep him quiet for a while."

"Thank you. Then you will help me?"

"Yes," she said and wondered, as if she were watching, not participating in this scene, with a kind of idle surprise at her own folly, where this decision would lead her. Yet perhaps it was not so important after all. "Yes," she repeated, "I'll help you if I can."

Catherine thought, people hardly ever admit the reasons for which they are quarrelling. That would be dangerous. There are forces, she decided, chaotic powers in rocks, storms, skies, behind locked doors, walls, in cellars, beneath floor-boards, which must not be called up. Unleashed, heaven only knew what damage they could do for they would then be uncontrollable, they could kill, drive you mad, reduce the earth to a desert, bring down the sky. She guessed that her mother knew this. Did Olive?

Things, even the most solid-seeming, were so fragile. She had seen a house fall in a street weakened by bombing, but on a harmless, post-war afternoon. There had been a man drilling the pavement. A plane had passed overhead. This, something like this, had set off the vibration which brought down the house. Since no one was hurt Olive had not seen the point of the story.

Olive came in late one evening, took off her coat, lit a cigarette and said to Mrs Armitage, "You lied to me. You never told me Dennis Rawston had rung."

"Didn't I? Did it matter?"

"Yes."

"I must have forgotten." But Mrs Armitage was shaken. She looked at Olive's hair and said nothing, at first.

"You didn't forget. You lied." Olive's voice was flat. Catherine could have wept for her sister's hair, as if Olive, like a widow, had been bereaved but of her beauty. What would Harold say?

"What Harold will say about your hair I cannot think." Mrs Armitage rallied and her expression of shock was overlaid by cunning. She understood well the relative virtues of defence and attack. Also she was trying to avert the forces Catherine felt to be gathering, breaking. There was no danger in a row about hair.

"I'm not talking about hair. What I'm saying has nothing to do with Harold." Don't, Catherine wanted to say, stop, before you kill us all. Yet she was impressed. She could not leave the room. They had forgotten her in any case.

"I should have thought . . ."

"But you don't think, do you? You don't think about Dennis Rawston so as far as you are concerned he has no needs, he doesn't exist. You don't even know you're lying because you have your own scheme of things and nothing that doesn't fit is true."

"I think you are very tired. You should go to bed."

Catherine remembered Olive raging in the sun in Aunt Cat's garden. Then she had simply turned on her heel and walked away. Now she stood her ground. She was trembling and had an odd, pleading look as though beneath the row there were another secret dialogue between herself and their mother, excluding Catherine. Mrs Armitage seemed to see it. Her gaze flickered. She too appeared as bewildered as Olive by the hatred they had called up. She wanted the best for her children which meant that their lives should be as different as possible from her own. How then, even for a moment, could she hate them? And she did, often, especially Olive. She knew she would lie in bed tonight and recite to some mysterious, sympathetic being, God-in-Teddy-Asher yet neither God nor Teddy but someone she had been waiting all her life to meet and despaired of meeting, the wrongs done to her. In these waking dreams the words she used were sometimes obscene. Tomorrow she would be busy and cheerful. She would find something to do, or to seem to do. It was odd how no one noticed she was burning.

When Mrs Armitage had gone to bed Catherine made tea and waited for Olive to explain. It seemed a tremendous fuss about a telephone message. Olive said nothing but kept touching her neck where her hair had been. Catherine was out of her depth. She improvised.

"Was it very important?"

"What?"

"The message?"

"Not particularly."

"Oh."

Catherine understood she had been warned. Whatever was happening to Olive, she would have no part in it. She was afraid.

12

IN the end Catherine told Rebecca, as she knew she would. They had had a marvellous Saturday afternoon. Sam, who was normally up to some mysterious business of his own at weekends, took them rowing on the Serpentine. Or rather, he sat under a rug, his hat tipped over his eyes and allowed the girls to row. Afterwards he bought them ice-cream. Miraculously, as if he had created her from the air, a long-legged girl appeared. It seemed they had arranged to meet. The girl wore silk stockings and a grey coat trimmed with fur, like a Russian heroine. She carried a small dog. She slipped her white hand under Sam's arm and took him away. Rebecca began to tell Catherine how it was all quite absurd, she must be at least twenty-five. She was engaged to be married. She gave Sam presents. She had a flat of her own near Marble Arch. Mrs Davies would die if she knew. Suddenly Catherine burst into tears. She had not expected to. She rarely cried and she was happy. It had been a perfect afternoon. She tried to explain: "I don't even know what they're quarrelling *about*."

Rebecca was not embarrassed. She often cried in public, fainted, howled, got herself taxis, attention, policemen. It was in the family. It was known you could not tell Sara Davies an unhappy story out of doors. Rebecca's grandmother had once sat down on the pavement in Piccadilly. She had some new shoes which hurt her feet. When she felt better she got up, took off her shoes and went into Fortnum's for tea.

Rebecca said, "I think she's in love with Dennis Rawston."

"But she's going to marry Harold."

"Oh, Hog," said Rebecca, "you mean well. But will you *ever* grow up?"

At first, guarded and set on detachment, Olive simply watched. It was just a matter, she told herself, of separating one thing from another in her mind. There was the row with her mother. There was Harold. There was Dennis. The three were not connected unless she herself chose to connect them. It was from the connection she must detach herself: she must resist the suggestion, implicit in the quarrel with her mother, that concern for Dennis was disloyalty to Harold. This was clearly absurd. Harold would be the last to expect that in marrying him she should turn her back on the rest of the world.

It was in the same mood she visited Dennis. She had agreed to help him (without quite knowing what the help amounted to) and she could tell Maurice Leverett truthfully that she was talking to Dennis. Besides, she had nothing else to do. She was on days at the hospital and evenings at home were unendurable.

Dennis's room and what went on there were a revelation to Olive. She had understood, of course, that there was more than talk to Dennis's idealism, there must be a practical aspect. She had thought vaguely of meetings, letters, plans, but had imagined nothing like the ceaseless talk and activity, the comings and goings, tea-making, the way these people seemed to take him over, the apparent tirelessness with which he responded. Yet he was not a politician or a social worker or a priest, he had no obligation to any of them but he was always ready with attention, advice, action where action was possible. She was impressed and ashamed that she had ever thought him irresponsible and egotistical. At the end of such an evening he was grey and drained, yet that was the time he seemed most eager to talk. Fresh tea would be made and those who were left, helpers or 'clients', would stay while Olive too sat on, heavy-lidded. What were they talking about? Utopia? The shortcomings of politicians? How to get

Mrs X and her five children out of one stinking room? Whether a certain landlord could be persuaded to put the drains right and repair the roof? To what degree they were willing to commit themselves politically? If so-and-so would pay up as he had promised and if not where the next pound, shilling, penny for hand-outs, paper, stamps, medicines, baby-food, was to come from? Someone started a collection for an immediate emergency. Dulcie brought in fish and chips and a bottle of beer. A professional social worker stood up and made a short speech about the attitude of the Labour Party. There were derisive cheers. It was all, to Olive, an incredible muddle of good intentions, pathetically small achievements, absurd rhetoric, impossible obstacles and passion so strong it must vault all obstacles. She went home late, her head throbbing, and hardly slept. Each morning she decided that she would not go again.

As far as Olive could gather most of the group was vaguely left-wing, disenchanted with the Socialist government and lost for any more hopeful allegiance. To this degree they were bewildered, reluctant to believe that they had been let down. A couple, who were Communists (including Dulcie's husband, Tim), were inclined to make speeches and were invariably shouted down, but with good nature. There emerged, gradually through the confusion, the pattern which held them all together: the urge to right wrongs done by war or the negligence of politicians. None was over thirty. They were, in their attitude to those who came for help, like grave children apologising in a practical way for the shortcomings of their parents. If the Socialists had failed to produce Jerusalem, then Dennis and his friends could at least, pending heaven, write letters, argue with landlords, imitate in their small, frequently defeated efforts, a larger justice.

They all assumed from the start that simply by coming to this room Olive had committed herself to join them. They never seemed to imagine for a moment that she might be just a friend, or a girl-friend, of Dennis's. She said little and they asked her few questions so she was free to study them.

87

The clients reminded her of the squatters she had seen on the road in Kent but she began now to distinguish between the shades of hardship and resentment, degrees of need; the least hard hit were the most vociferous and there was a special tone of whining self-pity she learned to recognise— those who had really suffered to an intense degree, the homeless and the hungry, were stunned, inarticulate, so confused by their plight it often took Dennis an hour or more of steady, sometimes ruthless questioning to establish the facts of the case. Perhaps it was because they were inarticulate in the first place they had become victims. Or there was a point at which misery becomes the air you breathe, the way you live, anything better, even protest, unimaginable.

She had seen a little of this in the hospital, of course. She had heard of it from Dennis, and glimpsed it in faces in the street. A friend of Harold's had been into Hiroshima, someone Chris knew to Belsen. Olive was at once afraid and desperate to question them. There was this awful urge to know the worst, however appalling, as if only then you could act, make up your mind. As though there were anything one could do . . . Mrs Armitage, slicing a peach, said there was nothing new about the state of the world. It had always been the same cycle of violence, victim, reparation, violence. Each generation believed its conscience to be unique. Olive could not accept this. She had a blind faith in the breaking point, the point at which you give in or grow sane, the moment when the pattern must be broken or surely there was no sense in life at all? If this were true of the individual, why not of the human race? Was this the moment? She didn't know. Her thoughts were too vague to express. She had been brought up not to make a fuss.

If she had hoped someone in Dennis's group might put into words her own feelings she was disappointed. Dennis was far too busy to make speeches in public or in private. Among the helpers was a tense, angry girl called Polly who asked Olive to find out through the hospital about getting bandages wholesale. Olive could not imagine what they

wanted bandages for but she got the information and this
was the first job she did for the group. Then she volunteered
to address some envelopes. She had no intention of becoming
involved but she was bored doing nothing. Of the helpers
she found Polly most sympathetic, though alarming. There
was one tired-looking, palely pretty girl, Lucy, who did
much of the donkey work, appeared to worship Dennis, and
smiled shyly at Olive. But it was Dulcie Connor from downstairs who first made any serious gesture of interest towards
Olive. She was odd. She took no active part in meetings. Olive
could not make out if she was a client or a helper or if, like
Olive herself, she had nothing better to do. She looked a bit
of a slut, she was clearly unimpressed by anything that happened in this room, but most evenings she drifted up, smoking continuously, leaning against the wall, watching with
sharp eyes everything that went on. One night she found
Olive alone addressing envelopes. The others had gone out
for a beer.

"It feels like thunder. When it's like this I could drink
and drink. I get so dry."

"Why didn't you go out with the others?" Olive looked
up. She was thirsty too.

Dulcie shrugged. "The kids. They yell. The neighbours
complain. Not Dennis. Would you like some tea?"

"I'd love it."

Olive thought Dulcie would bring it up.

"Right. See you down there in five minutes."

Olive hardly knew what to expect. It was one room, quite
large. She took in a brass bedstead and another, smaller bed,
a divan in the corner away from the window on which three
or four children lay curled together. There was a cot by the
big bed. Washing was strung across the corner of the room
on a line. There was a smell of sleep she had encountered
before, in the hospital, in the early morning before the floor
was washed with disinfectant. In sleep the body seemed to
give off its chemicals, some acrid, some not unpleasant. The
table in the centre of the room, covered with American

cloth, held the tea Dulcie had prepared, the remains of a meal and a pile of books. Olive touched them. Marx, Lenin, names she had never read, but thought of vaguely as dangerous, difficult, magical (if you were susceptible to that kind of magic), but most of all, difficult. The dull bindings seemed wrong, they should be in blazing covers. She was ashamed not to have read them. How could one claim to care at all and have read nothing, know nothing? Yet Larry Towers must have read them and his mind seemed to Olive narrower even than her own, locked, finished for ever. She was repelled and intrigued by such certainty.

Dulcie was pouring the tea. She jerked her head towards the books.

"Tim's. He reads his eyes out. He's even learning Russian. Ready for when they come, I suppose. Though I tell him, God knows why he thinks they'd be better than this lot. Worse, I'd say."

"You don't like him doing this?"

Dulcie shrugged. She kicked off her sandals and put up her feet. The soles were dirty.

"I don't care. If he wants to, that's his business. It's cheaper than drink."

"How does he find the time?" Olive wondered why Dulcie had asked her down. Now she was here she seemed not only indifferent to Olive's presence, but almost angry, as if she wanted to be alone and Olive had intruded. She decided she would drink her tea and go.

"Didn't you know, he's out of work? No jobs, no homes fit for heroes. We live like pigs, no money, too many kids. You can't blame him."

For what Tim could not be blamed, Olive was not clear. The children? The Russian? Dulcie drank her tea and grimaced. Suddenly she looked up at Olive with an open face, child-like, "I used to love sugar. That's what I miss. Sugar."

They drank and smoked, two women in a room. A child stirred and murmured in its sleep. Olive was so tired she felt

90

she too might fall asleep in this room when at home she lay awake all hours of the night. Dulcie was talking again. "I can never make out if he really thinks Stalin is Father Christmas or if he's just bored. If he does this to stop going mad."

"You do funny things when you're bored."

"Dennis says you're getting married. Someone stinking rich."

"Yes."

"Then what are you doing here?"

"I don't know. I honestly don't know." Olive felt tired of watching herself, tempted in this odd complicity of women to tell Dulcie. What? And if she told she would regret tomorrow.

"Then that's two of us. Only you needn't be here. You're free."

"I suppose I am."

The two women smiled, as if they had reached an understanding. Then the baby woke and cried. Dulcie scooped it up and put it to her breast, still smoking. Olive could not look away. She was fascinated by this small, tugging creature, ruthless in its passion for life. She wondered if it hurt.

13

OLIVE had realised for a week that there was something extraordinary in the wind. Once or twice when she arrived at Dennis's room in the early evening she found what she had recognised to be the hard core of the group—Dennis, Polly and Dulcie's husband, Tim—several times arguing. It took her a while to understand that she was being tactfully dismissed, sent to post letters, fetch beer, until one evening the pretext had grown so thin she was embarrassed and wondered if she had made a fool of herself over the whole affair. She told herself this was an interlude. Harold would be back in a few days, then her real life would begin again. Yet this life, as yet unknown, held no reality for her. She was puzzled and depressed. In the end she tackled Dulcie. Later she confronted Dennis.

"Dulcie says you're working with Larry Towers. There's going to be some kind of demonstration."

"Something like that."

"Why didn't you tell me?"

Dennis looked so tired she was ashamed to bother him. Yet surely she had a right to know. He had been sitting on the edge of the bed. Olive had been standing over him—as she saw it, getting a harsh mental glimpse of herself—like a spoiled child wanting to know why it was left out of a game. He might easily and with justice refuse to answer. But he smiled and drew her down beside him, explaining as if she were indeed a child.

"We would have told you, but we weren't sure how committed you were."

"Committed?"

"You have your own life. This is only the smallest part. Something you'll give up when it suits you."

"You make it sound like games."

"Isn't it?"

"You think I'll tell Maurice Leverett."

"No. But we can't ask too much of you."

"You mean you don't trust me."

He shook his head. He was so tired.

"I'm sorry. You're tired. I'll go."

She had reached the door when he called her back, as she knew he would.

"No. Olive. Do stay. You do help. I will tell you."

He told her it was the same plan they had discussed with Larry Towers in the pub at the Elephant and Castle. On Sunday the homeless were to take over a block of flats in Kensington and later, they hoped, there would be others. The only trouble was they needed an organisation and that was what they had argued about. Tim was keen for them to go in with the Communists. Polly was against it. He, Dennis, had not been sure, but now he had decided. It was the only way.

"Can I come?"

"Do you really want to?"

"Yes."

"What about your respectable boy-friend?" This was the first time Dennis had mentioned Harold.

"He's away."

Dennis nodded. Apparently he was satisfied. At once he began to talk about their plans. There were ways she could be useful. There was always a dry part of Olive's mind which said you're a fool, you haven't thought this out; but already she was passionately rationalising a course of action she had settled on the moment she first entered this room.

Catherine was alone in the house when the telegram arrived. She took it to her room, laid it squarely in a patch of sunlight on the dressing-table, and looked at it. It was addressed to Olive. It must be from Harold. There was no one to ask. Did one open other people's telegrams?

A few months ago the question would not have arisen.

Catherine was caught short sometimes, shocked, by the small, secret ways in which she had changed; secret because these odd little hardenings within herself, like areas of dead skin, had grown without her knowing. She had felt lately, and told no one, that there was not only within her but all around, behind windows, doors, faces, in boxes, desks, cups, a world of secrets. She wondered if everyone felt this, if all offered one eye to the obvious and tangible, another to that inner darkness. Rebecca would not know what she was talking about; which might be why she had taken Rebecca for a friend, because she did not want to talk about it. It made no sense.

She was afraid her eye might be growing cold.

At seventeen she was frightened in a new, unchildlike way, by what she might see, if she looked. Better not to look. But the yellow envelope was urgent, it insisted. She touched it, carried it around the room, let it fall like a leaf, of no account. She watched it from a distance. Then the doorbell rang.

Harold said he would rather sit in the kitchen. He watched Catherine make tea.

"Did my cable arrive?"

"I think so. Just now. I didn't open it."

"Why not? Then you'd have known I was coming."

"I don't know. I was scared."

"What of?"

"Something I didn't know about."

He studied her gravely. They drank their tea and he watched her over the edge of the cup; she snatched up a cat and buried her face in its fur. It disliked the intensity of the embrace, understood perhaps that it was being used, and abandoned her. She was left empty-handed, near panic.

"Sorry. I'm not much good at entertaining."

"Something's wrong. What is it? Is it Olive?"

"No. I don't know. Harold, would it matter a lot to you if it were?"

95

"Very much. Catherine, if something's happened, you must tell me."

"I can't say anything has. I think I may have imagined it all."

"Tell me."

"She's out a lot. She's quarrelled with mother. She won't talk to me."

Catherine must have looked wretched because he took her hands in his across the table.

"I'm sorry," he said. "You shouldn't be upset."

That finished her, the fact that he was worried to death but could still think of her. She told him everything she knew or had guessed. It all came out, about the quarrel and Dennis Rawston, Olive cutting her hair, Catherine's suspicions about Chris; she did not mention her father because that was her secret, even from Harold. When she had finished she was appalled by the damage she might have done. There seemed no end to the ruin she had created as if she had brought down the house about their heads. Then Mrs Armitage came in and wondered what on earth they were doing in the kitchen, in the dark. Harold stayed till nearly midnight but Olive did not come in. They agreed she must be on nights. Mrs Armitage offered to ring the hospital but Harold said there was no point, it was too late.

When Dulcie Connor suggested that Olive might stay the night she agreed at once. She was tired, the meeting this evening might go on till all hours, and besides she still had a strange feeling that in this room she would sleep.

"But where?"

"Dennis has got a camp-bed. We'll fit you in somewhere."

Olive thought how queer it would be to lie down and wake in this room of breathing people, all those children, and Dulcie and Tim in the big bed. There were many who lived like this all the time. Those squatters on the road in Kent. One should be appalled. She was appalled, by that memory, by Dulcie's situation, and by her own sentimentality at enjoying as a visitor this closeness. Fine for her. Instructed by listening Olive could hold forth now on the housing situation, the plight of the homeless not only here but worse in Europe, the displaced, the exiled, the statistics, with which she was familiar after days of finding out for Polly (for what? what would Polly do with these figures?) the numbers of famine, disease, broken minds, the facts so far as they were known of Hiroshima, Nagasaki, Auschwitz, Belsen. To what end? Olive saw at one pole her mother who said, rightly, it had all happened before, at the other Polly, Dennis, the rest who seemed to imagine that by making lists they were actually doing something. Certainly they might tidy up their own backyard. But if you saw them in a larger context they were nothing more than industrious insects. It did not do to think too much along these lines. At the meeting on the evening before the squat, Olive found Dennis and his group faintly absurd.

Polly arrived red-eyed and made a small drama of not speaking to Tim Connor, who was looking pleased with himself. Dulcie told Olive that Polly had been crying because Tim had won, they were to act under the wing of the Communists.

"She came down when Tim was out, this afternoon, and made a scene. I said politics were Greek to me and as long as we got somewhere decent to live I didn't care how. She said I was a disgrace to the working class. I told her to mind her language, then she had a good howl. We got on like a house on fire after that. She's a nice kid, there's nothing wrong with her."

Someone frowned at them. Dennis came in with Larry Towers. The meeting had begun. Dennis spoke first, introducing Larry. No one applauded but Tim unfolded his long arms and, with the other Communist, leaned forward attentively. Lucy was taking notes. Polly was chain-smoking, her face creased, glaring at her feet.

Larry spoke in his grinding voice, explaining flatly how lists of the homeless had been made, they had been told

97

where to go, and to bring food and bedding. He said the squat had become a public secret. They must expect more than had been allowed for on the lists. Members of the London District Committee would themselves occupy one of the flats to oversee the demonstration. It struck Olive that behind all the soul-searching of Dennis's group, the high drama and baring of souls, was a system which made such theatricals ridiculous. Larry and his mates were neither devils nor angels, they would beg for no one's soul, they would proceed, blinkered, indifferent, regardless of Tim's loyalty or Polly's tantrums. This was both their strength and their weakness. For them, the system was stronger than the individual. Yet what was the system but the unanimous will of individuals? Everyone here, she guessed, would call themselves Socialists but even that was diminished by its shades of meaning. She and Dulcie were the only exceptions. Politics meant nothing to them. To Dennis they meant something because they were abhorrent but necessary. Perhaps he was right, for, short of violence, what could you achieve without them? If only you could use them, without being used.

Dulcie nudged Olive. She realised she had not been paying attention. Dulcie was grinning. Tim's friend, the other Communist, a sturdy, boiled young man, had climbed to his feet.

"I hope, Comrade Towers, the people will remember it is the Communist Party that fights for the workers." Delivered of his message he looked round, panicked and sat down. Larry nodded curtly. Dennis stared at the papers on the table before him. Polly said in a strained, unnatural voice, "Can Mr Towers give us any assurance of protection for our clients?"

"We can give no assurance. If this fails, if the Government choose to persecute the innocent, to override the will of the people, the blame is at their door, not ours."

"Then you can't lose, can you? Whichever way it goes, you're right." Polly looked as if she might cry again.

"You're mad," Dulcie said to Olive later, while they made

up the camp-bed between them. "You must be crazy to be here at all."

"I want to be here."

"Why? You're not like Polly and Tim. You're not like Dennis. You don't *have* to do this. You've got everything. Why do you bother with us?"

"I like it here."

"Then you are mad. You realise the risk tomorrow? We might all go to jail. It might be more comfortable, heaven knows. But not for you."

"I don't care about comfort."

Dulcie paused and stared at Olive, then she grinned. "I really believe you don't."

The children were fed and went to sleep. Olive and Dulcie stretched out on the big bed, smoking. Dennis and Tim were upstairs still with Larry Towers. Olive glanced at Dulcie, the thin girl, worn out by being a woman. Oh well, Dulcie would say, that's men, meaning children and war and nowhere fit to live and being tired. It seemed appalling that she should accept such a situation, yet at the same time she had a kind of splendour. Olive thought how easy her own life had been.

"Do you think Tim would tell me what to read?"

"He'd love it. He'd talk the hind leg off a dead donkey." Dulcie yawned and stretched. "But you don't want to know that. What's the point? They just stuff their heads and it's all the same in the end, if you're a woman. You're flat on your back and it's babies and you're yelling, then you're dead."

"It can't be. There must be more. How can you stand it?"

"It's not so bad."

Dulcie went to sleep. Tim came in. Olive thought of ringing home. She sat up for a while talking in whispers with Tim, then she went to bed and fell asleep at once in the softly breathing room.

14

MRS ARMITAGE slept late. She had troubled dreams of a city which she dimly recognised, ordered, peaceful, fountains playing, bland terraces and squares, invaded by marching columns. A child cried and was trampled underfoot. She woke and looked out. It was Sunday, yet the street was full of people.

Catherine should have gone to Rebecca's but she rang up.

"Why not?"

"There's a bit of a flap." Olive had not come home for breakfast, nor had she telephoned nor was she at the hospital. Harold had telephoned three times.

"We were going to play golf."

"Golf?"

Harold came round at midday. He said some kind of mob had got together to take over an empty block of flats. He and Catherine played cards. Catherine thought it was like waiting at the bedside when someone was fatally ill, boring and frightening at once. She wondered why one had to behave so well; at Rebecca's, in a situation like this, someone would be crying, fainting, praying; Sara Davies would be put to bed; Moshe would crack his long fingers. All would be ready for the worst and when it did not happen, this would be a matter for celebration.

If the worst did happen it might be that Olive was dead, dying at least, run over, suddenly ill, among strangers. At the best she would have run off with Dennis Rawston, or surely she would have telephoned.

She could not bear to think what it must be like to be

Harold at this moment. Catherine decided she would become extremely good at shorthand typing and have nothing to do with love.

As they approached the Duchess of Bedford House Olive was astonished by the ordinariness of the extraordinary. The police were baffled and polite. The ragged column of squatters, converging from all over London, pushed prams, bicycles and carts laden with household goods and food. They were orderly, cheerful, incredibly respectable. It was hard to believe that for the British this was a quite revolutionary piece of mass law-breaking on an unprecedented scale. Only the children, and some of the observers, seemed to sense the drama, the potentiality of the occasion. For the younger children, this would be their first significant memory of any world beyond the domestic. For the older ones, who had been born in war, could remember nothing but war, today was like a long-promised party. If this came to nothing, if they were defeated, the infants would assume that this was the structure of life; the adults would grouse, try again, retreat behind complaint and stoicism. The children, Olive thought, might never recover. She could not imagine what would happen if they were forced to grow in a world of dreariness and perpetual frustration. It seemed cruel to educate them, to persuade them on the one hand that there was a better way if it could only be snatched, on the other to let them down. She thought, they'll have the right to accuse us when they're grown, and we can plead only that we tried and failed. Yet that would be intolerable, the bleak answer given always by one generation to the next.

Olive was aware of being keyed up, of reading more into this occasion perhaps than there was, because, she realised suddenly, she desperately wanted it to be significant. It could be the challenge to everyone who said the world could not be changed, it had become too complex and dangerous for the will of any but the most sophisticated and powerful to alter the substance of life. Maurice Leverett and his

102

masters. Most of the people here, she understood, were self-absorbed, indifferent to anything but their own inarticulate dissatisfaction. Yet collectively they were a force.

She looked for Dennis but he was ahead with Tim and Polly. There was no sign of Larry Towers, only a couple of people who might be Communist organisers. For the most part, Olive guessed, hardly anyone here realised that the squat was politically inspired. An angry-looking youth began to sing the 'Internationale' but no one took it up.

Dulcie was pushing a laden pram, containing the baby, food and saucepans. The rest of the children trailed behind her. She wore an old leather jacket of Tim's and slacks. She turned, saw Olive watching her, and grinned.

"So far so good."

"Shall I push the pram for a bit?"

"If you like. But you ought to be up front with the revolutionaries. We're only odds and sods back here."

Olive shook her head.

"Why not? Don't you agree with them?"

"Yes, I do." Olive was about to say more but they had arrived. She had a feeling, at once uneasy and attractive, that Dulcie knew, perhaps without ever formulating her conclusions, what went on in people's minds. That was why one sought her company. She understood but was too easy-going to criticise. Oh well, she would say of someone, of Dennis, or her husband's politics, presumably of Olive, oh well, he's like that. Intimacy with women—with anyone for that matter—had never come easily to Olive. So it was a surprising experience to feel instinctively that in Dulcie she had an ally.

"Olive!" Dennis was calling her. "Would you go round the flats and make sure everyone has food and water." They were standing on the steps. Looking back the street was full of people but there was a holiday feeling, no coherence. Babies were crying, children playing. Adults waited to be told what to do.

The next few days were in Olive's memory an experience

103

of weariness, confusion, achievement and disappointment, and of closeness. Once she remembered ringing home and Catherine's voice from a great distance saying that Harold was back. It was like a message from another world.

In the course of the week several other blocks were taken over and a pattern became established. The authorities grew shrewd. As soon as a house was occupied gas, water and electricity were cut off and a police cordon prevented food deliveries.

They were forced to abandon the Kensington house. Between jobs for Dennis (he was still going to the Ministry every day) Olive helped Dulcie to move back into her one room. At least Dulcie had somewhere to go. Those who had not were sent to hostels.

Yet there was a strange feeling of triumph in the air. Olive, who never again experienced to the same degree the euphoria of those days, felt that you could reach out, touch, breathe, smell the glory. They had failed, but nothing would be the same again. After this who but the most complacent and totally blind could accept things as they were? She felt this because she was constantly occupied, busy in a way she had never been before, even in the war, so that at night she slept deeply in Dulcie's room, woke to children crying, a fine morning, more work. Her limbs ached, she had the curse, her head throbbed, she was happy.

She began to realise that behind the apparent spontaneity, even behind the workings of their own little group, and Larry Towers, was a complex machinery. Every move had been worked out. Behind Larry Towers was another boss and behind him another boss. At the top someone, presumably, who had calculated the exact degree to which success was possible. Failure too. Yet they must succeed. The whole exercise must have been based on the assumption of success, or it would be pointless.

Olive saw Harold once. After an awkward telephone call they met in neutral territory at a café down the road from the B.B.C. The meeting was inconclusive. Harold looked

104

strained. For the first time for days Olive was aware of how drab she must appear; exhausted, she had come out without looking in the mirror. Now she saw herself as Harold must see her, some kind of decadent vicar's wife, down at heel, shabby, too bright. As for Harold, she was appalled, incredulous that she felt so little for this man who had become a total stranger.

She had never before realised that the most important decisions, even between two people, are frequently made in silence. Somehow, the engagement had broken itself without a word being spoken.

"When do you go back?"

"I'm not sure I'll go at all. Not yet anyhow. I may see a bit of Europe first."

"That's what you always wanted. I mean . . ." Olive was appalled by herself. Who was this man, this blurred, receding creature who made her behave with such hideous, sparkling, official kindness, like a social worker? In a moment she would be telling him that Europe might be good for him. They had no language even, in common, so how could they talk? For Harold Europe was pulling strings, getting into private collections, decent hotels, monuments, Venice, Rome, the loving excavation of the unchanged, Mrs Armitage's Europe. Continental Europe meant to Olive, who had never been there, Polly's awful statistics, so many dead and starving. No more real, in the context of her own experience, than Harold's. Doubtless both were true and it would be arrogant to assume as correct either posture. Yet she did assume a posture which made her right and Harold wrong. Only in meeting Harold did she understand how completely she had committed herself to the group. Time away from them was wasted. She could not bear to go home. She resented the time spent earning a living at the hospital. One could not live like this, it was mad. Yet she did.

They walked out together into the street. They could hardly shake hands. There was no question of kissing, yet there had to be some gesture. Olive had a mad impulse to hug him and say, you're the best man I've met. She almost wished he would argue or protest. She was struck for the first time by the finality, struggled against it, "I'll see you when you get back? You'll let us know how you are?"

"If I come back."

"Well . . ."

He touched her cheek lightly with his finger. "Look after yourself. Be careful."

"I'm in no danger. I'm not important enough."

"If you have time, ring Catherine."

"Cat?" She was puzzled. But he had gone.

That day two thousand people sat down in the street in Regent's Park. Squatters had taken over a block and baffled police allowed through bread and milk. There was no violence. After a while the Communists sent them home. A point had been made.

The same evening they all met at Toni's, a café run by a cockney Greek. Lucy was sitting in with Dulcie's children. The café was one of two surviving buildings shored up on a bomb site. At this time and for many years after there were areas of such desolation in London. Already they had ceased to shock, one grew blind to them, they were covered by a purple weed. When visitors were appalled, Londoners looked surprised, as if they had always lived like this. No one knew where the weed had come from. It must have been blown by the wind or waited in the dark subsoil for release. It masked less graceful signs: rats, craters, scorched foundations.

Dennis had hardly slept for a week, his eyes burned. Olive felt protective and at the same time impatient, because he took on too much. He would be ill again. People came to him to be comforted, encouraged, recharged. Without him they would be merely individuals of vague goodwill and no direction. He held them together but he could not afford to spend himself like this. She was impatient with him yet she had to admire him. Something about her short, pointless talk with Harold had made it all the more necessary to admire Dennis Rawston.

This was not an official meeting, more of a party. They had drunk beer first, and some sherry Polly produced, in Dulcie's room while the children were put to bed. Olive had noticed that for once, Dennis too was drinking. In the mood of the day this was understandable, yet she was disturbed. Perhaps she felt Dennis should be above such things. Yet why should he be? She was drinking herself.

She sat at the end of the table, which was covered in greasy oilcloth, and listened. Tim Connor, Dulcie's husband, was flirting with Polly, on behalf of the group. In the flush of victory, there was an urge to solidarity. Tim had been born in Australia of Irish parents. He had met Dennis in the Air Force and like him, but possibly for different reasons, stayed in the ranks. He was mysteriously classless and had worked as a bus-driver, a labourer and for a time briefly, after the war, on a farm. Olive doubted his intelligence but there was a vitality about his political convictions she found attractive. By the side of Larry Towers he was, she guessed, politically naïf. He was limited. In his passionate self-education he would find only the answers he wished to find but, unlike Larry, he would enjoy himself. Both were ruthless but while Larry would kill coldly along the devious path to some distant, precisely formulated objective, Tim would strike out in a hot rage. When he could afford it, and even when he couldn't, he drank too much. In the first stages of drunkenness, as now, he was charming.

"We'll make a red of Polly yet." He was looking at her breasts, which were very fine. Polly's father was a Tory M.P. Somewhere in the country she had her own horse. Her mother had run a settlement in Stepney. Her daughter, doubtless, if she had one, would burn down London or regard the whole business of helping the underprivileged as nonsense. Polly was caught between, awkward, well-meaning, worried, large. "Come on, Polly, love, you lovely woman."

107

"Leave her alone."

Tim sighed. Polly smiled, vaguely, then with radiance. She had given in. In her way, she was a beauty.

"You're wrong all the same," she said, "that's not the way."

Dennis told them that Larry and his comrades were writing to the Minister of Health. He told Olive, "I think I might go over to them. At least they get something done."

Tim said, "Polly's got a horse."

"For God's sake."

Toni was handing out some dubious chunks of meat on skewers. Quite suddenly Olive felt sick. Dulcie took advantage of the racket.

"You've chucked him, haven't you?"

"Who?"

"That Yank."

Dennis was saying that if Larry was to be arrested he should join the party so that he should be arrested too. No one was listening. Dennis went on and on talking to himself. Olive wanted to cry.

"I don't know about chucked. But it's finished, anyway."

"You must be off your head."

"Perhaps I am."

Olive sounded so desolate Dulcie turned to face her. At the other end of the table a row, still cheerful for the moment, was brewing up between Dennis and Tim. Tim was waving his long arms like flags declaring that the whole business of the squat had been a victory for the solidarity of the working class. Dennis was shaking his head. With the effects of the drink, exhaustion, the first chance to relax for days, he was seized by a weary bitterness. Olive saw him from a great distance and heard Dulcie say, "Take it easy, love. It's not the end of the world." She looked worried.

Dulcie treated Olive with the careless affection she dispensed to her own children. It was a treatment quite new to Olive, who found herself responding with astonishing intensity. With everyone else she knew she had to guard herself for her own sake; with Catherine, for Catherine's sake. What Dulcie said was unimportant and she rarely said anything striking: oh well, that's the world, that's men, that's peace, war, the price of things. That's life. Harold had said something once about the roots of life. Was that what she felt about Dulcie? Yet Dulcie seemed to live easily, on the surface of things. Because she was stupid, or too tired or too wise to live any other way? Olive shivered. "You take things too hard. It's not that Yank, is it?"

"Not altogether. Harold's just part of it, or perhaps he simply confuses the issue. Perhaps I'm just tired."

"No wonder. We're all tired." Dulcie leaned back and grinned. "I used to think what I'll do after the war is sleep. I'll just lie down and sleep and sleep and Tim'll be back and there'll be more kids but I'll just lie there and once a year I'll pop and peace will take care of them. I thought, you know—just because we'd stopped killing each other we'd all be angels or something. But it seems to go on, just the same. I suppose it always did."

"Are you happy, Dulcie?"

Before Dulcie could answer Tim called down the table, "Olive, for God's sake tell him. You're the only sane one here."

"Tell him what?"

"That we've won."

Olive looked round at Tim Connor, Polly, Dulcie and Dennis staring at the table. How could anyone say 'we'? There was no such thing as the group, it did not exist. Dennis was perhaps the only one here whose motives were pure. Olive herself in this last week might have mistaken action for triumph, protest for action, might be no more admirable than Dulcie, less so because Dulcie at least acknowledged the selfishness of her motives. When you came down to it what could you say they had achieved? The squatters might or might not be allowed to stay. Many had already been evicted. Two thousand people had sat down quietly in the street. It had been a moving moment, historical, possibly prophetic. But only a moment. Nothing was changed. Had they won?

They were all watching her: Dulcie grinning, Polly frowning. Tim flushed. They needed so much to believe that this had been a victory. Olive understood how tired she was. Her own flicker of despair, like Dennis's, was a matter of exhaustion. This would pass. Olive knew herself to be tough, not in the sense of resilience but of surviving; her nerve might falter but she could not imagine it breaking. This was something new she had discovered about herself. The others must have sensed this strength.

"Of course we've won," she said lightly. "We're just worn out, that's all."

She had released them. Toni brought on more skewers loaded with unspeakable meat. He was worried about the Greek situation. He puffed and sighed. "Your war is finished, but you see ours goes on. You will pull out. Now it will be the Americans."

"Or the Russians."

He shrugged. "Whichever, there will never be democracy in Greece."

No one took Toni's depression very seriously. He had not been home for forty years. Tim began one of his long explanations, at once excited and earnest, that Communism was inevitable in Greece and Western intervention was not only futile but provocative. It might even lead to a direct confrontation with Moscow, another world war.

Dennis smiled. "Who'd win? Your pals, I suppose. One thing's certain: that's the only way you'll ever get Communism here. By force."

Dulcie groaned. "Don't start him off. We'll be here all night."

"Look," said Tim. He spread his arms, leaned back, took one of Polly's cigarettes, as if by right, lit it, then hunched himself, elbows in as if under starter's orders. "Look, you tell me, what do you want? Olive?"

"Peace, I suppose. Freedom and tolerance within an

ordered society. Some kind of purpose. Most of all, peace. Till you've got that you can't start, can you?"

"And you think we've got that? Here?"

"No. But I think if in some way you could find out what everyone wanted it would be the same thing; people are basically sane. They must see that we can't go on like this." Olive was aware of being pushed into a corner, trapped.

Tim grinned with triumph: "And these basically sane people in a western democracy were consulted about the atomic bomb, are being consulted now about a situation which could start another war that would kill not fifty million but wipe out the earth? You mean well, Olive, but you're a liberal of the worst kind. Live and let live and they'll dig their own graves. The so-called balance of power has always been a bomb. A single ideology is the only hope, and you won't get that from your wet-arsed Socialists or chinless Tories. You must see. It's the only way. It makes sense."

"I don't know." Olive shook her head. Polly was pink. Dennis had been watching with a peculiar intensity. Dulcie saved them.

"Come back home and I'll make some tea."

They walked back through the evening which Tim had failed to spoil. They still had the feeling of paraplegics risen from their beds to go about the world and stir the dead to life. Dennis was walking in his sleep. Tim was singing. When they got to the flat the children woke, one by one, rubbing their eyes. Olive held the smallest girl and comforted her. Perhaps that was what she really wanted, the warmth of another person, husband or children? For the first time that day she was mindless and happy, happy because she was mindless.

15

A FEW days later Olive found Catherine waiting for her outside the hospital. Rebecca had said, "For heaven's sake stop moping and go and see her."

A cold wind whipped up the street. Winter was here. In a month Catherine would have chilblains. Olive wore Dennis's thick woollen scarf round her head and her throat. She walked quickly, head down against the wind. Catherine had to step forward and catch her arm. "Cat!"

"I wasn't sure you'd be here. I thought you might be on nights."

"Not this week."

"Which way are you going?"

"To the tube."

"I'll walk with you."

"It's out of your way."

"I don't mind."

They were both embarrassed. Catherine glanced sideways at her stepsister and Olive guessed what she saw; she had seen it herself: something too bright, too sharp about her. Her cropped hair was hidden beneath the scarf. She was, in her own mirror, all eyes and bones. They talked about nothing as if they had met accidentally, and then were were at the Underground station.

"Well."

"Olive, you wouldn't come home?"

"Did she send you?"

"No."

Olive softened. "Cat, I'm sorry if it's awful for you. I seem to have messed up a lot of people. But I can't come back."

Catherine was hunched, hands deep in her pockets. Olive

thought, she was seventeen, capable of marrying, bearing a child, entering the mystery, but she looked like a sulky schoolgirl.

"You're angry with me." Olive was genuinely puzzled. She could imagine how it would be at home alone with Madam but not bad enough, surely, to make Catherine hate her. "Come on, Cat, what have I done?" Her voice, in her own ears, sounded hideously jolly. The rush-hour travellers were arriving, pouring into the black hole of the tube, tearing the sisters apart. Olive was tired, she wanted to get back to the house, to have tea with Dulcie, hear what had happened and start on a book Tim had lent her. There would be a racket, the children being fed, people coming in, staying too long, the kids crying, someone bringing beer, making a speech; and Dulcie saying, oh well, what the hell. The pulse of life. Olive would be referred to as the sensible, objective one. She would smile and shake her head. The talk would go on. They would get to bed after midnight and at about four a child would cry.

"You've ruined Harold's life."

"Cat, it's not like that, you don't know. Truly. He'll live."

"Oh yes. He won't kill himself or anything."

"Cat . . ."

"All this suffering."

Suddenly, Olive was alarmed. People pressed against them, thrusting them downwards and Catherine made no effort to resist. Olive had to grab her elbow and shout, "We can't talk here. Come back with me."

Catherine pressed her lips tight and shook her head. The world filed past her, face by stricken face. She was afraid to wake in the morning, to open her eyes. How could she tell Olive? The roof was pressing down. They would be buried alive.

"Cat!"

The dark waves came between them, as Catherine had know they would, and pressed them apart. When Olive looked frantically back Catherine was stranded light years

114

away. They waved. Catherine turned to a complete stranger, a woman with a shopping bag, and told her in a voice which sounded in her own ears perfectly sane, that she was terribly sorry but she wasn't feeling very well. Apparently she had not spoken loudly enough because no one heard her. But after a time, as the tide diminished, she felt strong enough to go home.

When Olive got back Dulcie told her that Larry and Tim had been arrested and Dennis had lost his job. In a way they had been expecting this but it was hard at first to realise the shock of the two calamities in a single day. The baby was in its cot. Polly had taken the older children to the park. Dulcie was sitting smoking. She wore an old sweater of Tim's.

"She ought to get married."

"Who?"

"Polly. She's crazy about kids. Here am I going off my head like the old woman in the shoe and Polly loves every minute of it. It doesn't make sense."

Olive sat down. "Where have they taken him?"

Dulcie shrugged. "He's only in for questioning. He'll be back. It's the big wheels they were after. You know they're evicting all the squatters?"

Olive shook her head. So it had all been for nothing. She should cry, feel something, but there was Dulcie to think of, and the others. One lives up or down to expectations and Olive knew she was expected to be competent and optimistic. That was the role assigned her. Dulcie was perhaps the only one who would expect nothing of her. Which was just as well as Olive had no idea how to help. She guessed Dulcie had not eaten and began to make sandwiches. The children would need feeding when they came in. "Where's Dennis?"

"Upstairs brooding. It's been quite a day."

"I'll take him some tea."

"I shouldn't, you'd get your head bitten off. When he's like this he locks the door."

"He's done this before?"

115

"About once a month. For three days once. Tim was just going to break down the door when he came out."

Olive put down the sandwiches in the middle of the table. She made some fresh tea. It was a relief to do something. Dulcie's calmness astonished her. It was rather like the war when one sat out the crisis, drinking tea, talking about everything but the matter of immediate concern. It was only when the war was won that people started to have nervous breakdowns.

"You may be right about Polly. It's obvious now I think of it. Is there anyone? A man, I mean."

Dulcie grinned. "She can't stand them. Isn't that awful? Mad for kids but she'll run a mile from a man. Me, I'm the other way round. Oh, I don't mind the babies but the only reason I don't stop them is it would spoil the other thing. I went to the doctor and he showed me and I even tried once, and Tim said it was all right, but it wasn't. It was foul. I suppose I'm sex mad. Does that shock you, Olive? D'you think I'm bad? I mean, when you come down to it there ought to be a law to stop people like me. Oh God, Olive, I want him back and he can have Stalin and all his pals and talk Russian if only." Dulcie jumped up and began to wash the dirty pots at the sink. They must have been piled up for two or three days. The darkening room was squalid. It was next door to a fish and chip shop. The house opposite was a cliff, cutting out the light. There was nowhere to hide.

Dulcie had been crying over the sink. She came back with half a bottle of brandy she must have been hoarding for years, since before the war.

"Sorry about that. It's just that there's a limit. You know your job is to be there and he comes back and then it all starts again. I'll get used to it. But can you live like that, Olive, to eighty or ninety or a hundred?"

"Some of us can. I don't know, Dulcie. I hope not. We may have to."

"We spend all our lives worrying about men. Then half the time they're not there. What sense can you make of that?" Dulcie smiled. With the brandy her bravado was coming back, shakily. Her tone now was half wistful, half mocking. "We'd be all right without men, wouldn't we? And bloody bored."

"Dulcie, would you like me to go to the station, wherever he is, and find out what's going on?"

"No, love. Honestly, he'll be all right. He'll roll back in the morning yelling his head off." Dulcie turned the glass in her hands, then she looked up. "You know what they're on about, don't you?"

"Roughly. But——"

"Then you know more than me. Oh, I'm sorry for those poor sods who've been thrown out. But somehow I can't think about people I've never seen. You know, they say so many millions this and that and I listen and listen but I can't take it in. All I can think of is Tim won't be home tonight and we'll go on for ever, if we're lucky, living in this dump. Sorry, I'm going on. I love brandy. I was saving this till peace broke out. That's funny."

"I'm going, anyway. They might give him bail or something. At least we'll know what's happening."

On the way to the police station Olive thought this was the first time she had been, even by association, on the wrong side of the law. One was brought up a certain way and if the police entered one's life at all it was as amiable not very intelligent creatures without faces, whom Mrs Armitage would address in a particular voice. Now they were a force to be cajoled and placated. She thought she was seeing the edge of a dark world she had entered almost haphazardly, expecting an illumination, a blaze of light, and found only the usual compromises and besides, bleakness, violence, a sign of the times, of anarchy, heaven knows what to come. It was enough to drive you mad, and perhaps that was the only way to ultimate sanity? The twentieth-century way of losing your soul to find it? But she continued to believe in the making or breaking point, the basic common sense of the human race. Otherwise the Mrs Armitages, the Maurice Leveretts, would win and there would be no point in living at all.

She brought Tim home, sheepish and truculent. Larry Towers too was released, and five other Communists were charged and held. When she got back Polly was putting the children to bed. Having delivered Tim to Dulcie she felt useless. She went upstairs to Dennis.

The door was not locked, after all.

"Would you like some tea?"

Dennis was lying on the bed. She had expected to find him angry or ill but he smiled and shook his head. Olive turned on a light and he sat up looking pleased with himself.

"I'm sorry about the job."

"That doesn't matter. I'll find something. Oddly, your friend Leverett was charming. He shot me down in the nicest possible way. Everyone has a right to their opinions but in the Civil Service no room for the rights of the individual—embarrassment to the department and so on."

"I never trusted him."

"You judge people harshly, Olive."

"I never thought you liked him."

"I don't. I simply don't waste time judging him."

"What are you going to do?"

"What I said I'd do. Join them."

Olive felt angry with herself as much as Dennis, but she took it out on him. "For heaven's sake no one here takes the Communists seriously. You said yourself it couldn't happen here."

"They've arrested Larry and Tim. That's serious isn't it?"

"People like Larry Towers——"

"And Tim?"

"He doesn't know what he's doing."

"Do you?"

Olive shook her head. She felt worn out, defeated and entirely committed to all the people in this house. "But I

118

used to think, if there was something you really wanted, something important, and you went on trying hard enough, you'd get it."

Dennis sat down beside her and took her hands. "But that's true, Olive."

"Not that way. I sound like Polly, don't I? But we have failed, haven't we?" Olive could not distinguish between her feelings for Dennis, and the people in the house, and the others outside they had let down, the ones they had tried to help and those they had never seen. "I saw my sister. I couldn't talk to her. We love each other but we can't talk. She'd never understand this. And yet, in a way—she understands more deeply than I ever will. It's a bore being practical. You rush around trying to tidy things up while everyone else goes off their heads. Sometimes I wish I were mad. Perhaps I am. Perhaps that's being mad, thinking you're sane."

"Olive, I had something I wanted to say to you."

She wondered if he was going to ask her to marry him, or sleep with him, or become a Communist, or tell her to go because she was a friend of Maurice Leverett's, Mrs Armitage's daughter.

"Will you stay here? We need you. I'm not sure we could manage without you."

There was no need to ask what he meant. She guessed at some time she would become his mistress, possibly his wife, and meanwhile her function was to be there, to keep things going, not to ask what her function was.

He said there was a room in the attic, she could do as she liked with it. That night she slept with him and he woke crying in the night and she held him and went back to sleep and had a strange dream of a catastrophe and digging in ruins for Catherine's body. In the morning she made him breakfast and went down to help Dulcie with the children. She had made up her mind Dulcie's life was absurd, something must be done about it. Then Dulcie said she was pregnant again, she'd missed twice and wasn't that too bloody silly?

119

Part
Two

16

Olive had been home only once after she decided to stay in the house with Dennis and the Connors. She had thought of arriving without warning but in the end she telephoned Catherine and asked her to pack up her clothes.

On the day she went to Kensington it had been snowing for a week. Most of her winter clothes were at home and she wore a thick old skirt of Dulcie's and several sweaters. There was a grace about the snow which covered the bleaker aspects of the city, though soon the white would be dirty and the streets rutted with frozen slush. It was odd how in some people the bitter cold had awakened a new vigour. Strangers smiled and grumbled; the snow was at least something to talk about, a positive enemy. What was known as the war-time spirit reasserted itself, for the moment at least.

It was a Saturday afternoon. Catherine was out. The flat seemed musty and chilly. Dennis's house was cold, of course, but there at least there was brightness, movement, a sense of life. Two cases were standing in the hall; Olive thought, thank God, I can carry them if I have to.

"Mother?" Mrs Armitage appeared at the sitting-room door in a pink dressing-gown. Her hair hung down almost to her shoulders. She was holding a hot-water bottle. Through Olive's mind flashed two thoughts: she's set this up to blackmail me; she's an old woman, she'll die. But she did not for one moment believe that Mrs Armitage was really ill.

Her mother's expression was a mixture of slyness and conciliation. Olive paused, her hands on the cases, then she straightened and reluctantly followed Mrs Armitage into the sitting room.

"I'm all alone, you see."

"Where's Catherine?"

"Out."

"Why don't you turn on the fire," said Olive briskly, "it's after four o'clock?" She bent and snapped on the fire. "Now I'll make some tea and then I must go." She recognised her own nurse voice, ruthless, bright and chilling. In fact it was only to the least ill and most tiresome patients she ever spoke like this. "Are you ill? Why aren't you dressed? If you're ill you should be in bed."

"It's cold in bed."

Olive made the tea. When she came back Mrs Armitage was sitting in the same chair, with her eyes shut; from the flicker of her lids Olive felt sure she had only just closed them.

She sat down and lit a cigarette. Very well, let her mother put on this act, but it would be a one-sided drama to which she had no intention of contributing. Then she began to imagine that Mrs Armitage might really be ill. Certainly she was a bad colour. Olive thought how absurd it was, how little she had to lose, since she was leaving anyway, by the kind of gesture for which her mother was obviously pleading, ill or not; simply the appearance of concern she handed out every day to strangers at the hospital. That cost her nothing, it helped them. For reasons she could not understand she would find her mother's death almost intolerable, yet she withheld pity as though she were actually afraid this slightly pathetic, tiresome old woman, whose life after all had been a failure, could destroy her. She said, more gently, "I should drink your tea, mother, before it goes cold."

Mrs Armitage opened her eyes. "You're not looking well yourself."

Immediately Olive stiffened behind her defences. "I'm perfectly all right. No one looks well this winter."

Mrs Armitage sighed. She frowned slightly. Olive had brought in the thick kitchen cups. "I'm sure you don't look after yourself. You're determined to stay in that place, with those people?"

"It's a decent room and those people are my friends." She looked at her watch and got up to go. "I don't want to lug those cases about in the dark."

"How you will live, I can't think."

"I'm doing shorthand-typing, a crash course. I could earn quite good money."

Outside, struggling through the snow with the heavy cases, Olive was glad of a positive nuisance against which to vent the usual helpless anger her mother inspired. As she stood in the street looking round, without much hope, for a taxi, she turned once and saw the corner of a curtain twitch then fall again.

Tim was back on the buses. Dennis was ill for a while, not with psoriasis but some kind of flu, then he got a job, as a clerk again, in an insurance office. The boss was a philanthropist. He ran a boys' club. He found Dennis had been in some welfare department of the R.A.F. and for a drop in salary gave him the job of keeping the club going, organising activities, building up a piece of vague goodwill into a practical working unit. The hall, not far from the flat, on the same bomb site as Toni's café, was literally falling down: at first it was simply a matter of the roof leaking, the lavatory blocked, drains broken, no heating, the floor rotten, pitted with traps; then as the snow fell and continued to fall the killing winter, like a punishment for the madness of the last five years (a Greek judge, whimsical, amoral), worked at the deeper, secret fabric of the building, undermining foundations, in one blizzard tearing half the roof away, whipping windows from their frames, doors from their joists.

At first the boys for whom the club was intended kept away, then they hung around like starlings, shivering and watching. Dennis was patient, he worked steadily on. Mortar between the bricks would not set in the frost, so he searched the site for corrugated iron. He put this up and the wind blew it down. Tim got some wood, it was better not to ask where, and showed Dennis how to fix it against battens.

125

They used the corrugated iron on the roof. They put in a window and in the night it was broken. Even Tim could not produce more glass and there was a limit to the help he could give. Dennis was at the hall at nine every morning and worked by torchlight far into the dark. He would come home at nine or ten or eleven and drink some soup and fall asleep.

About seven, if she was off duty at the hospital, Olive would go down to the hall with coffee and sandwiches. She was working hard at typing with the idea of a better job and helping the group; if she could finish the course she might get a decently paid job in the registrar's office. Also she felt the need to keep busy. Also she was waiting still to know what her role was to be in Dennis's house. They had slept together only once since that first night. She had thought this might be her own inadequacy, her inexperience. Dennis seemed satisfied and untroubled. They never spoke by day of their love-making. She watched him move in his clothes, in a cloud of plaster, and would have liked him to hold her face in his dusty hands but he was kind, patient, correct, committed.

One night she turned on the boys, astonished by her rage, and forced them to help. A few drifted away. She got one or two sweeping the floor, another scrubbing the walls. One actually produced a watchman's brazier from among the ruins and managed to get it alight. For the first time the hall seemed possible, as a domestic interior. When they had finished for the day and the boys had gone they sat huddled over the brazier drinking coffee. Part of the roof still gaped but the night was dry and the wind had dropped. Olive thought that since the war she had never really looked at the sky. It was odd to think that it contained no threat worse than inconvenience or discomfort. Sagging with stars, it appeared now very pure and calming, innocent of the danger it had held. Of course, it was absurd to think along these lines. Man is the only moral force in the solar system. A tree is only a cross if man makes it so. It was pleasant to see great currents out there, tides of stars, an order to the vacuum of space, an ordering consciousness. But the truth was that we were stuck on our own.

"What's that all about?" Someone had written on the wall in small chalked letters Olive had never noticed before:

SCREW THE REDS

Dennis shrugged. They sat for a while without talking. Then Dennis began to explain his plans for the club, how he hoped after a year to extend it, in a month or two he might put in a kitchen, a small office, if they put up a partition there might be two or three activities at once. He sounded like a medieval mason planning a cathedral, knowing it might not be finished in his lifetime, certain only that it would stand. He looked the part. He wore an old painting smock over several sweaters, his hands were chapped and his brown hair dusted with plaster.

"I really believe you'll do it."

"I hope so."

She stared at the dancing flames, cradling her mug in her hands. "You didn't like the way I spoke to them, did you?"

"I don't like violence." He smiled, to soften his reply.

She mumbled, "I can't bear to see you getting so tired."

"I'm well."

"But without help you could go on like this for months, years. We never seem to have time to——" She was shocked. She could have bitten out her tongue. She was behaving as less than Dulcie, a female with a grievance using it to bring the male to heel, the kind of woman she most despised. If she had slept with Dennis, twice, that was no more significant nowadays than shaking hands; no contract had been sealed, no promise made. She had come to the house simply because she felt slightly less useless there than she did at home, because she liked them all, enjoyed the chaos and the sense of purpose. She finished limply, "I mean there's no time to talk."

127

"What do you want to talk about, Olive?"

She lit a cigarette from the fire, her face flamed. "If you don't believe in violence why are you a Communist?"

"I'm a Communist who does not believe in violence."

"There's no such thing."

"I think there is."

"Larry Towers wouldn't agree with you. Or Tim. Anyway, in a few years Communism will be a joke in England. Politics will be as out of date as religion is now. At least, they'll still exist, but no one of any intelligence will take them seriously."

"Who'll be our master then? Maurice Leverett?"

"If he is, I'll resign from the human race."

"But that's not what you're talking about, is it?"

Olive shook her head. The fire was sinking. It would be too cold to sit on in the hall much longer. She had thought of Dennis as mercurial, changing, easily discouraged, but she saw now and envied the astonishing certainty at the centre of his existence. She dismissed the idea that his goodness might be blind and narrow and wondered why she was irritated by the picture of this small brown man, working with such steadiness to rebuild a totally rotten construction which had survived an acre of destruction by the merest accident and might have been better wiped out. She looked round. It was an ugly building, whose fabric had always been flimsy. Once attached to a church, its high roof and vaulted beams mirrored ecclesiastical connections. The stage at one end suggested an altar. But the original materials had been poor and the only remarkable feature about the place was that it had stood while all round was levelled, including the church of stone.

What was she talking about? The pointlessness of Dennis's small exercise in a pointless world? She had never felt that before, even in her blackest moments; even when she saw the group as absurd, she saw too that it was important, as anything was important which challenged the lethargy she sensed around her. She shivered and concluded

128

she must be ill. With a shamed part of her mind she hoped to be ill, to give way to fever, dreams, sleep, whims, to be weak, dependent, feminine. She wondered how Dennis would react if she said, quite simply, I am ill, and was afraid to find out. He had been much steadier lately. This new project had more than made up for the disappointment of the squat. He was childishly pleased to have joined the Party, a step which seemed to have eased him much as another man might find peace in some peculiarly harsh monastic order. Yet this parallel was inexact. The kind of monk Dennis might have become would be vowed to the inward life; the essence of any political affiliation was that you could at any time be required to measure your ideals against action—action determined not by your own inclinations but by the Party. So far Dennis had been let off most of the duties demanded of comrades because of his work at the club. He could hold himself above the row between Polly and Tim, which had now become a feud, as to whether or not the group should go in piecemeal with the Communists. He could enjoy the sacraments and avoid the duties. In a way, Olive thought, shocked by the bitterness her illness or her mood induced, he holds himself above everything. She felt mean to grudge him his happiness, for Dennis was happy. She could no longer see his face across the embers. "I was thinking of my stepsister. She wouldn't understand any of this."

"She's quite young, isn't she?"

"In a way. I think she's rather unhappy. She makes me ashamed."

"Why?"

"She's innocent but she's practical. All the words we use would mean nothing to her. We've built up defences ... attitudes. She has no standpoint because she's had no experience of anything but this. I think Catherine feels the only thing that matters is private happiness, not hurting. She wouldn't see hunger or pain or grief like Polly does with those ghastly figures, as a world problem or a national prob-

129

lem or an historical problem, but as a personal, individual thing, not to be borne. That must make her very vulnerable." Olive shook her head. She was probably wrong about Catherine and in any case Dennis was the last person to understand.

It was quite dark now. They took a short cut home across the bomb site. The snow was falling again. Olive stumbled and Dennis caught her elbow. Briefly there was a pleasant sense of closeness, of walking together in the same direction through the dark. It didn't seem to matter now if they were comrades or lovers. Then they got in and at once there was the feeling of crisis again. Tim had had a row with the inspector and lost his job. He had come home drunk and upset Polly who had burst into tears and flounced out. One of the children was ill. Olive realised there was no question of being ill herself. Life had returned to normal.

17

"So we were wrong about him."

In February 1947 Olive and Catherine were discussing Maurice Leverett in the Kensington flat. Mrs Armitage was really ill this time, nothing worse than flu but alarming enough for Catherine to fetch Olive. Chris was upstairs kicking his heels; he had appeared on and off for several weeks that winter. He said it was too bloody cold in Hampshire, there was nothing doing in the yard because of the terrible winter and a chap got fed up. There was still a good time in London if you knew where to find it and he always seemed to have money. Mrs Armitage, who nowadays regarded Olive as good as dead, had taken to speaking of 'my son'. At Chris's arrival her vitality, which had been precarious that winter, invariably recovered. She was ill now because she had insisted on redecorating his room on a freezing afternoon with the windows open. Chris probably never noticed that the room had been painted but he responded to her attentions with his usual vague amiability. When he scored, even if it was with someone who had previously neglected or even offended him, he was happy. His need to be liked was deep. Mrs Armitage was thankful that one of her children, at least, appeared settled, contented and successful. She despaired of Catherine. Of Olive she could not bear to speak. When Olive was not there Mrs Armitage was quite clear in her mind about the things she would say to her. She even imagined a reconciliation, after concessions on both sides. She would be magnanimous. Olive could keep up with her peculiar friends, her politics or social work or whatever it was, this Rawston man, if she would only come home to live. The way she lived now was absurd and unnecessary.

Mrs Armitage had been one afternoon to look at the house; it was no better than a slum and a sluttish pregnant girl (one of the friends, presumably, for whom Olive had turned her back on her own home) was shouting at her children whose faces and clothes were filthy, who had nowhere to play but the street. But whenever she saw her daughter Mrs Armitage became querulous. It was for Olive—whose responses were invariably chilly—she saved up her complaints about her pains, her headaches, the leaks in the roof, the mice in the cellar, the window that would not open, the door that would not close. It was shocking in a way how she offered, to this daughter only, the petulant, grave-marked features of an old woman. Olive thought, with a shudder, she wants to pull me into the grave with her and I suppose that's how we'll all feel in the end. But she said, in her nurse voice, it's all right, mother, the plumber will come, Chris will mend the door, the roof will not fall. Mrs Armitage was still known for her vitality. Olive saw her once or twice in dreams as death itself raising a cold finger of denial against every effort, every hope.

Catherine told Olive that Maurice Leverett was planning to stand at the next election.

"He told mother he was sure to be adopted—by the Tories, of course."

Olive pulled a face. "It's funny. I thought he didn't want that sort of power. That'll be another reason not to vote Tory, anyway."

"He's got terribly fussy, like the Queen or the Pope or something. Mother said he was going to some very grand dinner and at the last moment he pretended to have flu because he found someone a bit notorious was going to be there."

Olive said lightly, "I suppose that business with Dennis shook him up—a black mark against his department." She glanced at Catherine, sitting in the window-seat well back from the fire because of her chilblains. Her hair fell in a dark mesh across her cheek, her feet were tucked under her

and her arms folded roundly under her breasts in the attitude, almost, of a woman nursing a child. But she was only a
child herself. Olive remembered an occasion, six months, a
year ago, when they still shared a room and she had been
startled by the rich, ripe beauty of Catherine's naked body,
the deep whiteness of her flesh and the calm, contemplative
curves which seemed to hold a knowledge of which the girl
could not yet be aware. The splendour had yet to reach her
face but at thirty Catherine would be a beauty, magnificent
at forty; Catherine, she felt sure, knew nothing of this, she
thought she was plain. Olive thought how absurd it was, you
couldn't tell your own sister she would be a beauty. So unless
she met a man of extraordinary perception she would marry
late, suffer for years for her height and her large breasts.

Olive sat as close as she could to the small fire. Catherine
was lit from below by a table lamp which emphasised the
unconscious beauty, the attitude of sleep and waiting in her
posture. Her face was half turned to the frosty glass. When
they had started talking the room was dimmer than the late
afternoon. Now the single table lamp was brighter than
street and the sky veiled by more snow to come. Between the
sisters was an area of darkness. This was the first time Olive
had mentioned Dennis in this house since she left home. She
knew that Harold sent postcards to Catherine. He had got
some kind of job with an American cultural delegation in
Rome which sounded like coals to Newcastle but was, in
fact, more practical. He was concerned with recovering
looted masterpieces for the Italian state. Olive thought he
would like that.

Catherine did not reply at once. She seemed to have forgotten the question. They could hear Chris moving around
upstairs. She said, "Mary Owens's coming."

"Who's Mary Owens?"

"Chris's latest."

"What's she like?"

"We haven't met her yet. The last one was awful. She
looked like a film star and said pardon. Mother behaved like

133

Queen Mary, with flu. Are you going to marry Dennis?"

"I don't know. I think . . ."

"I don't know how anyone could get married."

Chris was thumping down the stairs. Mrs Armitage called and Olive went to shake up her pillows. When she came back into the sitting room, hoping to continue the conversation with Catherine, the lights had all been turned on and a rather ordinary-looking girl, with reddish fluffy hair, was sitting, dazzled, on the edge of the most uncomfortable chair.

"You must be Olive."

"Yes?"

"I'm Mary Owens."

Catherine had gone to fetch Chris. From the rattling of the pipes he appeared to be having a bath. Mary Owens refused a cigarette. It was too late for tea, too early for a drink. Olive wondered what on earth to do with her. She cursed Chris.

"He's in the bath."

"Yes."

"Have you known him long?"

"A week." Mary Owens fiddled with her handbag and looked round for rescue. "It's a lovely room. You're lucky to have such a nice flat. That's nice." She fixed her flittering gaze on a peculiarly nasty porcelain duck Maurice Leverett had given Mrs Armitage one Christmas. Eleanor of Aquitaine must have chosen it. "That's lovely." But her attention was off again already.

Suddenly Olive felt sorry for her. "Would you like it?"

"What?"

"The duck." On an impulse which somehow felt altogether right but must, surely, be quite mad, Olive snatched up an old newspaper, wrapped the duck and thrust it into Mary Owens's lap. "You could put it in your handbag. It's not very big."

"But I couldn't!"

"Of course you can."

There was the sound of feet in the corridor. To Olive's

134

relief Mary Owens had pushed the parcel into her bag before the door was opened. Chris came in and Olive, watching Mary, was struck by the sudden beauty in her face, a smile of extraordinary radiance which lifted her, momentarily, far above the ordinary. It must be simplifying, and dangerous, she thought, to build your life upon one person. She knew herself to be capable of this and wondered if she had, in fact, already done so. A few months ago she would have imagined the difference between herself and Mary Owens to be so great they might have been born on different planets. Now she was not so sure, and the thought scared Olive. None of the far more dramatic commitments she had made in the last six months seemed as startling as this second in which she felt briefly a bond of shared experience between herself and Mary Owens. It passed. Chris and Mary were going to the cinema.

Chris grinned. His face was shining from the bath and he smelled of soap. He surveyed the two women.

"So you've met."

"Yes."

"Olive is going to blow up all us filthy capitalists."

"He's talking nonsense."

"I know." Mary Owens smiled at Olive. Now Chris was here she was easier, more confident. She could afford to take a small stand against him. "He often does."

"Mutiny!" Chris tapped her bottom lightly and they were off.

Olive turned off the ceiling light and lay on the sofa. Mary Owens was right, it was, in a way, a nice room. She felt faintly ashamed of noticing the contrast between the flat and Dennis's house, at its worst now in the winter when no amount of life could defeat the cold. She had been happy enough to leave here and had no desire to return, and Dennis, of course, was right, surroundings did not matter. He was as unaware of the discomforts of his own house as he would be of the comforts of this one. He never noticed what he ate. Lying here, on the edge of the soft pool of light from

135

the silk shaded lamp, it was hard to believe in the grim stories Dennis's clients had to tell, the tales of privation that came in letters from Polly's contacts abroad, some hideously true, some surely false, like the rumours of cannibalism in Berlin. In this mood it was possible to believe they had all exaggerated the state of things, perhaps to their own ends. For where would they all be without the group? Dennis would be filing papers in Maurice Leverett's ministry. Polly would be riding her horses, pining for a husband; Tim, without his Communism, a layabout of diminishing charm who couldn't hold down a job and drank too much. She herself, she supposed, would be married to Harold. She had a vision of herself in a centrally heated flat: there were many large rooms through which she moved, touching waxy flowers, out of season, waiting for Harold. But she did not love Harold.

She decided she had been away from the other house too long. Her mother no longer needed nursing. Now she had thought of it she wished to be back there at once.

"I thought you were asleep." Catherine was dressed to go out. "I wondered if you'd be here for an hour or two."

Olive thought, no, I should never have come, but she said, "Yes, of course. Are you going out?"

"For a while. I won't be long."

"There's no hurry."

"What did you think of Mary Owens?"

"Not what I expected."

Catherine agreed. She stood with her hands pushed down in her pockets, very serious. "I thought she was a bit dotty about him. Where do you think he gets the money?"

"I never thought."

Only when Catherine had left and Mrs Armitage was calling and it would be necessary to go and listen to her complaints, all the more irritable now she was getting better, did Olive wonder where her sister had gone at this time on a winter night.

18

"HELLO, old lady."

Catherine had never before been in their bedroom. The carpet was deep, the bed large, the small room tortured by frills and dots: frills skirted the bed, the kidney-shaped dressing-table, the curtains and the bedside chair. Curtains and bedspread were dotted. On Mrs Riley's side of the bed was a small table on which stood a number of bottles and pill-boxes, several glass animals and a panda. On the bed was the panda's mother or father. Presumably it held her nightdress. Since Charlie Armitage and Mrs Riley were not married this was, Catherine supposed, a bed of shame; she had never in her life seen a more innocent room.

"How are you?" Charlie was sitting up in bed looking at a stamp book. On his table was a damp sponge, a pair of tweezers and a pile of stamps. In his blue-striped pyjamas he looked like Chris after his bath: scrubbed, cheerful and healthy. He seemed shy to be caught in bed.

"There's nothing the matter. Marjorie fusses. I'm the better for seeing you. I'll get up soon."

"Do you think you should?"

"She can't manage on her own. She's never been strong, you know."

"No."

They were stuck. They listened for Mrs Riley but she had the wireless on. Catherine felt, as she always did, too large for this house, Alice when she grew, her fault, not theirs.

But she had discovered, if she waited, she found ease here.

"You wouldn't like to see the stamps?"

"I would."

He showed her. Some of them were marvellous and she could understand his delight in them, but in a way too they appalled her. Something was wrong, the room was too small, there was no comfort here. Everything seemed suddenly very sad. Catherine could think of no one who was truly happy. Rebecca was adorable but mindless. Sam was a mystery. Olive looked so thin and pale, burned up as if she had seen something terrible. Catherine thought she would like not to come to Battersea any more.

Now she looked round there were signs of decay in the house: a patch of damp, a creeping flaw, peeling paper. In places the carpet was worn thin and the dressing-table, under its frills, was the cheapest whitewood. There was a feeling not of actual poverty or hardship but of bravado, a thin façade, precariously propped up against an invading darkness. One crack, one small calamity and they would be helpless as children—more helpless, since they were not children and no one would help them. There was a blankness sometimes in Charlie's eyes which frightened her. It had been important to Catherine that he should be strong.

"I'd better go."

"So soon? Marjorie will be disappointed. She was getting a bit of supper."

"Mother's ill and Olive wants to get home."

He nodded. He did not ask about Mrs Armitage's illness.

Catherine had noticed before that both he and Mrs Riley preferred not to hear bad news. They took no newspapers. They listened almost constantly to the wireless in winter, but never to the news. Mrs Riley said there was enough misery in the world without thinking about it. Charlie nodded but looked embarrassed. Catherine guessed that he realised Mrs Riley was extremely stupid. His own evasions were more subtle.

Olive would despise them, yet were they so wrong? If they were wrong, then so was Harold, so was anyone who tried to be happy. And if happiness were wrong there was no point in living. Suddenly, she thought she would like to talk to

Sam Davies about this but she knew, if she tried, she would be struck dumb.

Mrs Riley came up with a tray and left them. There was something she wanted to hear on the wireless. They ate beans on toast and talked or were comfortably silent. Catherine said no more about leaving. Charlie said, "We're all right, the three of us, aren't we? We get on."

Catherine smiled. The ease had come. She could not bear the thought of going back through the dark to the flat. Olive would go and Chris would not be home till late. Chris too would go, tomorrow or the next day and the fires and the lights would be turned off, the curtains drawn, the door bolted and Mrs Armitage, in the deepest inner room of the house would close her eyes, sigh, rustle and criticise, affirm the end of things. Catherine would hold her breath, walk in shame of her clumsiness, her vision. She said to her father, "I've been wondering if I could come and live here."

Even while she had decided never to visit this house again, she had thought it out. Her fees were paid up to the end of the course. She could work in the evenings. She could help in all kinds of ways.

Charlie looked pleased and startled. "Of course we'd love to have you to stay for a bit. But what would your mother say?"

"I don't mean for a while. I mean to live. And I don't think mother would mind at all."

Her father wagged his head. "Well that's a poser. But, Cathy love, you're better off with her. And she'd miss you, you know, more than you think."

"She wouldn't."

Charlie sighed. He pushed aside the stamps in a gesture that was almost petulant. She remembered her first sight of him, Charlie the ordinary chap, the joker. She always suspected him of having an act up his sleeve but his tone was embarrassed and serious. "She's not so young you know, old lady, any more than me. It's not so good growing old. What no one ever understands is you still feel young inside but

139

your legs don't know it. You know when someone goes and they say it's a mercy, well I don't believe that; I don't believe there's anyone who wants to die. It would be bad for her, worse than most. She was a beauty, you see."

"I suppose that's why she doesn't like me much, because I'm such a lump."

"You're lovely," he said, and shyly touched her cheek. "She was all spikes and flowers but you're lovely, in a steady sort of way that gets better and deeper, or you will be when you know it. And don't let anyone tell you otherwise."

"I do so want to come."

"Well we'll have to think about that, won't we. We'll have to ask Marjorie."

She knew then they would not have her. Unless she brought the subject up it would never be mentioned again. She stayed for a while playing draughts with her father until he seemed tired. The moment she left the room she heard him coughing, a dry, scraping cough that frightened her. On the way home she rang Rebecca, but there was no reply. There was nowhere to go.

Mrs Armitage heard Olive leave. When her daughter came in to say good night she had pretended to be asleep, fearful of the things she might say, knowing her intentions to be good but her mouth full of serpents. She was well now, in her body, but her mind ran on, crashing blindly against a fine mesh of dread and regret. She would dress, give a party, move around her home, but see beneath the surface of the house a dissolution, a rent in the fabric of life; the fabric, that was it, which had once, with Teddy, seemed so smooth, so certain, was now jagged and flawed. Even after Teddy one managed; one came to terms with the kind of war to which one was not accustomed. It was the peace that had defeated Mrs Armitage. Peace and her daughters. She was drowsy. Children should be a comfort but her daughters brought her nothing. Once she had looked elsewhere, got on well, so she thought, with young people; now she wondered if they found her picturesque, if they laughed behind their hands. Perhaps genuine friendship between the young and the old was impossible, it was love or nothing? Had she made herself absurd? How did one ask for love, how did one take it? Had she ever known? This was sacrilege against Teddy, a place not to visit. Charlie had loved her. She dozed. Charlie had been impossible. One did not marry people like Charlie or bear their children. The most terrible thing of all was that now even Charlie would have seemed better than nothing. She was cold. She scratched up the blanket, harsh against her cheek. If she could sleep. If she could feel once more before the vision ended . . . If she had ever felt was a question, another of those places not to linger. The darkness was like a cataract growing from the corner of her eye. A little vision lost and then a little more until one was blind, thrust finally into that inner blackness.

She must sleep. Her father said, go to sleep. As a child, Olive never slept, or so it seemed. She came downstairs in the middle of dinner and Mrs Armitage let her stay. She fell asleep, standing up, with her head in her mother's lap. Teddy had not approved. That was a quarrel. Don't go there.

Charlie adored Catherine. He loved Mrs Armitage, but he adored his daughter. It would have been absurd to let him see her, bad for them all, bad for the child. One could only feel what one could feel. Catherine was a child of circumstance, not of the mind. In her mind it had never been necessary to marry Charles Armitage, Catherine had never been born.

She was so tired. Her thoughts raced while her body was more than ready for sleep. Her mind rested on Christopher. She slept.

Catherine came in with a hot drink. Mrs Armitage woke. Her sleep had been light and fretful. "Is Christopher in yet? I want to see Christopher."

"No. Is there anything I can get?"

Mrs Armitage shook her head. A skin had formed on the

141

milk and she pushed it aside. "You'll tell him when he comes in?"

"Yes, mother."

Mrs Armitage seemed more cheeful. "I must look a fright. Pass my things." She peered in the mirror with a sharp bird-eye, combed her hair and patted powder on her face. Chris was coming. Chris was doing well. She felt generous. "What's the new girl like? She sounds a bit of a rabbit."

"I don't know really. She seemed nice."

"And where have you been?" Mrs Armitage took a small, tipped cigarette from a box by her bed. Lately she had begun to smoke again. She found she liked it. When Chris came in at night they drank tea and smoked.

Catherine closed her eyes. She felt she was falling. "To see my father."

If Mrs Armitage was startled, Catherine was shattered. She found she was trembling. Her face burned. Then there was a thump in the hall and Chris came in, his breath still steamy like a young horse from the cold night air. Any explosion was suppressed. He appeared oblivious of the atmosphere and perhaps he was. He began to tell them in detail about the film he had seen with Mary Owens and some old war-time pal they had met in a pub. He seemed impressed that this man had what he called done all right for himself but he had married the most awful female, a real horror. She had got a bit tight and there had been rather a scene. The incident had clearly been far from funny, but Chris made it so. Catherine slipped from the room.

Half an hour later Chris came out and found her in the sitting room in the dark. He turned on the lights. Whatever had happened in Mrs Armitage's room had robbed him of his bounce. He looked puffy and exhausted, like someone who has been drunk and been sick and is forced abruptly to face sobriety. He collapsed in a chair, still wearing his duffle coat. He was shivering. "This damn cold. If Maurice and his pals don't starve us, we'll freeze to death. Well, I've settled her down at last."

Catherine sat huddled on the rug, level with Chris's feet. He was wearing rather smart dark brown suède brogues. Catherine wondered how he could afford such expensive shoes and where he got the coupons. "Was she very angry?"

He grinned weakly. "Spitting. You've done it this time."

"What did she say?"

"Oh, a lot about loyalty and all that stuff. I don't know. But I wouldn't mind a cup of tea."

Catherine brought in a tray. Chris dug a flask from his pocket and tipped a measure into the cup. He offered it to Catherine, but she shook her head. He drank, lit a cigarette, then sighed, but he seemed more himself again. "What I can't understand is what possessed you to tell her?"

"I think I went a bit mad."

Chris nodded. "I liked Charlie. He was a good sort. The only mistake he made was marrying her. Funny how some people look for trouble. Or it looks for them. How's he getting on? Is he still with the stunner?"

"Yes. Chris, what happened between them, mother and Charlie?"

"What happens between anyone?" He shrugged. Chris had his own instinctive sense of life, but his curiosity into the workings of the human mind was limited. By innocence and by accident he worked some good. Until it proved itself otherwise, he believed life to be benevolent. He was out for what he could get not from greed but simplicity: because it would be ungrateful to turn down any pleasure life might offer. Morality puzzled him. He knew when he was happy and when he was unhappy, hot or cold, hungry or thirsty. His only superstition was his luck, which held.

Catherine knew all this without formulating it. "I'm sorry I let you in for this."

"That's all right. It'll blow over. Madam's as tough as old boots. I'm for bed."

"I don't know what to do. I don't know what will happen to Olive."

"Poor old Cat, you think too much; that's your trouble."

143

"I suppose I do."

Olive was ill after all. The symptoms she had dismissed as hysterical failed to go away. By the time she got home after the visit to her mother's flat she was dizzy and sick. The tube was not running, there were no taxis, even if she could have afforded one, and she had to change buses twice and walk the last half mile. She had hoped to go straight to bed but the Connors' door was open. They called her and she had to go in.

This was clearly a special occasion. Normally, once the children were in bed meetings, social or concerned with the group, were held elsewhere, in Dennis's room or Olive's, or in a pub, or at Toni's. Dulcie, who was now seven months pregnant, was sitting up in bed, smoking and coughing; this had been a bad pregnancy, she had been ill, the doctor had said it should be terminated, she had refused, eloquently obscene. Ever since, she had kept away from doctors, clinics, hospitals. She was often sick. The child had quickened early and now wore her out, heavy and active. Once she had made up her mind to keep it her mood of despondency passed and, ill as she was, she was cheerful enough. At the moment she was knitting clumsily on thick needles a garment that had once been white but was turning rapidly into a grey mat of dubious intention. Olive had opened an old trunk once and found an amazing collection of similar disasters. They made her feel odd, like stillborn children. Dulcie didn't seem to mind. She couldn't afford the wool so she went from time to time to the trunk, unrove an old failure and started again. What the children actually wore were hand-on shop clothes, but Olive knew the disasters were important to Dulcie; they were flags of courage.

In the corners of the room, at the edge of the light, the babies slept and a couple of the older children sat up, rubbing their eyes. Olive too, coming in from the darkness, was dazzled. Tim had called her in. His bony face was flushed. Polly stared at her lap. Newcomers to the group, a couple who had been clients but fallen on happier times, smiled nervously. They were teachers. Olive sat next to Dennis, and refused beer.

Apparently, there had been a showdown. As far as Olive could gather, through waves of nausea, the group was finished. Tim and Polly had quarrelled beyond mending. Both had proposed that as it stood the group was ineffectual, it needed the support and authority of a stronger affiliation. Big fish, thought Olive, now warmer and light-headed, swallowing little fish, swallowing smaller fish. Polly, whose mother had a friend who knew someone in the L.C.C. who ran a settlement, wanted to go in with Mrs Craig-Cooper, Tim with the Communist Party. Which meant, indirectly, Maurice Leverett or Larry Towers. Or someone like Maurice or someone like Larry. It seemed to Olive a choice between sharks.

The female teacher, a good-looking girl with a fluff of bright hair, said, "But surely we're all Socialists?"

Tim said, "The Labour Government are tools of the capitalists. They have abandoned the workers."

Polly snorted, then she burst into tears. It was like watching a monument cry. No one, nothing, could make Polly weep except Tim; he alone had the power to dissolve her competence, her resolution, to expose the large white woman who wanted children. We're all cows, Olive thought, all trapped. But she didn't believe this at all. She was ill. From her fever she observed herself tenderly, like a child. She looked round at the startled faces. She was enjoying herself. It was like a play put on for her benefit. Under the cover of Polly's drama Dennis touched Olive's arm, "Are you all right?"

"Fine."

He nodded, satisfied. Polly was so formidable in her grief no one dared to comfort her. She twisted her head from side to side as if she were yoked, then as suddenly as she had started she mopped her eyes, blew her nose, and said, "Sorry about that. But we can't go on like this."

Someone said, "She's right."

The male teacher, a shy man with sore eyes, suggested, "We should think very carefully about any political allegiance. I can't see either that it would bring us any particular advantage."

"For God's sake!" Tim groaned. "You're all virgins. Not one of you has the faintest what I'm talking about. Don't you see? It's so simple. Even if you're not with the Party, you must see our only chance is a genuinely socialist state. We're supposed to have that now. Right? You look round. You see the same old pattern of power and privilege. In a socialist state we would be unnecessary, we would have no function. The very fact that we can sit here fussing about our virginity means the socialist revolution has not been accomplished."

Olive glanced round. Dennis was watching Tim with steady attention; he gave a slight nod. A few months ago he would have smiled at this Party claptrap and it was hard to believe, even now, that he took it seriously. Tim was, as always, inflamed by his own words and Olive could see that the female teacher had been hooked. Her lips were slightly parted, her eyes bright. She looked very young, about twenty-two, and her husband no older. It made Olive feel that it had been for years, not months, she had heard in this room, or upstairs, or at Toni's, the same arguments, the same self-defeating cycle of reasonable discussion, impassioned protest and rational, inconclusive conclusions. She knew, if she turned to Dulcie she would be grinning through a cloud of smoke. She turned. The two women smiled at each other and Dulcie shrugged. Olive thought in conspiring with Dulcie she had betrayed something, but she was too light-headed to care.

Someone asked Dennis to speak but he shook his head. Olive saw, with the clairvoyance of fever, that he might withdraw his strength from the group. If he did it would certainly collapse. It would disintegrate or go in with Larry Towers. Either way its purpose would be lost.

"The only hope," Tim was saying, crouched over the

146

table, his hands locked so that the knuckles stood out, "is a genuine revolution by any means."

"I thought force was out of date in the Marxist-Leninist dogma?" Polly was twisting a man's handkerchief in her lap.

"It's a last resort."

"That's self-justification. I doubt if you'd get much support for that, even among your comrades. I think you're pathetic. I think in a way we all are. I don't see there's much point in going on."

One of the children began to cry. Dulcie heaved herself out of bed and soothed it. "They'll never sleep if you go on like this."

"Olive?"

Olive had a terrible sense of having lived all this before, of having been in some other existence Tim and Polly, the bright new girl enchanted by Tim, Dulcie all bones and belly holding a hungry child against an empty breast. She looked at Dennis's hands, like small brown animals sleeping, his reasonable, smiling look.

She was the sensible one. They counted on her. Which was absurd considering her reputation at home with her mother, Catherine, Chris, Harold for that matter.

She remembered the people on the road in Kent, her rage at everyone who was blind, her nameless fears for Catherine, her hopes when she had come to live in this house. She felt she knew everything and nothing. She had sat by the dying in the hospital, not at the dramatic, literary moment, but in the long-drawn-out hours of fear, sleep, waking and terror in which she learned that no one, even the most cancered, broken, abandoned, wished to die. Even the most terrible life was better than death. She had learned not to feel too much, to let them go. After her first death she had walked all night. She knew better now.

Harold's friend, who had been in Hiroshima, had had a nervous breakdown. Olive saw him sometimes. He had recovered enough to go back to work but he would only go out in the streets at night. He was a pleasant, rather ordinary

147

young American. He talked a lot about his childhood.

She thought about Harold, looking at pictures in Rome, and Mary Owens' bright face when Chris came in.

She could tell that the female teacher resented her, because Olive was good-looking, clearly important to the group; but most of all because she had once been enchanted too. Also because her husband was struck by Olive.

"Perhaps Miss Asher can give us a lead?"

Tim growled, "Go on, Olive, tell them."

"I think you're all saying the same thing, really. It's hopeless like this. I simply don't see what you can do about it." She did not include herself, and they noticed. She stood. It was necessary to get up to her room as quickly as possible. "I'm sorry. I think I'm rather ill."

Dennis took her upstairs. He was astonishing, all self-reproach.

"I should have noticed."

"I let you down."

"You're ill."

It was true, she was ill. It was rather marvellous to give way. She lay for a long time at the edge of the world in wakeful sleep. She thought that Catherine came to see her, but that was a dream, and one day in the early evening she agreed to marry Dennis. She woke in the middle of a mound of grapes and flowers and found that in her absence her life had been settled. Dulcie said that Dennis had gone nearly out of his mind and a van had come from Fortnum's with all this clobber and would it be all the same if she took some grapes for the kids?

19

MEANWHILE Mrs Armitage and Catherine had several talks about loyalty. Christopher went back to Hampshire, and Rebecca was madly in love with the most marvellous, penniless, beautiful, unsuitable gentile architect. In class she no longer even pretended to work but sighed and groaned and smiled and shredded her handkerchief. From Catherine's point of view, she might as well have been dead. Catherine walked home slowly through all kinds of weather knowing that the moment she entered the flat her mother would pounce.

"Where have I failed? What is it you want that I have not given you?"

"Nothing, mother."

"Your father is a stupid, shallow man. First he betrayed me, now you."

First she forbade Catherine, then she begged her not to see her father. Catherine put on the kettle, still wearing her coat. She cut some bread, then she sat down and looked at her hands. Then she got up and went out and walked about the streets. She could not understand the intensity of her mother's feeling. It seemed to come from a chaos outside Catherine's known world. She knew her mother had not loved Charlie. Perhaps guilt made people angry? There was no one to ask.

One day Catherine bumped into Sam Davies. He drew up in a taxi when she was waiting at a bus stop. He gave her a lift. The interior of the taxi seemed rich, warm and voluptuous. Sam was wearing a thick, dark overcoat with a black fur collar. He said it had been his grandfather's, and now she looked the cuffs were frayed and the whole garment was touched with a greenish patina, like moss. Sam called it his Smyrna merchant coat. Catherine thought it was superb. Catherine was painfully conscious of her own appearance in a hand-down coat of Olive's. Olive was smaller and slimmer than Catherine, and Mrs Armitage, in her make-do-and-mend phase, had sewn a band of chewed fur round the hem: Chris said it was dead cats.

Catherine closed her eyes. She was so tired. Then she sensed that Sam was looking at her. His eyes glittered in his large, pale face. She could not tell if he was smiling. She thought of him with that girl who was supposed to be shocking. Perhaps he was going there now?

"Why haven't you been to see us, Catherine?"

"Rebecca's a bit busy, isn't she?"

"But we'd like to see you."

She was embarrassed. "I get out here." She had no idea where she was but suddenly the interior of the taxi which had seemed so comforting was now threatening. This had happened increasingly lately. She would seek a familiar place of consolation—the kitchen, for instance, in the corner by the cat basket—and it would turn against her. The cats watched her with knowledgeable, complacent eyes and she wondered why she had never noticed before how cruel they were.

She looked straight ahead, asking to get out.

"No you don't."

They were at Marble Arch. That was where the shocking girl lived. "Don't let me take you out of your way." She imagined a hot scented room, the girl waiting for Sam. They would make love. She felt odd. She wound down the window. The rain lashed in. Floods had followed the snow. Sam, in his grandfather's overcoat going to his mistress, was a creature from another world.

They had arrived. Sam rapped on the glass. The taxi stopped.

"Thank you very much." She started to get out.

"Wait."

Sam leaped out, walked round behind the taxi and opened the door for Catherine.

"You'll spoil your lovely coat."

They shook hands, rather solemnly. With his hair plastered in whorls around his face, Sam looked quite human, younger and less certain. "You'll come and see us, then?"

She nodded and ran up the steps. At the door she glanced back and saw he was watching from behind the streaming glass. It was only then that she wondered how he knew where she lived.

One afternoon in class Catherine's head grew larger. All day it had been tight as a pea, riveted to her spine by metal bolts, then quite suddenly the pressure eased and her head floated easily like a giant empty pod on a waving stem. Someone was crying. Apparently it was Catherine Armitage. Willy said Catherine Armitage had better go home.

Catherine Armitage went to see her stepsister, Olive. She had never been to the house before. Olive was asleep and a tired-looking girl with a cigarette in her mouth offered Catherine a cup of tea. Dennis Rawston was out.

"I could wake her up?"

"No. I didn't know she'd been ill."

"Neither would we if she hadn't passed out on us." Dulcie Connor took Catherine downstairs to a big room full of children. Nappies were boiling on the stove and the wireless was blaring. It was a filthy, cheerful room. "She'll probably wake about seven."

"I've got to be home by then."

Dulcie nodded. Catherine drank her tea too fast, burning her throat. A child came and put a broken toy on her lap. Catherine looked at the toy.

"You like kids?"

"I don't know."

Dulcie grinned. "You're right there. Neither do I. Never had time to make up my mind."

Catherine liked Dulcie. Dulcie took her cup. "You don't

151

look too marvellous yourself. Look, you pop up and see if she's awake. You might as well."

Olive was dreaming. Waking and dreaming ran into each other.

"Cat?"

It seemed that Catherine had caught her hand and was crying. Olive would have sat up but the effort was too much. Fever pressed her down.

"Cat, it's all right. I'm not dying. It's only flu you know."

She must have fallen into another of those bottomless pits of sleep because when she next looked round it was dark and Catherine had left, if she had ever been in the room at all.

Catherine ran downstairs. Someone called after her but she stumbled on. Only when she got outside did she see that the house was falling down. The windows on the ground floor were patched with cardboard. A skeletal cat was dragging something nameless out of a dustbin. There was not a tree or a flower in the whole street. The railings had been taken away for the war effort. She walked through an endless maze of streets before she found the lighted high street and a bus.

As soon as she opened the door of the flat she knew Maurice Leverett was there. She could smell him. He was fastidious, but there was about him a faintly acid smell which went with his sallow complexion. Sam Davies smelled of musk. She tried to slip past the door but her mother called. Mrs Armitage was sunny, Maurice unbecomingly jolly. As Catherine opened the door one of the cats shot out. The omens were bad.

"Maurice has a plan." Catherine stood just inside the room, as far from the fire as possible. Her chilblains tingled. By the pricking of my thumbs.

Catherine would be leaving Miss Wilson's next month. She would need a job and Maurice and Mrs Armitage, well Maurice really, had found one. A friend of his had started a firm in Manchester and needed a first-class secretary. There was a lovely bed-sitting room with a nice widow. Catherine needed a change, she'd looked peaky lately. It was marvellous how things had worked out for the best. She should be very grateful to Maurice.

Catherine breathed deeply. This was supposed to stop you fainting. "Thank you, Maurice, but I don't want to go to Manchester."

There were chances of travel abroad.

"I don't want to go abroad."

Mrs Armitage's gaze flickered. "The child's tired. She should see a doctor."

Maurice wagged his long chin. "It's a strain on us all."

Catherine retreated to the kitchen but she could not eat, she could not even cry. She heard Mrs Armitage laughing with Maurice in the hall.

"I'm not going."

"You're behaving like a child."

"Because you treat me like a child." Mrs Armitage was astonished by Catherine's rebellion. The girl was dull and plain, but she had always thought her sensible. It must be her age. Her plumpness was becoming a full, almost voluptuous figure. It was shocking, like something indecent growing in the house. Olive was so slim and handsome. Mrs Armitage averted her gaze. 'That jumper's too tight."

"It shrank. You're trying to get me away from my father."

"We'll talk in the morning. I think you're ill. I think you should see a doctor. Perhaps you're growing too fast. Even children have nerves nowadays. We never used to have nerves."

"I'm seventeen. I've stopped growing. I'm going to see him. You can't stop me."

"You'd better have a holiday. Go to Aunt Cat's. I'll write to Miss Wilson."

It was Mrs Armitage who cried. Alone in her room she locked the door, as if anyone would try to come in. If only Chris were here. Filthy, filthy, filthy, she cried, rocking herself against the pillows. Love me, love me, love. Me. Teddy was as cool and unresponsive as a carved figure on a tomb.

153

Charlie? Before he left Charlie had gone through her desk, all her secrets, reading and taking things. If Catherine went, as she must, she would be left alone. In a vacuum vitality is useless. Perhaps Chris could be persuaded to move back to London? Or she could find a little cottage in Hampshire? She soothed herself, like a mother tending a child, with plans for this little house, near Chris, somewhere for him to come, a proper home. At last she slept.

Catherine could not cry. She sat for so long in the kitchen that the cats sensed something unusual and began to fret, to move away from her. In their high-stepping distaste they seemed to smell disaster. There was nowhere to go. They were cats who lived indoors. They watched her, from corners.

At last she rose and went to her room, where she began to pack things very carefully in a grip. It seemed important to forget nothing. The packing took a long time. She admired her own cunning.

She left the flat very quietly and only when she reached the tube station did she realise that she had forgotten to bring any money. In any case the last tube had probably gone. It was past midnight. At first she walked slowly, watchfully through the empty streets; once she thought she was followed; once an empty double-decker bus swayed past brilliantly lit. She was dazzled. She could smell the river. She began to see more clearly as her eyes grew accustomed to the dark and she became aware of shadows, hunched, moving, following, running before, dwarfs and giants, curled, coiled. A large black car, longer surely than was normal, was parked outside Olive's hospital. Something touched her, someone spoke. One of the cats had followed her. She flung a stone at it but it came on. She heard strange movements from empty places where there had once been buildings and people. She walked quickly, then she ran, then she threw away her bag and ran faster.

All the windows in the house were blazing with light. A stranger opened the door. Charlie had been taken to hospital that evening. Mrs Riley had gone in the ambulance. Catherine explained and someone offered to take her to the hospital. She saw Charlie about two o'clock in the morning. He died an hour later. Catherine refused to leave him. She was put under sedation which she fought, physically, smashing at the needle with her fist. She woke screaming and was moved out of the public ward. It was clear she had had a nervous breakdown. She was quite a problem. Nothing, short of a killing dose, could give her the quiet sleep she needed if she was to benefit from treatment. Since they could do nothing more to help her she was left strapped to a high white bed until she could tell them her name and the reason for her distress.

⟶ 20 ⟵

DULCIE's child was born in April, a fortnight early. Olive and Dennis were married in March but so that there should be someone to look after the children they waited to go away until Dulcie was out of hospital. The baby, a boy, was a fine-looking child but underweight. It was to stay in the hospital for care and observation for a few weeks. Olive was relieved that Dulcie seemed to have got over the birth very quickly and showed no signs of pining for the baby. She was bright and more energetic than Olive had ever seen her.

"While you're away I'm going to paint the room. You won't know it."

"Don't overdo things."

"Oh me, I'm tough as boots. If there's one thing I know about it's having kids. I just shut my eyes and yell."

"Now I'm in with Dennis you could have my room."

"We're all right here, we're used to it. In a way I'm quite fond of it, whatever I say. But thanks all the same. Anyhow, you'll be needing it yourself before long."

Dulcie could never be coy, her tone was matter-of-fact, and for a moment Olive could not think what she meant. When she did understand she said quickly, "Oh, we're not having children for at least two years. We couldn't have them here." Appalled, she tried to correct herself, "I mean——"

Dulcie laughed. Olive had never known anyone so innocent of pride. "Don't worry, love, I know what you mean. You've got more sense than me, you'll be all right."

Olive realised she and Dennis had never, in fact, discussed the matter. She had no idea what he felt. She had simply gone, in her competent role, to a doctor, held herself mentally aloof through a faintly embarrassing physical demonstration and carried out his instructions. The method was said to be ninety per cent reliable and she had every intention of sticking to it, but like Dulcie, she found it distasteful. Dulcie's reasons were sexual. Olive suspected that her own were aesthetic and therefore less admissible. She would have liked to discuss the matter with someone, and Dulcie was the only woman to whom she could have spoken of such things but she had felt lately an area of awkwardness between them. Dulcie moaning about being the old woman in the shoe was familiar and accessible; in her maternal role, however much she made light of it, she was formidable. In a strange way, for reasons Olive could not detect, she made light of it too much. Olive decided she had imagined this but she had not imagined that Dulcie disapproved of the marriage. She had talked of this only once, obliquely, but her meaning was clear.

Polly had broken from the group but suffered. Signs of her loneliness for them were the extravagant tributes of flowers and fruit she had sent when Olive was ill, an expensive wedding present and a silver rattle for Dulcie's baby. She had come once or twice when the women were alone but seemed nervous that Tim or Dennis might arrive home and find her there. She said she might be getting married but appeared reluctant to talk about herself.

Olive and Dennis could afford neither the time nor the money for a proper honeymoon. Olive had finished her crash course and was to start work in the registrar's office, where the hours would be short and regular. Her shorthand was indifferent but she could manage the typing and filing well enough. In her glass cage she knew she would feel cut off from the life of the hospital but she could not have kept up her old job in her new circumstances.

They went to see Dennis's father for a long weekend in Derbyshire. Olive thought about Catherine, staring at her hands in a hospital in Surrey where she had been for the weeks since Charlie's death. After her early violence she had been mild and passive, quite coherent when she spoke but disturbed by visitors, even Olive; then she would grow restless and fretful like someone struggling to wake from a terrifying dream. This was apparently a better sign than complete passivity but Olive found the visits an ordeal. She spoke of them to no one, not even to Dennis.

Brushing her hair in front of the low mirror she realised how tiring the last few months had been, how wonderful it was to have these few days ahead in which she would be simply Dennis's wife, in his father's house. Mr Rawston was a retired schoolteacher. A new building had been put up on the outskirts of the village and he had bought the old school house where he had lived for twenty years of his life. He was active, he cooked and cleaned for himself, walked, read, wrote a local history and stood in occasionally at the school. Olive's first impression was of a man who had invented a totally contained and satisfying life; she could not guess how he would react to change because she could not imagine him outside this world. Yet he was still flexible. He seemed delighted to see them but he would probably suffer little when they left. He entertained them well, but once or twice she saw his hand move to the deep pile of papers (his history) on the fireside table; he patted them without ever once breaking the pleased attention he offered Dennis and Olive, especially Olive. She asked what he thought of modern teaching methods and found him surprisingly well-informed and open-minded. Physically, he resembled Dennis, short and slim, with the same air of explosive energy, but less driven; she wondered if they were alike in other ways and watched for signs. In any case, she liked her father-in-law at once.

"You realise we're honoured? This was their room." Dennis sat on the wide bed. The architecture was the Victorian dream of a cottage. Windows were arched and leaded. Beneath the pale blue paint William Morris lurked. Outside no area of wall was unclothed by creeper, honeysuckle or roses. It was a nice room.

"I hope he didn't move out for us."

159

"He hasn't slept here since she died."

Later, Olive caught a glimpse of Mr Rawston's room: it was narrow, white-painted, simple to the point either of arrogance or of genuine disinterest in worldly comfort. It resembled Dennis's room in London, which was now also hers. "What was your mother like?"

"Sensible."

"What a frightful epitaph. Did he love her?"

"I don't know. I suppose he did. He tried to kill himself when she died. They were wrapped up in each other."

"He doesn't seem that kind of person at all."

She sat by him on the bed fiddling with a brooch, feeling guilty because she was happy in this house and he was not.

"He'll be waiting for us to go down."

"I'm glad we came. I like this house and I like your father."

He smiled. "I wish I could have given you a proper honeymoon."

"I'd rather be here." She stood and caught a glimpse of her white triangular face beneath the thick cap of dark hair. She still regretted the abundance she had lost. She felt him watching her and turned, smiling, to ask if she should grow it again, when another thought occurred to her. "Have you got a picture of your mother?"

"No," he said abruptly, "no, I haven't."

Downstairs Mr Rawston was waiting for them with the fire lit and a bottle of sherry on the table. The evenings were lighter now, the air the fragile windy violet of early spring. The snow here had been bad, enough to cut the village off for a month; floods had followed and the stream at the end of the garden still boiled. Many of the plants had blackened under the snow, but the earth was pricked with stiff green shoots. There was a bowl of hyacinths in the window. Olive stood there for a moment looking out at the stream and the sloping hill beyond. Mr Rawston came up beside her with a glass of sherry. "There'll be a lot to do when it dries out." The prospect seemed to please him and his delight was infectious. Olive asked him about the garden and he told her about his lilies. She knew nothing about flowers. He brought out a heavy nineteenth-century book of lilies with plates by a French engraver.

"I'd like to see the garden in the summer."

"I hope you will. I hope you'll come often."

"I wish we could."

He filled her glass again and she saw that his was still three-quarters full. She realised he had been drinking to keep her company. Dennis had refused and gone out to the garden where he stood with his hands in his pockets looking down at the stream. Mr Rawston got up to pull the curtains and Dennis turned his head. Mr Rawston made an odd little gesture, a half wave, then came back to the fire. "I must say," he said, "you're a delightful surprise. I just hope you haven't taken on too much."

"Too much?"

"He's a strange boy."

"I think he's rather like you."

"Perhaps that's why I don't understand him. We are reluctant to face ourselves. That may be half the trouble between parents and children. There is something I would like to say before he comes back. If you should ever need somewhere to go, I hope you will remember that this house is here." He went on at once to talk about something else before Olive could reply. Dennis came in and they ate. Mr Rawston would not allow Olive to cook. After dinner Mr Rawston and Olive talked while Dennis prowled around the bookshelves. Olive tried to explain about the group and Dennis's project and their friends. Every so often she would refer to Dennis. Her father-in-law was a good listener; he was interested; he asked questions, but Olive felt she was failing somehow to present him with the whole picture. It sounded like gossip. She glossed over difficulties as if it were important to impress him with their success while he was not at all the sort of person she needed to impress.

She wondered if she had lost something by marrying. She

thought about the desperate homeless on the road in Kent, and Harold looking at pictures in Rome, and Catherine staring at her hands in a hospital in Surrey. One goes down. Life becomes smaller. Mary Owens was more her sister than Catherine. Up to a point you believe in limitless horizons and in a way you still do, but conditionally.

Dennis said suddenly, "I've joined the Party."

Mr Rawston was interested. Dennis had been tense when he first made his statement—he must have been working up to it all evening—but gradually he relaxed. Olive wondered why they all referred to it as The Party, as if it were the only one. She would never have thought this six months ago. But she was glad Dennis was getting on with his father. She guessed her father-in-law would have reacted in the same way if Dennis had said he was becoming a conjurer or a hairdresser. Mr Rawston was interested in all the phenomena of life. They talked about the implications, pre-war Communism, the way the Party had become respectable when the Russians joined the Allies, post-war problems.

Mr Rawston said, "I must admit I don't see much future in it."

"There must be. It's the only way that makes sense. The Socialists have sold out the people." This sounded so like Tim that Olive smiled. There was so much to worry about yet she felt very happy.

Mr Rawston shook his head. "I suppose it must be a vocation. Like the Church or marriage." He banged out his pipe on a heavy ashtray. "There was a time when I nearly went into the Church."

Olive wondered what he meant about marriage being a vocation. Was it a warning? In marriage, she supposed, there was always one who must, like anyone vowed, subdue the will. She had always regarded her will as sacred. Dennis was vowed elsewhere. She must be the one to bend. In this house she felt it might really be possible.

They made very deep love that night on the creaking bed, in the sense that for the first time she felt entirely committed and if he was still looking over her shoulder she did not feel it. Afterwards he got up to find a cigarette and had some kind of spasm. He sat on the edge of the bed, his naked body knifed double so that his head nearly touched his knees. Then he seemed to recover. "It seems queer here, in this room. I never came in here."

"What was she really like?"

"She was clever. She had been a teacher too. It was a perfect marriage. They should have had no children and died together. Olive, I think I'm mad. You've married a madman."

"Not that mad."

"No one can think as I do and be sane."

"That's quite a common feeling. People who are really crazy never know it." She was thinking of Catherine. Yet she had not convinced herself. She shivered and pulled up the blanket. She saw the luxury of her own flesh and thought of Mr Rawston in that white cell. It had been Dennis's room as a boy and now his father slept there.

"But——" He shook his head. "I had no right to bring you into it."

"You must have been very lonely here."

"I can't imagine why you married me."

"Perhaps I'm the one who's mad?"

"No." He smiled and climbed in beside her. "You're the sanest person I know."

"I've been wondering, what will you do when the club's finished?"

"Run it."

She said lightly, her face against his shoulder, "I suppose you wouldn't think of leaving London? He'd never ask, but I get the feeling your father would be very happy to have us here. I'm sure you'd find something. It might be nice in the country."

He drew away, his narrow shoulders hunched. His back was smooth and white, like a boy's. She was torn between a spurt of rage that for all his compassion he should refuse

163

even to consider her inclinations and an instinct, stronger, to support him. "I thought you were with me?" He showed her the face his clients never saw. "You must realise I have to be in London."

"Yes, of course," she said. "Of course we'll stay in London."

Now she held him until he fell asleep. Olive slid her arm from under his back and tried to sleep herself. It was not his fear or his loneliness that worried her or even his dedication. She had understood long ago that this would be a difficult marriage, something to be guarded, watched and worked for every day if it were to survive. She would have, in a way, to make herself again, going against her nature. All this was possible. It was his goodness which worried her. She had admired it, envied it, married it, but she wondered if she could live with it.

21

THE incredible summer rose. It was too theatrical to be believed. Each morning the same light blue sky was rolled out, white by midday, deepening, as the day sank, to a steady, searing, un-British intensity of colour through all shades from violet to cerulean to black. It was war weather. It was a freak. It couldn't last. It did.

Catherine was sent into the grounds of the hospital, like a child put out to play. Some nerve not dulled by drugs recognised the warmth of the sun, but she was as indifferent to the beauty of the summer as if it were a picture. Reality was a veil across a void. After one disastrous attempt it was considered inadvisable for her mother to visit her. Olive came every week, Chris a couple of times, embarrassed with flowers. Rebecca brought chocolates and ate them all herself.

"I'm terribly sorry you're ill, Hog." They walked twice round the gravel path, then sat in deckchairs. There was something beautiful and hideously pointless about the circlings of the other patients, some in couples, mostly singly, making invisible tracks across the clipped lawns, like aimless snails. They walked so as not to stand still. One woman was frightened of flowers. Rebecca was the least tiring of the visitors because once she has grasped that Catherine was not frothing at the mouth she chattered as usual about herself. She had finished at the typing school and supposed some time she would have to get a job but it was such a marvellous summer, there was no hurry. If only Catherine could get better . . . "You are getting better, aren't you?"

"I don't know. I suppose I am."

"Uncle Absalom went mad, you know. He thought he was

Ivan the Terrible. Mother wouldn't go to see him after a while. I don't mean you're mad. I mean, you don't think you're anyone, do you? You've just got nerves." Quite suddenly Rebecca began to cry. "Oh, Hog, I wish you'd get better!"

Olive and Dulcie were sitting in the newly painted room. It was dazzling, an achievement all the more astonishing because such single-minded effort was not in Dulcie's nature. She was always planning to make the children new clothes, change her hair, cook something special, remake a life she admitted frankly to be a mess, but most of her projects finished like the grey aborted baby clothes. "What's the point?" she would say, cheerfully, and then there would be a party, or Tim would lose his job or find a job or Dulcie would get pregnant again and the chaotic life of this room, which Olive enjoyed but could never have borne herself, would reassert itself. Tim's ebullience, always at its lowest in Dulcie's brief spurts of competence, would revive. They were well matched. He throve on danger, chaos and muddle, and when there was none he made it.

Dulcie was lying on the bed in her bra and pants. They had tried opening the windows but the smell of fish and chips rose from the street on waves of hot air. The older children were at school. The infant was playing on the linoleum with a bowl of water. The baby lay naked in its cot. It was still small, but perfectly formed and remarkably contented. Dulcie rolled to the edge of the bed and scooped up the infant. She held it on its side, facing her, then kissed it on the lips. It crowed and reached for her hair, its eyes large with pleasure and wonder. "You're the best, aren't you, Stevie, you're the best." Olive watched. Dulcie was slapdash with her children. She breast-fed them, blowing smoke in their faces, neglecting to wind them. Presumably, she and Tim made love in front of them, in the big room. They stayed up all hours and ate too much or nothing at all. She cuffed them, but Olive had always been amused, and awed, by the intimate relationship between Dulcie and her children. The contact between them was so physical it was almost sexual. Now Steven looked like a solemn, wrinkled old man; Dulcie was murmuring into his face as if she had forgotten Olive was there. "You're a bloody marvel." They stayed like that, both tranced, Dulcie whispering, the child watching. With each child Dulcie seemed to grow thinner. Olive scraped a cup across a table. Someone shouted in the street. Dulcie rocked away from Steven and looked down her front between her narrow, elongated breasts. Her stomach was concave, a dip between fragile bird bones. "I'm the vanishing lady."

"You've kept your figure."

"I never had one. I'd got nothing to lose." She groaned. "I'm bursting." Steven, apparently, did not take enough milk. Enough for him but not for Dulcie, who smelled most of the time, sweetly and sourly, of milk. She told Olive when he cried she leaked. While he was in the hospital she went three times a day to feed him. At night they gave him bottles. Polly had a picture of a native woman in Africa suckling a child at one breast, a pig at the other. Olive was appalled and fascinated by the photograph.

"Can't you take something? Don't they have injections nowadays?"

"You know me. I can't be bothered. What I need is Polly's pig."

"I thought that was horrible."

Dulcie grinned. "I don't fancy it much myself."

"I don't think I fancy any of it."

"You've got brains, Olive, that's your trouble. Or maybe you're lucky." Dulcie put on the baby's nappy, put it back in the cot and began to dress. It was half past four. Olive got back from the hospital at four. The children would be home soon, then Tim, then Dennis. There was something both drugging and dangerous, Olive felt, about these afternoons spent, or rather wasted, with Dulcie. She was drifting in warm shallows. The air in the room was thick and dark. It

167

was so hot. They drank black tea which they found more cooling than lemonade. Sometimes Polly joined them, or Lucy. All the women smoked too much and made too many confessions, of which they were later ashamed. Olive was always tired when she left the room. She had tried to explain to Dennis but he had said, it's natural, why shouldn't you spend the afternoon with your friends? Olive thought of Mr Rawston's garden, but said nothing. Dennis was so reasonable.

It seemed to Olive that Steven was underweight. Polly and Dulcie had a mild row about this. In the end, out of lazy good nature rather than real concern, Dulcie gave in. She agreed to take him back to the hospital for tests. Polly would drive her there and bring her back, tomorrow.

And yet, in spite of the wasted afternoons Olive was not displeased with her life. It had been easier than she expected to remake herself to suit Dennis and yet to retain what she felt to be the inner core of her own nature. Which was what? What was the point in clinging to something she could not define? And she had not, in any case, been required to give up anything. Dennis liked her to work, even if they had not needed the money. He accepted the changes she made to their room because he did not notice them. In their love-making there had been nothing again like the violence, the drowning depths, the submarine splendour and sea-caves of that night in Derbyshire; but then he was working hard for the club opening and she was tired. The winter had drained her and she wanted now to lie in the sun and warm her bones and sleep.

Though she was still divided. Part of herself despised this slumbering woman. Then she would borrow books from Tim and drop off in the middle. She would offer to go down to the club after work, come home to change and fall asleep. It seemed a lifetime since she had spoken, not altogether jokingly, of walking to Hiroshima. Her mother, who imagined her living among anarchists, would be surprised by how staid her life had become.

Sometimes she woke feeling dizzy from a short precarious dream in which she looked down from a great height on the sleeping woman who lay curled and peaceful, hugging her breasts in the middle of a holocaust in which flaming houses fell in on themselves and running feet thudded by her head. After the war, she told herself, many had such dreams, even children. It was a way of getting the violence out of yourself.

The group staggered on, frail and reduced, and Olive helped, though she wondered sometimes whom they were all trying to liberate, their clients or themselves. Not that they had many clients now. Since Polly had left and Dennis was so busy at the club, meetings were repetitive airings of political theory. Tim had his victory. New recruits, as innocent as Olive had been when she first came to this house, would arrive full of zeal to find themselves listening to a reading from Lenin or a lecture by Larry Towers. Puzzled clients would be asked if they took the *Daily Worker*, were they members of trade unions, had they a Communist candidate for the local council, whom did they vote for. Olive was able to help a few of them to find somewhere to live or to get a job or simply to unravel the mad knitting of bureaucracy. She thought sometimes of Maurice Leverett sitting like a white spider, spinning neither from malice nor conviction, but instinct, this sticky web.

One family in particular interested her. Bob Wilson was a tally clerk at the docks, a member of the Party and a councillor. His wife was dead and he had a son whom Olive remembered seeing once or twice at Dennis's club. Alan Wilson was a good-looking boy, like his father thin-faced, dark, but with a brilliantly irradiating smile. He stood out from the other boys, but Dennis said there was a problem about him. He helped with the work and joined in the activities, but Dennis could never get him to talk.

Olive tried and found that his passion was wirelesses; he

169

worked in a radio shop and always had one broken-down, cast-off set at home on which he would spend loving hours. Invariably he was successful and his greatest triumph was in getting a foreign station, even though he spoke no languages. Olive, who had visited the house several times, imagined him alone high up in his little attic eyrie, his ear as finely tuned as a coastguard's to signals in the dark. She asked him once what was the point, if he didn't know what they were talking about, and he said he was sick to death of living on an island. If he could, he'd just take off, go everywhere he could in the world and everywhere he went he'd build a bridge and people would cross it every hour and every minute and every day. Listening to these voices in the dark was the next best thing. If he had a transmitter he'd tell them how sick he was of his father's rotten war, of England and Russia and Germany, when people were the same all over. He reminded Olive of Catherine.

She told Dennis, "I don't know what to say to him. I know what he means. If I didn't it might be easier. There's a tremendous energy about him, but it's unharnessed. And what on earth can you tell him to do with it?"

"He'll be all right. Bob Wilson's decent."

"He's a Communist."

"So am I."

"No, I mean Alan doesn't want his father's politics."

"Has he anything to put in their place?"

"No. I think perhaps he would like to do away with politics altogether. You felt the same once."

"I tried to ignore them, that's not the same at all. And I came to the conclusion that they can't be ignored because that is the only way we have of talking to each other, getting things done. Christians and philosophers can go on dreaming of cloud cuckoo-land but what has Christianity achieved in nearly two thousand years? Genocide, holy wars, torture, a few dozen dubious saints. It doesn't work."

He was right, of course. Yet Olive was haunted by the picture of Alan Wilson listening for the impossible and the

170

unattainable, in a rage of desire as she had once been. As she still was, surely?

When Bob Wilson came to see Tim it was quite different from the airy discussions between Tim and Dennis. Wilson was another professional and his presence in the Connors' room twice or three times a week reminded Olive how far Dennis still was from the action. He had the dream and she hoped it would never be spoiled; she would have liked to keep it whole for him and so far she had succeeded.

Bob Wilson and Tim talked about the Marshall Plan which was designed to undermine the proletariat, and the new hard line from Moscow. Tim was excited. 'The coming revolution' was a phrase to which he constantly returned, rolling it lovingly on his tongue. "At last they've seen that there can be no compromise with capitalism. Europe's ripe. It's only a matter of time."

Wilson smiled. He was impressive, much more attractive than Larry Towers and more stable than Tim. He was realistic, he appeared to have no chip on his shoulder, and of all the Communists she had met Olive found him the most convincing. The leaders like Larry Towers repelled her with their narrowness, their pat arrogant dogma and their assumption of Moscow's infallibility. She knew they despised the so-called intellectuals like Dennis and for Dennis's sake she resented this. The fire-eaters, of which Tim was one, were beguiling, but there were very few now in England. In Communism as in government the grey men had taken over, and as far as Olive was concerned there was nothing to choose between Larry Towers and Maurice Leverett except that Maurice had the power. Bob Wilson, she felt, combined Tim's passion with experience and as much degree of foresight as anyone could have who committed themselves to a radical cause. Larry could see no further than the number of copies of the *Daily Worker* sold in Hackney, or the latest pronouncement from the Kremlin. Tim was at heart an anarchist who could imagine nothing beyond the moment at which the present system would be fired and burst into flames. This was sympathetic. Anyone living now, Olive could see, sewing as they talked, was dead if he was not in some sense or another a revolutionary. It could be quite personal and private, as it was for her. As for Dennis, he was good, there was no doubt about that, he actually did good in a way which could be written down and measured; yet she wondered sometimes, most of all since Derbyshire, if the core of certainty she believed he possessed were not, as he himself clearly imagined, an ember of madness. The others might be saved by revolution or dreams of revolution, violence, action, courage, stupidity, subversion. Anyone who is not the living dead has in themselves an image, or several images. Deny them, try to tame them as perhaps Dennis was doing, and they will become at the least an itch you will never soothe for the rest of your life, at the worst a smouldering brand which will burn the house from within. With Dennis the fires might be banked indefinitely, secretly, for years.

Bob Wilson was explaining to Tim that Communist influence in the coming dock strike must be played down. He leaned back in his chair, hands spread on the table, face open with reasonableness "It's for their own good but there's no reason why they should see that. If they think they're being used they'll resent it. They're interested in the money to live decently. So are we. It's just that we see farther."

Tim grumbled. "We're lagging behind the rest. I've heard from comrades in France. They're red-hot. It's the same everywhere. One word and they'd all rise. Moscow couldn't let us down."

"What do you think would happen then? Do you really imagine the Russians would come marching in?" Bob shook his head. "They're waiting for the West to cut its own throat. It will. There'll be war in the West in ten years, military or economic, or a military war for economic and colonial reasons. That will be our time."

Tim looked sulky, then he grinned and began to roar with

172

laughter. "For God's sake I'll be forty in ten years time. Forty!"

Olive made them tea. Bob Wilson thanked her. He seemed at pains to please her. "Alan's talked about you. I'm grateful. I'm grateful for everything you've done for us."

"I haven't done anything. I like talking to him. At least he talks and I listen. He's a nice boy."

"You're luckier than me. I can't make sense of Alan. It's mutual."

Olive had an odd, crazy moment in which she could have loved this man. Perhaps she would. In her present mood she could see no farther than the morning. Then Dennis came in, very cheerful. The club was finished and some nob was going to open it next week. He was full of plans. Dulcie came back from the hospital with Steven but Polly did not come in. They heard her new, perfectly tuned, low black car, a present from Daddy, slide off through the night, like a dark ship launched from a sightless beach into a mindless sea.

22

OLIVE had refused to sit on the platform. She had given as her reason that Dulcie should not be left alone too long so she would have to slip away, but the truth was she hated these occasions. So, she knew, did Dennis, looking smaller than usual behind a bank of flowers, but then it was his triumph and his hard luck that he had to put up with it. All the same she felt a twinge of sympathy that he should have to be bothered with Polly's nob and the local council, tea and biscuits, flowers and speeches, all to placate and seduce people who would never come here again but might at some time, or might not, write a decent cheque. Never mind his motives, anyone who actually tries to do any good is a beggar. The club was finished and would now be officially opened and God save the L.C.C. and the local council and the Labour Government and Queen Mary.

It was so hot. Polly, who had produced the nob, was sweating stoically in a perfectly awful flower print dress. Olive wondered if she were becoming cynical to see things in such a harsh light. This was the most important thing to Dennis, the crown of his life. She should care, she did care. It was just that she had been so tired lately the heat finished her. She saw Dennis was watching her from the platform, and grinned. They had been up half the night putting finishing touches to the club and concealing deficiencies. The lavatory still did not work and by midnight they had become childish and mildly hysterical at the thought that someone might need to use it.

Tim had said they'd have to wet their knickers and gone off to his night job. He was working as a watchman to give him more time in the day for the Communist cell he had started with Bob Wilson. Ironically, he was in some government office in Holborn where you had to show your identity card to get in. He knew a bit about explosives from the war and from a book he'd pinched from the library, and said one day he'd blow the place sky-high. He spent the nights reading all the stuff he could lay his hands on in the offices.

Olive said they'd just have to take them over the road to Toni's. Then they found they were short of chairs and rang up Polly at her sister's in Chelsea. The chairs arrived ten minutes before the nobs and Polly being Polly they were gilt.

Polly's duchess had made her speech and subsided into a hedge of hydrangeas. Olive slipped out, checked that the tea was ready and walked back to the house. She was too weary to cross to the shady side of the street and had a stitch, which had persisted for several weeks, in her side. She passed Toni's café, waved and saw her reflection, cool and slim in the watery glass of the window. Toni, smiling and weaving around the tables with a half-hearted cloth, looked like a fat fish in a stagnant pool, an old carp. He kept talking about going back to Greece but he never went.

Olive was not used to high heels and walking across the bomb site was painful. She turned her ankle and a jagged stone cut her, drawing blood, but she was too stunned to care or even to feel. She felt sick, which must have been the sun, and bending to retrieve her shoe saw all around her, on the fringes of the bomb site, the buildings shaking and quivering, about to fall.

Yet reaching the house she was reluctant to go in. The high sun divided the street sharply in two. The house was like a dark cliff which she suspected to be teeming with dangerous life within. Though at this time of day there was only the old woman in the basement, and Dulcie and the child.

Dulcie would have heard the results from the hospital at two o'clock, when she was supposed to telephone. Tim had offered to stay in but he had been packed off, with everyone

176

else, to the club opening. He said he'd have a kip on the job tonight.

"What did they say?" Olive undid her zip and plunged her wrists in the sink.

"No, tell me first how did it go?"

"All right. I can't stand that sort of thing. Dennis looked like something in a zoo. I think Polly disapproved of me leaving. It'll be all right."

Dulcie poured the tea. "Someone's been ringing. Every hour on the hour. A girl. She sounded up the spout. She couldn't leave a number but she said she'd ring again."

Olive shook her head. They drank tea and smoked. Dulcie said, "He'll never grow. He'll grow till he's four, then he'll stop. Isn't that crazy, after all this time the best of the lot, and he's a bleeding dwarf. They want me to go in to tell me all about it. As if I want to know. Who'd do that, Olive, to a kid? I can't make it out. I can't think who'd want to live in a world like that. If there's a God he must be off his head. Who could put up with that? How can anyone bear to live?"

The telephone rang. Olive ignored it. Dulcie raised her face, sharp, puzzled rather than angry. "I knew. I think I knew all the time. I must have done something bloody awful to be punished like this. But that poor kid, what's he done? What's he paying for? Some gland. Up in the back of the head, I forget its name. Because of some gland he'd be better dead. I thought at first of killing him, but I can't, Olive. That's why they want me up at the hospital, I know, to stop me killing him. Because human life is sacred even if it's some kind of stinking joke. I wouldn't mind so much if he were one of those idiots, but he'll know, Olive, he'll know. His brain's all right. He's a lovely kid. And he'll never forgive me for not choking the life out of him the moment he was born."

"You can't be sure of that. I don't know what to say, Dulcie, it's terrible. But once you've got life it's curious how reluctant you are to part with it. I don't see why Steven should be any different from the rest of us." She thought, we're all deformed, life is a constant struggle against limitations, but she had not the heart to put this to Dulcie. Dennis is crippled because his father loved his mother too much. Catherine... Polly's many dead or broken, everywhere, all over the world. Bad times.

Steven woke, smiling.

"Shall I take him? You can send the children up to me. Tim will be home soon."

Dulcie seemed not to hear her. As Olive guessed, she had been talking to herself all this time and might never speak like this again, even to Tim.

"What shall we do with you? Shall we put you in a circus?"

Tim came back, and Dennis, and then the telephone rang again.

"Mrs Rawston?" The voice was a woman's, familiar, faintly London-accented, breathless.

"Who's that?"

"It's Mary Owens." Before Olive could answer she went on, "I wonder if you could come round to my place? Now? It's rather urgent."

"Well, it's a bit difficult. Can you tell me over the phone, or could you come here?"

"I can't, I'm sorry. It really is important or I wouldn't ask."

"All right. Give me the address."

The telephone was in the hall. Olive went upstairs. The door of the Connors' room was shut. In their own room she stripped off her stockings, changed into sandals and told Dennis, "That girl Chris was taking out, there seems to be some alarm on. I'd better go round. I only hope to God he hasn't got her pregnant. It's funny, I thought he'd finished with her."

"You look all in. Do you have to go?" He was pulling off his tie. "Thank heaven that's over."

"It went well? No one had to pee?"

He smiled. He looked exhausted but happy. "No. Perhaps duchesses don't. Now we can start."

"I'm glad. I'm really glad." She kissed him, then remembered. "I should leave the Connors alone tonight. I'll tell you later."

Olive was surprised to find that Mary Owens had a flat. She had expected, for some reason, that she would live in the suburbs with her parents. The flat was at the top of a block in Bayswater, a converted house of partition walls which held, doubtless, a warren of Mary Owenses, judging from the number of buttons at the front door. Beside Owens there were two other names, so presumably she shared. Olive pressed the bell and went in. Mary Owens met her on the stairs. "I'm so glad you could come. I was sorry to drag you over in this heat, but it seemed the best way. You see, I couldn't think of anyone else." She looked flustered, but prettier than Olive remembered, in a pink cotton dress and white cardigan.

"I can't stay long, I'm afraid."

Mary Owens led the way. The door was propped open and the flat was large, ordinary and cool. Through a bathroom door Olive saw stockings hanging to dry, signs of women living together. The room at the end of the corridor was small, cheaply and cleanly prettified, and so dark all the lights were on.

Chris turned as they came in. His face, normally ruddy with health, was blotchy as if he had been ill. Mary Owens led him to the sofa like a child. He looked up. "Have you told her? You tell her." He lit a cigarette. His hands were shaking like an old man's. He had not greeted Olive.

Mary Owens said, "Chris has been charged with smuggling brandy. It's quite serious. He could go to jail." While she spoke she stood by him, as though to protect him. Olive sat down heavily. She too lit a cigarette, but felt sick and put it out. Soon she would be anxious, frantic, probably competent, since competence was asked of her, but for the moment she was unreasonably irritated by Chris's sheepishness,

179

the pair of them side by side like children. She felt like a nurse running from room to room, to Dulcie and Dennis and Catherine and now this nonsense.

"Could we have a cup of tea?" she said. "And then perhaps someone would explain?"

Mary brought out a bottle of sweet sherry. Apparently Chris had been smuggling by motor-boat from Cherbourg to the Hampshire boatyard for about eighteen months. He had also taken people, no questions asked, from England to what he called a soft spot on the French coast. Toby Tait had fixed it. At first Chris had had no idea what he was carrying. Once he understood it was too late and anyhow, even if he'd known from the beginning, he'd have done the same. It was a living. It was better than scraping to some bloody bureaucrat and why should the froggies drink themselves stupid while we'd won the bloody war and had to say thanks and pardon for a cup of tea? No one knew how hard Toby had had it. He'd got iron in his leg and he screamed in the night and he owed no one anything. You took what you could get and if that meant helping a few chaps over the water that was just one down to the grey men who'd greased their bums in the war and taught you to kill and be killed and then you were supposed to come back and sing God Save the King. The sherry had worked on Chris. He was flushed and frighteningly detached from the consequences of his actions. This was a first sign of madness, yet he was not mad, which made it all the more appalling, just as Steven's deformity, Catherine's illness and Mrs Armitage's despair seemed like mad weeds sprung from a burned earth. It was important to keep these things separate from each other. Once you saw a common denominator in this universal suffering you might go mad yourself and then you'd be no use to anyone.

"What about Toby Tait? Where is he?"

Chris shrugged, then grinned. "They won't get him. Cheers for Toby." His voice was blurred.

Mary said coldly, "The police seem to think he's gone abroad. The boat was missing. He must have known they were on to him but he said nothing to Chris. I hope they get him."

"Steady, old love. He's a good pal." Chris was embarrassed. At any other time Olive would have been interested in this rocky core of implacability in Mary Owens, and in Chris's half-hearted protest. Now she asked exactly what had happened, in what order, and tried to work out what was to be done. Chris had been charged that morning in Hampshire and released on bail. He had gone at once to Mary's. As far as Olive could gather, they had done nothing.

"The first thing is to find a solicitor."

Chris nodded. "What I dread is Madam. She'll go out of her mind."

Olive heard her own voice from a great distance, speaking quite sensibly through the exhaustion of the last night and the day. One had crossed the desert and reached the end only to find another unrolling, the need to walk another hundred miles. One coped for the simple reason there was no one to cope in one's place, even Dennis, least of all Dennis, who was so vulnerable in his goodness she feared for him and for them both. "She'll have to be told. If it gets in the papers it would be worse."

"I can't tell her. She's got some cracked idea in her head I'm the Holy Ghost."

"All right." Olive wondered if they realised how much, exactly, they were asking of her. "I'll see mother and I'll get a solicitor. Maurice Leverett's a lawyer. He might know someone. I'll see him first. He might be able to do something, though I don't see why he should. You've been an idiot."

"He knows that." Mary had the grace to thank Olive, obliquely. "But if you can do something, we would be grateful." Olive noted the 'we'. She asked to go to the bathroom and plunged her face in a bowl of cold water. Only water could assuage her infinite weariness and this was not enough. Mary Owens was waiting outside the door. "You won't be too hard on him?"

181

"He doesn't seem to have the first idea of the trouble he's in."

"He'll get enough punishment. They'll see to that."

"I'm not talking about punishment."

"I couldn't think of anyone else. I'm sorry."

"You're not sorry. This is the only way you could have got him." Olive could have killed her own tongue, for a serpent. What did motives matter, after all? Chris needed Mary as Dennis needed her, except Chris's instincts were franker. Love, where need is, was a slow death, a mutual slaughter, and need was always there once love was spoken; and the only alternative was loneliness and courage, bleak. "I'll do what I can."

Mary had the tact to leave them alone for a moment. Chris appeared to be asleep. Olive sat down, watching him. He stirred and whimpered like a child waking from a bad dream. "What can a chap do, Olive?" While Mary was there he had made some attempt to hold himself together. Now he seemed, physically, to be falling apart. His mouth sagged and he supported his head in trembling hands as if it were too heavy to bear. His gaze was imploring, his eyes watery. She turned away. It was like watching an animal that had been run over. Dulcie's rage and bewilderment were heroic beside this disintegration which was, Olive imagined, as low as you could go.

"You'll just have to put up with it, that's all. I've said I'll do what I can."

"I could scarper, like Toby?"

"You'd last ten minutes."

He nodded. "You don't think much of me, do you, Olly?"

"I don't think anything. I don't think we've ever had much to say to one another."

"It's so simple for you, black and white. You've always known your mind. You'd never get in this kind of mess. I suppose you despise me."

Olive moved her head from side to side against the high

back of the chair. Her shoulders, her neck, her whole spine, were knotted. Chris would be astonished if he knew how deep were her dreams of sleep, inaction, rest, death. For if one felt like this and gave in what was the end, but death? She was aware that most people admired her, some even found her frightening, so she was admirable and alarming, energetic and positive, yet the response was no more evidence of her true nature than this present weariness. She felt at this moment she was no one. And she was everyone who cared to demand anything of her. She was as mad as Catherine, as brave, feckless and tormented as Dulcie, as hopeful and blinkered as Dennis, as broken as Chris.

'I'm sorry.'' She made an effort to smile. "I'm just tired, it's been quite a day. I honestly don't despise you. That would take more courage than I've got. Anyone who can judge anyone else must be either a saint or an arrogant imbecile. It seems to me we're wasting time. The point is to decide what to do next. Where will you stay? I imagine mother will produce the fatted calf, but that might take a day or two. I'd put you up, but we live like rabbits.''

"Mary's friends are away. I can stay here.''

"That's all right, then. But don't start something you don't mean to finish.''

"She's been marvellous. I owe her a lot.''

"That's your business.''

"You've got hard, Olly.''

"Oh, Chris, for God's sake.'' At that moment Mary came back into the room and Olive heaved herself up from the chair. "Look, Chris, we're both trying to help you, Mary and I. What use would it be if we broke down?'' He made a movement with his hand and she finished, "And please don't thank me or I shall break down. Just try not to worry too much.''

"I'm sorry. I don't know what I'm saying. I'm half out of my mind.'' He grinned shakily. "In a way I'm on your side, even if it's only brandy for the parson. I expect your anarchists would despise us but we're all at the same game really,

183

striking another blow at the rotten system." His voice was pleading.

"Oh yes," she said brusquely, but could not bring herself quite to touch him. "The system's rotten all right."

Mary saw her out. Her face was burning as if Olive had physically struck her a blow. "I really do care for him, you know."

"I know. I didn't mean what I said."

"I expect it will turn out all right."

"Yes," said Olive lightly, leaving to go into the furnace of the late afternoon, "we'll all survive one way or another."

When she got back Dennis was out and the Connors' door was shut, which meant they too were out or they wanted to be left alone. Olive bathed and changed for the second time that day, then she went down to Toni's with the vague idea that she might find Dennis there or Tim. There was a man eating with his back to the door. Toni came up. Dennis had said he was going back to the club and Toni's wife Maria was sitting for the Connors while they went out. Perhaps Olive would like something to eat? She looked tired. This weather was good but it was hard if you had to work.

"No thanks, Toni. Just coffee." Olive knew that with the slightest encouragement Toni would be sitting down opposite her pouring out his troubles, demanding hers, talking about politics, the price of eggs, Greece, Maria, life, death, the pointlessness of talking about anything. Olive did not feel up to it. She asked for the evening paper and wondered how to tackle her mother and Maurice Leverett, and what she was doing sitting aimlessly when she was neither hungry nor thirsty, in this awful, fatty, steamy hole when the bright evening was all outside and there was so much to be done before she could sleep.

"You look as if you'd lost a pound and won a penny."

"It's been rather a day."

Bob Wilson sat down in front of her. He offered her a cigarette and lit it. He had large, rather square hands, but

184

nails cut short and clean. She saw as he bent to the match that his hair was brown, cropped close to the head, greying around the temples. He leaned back and looked at her, smiling. There was something open about his face and at the same time contained, as if he had resources, a different kind of certainty from Dennis. Dennis believed in principles. Olive guessed that Bob Wilson had something much rarer: faith in himself, without any particular self-regard. This was rare and she could of course be wrong. "Do you want to tell me? It can help. Or perhaps you'd rather not. Or can I help without you telling me?" He told her later that she scared him that day, she looked so angry he almost decided not to approach her.

"No. Well yes, I suppose you could if you had a car. I've got to get to Kensington rather urgently and see two people. My brother's got himself in a scrape. I don't feel quite up to a trek across London, so I suppose it'll have to wait till tomorrow. It's not the kind of thing you can do on the telephone." She made an effort to smile. "I'm in the sort of state where you feel no one in the history of the world has been so put upon. I've no right to bother you with this."

"Nothing easier. I've got a car for the evening and nowhere to go. It's not up to much but I was mending it for a mate and it's mended, so it's all mine tonight."

"I don't see why on earth you should."

"Because I want to."

While they drove she told him about Chris. "It's rather awful for my mother because she'd more or less written me off, and my sister's ill—they'd quarrelled, anyway. So Chris was all that mattered to her really. She thought he could do no wrong."

"Poor blighter."

"Chris? Yes, I suppose that's the worst thing a parent can do to a child. Except not to love them at all. I'm not sure which is worse, who's suffered most from my mother, Catherine or Chris. Thank heaven I haven't any children."

"But you will have, I've no doubt." She glanced sideways

185

to see if he was smiling, but he looked quite serious.

"No. I don't think I will, if I have any choice." She realised now this was a decision she had made quite lately, without realising it. "Do you think that's awful?"

"You might regret it."

"I hadn't seen you as that kind of man. I mean the sort who'd see a woman's function as child-bearing."

"That means, then, you'd seen me as something. I'm flattered." Now he did turn and grin. His shirt-sleeves were rolled up and his hands on the wheel were brown and competent. She looked away. "You're right, of course. I don't. All I mean is, any intelligent woman's a battlefield—mind against nerves, body, instinct. More than a man, her body makes decisions for her and it can be unwise to go against them."

"What does one do then? Become a cow?"

"Someone like you would do best to put up with the tension, try not to deny any part of yourself. It'd be tough but you could lump it."

"You seem to know a lot about women."

"No. But they interest me. I'm sorry for them and I admire them. I like them, I admit that."

Olive wondered how he managed, with his wife dead. She had never heard anything about him and women. The car braked suddenly at traffic lights and their bare arms touched.

"How's Alan?"

"I don't know. I told you, we can't talk. As you said, who'd have kids?"

They had reached the Kensington flat. "I might be half an hour. Don't wait."

He nodded, but when she came out he was still there. He drove her on to Maurice Leverett's and then home. She must have fallen asleep on the way back because she woke to find the car had stopped outside the house and it was dark.

"You should have woken me. How long have we been sitting here?"

He shrugged. "You needed the sleep. I'm in no hurry."

Olive felt caught out. She had always had a superstitious horror of being watched in her sleep. She sensed herself retreating from him. "I am grateful. Won't you come in?" She heard her own voice, high, charming, chilling, what Dulcie called her posh voice.

"There's no need for that. We're past that." She leaned against the car window smiling, stupidly, she felt. She wanted to go in and sleep for ever, but was unable to leave the car until he released her. She told herself, it was unreasonable, she was tired, she was imagining things, he was taking too much for granted, yet she could not altogether draw away from him. He lit a cigarette and against her better judgement, Olive took one. It was absurd to look for fresh complications in her life, though this, she suspected, would be more an earthquake than a complication. "Why did you marry him?"

"Dennis? He needed me. And I suppose I felt . . . he thought as I did but he carried the ideas through. Oh, for heaven's sake, why does anyone marry anyone? You've been married. Everyone does it. I'm sorry, I'm simply not up to this kind of conversation."

"You can't get off with being tired all the time. One day I'll catch you wide awake, then I won't let you off so easily. I want to know why you bury yourself in other people's problems."

"There doesn't seem much else, nowadays, does there, unless you're blind and deaf."

"Well." He touched her cheek lightly with his finger and it was an effort like standing upright before a wind not to fall against him. "You do look ill. I wish you'd see a doctor."

"There's nothing the matter with me."

"Shall I see you tomorrow?"

"If I'm in I'll see you at the cell meeting."

When she got in she rang Chris at Mary Owens', and gave him an edited version of her two interviews that evening.

"Mother will come round, but I should leave her alone for

a day or two. I'm afraid Maurice was no use. He gave me the name of a solicitor but he won't help otherwise of course, there's no reason why we should expect him to. Try to get some sleep. I'll come over tomorrow."

23

Tonight the cell meeting was at Dennis's house. Olive could not be there because Mary Owens had rung on the Saturday morning to say that Chris had had some kind of collapse. The night before he had been upset but more or less under control. He had drunk quite a lot, slept heavily for two hours, then woken and apparently tried to break up the flat. She had finally got him to bed and called a doctor. He was under sedation, but she was not sure she could cope, physically, when the drug wore off. He seemed obsessed by the idea that there was a conspiracy against him.

Olive had to ring the hospital to say she could not visit Catherine that day. The matron sounded disapproving. Catherine had improved to a point, but not enough. Contact with the outside world was important, if she was to make a complete recovery. There was always the risk of a relapse. The matron had hoped to discuss with Olive where Catherine could go when she left the hospital. It was worrying that there seemed nowhere she wanted to go. "They are rather like long-term prisoners, you see, Mrs Rawston. There comes a point when they lose the will to leave." Olive agreed that something would have to be settled. As she listened to her own competent voice, soothing, placatory, she was appalled by her own efficiency. Was Bob Wilson right? Did she spend so much on other people she had become impoverished herself? Was her strength really weakness, a deep fear? She looked at her face in the cracked mirror above the telephone. She felt well and energetic, but she looked drawn and sick. At least she need not worry about Dennis. He was happy and had made love to her last night, some kind of celebration, she guessed. He wanted to fill her with his triumph, but he was an enemy in her body. She had deceived him, or thought she had, but afterwards she had been sick, a terrible gasping sickness.

And her mother was off her hands. She had gone for the weekend to Aunt Cat's. She had rung Olive early in the morning to say that Christopher must come home on Monday. Olive must arrange this. Whatever he had done his place was with his family. Olive guessed Mrs Armitage had spent a sleepless night, after the hysterics of the evening before, spinning this fine thread of self-deception. Soon, she would join with Chris in the theory that there was a conspiracy against him.

After all, Chris was not violent when he woke. Olive said she had made an appointment for him with the solicitor on Monday. He seemed grateful and pathetically eager to please both her and Mary, which was worse than his first self-pity. "You said she'd come round."

"She wants you to go home."

"Do you think I should?"

"If you do, you'll never come out alive."

Mary brought them in a cold lunch of bread and cheese and beer. They could have gone to a pub, but there was a feeling of siege or vigil which Mary implicitly encouraged. When they had finished Olive said, "Come on, Chris. I'm going out for some cigarettes. You need air."

Mary looked worried. "Do you think that's wise?"

"He's a criminal, not an invalid."

In the street Chris said, "That was a bit rough, Olly."

"Rough on whom?"

"Well, Mary, I suppose. She's put up with a lot, you know. She really seems fond of me, though God knows why."

"It's nothing to do with Mary. It's because I'm fond of you I do care what happens, I can't bear to see you give in like this. It was a stupid, weak thing to do, but that doesn't matter. What bothers me is the way you're making yourself vulnerable, now. You're asking to be walled up, by mother or Mary, it doesn't matter which. If you're just going to lie down and die, I can't help you."

"Doesn't love always make you vulnerable? That's the price you pay."

"Don't be wet. You never liked mother much and you certainly don't love Mary Owens."

"What's wrong, Olive? What's hurt you?" She shook her head. He went on. "You're right, of course. But I don't think I could manage without her."

"I won't come back, if you don't mind. There's a lot to do."

"Whoever he is, tell him from me he's a bastard."

"I don't know what you mean. Don't forget the appointment on Monday."

At last, after all the postures of self-pity he said quite simply, looking at the corner of the street where children played in a triangle of sun, "I'm not sure I could stick prison."

"Perhaps it won't come to that. Maurice did say if Toby Tait could be found, and if it could be proved that he set the whole thing up, you might get off lightly. He was a lawyer once, he ought to know."

"But they won't get him. In a way I still hope they don't. At least it would prove they don't win every round."

Olive would have liked to jolt Chris out of his paranoia, to convince him that 'they' did not exist as persecutors: the law was necessary, he had broken the law and must expect to be punished. This was the reasonable view, but she could not put it because she was aware that to some degree she shared his paranoia just as she sympathised with Tim Connor and Bob Wilson and his son, with all who, in their different ways, rejected the system. Yet she was not sure enough of the roots of her own anger to join any of them, actively. She was angry about Dulcie's child deformed, Catherine broken, yet no system, except perhaps a cosmic one, was responsible for these casualties. Perhaps the peace had let them down, life was greyer and meaner than those who believed in reward, like Chris, had a right to expect. Or were they, in the end, with their politics and good works and Chris's fumbling pathetic criminality, circling and avoiding the true issue, that life was unendurable? How can anyone bear to live? Dulcie had asked and Olive had not been able to answer her.

She kissed Chris lightly on the cheek. "Give me a ring when you've seen the solicitor. I'll be at the hospital on Monday. On the whole, I think you should stay with Mary."

"I'm not sleeping with her, you know. On that level she seems to find my charms resistible. Quite a blow to my pride."

Olive grinned. "You'll live." She turned to go.

"It's hard, all the same. Don't forget, whoever it is who's holding out on you, tell him he's a bastard."

Olive waved and walked off. She was aware that she looked attractive today, slim and cool, purposeful, yet she was irritated and restless. After all, Chris and Mary could have managed quite well without her, but now it was too late to go out to the hospital to see Catherine.

She walked past Toni's and looked in at the club. Some of the older boys were helping Dennis to set up table tennis equipment. The gramophone was blaring 'Yes, we have no Bananas', and the atmosphere was stifling. Olive gazed blankly at this curious scoutmaster of a husband and wondered who on earth he was. She refused a cup of tea, but smiled, which was expected of her.

"Is there anything I can do?"

"If you've time, you might call at the Wilsons'. Alan hasn't been in lately."

The Wilsons' house was a brave effort in a dingy row. Inside it was a place where two males lived together. Both Bob and Alan were fastidious so there was no squalor, simply the feeling of a transit camp, of so little put down there would be next to nothing to take up if they left. This was right because, Olive sensed, they both lived like this. Women are drawn, frightened, cherished, betrayed by houses. There is an endless give and take between women

192

and houses. Some women go mad when they are forced to leave their houses. Bob and his son could flit overnight. There would be nothing lost, left or taken. They could move off in the night, packs on their backs, and go anywhere because they had nowhere to stay. Men can walk away.

"You're shivering."

"It's so hot in the streets." Lost, she moved around, touching things. Alan was out. There were summer noises, of children playing in the street, a hose spraying a small patch that would not grow, an intensity of life in this narrow place. She felt sick again.

"Tea. I'll get it. Put your feet up."

"What would the neighbours say?"

"I'm having it off with a lady social worker."

"I'm not a social worker."

It was easy between them as if in their time apart they had made progress towards one another. One thumps around the world, Olive thought, talking one's head off and in darkness and silence decisions are made. She followed Bob into the kitchen. He was neat and quick about making tea. She watched and made no attempt to help, aware that in this house the necessary jobs were done quickly, without interest or the infinite weariness that oppressed her in the day to day managing of her life. Sometimes she felt pleasure in a meal well cooked. Most of the time it was pushing a bus up a hill.

"What are you smiling at?"

"It's like a camp."

"It lacks women."

"I like it." She did. She felt free here.

They went back to the small sitting room and drank. He seemed massive in this room and collected, ready for war, resting but watchful. "How's your brother?"

"He thinks the world owes him a living. He can't understand why he isn't happy."

"He's alive, that's something. I can't think why people go on so much about happiness. It doesn't matter. It's the sickness of the times we live in. There are more people unhappy because they think they've the right to be happy than hot dinners. And it's so damned unimportant. The moment you know you're happy, you start worrying about losing it. That's the fear at the root of the capitalist system. The pursuit of happiness was the worst bloody phrase anyone ever coined."

"What does matter, then? And I don't mean politics."

He shrugged. "I used to think, guts and a knife."

"That sounds like Tim Connor."

"Everyone sounds like Tim Connor at some time or another, unless they're dead. Then you realise that doesn't work. I suppose what matters is people living freely together."

"Love?"

"Nowadays that's mostly eat or be eaten. It's a bad word, anyway, for things that really matter. I'll admit your husband makes me spew. No one has the right to live off anyone like that."

"What do you do, then?"

"You give people a framework within which they have the chance to fulfil themselves. As far as I'm concerned that is the Communist state. Then, once you're free, you've the right to talk about understanding and needing and loving. Most of the people I know are a lot of kids playing about. Who has any right to talk about peace? There's always a war on somewhere. We're used to it. We were bred in it. It's a factor we take into account, but the young like Alan don't understand this and why the hell should they? We weren't so clever we can tell them."

She shook her head. "Bob . . . I'm all right. Truly. Dennis was worried about Alan. I'd better go."

He touched her breast. They moved upstairs leaning against one another. It was so urgent they had no chance, this first time, to speak, and when she tried to speak he covered her mouth. She loved, without understanding, every part of his body and mind. Towards evening he said the meeting had been cancelled and at last they smoked and undressed completely. He had pulled the curtains and pushed a chest against the door. He even brought in food: bread and beer and apples, but she ate nothing. She was aware only of being filled, completed, finished, released, until she cried out and knowing he could not help her, he held his hands, hooped below her body, until it was over and they could speak again.

24

BOB was on strike for a fortnight, so they could meet at the house every day while Alan was at work. Olive went straight there when she left the hospital at four o'clock. Dennis was always at the club at that time in the afternoon and Dulcie did not ask, she was so wrapped up in Steven. After that first cry of pain she spoke rarely of Steven's tragedy, and then lightly. Olive was ashamed beside such courage. She tried to explain to Bob. "I suppose we all used to think of her as good old Dulcie, a bit of a joke. Everyone was fond of her but no one took her seriously. What's so marvellous is, I don't think she's evading anything. She's looked at the worst and gone on all the same."

"You think you're a coward?"

She pondered. "I think I could be brave in some situations, but not Dulcie's. Maybe that's because I've never had a child, so I can't imagine what I would feel, except horror. It's not true, you know, that all women have the maternal instinct. I've seen enough around here to understand that. Women who look perfectly normal, terribly respectable, what Polly would call decent gells, beating their children, abandoning them, locking them up, tying them to table legs. I used to get angry, but that's pointless of course."

"It's pointless, too, the way you run yourself down." Bob was sitting up smoking, Olive lay curled on the bed. Some days they did not make love at all, but simply talked. But they always came up here. The moment she entered this room Olive's tiredness lifted. She felt as if she had been running all her life, till now.

"I never used to. I had a very high opinion of myself and my capacities."

197

"And now?" They were naked. He touched the jutting bones of her pelvis. "I like that, you being thin." He smiled. "I've always liked skinny women."

She shook her head. "Things have got blurred, confused. I had this terrific reforming zeal, I was always in a rage about the way things were going, and I suppose, in a way, I still am. But then you see things that make you qualify your attitudes. People like Dennis who have this tremendous universal love but can't begin to build a personal relationship. Dulcie, who couldn't care less if the world goes down the drain tomorrow as long as Tim and the children are all right. Then someone like my sister who never began to understand what I was up to—all she cared about were the individuals she loved. Then she goes half off her head as if she'd got some hideous cosmic message. Part of me is in a fine rage about it all, and the other half just wants to give in and say, oh well, that's living, it erodes you. All you want is a warm, quiet place. I begin to understand my mother, which doesn't make me like her. But I can see, once you've been in Eden, or think you have, everything thereafter is a fall."

"So where do we stand?"

"I honestly don't know. I don't even care very much. Sometimes you have to go by instinct. I know till I met you I had been on the edge of giving way to something."

He was tracing the line of her ribs, bones, as if to reach the essential, asexual part of her which could never be reached but they both believed to be there. "You're getting even thinner. You'll burn up. You'll be ashes. I cremated my first wife and I could do without that again."

"So how many wives have you had?"

"Her and you. Olive, will you see a doctor?" Bob was astonishingly serious.

"But there's nothing the matter with me. All right, I will. And he'll say I'm a perfectly healthy young woman who ought to have babies. Doctors have a curiously Old Testament view of women. Alan will be home soon, won't he?

And shouldn't you be picketing or making a speech or something?"

He eased her legs apart, kissing her on the belly and the breasts. They both looked at her spread body, as if it were a patient between them. "I'm taking a back seat, as a well-known red. They'll do better without me. No one likes to be used."

"But you are using them?"

"The only weapons are the ones that come to hand. In England the proletariat is a dead loss, politically. We'll use their greed, we'll do them good in spite of themselves. Pure Marxist–Leninism doesn't work any more. You have to make it up as you go along. That's what Larry Towers and his lot don't understand." He grinned, and rubbed his hand through his close-cut hair, a characteristic gesture. "I can't stand politics. They stink. As far as I'm concerned they're just a filthy way of giving people a chance to live as they should. Communism happens to be the way that stinks least."

"Dennis said something like that."

"Your husband's a good weak man who wouldn't know how to use a spanner if he saw it. He's the kind who'd have gone to Spain when politics were a simple matter of right and wrong. He ought to be locked up. That kind of innocence is a flaming nuisance. It's guerrilla war now. You've got to be cunning and mean. You realise you are about to be screwed by the meanest bastard you ever knew?"

"If I believed a word you said I'd run a mile."

"Your breasts are swollen. I love them."

"They're sore. It's like a kind of burning."

He entered her slowly, easefully, taking possession again of a country he knew well whose cartography was never, from one delight to the next, exactly the same. You were at once knowing and blind, tumbling down familiar slopes, meeting unexpected obstacles and dangers.

"What's the matter?"

"I don't know." She turned her head and bit the pillow.

199

"You're too tight. I can't make it."

"Sorry."

"We've talked too much."

"No."

"It doesn't matter, love. There's time. We're not catching a train."

"There's so little. I keep thinking every minute Alan will be in. I love this room but it's not safe."

He dressed and opened the curtains. Between chimneys there was a patch of brassy blue sky; a meaningless aircraft passed leaving a vapour trail, a silent, indecipherable message. On a bird-run of a roof a girl was sunbathing in a white swimsuit. Here, in the city, the sun was filtered through dirt and God knows what else men threw up to spoil their marvellous world. Nature will turn against us, he thought, we've pushed her too far. And the rain was poisoned and monsters walked the earth. Who was Eugene Aram? "Who was Eugene Aram?"

"I don't know. Why?" She was dressing, quickly, listening, on guard. Watch and wait. On guard.

"That book you lent me. Orwell. *Between the priest and the commissar I walk like Eugene Aram.*"

"Oh yes. I'd forgotten. I haven't read that for ages."

"I'd like to know who he was, that Eugene. We might go to the country for a couple of days. If your lame dogs can hobble on without you."

She was preparing herself to re-enter the world, dressed, brisk, practical. "I'll see Catherine tomorrow. Chris is still on bail. Since Mary wants him she can have him for forty-eight hours. Dennis had some do at the club. I'll say I'm going to my aunt's, I'm tired."

"That's true enough. Bring some books."

"So we're going to read?"

"In between. Where would you like to go?"

Of all places, Olive had an irrational desire to take him to Mr Rawston's. They would get on. Bob would like the country and the house. She smiled. Dennis can't come because he doesn't know I'm here but this is my lover. "I don't mind."

"It won't be Mr and Mrs Smith in a plush hotel. I can't afford it. No gin or early morning tea. Can you stand it?"

"As long as it's somewhere I've never been before I don't care if it's under a bush in a field."

They faced one another across the room. Bob said, "I don't want you to be disappointed." He was serious.

"Have you any idea how much I love you?"

He kissed her, looking over her shoulder at the hard blue roof of the sky and then it was time for Alan to come in and Olive to go home, and the girl in the dusty white swimsuit to shiver and feel the prickle of burning on her skin and groan and try to sleep, then climb back, complaining, through the window. The sun would not set yet but the moon was already up, low in the eastern sky.

The flowers were so noisy. They stood, stiff and thirsty in their trim beds, and screamed for water. Catherine wanted to stay indoors. The garden was deafening. Officious ants crossed a dry patch of sand. Catherine traced a line, a trap for them across the baked earth, but they paused, dipped, climbed and continued their inexorable track. They were fat this summer. Some had wings. Ants had perfected, smoothed, polished indifference beyond malice or desire. Catherine tried to explain. They listened gravely, holding their chins and nodded. The shock treatment plunged her into a pit deeper and darker than the knowledge of ants. It left her with a headache and a terrifying forgetfulness.

"Cat?"

She was dead and people visited her in her grave and brought flowers. Roots tangled with her hair and she anticipated the closeness of snow, the seasonal pricking of buds. Charlie whispered from his own place through the dark earth, Well, old lady, what's all this? Iron feet on hard earth. Leave me alone!

201

"We've been a bit naughty, Mrs Rawston, but we're on the mend again."

A flash of orange in the sun, shook, vanished, trembled and formed. It must be my sister, Olive. A breath on the cheek, a kiss? But the dead feel nothing?

Olive smelled of the world, rich and impatient to get on, but something extra, an acid sharpness of life rampant, triumphant. Beneath her arms were two triangular stains of life. "It's better out here. London's an oven. Would you think of going to Aunt Cat's? You can't stay in this ghastly place for the rest of your life."

"It's not so bad. People come to see me."

"Why won't you go in the garden?"

"I can't remember. Honestly, I'm all right. I'm quite busy really."

What had been an area of darkness was now a desert between the sisters. There was no crossing it. They touched cool cheeks in the darkened room and parted. It took Olive two hours to get home by train and tube and tram. Catherine played table tennis, then she listened to the wireless, or appeared to listen until it was time to eat and wash and go to bed. Like the ants she had learned to observe the system. She was proud of her cunning. She even pretended to sleep. If you wished to survive—which obscurely she still did—there was not a moment, night or day, when you could go off watch.

"His place is with me. How can that rabbit look after him properly? How must it look, living with that creature at a time like this?"

Mrs Armitage buzzed. Olive sighed. Bob had armed her against her mother. She could wait, let the old woman finish, why not?

"Really, mother, Chris is not living with Mary Owens, he is sleeping in a room in her flat."

Mrs Armitage had found Mary's address, gone round, made a scene and carted Chris home with her. He had stayed

202

one night and in the dawn crept back to Mary Owens. Mrs Armitage had gone after him. Mary had slammed the door in her face. Olive had been summoned to hear Mrs Armitage's list of wrongs. Her mother had put on weight, lost her style. Beware pity.

Yet she did pity her. She had been a power. She was a victim. You can drown trying to save someone's life.

"I must go, mother. Try not to worry."

Mrs Armitage nodded with surprising resignation and rocked in the chair in the overstuffed room in the sun. Portrait of an old woman with cats. Another trick? Not so old, after all, and sly, flirting, sideways head. "Where are you off to now? I never know what you young people will get up to next. But then I forget, you're a married woman. How is Dennis?"

"Very well. His club's going well. He's busy."

"Ah, everyone's so busy."

She knew. It was fantastic and appalling but of the two Mrs Armitage was more woman: from the air she had sucked in secret female knowledge of Olive's affairs. "Off you go then." Perception had made her quite jovial. Her eyes were bright, as if she shared with Olive some obscene information barred to men. "Your husband will wonder where you are."

"I doubt it." But Olive spoke lightly, warding off this bleak, vaginal, offered conspiracy of women. Her mother made her prim in a way men never did. She felt Mrs Armitage was spying on her womb. They brushed dry cheeks. Olive walked out into the sun.

⌐⊃ *25* ⊂⌐

THEY had agreed to meet at the station. The strike was settled on the Thursday. Bob said he could take the three days, from four o'clock on the Friday when Olive left the hospital.

"What will you tell Alan?"

"That I'm going away for a couple of days."

"But if he wants to know where?"

"The truth. We may not have much to say to each other but at least we never lie."

"Aren't you expecting rather a lot of him?" She said no more. Alan was a potential query in their relationship she was not yet prepared to face: while she could keep them in separate cells she could continue to have the son's confidence, which she valued, and the father's love. She was shocked by the deviousness, cunning and determination she applied to this situation, and wondered if it were Alan or herself she was trying to preserve. Bob would have been happy, she guessed, to bring everything into the open. She did not tell him that Alan had not been at the club for three weeks. There was another motive for her silence on the subject: a desire, almost superstitious, to go to Bob free, empty-handed even of the bribe of getting on with his son. There was a female part of her which might have used this. She rejected it.

She even tried, and in this over-populated house failed, to avoid Dulcie. The eye in her womb was as sharp as Mrs Armitage's, but benign. After all, Olive was glad of the blessing.

She was lying in tepid shallow water in the bath when Dulcie came in with Steven on one hip and a bucket of nappies on the other. The lock was broken which in this house was a matter of no importance. Olive was the only one who might ever, in a passing shudder of fastidiousness, resent the way they lived without secrets.

"Sorry. D'you want to bath him?"

"Don't move. Can I dump him while I put these to soak?" Polly had bought Dulcie fifty nappies from Harrods. Being Dulcie, these were sunk in deep ammoniac buckets five a day till one was left and washing was done in the middle of the night. Dulcie moved like a priestess through this house of milk and ammonia. Neither she nor Tim noticed the atmosphere. Dennis was never there. Olive woke to it, returned to it. Dulcie tipped Steven into the bath where he crowed and waved his hands like flippers, a man fish. He swam between Olive's legs. A child screamed downstairs. "Fuck." Dulcie went without alarm or acrimony to yell over the banisters. Olive started to climb out of the bath. Steven squealed, so she picked him up. He thumped her breasts like footballs; the sensation against her naked body of his bath-sweet tender flesh was extraordinary. She had had nothing to do with babies, and was torn between the urge to cover herself and to hold him. He was perfect. He offered her a windy smile and began to kick. He was entirely simple and natural. Growing was in his mind like a seed, so he kicked, to grow. The sensual life was now to him a simple matter of milk, excretion and sleep of which he was king. Later in what dwarf alleys would he learn his body, with what women? "Kids." Dulcie was back. "You're off tomorrow then? So's Bob Wilson."

"Dulcie . . ." Dulcie took Steven and laid him on a towel on the floor. He kicked and surveyed the two women. Olive was struck again by the thought that this was not a child.

"I'm not asking. Don't tell me. But I'm glad, Olive."

"I suppose it's pointless. I'm not much good at this kind of conversation. I never thought I'd be good at adultery, but I am."

"Then it's not adultery."

206

"What is it? Love? Sex?"

"I slept with a man once, in the war. Not Tim, I mean." Olive lay back in the water, now chilling. Dulcie tipped some washing powder into the nappies, sat down comfortably, like a larger woman, on the lavatory seat, and lit a cigarette from a battered packet in her apron. Olive thought, as she had before, how Dulcie and Tim were nomads, Dulcie the perfect nomad wife. Not homeless like the Wilsons. The Connors collected useless possessions like a dog gets fleas, but one jerk from Tim's long head and they could be off, a clumsy, cheerful, feckless but somehow admirable caravan thumping through the night till they reached the dump, setting for chaotic intermittent domestic bliss. They were not rootless, they carried their roots. "It's funny, Olive. I look easy come easy go, and I liked him and he liked me and we were lonely. He was a Yank, which is corny I know, but I really liked him. We talked. He showed me pictures of his wife and kids. You know, I've never told anyone about this before?

"Well. We talked a lot. I talked more that week than I have in the rest of my life. Don't ask me what about. Then one night he was on leave, he'd nowhere to go, we'd finished talking, there was nothing to say, it seemed bloody silly for him to sleep in the bath, so we went to bed. You know that bit in films, where they chew each other's ears and they won't show it but you know they've got to go to bed or bust? Well, it wasn't like that. What they don't know is half the time women get screwed by accident. It wasn't so bad except he talked about his wife.

"It was like talking, really, very polite."

"What happened?"

Dulcie looked vague, as if she had forgotten. She stood up and dropped the cigarette butt in the pan. "He brought presents for the kids and eggs and coffee. He sends a card every Christmas. He's got five girls now. I think I liked him more than any man I've ever known and that was the dirtiest thing I ever did. It was all right in my head and still is, but I

207

was sick in the morning and for a month after. That was a time I thought Tim was dead and this Yank wanted to divorce his wife and marry me. But you can't spend the rest of your life throwing up. If you don't love Bob Wilson I think I'll kill you; you married wrong, you might as well muck up your marriage for the right reasons."

"I hadn't really thought that far. I suppose I hadn't thought at all."

"Cheer up, it may never happen." Dulcie grinned. "The way we go on you'd think women had no sense of humour. But then, when you look at it, it's not so funny is it, being a woman?"

"It's not so funny being alive."

"Oh well," said Dulcie, "that's different, isn't it?"

"The country retreat of the bourgeoisie." But he grinned. "You meet such nice people in the Red Army."

They were shy and it helped to talk about the house. Bob had borrowed a cottage in Sussex from Patrick and Enid Green, a couple he had met through the Party, both teachers at an art school. Olive was struck, as she had been before, by how classless he was. He moved here, as in his own house, with a neat, sure touch. He possessed it for as long as it suited him but it left no mark on him, nor he on it. He seemed to need nothing, a class or home, to reassure him of his identity. She wondered how much he really needed her.

"Food?" she asked vaguely. "Should we buy some food?"

"You make the bed. The sheets are in the top drawer. Then put your feet up, I'll do the rest."

Here his camping instincts were valuable. The cottage was stone, bare, stark, the larder empty. She turned on the gas and struck a match. Nothing happened. "It won't light."

"Calor gas," he said. "There'll be another cylinder in the shed. I'll get it."

He lit the geyser. "Have a bath. I'll go to the shops."

The bottom of the bath was chalky and the water soon ran cold. He had said Enid was a slut. Olive lay for a while, then

208

dried herself on a grubby towel. The sheets in the drawer were damp, so she hung them out of the window and lay on a grey blanket. She had not meant to sleep but lately she fell into these deep greedy sleeps like traps. When she woke he was standing over her with the tea she had meant to make. "I should have done that. But I'll cook tonight."

"It's done. Casserole of tinned dead dog with spuds. The shops were shut."

"It smells marvellous. Where did you get it?"

"I had half a pint, then I walked into a house and said to a woman can you sell me a tin of meat and she did. I dug up the spuds. They had so many legs they practically ran into the pot. We might go down to the pub later, it's all right."

"Where did you learn all this?" She marvelled. There was something curiously sensual about Bob's domestic talents, usurping though they were. Usurping what? Cooking had always bored her. "If you go on like this I'll have nothing to do."

He lay down beside her, fully clothed. She had expected him to make love to her but he did not. She was still puzzled by her life being so entirely taken over and ordered. That was wrong, implying sanctions and limits; she was free within boundless limits, or could be if she chose. "You could marry me."

"That's a bit complicated, isn't it? In the first place I'm already married."

"That's no marriage."

"Why do you hate Dennis?"

"I don't, except for what he does to you. All these people living off you. You go on like this, one day you'll wake up dead. You think you're living through them but you're dying."

"But why bother to marry?" She was still smiling, arming herself against his quiet intensity. This holiday was precious, she was greedy for it and wished she had more wiles, women's cunning in its defence. "I'm here aren't I? And I shall be whenever you want me. I love you, isn't that enough? And I realise I've never loved anyone before. I didn't know that till I met you."

She sat up to drink the tea and saw her own reflection naked but oddly prim in the mirror. He was looking too. "Look at you, all skin and bones, because you're married to the wrong man and living the wrong life: There's always a part of your mind, your nerves, thinking about your brother, or your bloody husband, or the Connors who can perfectly well look after themselves. You can't do it, Olive Rawston, not single-handed. There's only two things left in this world that work, politics and private life. And politics are not Dennis Rawston's soup kitchen and private life isn't a couple of days of tinned steak and sex."

"So why are we here?"

"Because we want to be. Because we're human. Half a loaf isn't enough but you can starve on none. Which reminds me we've got a dog to eat. And I'm hungry and you want feeding up. You're marvellous, you know that, don't you? And if you don't marry me I'll put a bomb under London or walk off the edge of the earth."

"Does it matter so much?"

"You mean if you don't marry me, am I finished? No. At least I don't think so."

"I wish you could meet my father-in-law. I think you'd like him."

They made love and went down to the pub. It was the first time they had appeared together in public as a couple. It had never occurred to Olive that Bob might be known here, but he was, from staying with Patrick and Enid. This meant a small adjustment in her attitude. She had thought they would be an anonymous couple but they were not. She was amused at her own disappointment. As long as you're alone there's a chance you can set the pace. The people in the pub knowing Bob and therefore being interested in him would make assumptions which might, however obliquely, require that their relationship be explained.

210

Bob walked straight in while she hung back a little and began at once to ask questions about a third person, someone in the village she did not know. He did not introduce Olive but drew her into the conversation as if she were already known to the rest. That was tactful. She was happy to listen and watch and amazed, as always, by his constancy. He was himself everywhere. He played shove halfpenny with the same light seriousness he applied to cooking or reading, and he won. The sky, which had been thickening all day, broke and warm unwilling rain fell.

"I don't know anything about you. Where do you come from?"

"Essex. Before my grandfather's father. That's as far back as we go."

"Do you think much about your wife?" The rain was streaming down his face and he was enjoying it like a splashing dog. His greying hair was cut so short that plastered by the rain he looked like a monk; she'd had enough of that, the vowed man.

"Every day. I don't grieve for her for the simple reason I didn't love her. I don't believe in ghosts or spooks or the life ever after but the dead have a hold. A bit of anyone you've known well, lived with, moves in on you when they go. I have dreams."

"Bad?"

"Bloody boring mostly. Moira's more Moira now she's dead, if you know what I mean. While someone's alive there's always a chance, right up to the dying breath, you might arrive at some kind of truth between you, you put it off and put it off like going to the dentist. Then they're dead and you think, all right, it doesn't matter now. If you're riddled with guilt, which I'm not, you probably have nightmares or marvellous dreams of all the things you meant to say and ask. Asking's more important than saying. Confession's just making love to yourself, really. Anyway, the only place I got on with Moira was in bed, that is we both worked

211

like mad at it and by any standard of your sexual surveys our life in bed was a success. She crucified me. I died twice a night and thought I was God's gift to the vagina and it was like being swallowed by a great jelly fish. She was a Catholic and I managed to keep my head above water just long enough to take measures, so I suppose she was living in sin and is burning now in hell. And now I have these dreams.

"You see we could be having a row, which we usually were, and then there'd be this fantastic sex, then I'd bring her a cup of tea and she'd be off again about Alan or her mother or my politics, as if nothing had ever happened. Women can split up their lives into rooms, men can't do this or I can't. So I was always a mile behind her and I'd wake up every morning as if I'd run a race. You just go on doing the same things you did in life, no better, no worse."

"I didn't dream last night."

It was still raining. Olive wanted to lock the doors, mine the garden, cut the telephone wires and stop the clocks. She supposed this must be sexual greed. Bob wanted to chop wood and walk down to the village for the papers. He came back with enough food to hold off a siege for a week. Olive was still drifting around the house in her dressing-gown. Sleep stunned and killed her. He kissed her blurred face. She shook her head and drew away, but smiled to soften the rebuff. Then made herself busy cooking some of the things he had brought. Quite suddenly, at the stove, she began to cry. She never used to weep. Now her whole life seemed to be sleeping and crying, her visits to what she had always thought of as the real world increasingly an effort of will. She thought, if I go on like this I might as well move in with Catherine. There were three in a bed and the middle one said, move over I'm mad too.

He held her. Behind her the fat smoked and spat. With one hand he shoved the pan off the heat. "What's all this?"

When she had finished he pressed her down in a chair and brought black coffee. She shook her head and smiled weakly.

"I don't know. If I did I'd tell you."

He took her hands and turned them in his. "Neither of us will ever live easily."

Olive closed her eyes and lay back, her head against the wicker. "I never thought I would. If I had I wouldn't be here. I can't think. I can't imagine what will happen when we get back."

"Nothing, if you don't want it to."

On the last evening she told him she was pregnant. This was the third time he had asked her to marry him. "So you see it wouldn't be very practical. Whatever you think of Dennis he has a right to his child. And it is his, I know that, because it's three months. Which is why it doesn't show. The joke is, I've actually lost weight this summer. And if you hadn't sent me to the doctor I don't think I'd have realised even now. At least I suppose I did realise but I told myself I was just run down or anaemic. You think you've been careful and it couldn't possibly happen to you, but it does. It's all rather a mess, isn't it?"

"I don't see that. You can still come to me and bring twenty kids if you like. Unless Dennis wants it, which I doubt."

"But it's not your child. You wouldn't mind?"

"I don't have that sort of pride."

Nothing was settled. Olive suggested he might like to go out for a drink—she meant get drunk and told herself she would not have thought less of him for it—but he would not go. The next day there was a mild quarrel, provoked by Olive who found herself obscurely resenting his acceptance of the situation. In the end she did not want to leave.

"I wish we could stay here, in the country at least."

He shook his head and smiled, slamming the cottage door behind him. He put the key under a flower pot. "The country's an ancient monument. Nothing happens there now. The only life nowadays is in towns."

"Well, that's one thing you've got in common with Dennis, apart from me."

"You can hide in towns too."

She felt the child, which she could still not conceive of as a living being, had already put a distance between them. They no longer faced each other freely but through curtains of consideration and anxiety. On the way back in the train Olive decided that she would say nothing to him or to anyone, but she would get rid of it.

26

OLIVE spent her time in fragments of exhaustion between the house, the hospital, Bob Wilson and Mary Owens's flat. She went once a week to see Catherine. Now he was working again they could not meet at Bob's house. Sometimes they pretended to have run into each other by accident at Toni's, then they found a bombed house with cellars still intact. At first Bob did not care to make love there. From the grated high window of the cellar they could see Toni's café, Dennis's house and the bulldozers moving in from the edge of the site. This was a priority area for rebuilding. They would come one day and find their cellar gone. Bob brought in a mattress and fixed a padlock to the door and at last they felt safe enough as long as the bulldozers were silent. Olive lay beneath him and looked across his shoulder at the scrap of sky between the bars. Afterwards the child stirred, she felt it move within her like a fish. Daily it became more difficult to kill it, even if she had known how to set about a business which repelled her even more than the idea of birth. She rang a girl she had known in the war but she had moved. She felt her vagueness was an insult to her intelligence. She embarrassed the overworked doctor.

"Mrs Rawston, there are people now in this country, in London, who are actually starving."

"Which is surely one reason more for not bringing another mouth into the world." She hated her own clipped, smug voice. He was right. Things were worse than they had ever been in the war. Worse in a way, because in spite of everything the war had been a kind of childhood, in which issues were simple. This was a pointless hunger, a mindless fear, an anarchy of the body and the spirit.

He was quite young, he looked fifty. As a good left-wing humanist with a vocation to heal he disliked this well-fed educated female who had a whim to escape the implications of her humanity. "I'm sorry. I know you can't do anything. I shouldn't have asked."

He was placated. "Women are often depressed at this stage of the pregnancy. You'll find it sorts itself out in the end. It's natural. There's nothing to be frightened of." He took off his glasses and mopped his brow. His skin was boiled pink. He was inclined to be kind after all, to waste five minutes on this quite attractive young woman. "You'd be surprised, Mrs Rawston, how many mothers feel like you at first."

"But I'm not a mother."

"You see," she said to Bob, "I'm just too busy to have a baby. It's like climbing a mountain carrying a stone. Sometimes I can't stand women, except Dulcie and Catherine, the way they moan and whine, and here I am whining. That was how the doctor saw me, a whining woman. Everyone thinks, she'll come round in the end and the worst thing is that's probably true. Why don't you say something?"

"Because there's nothing to say." Now he too looked tired, she was wearing him out, the child had made her a shrew. His speechlessness enraged her. Sometimes she struck him. They went into love like soldiers to war. She loved him then best, when he was bruised and weary. "What does Dennis think?"

"I haven't told him."

"You'll have to."

"We can't come here in winter, can we? Even if it were still here it would be too cold. I suppose there are people who live like this all the time." She propped herself on an elbow. Outside the grating within a few yards of them a woman was calling to a child in the sun. A cat ran past on stiff legs, eyes blazing like a tiger. Toni came out of his café, a cloth on his arm, and basked, a beached whale, in the sun, richer now, dying, ending summer. "Tell me now, Mr

216

Councillor Communist Wilson, what is the news from the East?"

"If you don't tell him, I will."

Men couldn't split up their lives into rooms, yet an hour after they had been in the cellar Bob could be arguing with Tim Connor about the implications of the statement from the Cominform. Tim was exuberant, like a child at Christmas. "Don't you see! It's the red light. Europe's ripe. They've seen it at last." Olive, washing up with Dulcie, wondered sometimes if Tim was going mad. She saw him, the tall, thin, bony red man, prowling corridors at night, cracking his knuckles and planning world revolution. He was still, miraculously, night-watchman, pinching secrets he would never use, working out on yards of ministry paper more hideous and fearful weapons of destruction: fearful because the only person he was likely to blow up was himself. It was just like the British to build this paper palace of useless secrets and put an anarchist to guard it.

Bob tried to explain that while the Zhadonov statement was certainly an encouragement for the workers it was not a call to arms. It was not really so important, simply confirming a state of cold war which already existed. The capitalist system would destroy itself. Olive thought Bob seemed less confident, more disturbed than usual. He had confessed to her privately that he took the peaceful intentions of the Soviet Union with a pinch of salt. She could see he was worried. He rarely talked to her of politics and less now than ever. She was appalled by her blankness about politics. Tim said that India was the first blow to the capitalist colonial system and the six hundred thousand who had died were blissful martyrs. Olive saw them only as so many dead, victims of incompetence; the partition of India, a crazy Solomon's judgement, as only the first catastrophe of many to come. She had been told that many women, at this stage of pregnancy, had forebodings of disaster. She felt, in a mad way, she was moving closer to Catherine, though she herself

217

would never be mad. But the dark gulf had narrowed, somewhere they touched.

Over the washing-up Olive asked Dulcie, "Does Tim believe what he says?"

"Every word."

"Doesn't it worry you?"

"Why should it?"

Olive felt foolish. "I don't know. He might hurt himself."

"Well, I couldn't stop him, could I? He's got the right to blow himself to smithereens."

"You wouldn't mind?"

"Of course I would. It's corny, but I couldn't live without him. I would, I suppose, because of the kids. But he's a man. He's free."

"Bob said something like that. People living freely."

"Then he's right. Not that I think about it much." Dulcie looked at a saucepan, scowled and put it to soak. The washing-up in this house was never done. It would have been quite alarming to find the sink empty. There was in the inevitable, consoling, maddening greasy pan a continuity of life and idleness and delayed effort which suggested squalor on the surface, ease and richness beneath. Olive thought, this house is bad for me, now I'm getting romantic about dirt. Yet her own pin-neat, pleasant, comfortable flat above was barren. She laid traps for mice, tipped soda down drains, locked the door behind her on empty perfection. Dulcie was talking about Bob. "How's that going?"

Olive shrugged. "He wants me to marry him. I want to. I don't know. I can't see at the moment what will happen to any of us."

"Have you told Dennis about the kid?"

"No."

"It's bloody, isn't it," said Dulcie, cheerfully. "It's a bloody life."

Olive had a sudden burst of energy. Chris's case was to come up at the end of the month. He and Mary Owens seemed to have settled into a state of curious domestic euphoria, a condition of wilful innocence Olive found more maddening than touching. They looked at her like children, shocked and slightly reproachful, grateful, invulnerable, feckless, she felt, in the face of reality.

"I'm *not* trying to upset him," she said for the tenth time to Mary Owens. She had read them the usual lecture and Chris had stumped off like a whipped dog to the pub. Mary had said nothing, but she clearly blamed Olive. "But I think he knows where Toby Tait might be. I don't think Chris has begun to understand that if Toby isn't found he might go to jail for heaven knows how many years. I've nothing against Toby. I'm not judging anyone. But Chris has got to put up some kind of fight. He doesn't seem to care what happens to him."

"He's happy. I think this is probably the first time in his life he's been truly happy." Mary put down her knitting. It appeared to be some endless sexless pale pink garment. She smiled. "You expect too much of him. That's what we have in common, we're very ordinary people. Chris could never live up to you or any of the things that were expected of him."

"He couldn't stand prison. He's said so."

"He could if he had a reason for enduring it. You know we're getting married?"

"No, but I'm not surprised."

"You don't approve." Mary made this statement quite calmly, without hostility. Since this business began apparently she had found some certainty in herself. It no longer mattered to her what Olive felt. Her next remark confirmed this. "I don't mind for myself, though I'd hoped we might be friends. But I think Chris guesses and it worries him."

Olive thought, what does it matter? He'll marry her anyway. Why should I spoil it for him? I don't manage my own life so well I've a right to run anyone else's. She smiled. "Of course I approve." On an impulse she kissed Mary.

Chris came in as the two women were embracing. He

grinned sheepishly. "Don't I get kissed?"

Mary went to his side and took his arm. "I've got your special, some liver. You'll stay won't you, Olive? There's enough."

"Oh, I think I'd better . . ." Olive rose. She was now anxious to go. The sight of these two disturbed her unreasonably. Perhaps she did not like to see love as this kind of hiding—two small soft animals curled in a pocket of mutual consolation. Or was she jealous? Whatever the reason she had had enough of Chris and Mary Owens for today.

"Do stay, Olly, old chap. We don't see much of people now, we're getting dull. Give us a treat."

She gave way. Chris turned the dinner into a mild celebration.

He drank a little too much and Mary made no attempt to stop him. "Mary's told you the news, then?"

"Yes."

"We want to keep it quiet for a while. You know, better not tell mother. I don't think she understands what a marvellous person Mary is."

Mary was clearing the table. She looked down at the dish in her hands and said quietly, without venom, "Your mother is a wicked, evil woman."

"I think you're overrating her." Olive was making an effort to keep her temper. She had an irrational urge to defend her mother. Whatever Mrs Armitage was—lost, defeated, greedy, hungry, finished—she was not evil. "I really must get back."

Chris's eyes were bulging with sincerity. He said slowly, with the precision of a drunken man, "I don't know how you can say that, Olly. She put Catherine in the loony bin."

Olive said crisply, "Catherine's not mad."

"You two were always thick as thieves."

"Mother's old, she's lonely. That's how the old are. It's primitive. They want to eat the young to live." I hate her. She is the only person in the world I hate. And I will not

220

allow Mary Owens to speak a word against her. "She's lonely. I can't bear her. It doesn't matter. We can't talk any more, we never could. At least you talked to her, Chris."

"Who can you talk to, Olly?"

Only Bob, Bob only, alone together in a disreputable cellar even the rats despise. One day the snouty engines will move in and we'll be buried alive. I signal to Dulcie. I love her, but women cannot talk to each other, only signal.

Hating mother is family business, nothing to do with Mary Owens.

"I sometimes wonder," said Olive. She wanted to go at once to the cellar even though Bob would not be there and there was no way of getting him. Their life together was a precise, prearranged, finely determined business of time and place as set as a bus timetable. Each admitted they had, sometimes in embarrassingly hopeless circumstances, through the day, an urgent need for the other. It had to wait, and even then the slightest whim or accident could put off their meeting. Dennis came home early or Bob worked late. There was a crisis at the hospital, or in the house which bristled with emergencies like a beleaguered city. "I really ought to go."

"D'you remember, when we were kids, how she went on about father? I mean our father, yours and mine, which art in heaven, hallowed be his name till I could have thrown up. Poor Charlie. I bet he never screwed her."

"He must have done."

"What? Oh yes, Cat. Well, once, and she jammed her eyes shut and thought of Teddy in heaven. I think she saw Cat as an immaculate conception. Poor Charlie, I liked him, he was a good sort." Chris was very drunk. Mary touched his arm and he jerked awake and said quite clearly, "What's it all about, Olly, I don't understand?"

"He'll sleep now." Mary eased his head into a more comfortable position and brought an eiderdown from the bedroom.

At the door Mary said, "Come and see him again. It's not

221

good for him cooped up. I know what you think of us. You feel I should make him give Toby away. But that's the only pride he's got left, you see. If we take that away he'll never think anything of himself again. You do see?"

Olive shook her head. These lives baffled her. "It's funny," she murmured, as much to herself as Mary Owens, "we used to think he had a charmed life."

"I've been thinking we could be buried alive." There was a strange sickly yellow light, thick. Thunder had been gathering but would not break. The smell of the cellar, in spite of the summer, was damp. The walls sweated. She had left a slice of bread and the next day there was a fine, exquisitely worked lace of fungus. What diseases did you get from damp? Rheumatism? Nothing fatal but absurd music-hall ailments of creaking age. There was always the drip. A main had been broken and cut off but it still dripped somewhere in some private place outside houses or cellars. The engines will come one day when we are asleep and dust will fill our eyes, we'll be ploughed in, built over, children will run across our heads. We would make manure, fine roses. But we won't, Bob and I, because we watch, we have sharp eyes and bushy tails. Mother used to talk about the dead as if they had carelessly mislaid their lives. It can be done and not only by the dead. "I mean if they found us it would seem quite natural, wouldn't it, as if we'd died in the war?"

Sometimes they just lay quietly side by side. Olive had brought in an oil stove but he said it increased the humidity. They could rarely come till it was dark. Lately, the engines had begun to work at night under arc lamps. In the area they had cleared prefabs already sprouted, overnight match-box mushrooms. They were supposed to be a temporary measure. Bob said there was a model at the council, just like a rich kid's toy, of this place as it would be five or ten or fifteen or twenty years from now, or never, he added. Tower blocks, just like American skyscrapers, playgrounds, shops. Some maniac with nothing better to do had brought in toy

222

cars, wooden people, wooden trees and paper flowers. They'd played with it for one bleeding evening, grown men making car noises.

"It sounds awful."

"Just a waste of time. They'll get over it."

"No, I mean the plans. It sounds hideous."

Bob had been laughing easily. Now he turned away and shrugged into his shirt. "They've got to live somewhere. What do you want? Windsor Castle?"

"It just seems a pity. A chance missed. Even what there was before might have been better. At least it was human. Or is that a very sentimental upper-middle-class point of view?"

"It is. And as it happens your quaint old Victorian artisans' dwellings were death-traps and sewage pits. It was human, all right, like death and kids with rickets and no hope. A tree, just take a tree, you realise that in all these streets, as far as you can walk, there's not a tree?"

"We're quarrelling."

"No. It's just that there's no time for aesthetics. If you like to come up to the council offices I'll show you the figures. Anyway, I'm giving up the council. Did I tell you my brother had offered me a job? A partnership, in fact. A garage business. This will be over some time and then cars will be gold. I've not changed. Nothing will ever change the way I feel, if that's what you're thinking. But it's like wearing chains and carrying a leper bell being a red. I'm just fed up."

"That's not the reason."

He stood, dressed now and ready to go. She believed him when he said he would never leave her, or at least she believed his intention. This was the deep silence of their relationship, where the intention ended and the facts of his nature began. He was a man who could not be tied down, however much he wished. She brought things to this cellar like the kind of nest-building blackmailing female she most despised, but now understood a little better. He was always

223

going somewhere. This was where she finished.

Bob admitted, "I thought if I became a bloated capitalist you might come to me. I mean, we've got to live."

"It doesn't matter," she cried, and saw that the cellar was hopeless, beyond redemption or cure. "None of that matters."

He said gently, "There's Alan to think of too. The house is too small. If we set up there we'd be shoving his face in it all the time, that wouldn't be fair. And I don't imagine you'd want to live two streets from Dennis."

"It wouldn't embarrass me."

"No. But you don't like muddle, not that sort of mess. And you're right. Everyone's got something working against them, no need to increase the odds."

Thunder rumbled like the drums of an advancing army but no rain fell. The green silence was stronger than the small interferences of sound. She ought to get dressed. The truth was, he found this life in the cellar ran against his nature which had often been shrewd but never furtive. And it reminded him of the war and he could do without that. He had known a lot, especially men, who felt the war justified their existence. It had been a change for his politics to be respectable, but the price was too high, or was it that the prize was too small? He had known before so clearly what he was for, what against, but he had crawled through the dark tunnel of war, as it seemed to him, to no purpose. Down with Adolf, yes, and up with compromise, prevarication, shame. War, even when it seemed so clearly the conflict between darkness and light, was muddy, it messed, spoiled, confused the issue. *It is forbidden to dream again / We maim our joys or hide them.* Olive understood more than most but this was something he could never explain. Not at once, but now, the war got him down literally, so deeply he wondered sometimes if Tim Connor was right. This was a bad peace, it should be broken. You thought these things, but meanwhile you had to live, eat, sleep. Violence couldn't break you, you'd proved that, but necessity could? She was

224

talking, pulling on her clothes wearily, like someone loading themselves with chains. Her belly was now a little rounded and the planes of her face blurred, against her will. "We don't even speak any more. We just live in the same house. If anyone comes out of this in one piece, it will be Dennis." Saying this, she was sure of it. "He's the only person I know who's really got what he wants. I honestly don't think he'd notice if I walked out tomorrow."

"So why don't you?"

"It's just a matter of finding the right moment to tell him. I wish it would rain. I wish I didn't mind if it rained or not." She came and stood by him at the grating.

"Look." There were people already living in the prefabs. The gathering storm had darkened the sky. The sulphurous glow was intense but lights had been switched on early in most houses. It was odd to see from this worm's-eye view below the earth figures moving around inside the prefabs, imagining themselves unobserved. A woman was hanging curtains. A man was shaving. As a picture it was interestingly composed: in the foreground rubble and weeds, then the cluster of lighted dwellings, bright points of humanity on the raw, ugly site, and behind and above, the rumbling sky; while all around crouched the hungry yellow engines, resting now.

Olive thought how oddly complete and satisfactory other people's lives looked framed in windows. Bob was right, if they were to set up together it must be in a new place.

As they left the cellar the first warm drops fell. Their mood lifted and they smiled, in no hurry to get out of the rain. He took her arm to help her through the rubble and she felt suddenly optimistic. She would explain to Dennis quite reasonably and he would understand. He had outgrown the need for her support. The ending of their marriage would be no more than a formality. The child was a problem, but there was nothing that could not be sorted out with goodwill.

"You're not really taking that job, are you?"

225

He grinned. "I shouldn't think so."

Now it was raining heavily and they joined hands and began to run.

Rebecca seemed to think that getting wet would make Catherine madder. She fussed until Sam climbed out and heaved up the hood, like a perambulator roof. They sat, the three of them, Catherine in the middle, like three rich children in an expensive racing pram. Catherine wondered what would happen to the ants in the rain, then she remembered they were dead. The gardener had come and poured boiling water down the hole. "You never get them all," he said, "they always come up somewhere else. We'll have to watch for them." That was something for her to do or to seem to do. Since no one had noticed she was dead she led her seeming-life and wove weird, spiky dangerous baskets and ate. Apparently they wished her to eat so she stuffed till she was as white and fat as the grubs the ants had nourished. After death the hair continues to grow and the cells to multiply. Charlie? Does your beard grow?

It had been very still. There was a murmur and a rustle and Rebecca and Sam came to take her for a drive. They put her in a big cream car with a sun-roof and the tall tangled hedges began to race. She closed her eyes and smiled a tight little sewn-up smile. Sam had brought a picnic in a basket. There were scones and cream and jam.

Rebecca said, "You're the size of a battleship but you look better. You *are* better, aren't you, Hog?"

"Oh yes, I'm much, much better."

"It's marvellous to see you outside that awful place."

"Will there be a storm?"

"No. It's a lovely day. This really has been a perfect summer."

Rebecca had got engaged to her gentile architect. She touched her ring to stop herself from crying at the sight of Catherine. Catherine asked quite sensible questions. Rebecca answered them, at first embarrassed because of her load of happiness, then she chattered. Catherine smiled. Sam watched her. The sky creaked. Green flashed.

They tore back, ripping the air, racing but not beating the storm. Something in Catherine answered, she stirred. Chaos was one thing she understood. She was sorry when Sam pulled down the roof. He had hardly spoken all afternoon.

"Where's your Smyrna merchant coat?"

He drove well, fast but safely. Catherine wondered why he had come. She saw him riding in this car with his Marble Arch mistress. He had soft white hands, dark eyes.

"The moth got it."

"What did you do with it?"

"Buried it."

Rebecca giggled nervously, she was frightened of storms. "Oh, Sam, really!"

"I'm sorry," said Catherine. "It was a beautiful coat."

The heavy air had given Rebecca a headache. She sat with her face pressed against the glass, away from the others. Madness was something she had no conception of, except as family myth; as far as Rebecca was concerned you were happy or unhappy, rich or poor, alive or dead. Madness you could avoid. No one in their right mind was mad. She realised the folly of her logic but feared these visits. She yawned.

Sam said quietly, for Catherine alone, "Do you really believe you are mad?"

"No."

"Then why do you stay?"

"Because there is nowhere else I want to be."

Sam looked solemn. Any interior he possessed became exotic. The rich padded car moved silently between walls of dark rain. He pressed buttons and lights came on. Everything in here was oiled and mythical.

"You should get your hair done. Would you like me to buy you a dress?"

"There's no point. I'm so fat."

"You're beautiful," he said, or she thought he said and

227

could not believe it. "You should cry. That would be good."

"Oh, you're a filthy old Turk," said Rebecca, waking up.

That night Catherine cried for everything she had lost and never had, for being fat, for her father dying, for all those mysterious unnamed troubles, for the vigil she felt obliged to keep, for the persistent, reasonable, mindless power of ants. Does your beard grow, Charlie, can you hear the rain?

27

THE three women were sitting round the playpen, a present from Polly. It came with all the accessories and some one would never have thought of: a mattress, ducks on an elastic, solid base against draughts, cat net against cats. "Christ!" said Dulcie. "All it wants is a burglar alarm." But she was pleased. She had never had a playpen. When she needed to fence her children in she made a fortress of the furniture. Steven lolled like a sultan and regarded the women with complacent eye. Polly sent presents, but it was rare for her to come herself. She said vaguely she was busy. She had taken to wearing quietly expensive clothes, a little too old for her, which made her a formidable county matron. She had come today to tell Dulcie about a marvellous specialist in Birmingham who knew everything there was to know about dwarfism, which admittedly wasn't very much. But Steven should have every chance. It was Dulcie's duty. If Dulcie wouldn't go she would take him herself. She had brought, to impress Dulcie, papers from medical journals, a letter from the specialist and a couple of books on the function of the pituitary gland.

"Ugh," said Dulcie. "Well, if you think he ought to go, I suppose he'd better. As long as I don't have to read that stuff."

Polly was placated. Olive guessed that she had come prepared to make a scene. "Poor old Polly," Dulcie had said, "she'd steal Steven if she could. I've never known a woman who wanted babies so much and men so little."

They had speculated, when slightly high, on the subject of Polly's sex life and decided she had none. She was supposed to be getting married but she wore no ring and never spoke of her fiancé, except obliquely. She would say, "I am going out to dinner," but never "I am having dinner with Edward."

"May I?"

"Help yourself," said Dulcie, and Polly scooped Steven out of the playpen and held him. It was a moment of such intensity Olive could not watch. She thought of her own child and was ashamed of her sexual pride. Now she wanted it, or at least she could no longer imagine killing it. Everything would be settled soon, and while she could see no certain outcome—even the birth of the child—she had retreated or advanced (at least it was an improvement on the summer's hectic lethargy) into a strange state of peace. Dennis, her husband who shared her bed, was a friend she saw occasionally it would be necessary soon to leave. She was already doing up her skirt with a safety pin. She wished, above all things, to be with Bob, yet she had a sense of infinite time and would have liked this afternoon prolonged for ever. Polly had brought, along with the papers for Dulcie, a report she felt Olive should see, since Olive was interested in that sort of thing, on the survivors of the bomb. Some American friend of Polly's was helping out at the Japanese hospital which, knowing Polly, meant he was running the show. The pictures were not for publication, for obvious reasons, and they seemed to Olive appalling and yet distant, from legends long ago. Once she would have been angry, perhaps she would be again. She asked the right questions and Polly replied then said, over Steven's shoulder, "How's Dennis?"

"Busy. I hardly see him. He's got the club and he's on some L.C.C. committee. He's always speaking somewhere or writing lectures or sending off pamphlets or begging letters. He's turned out quite a professional beggar, very smooth, you'd be surprised. He had lunch the other day with some double-barrelled female—I expect you'd know her—and she actually took off all her jewellery on the spot and handed it over. He'd make a marvellous crook."

"Of course he was always ruthless." Polly bounced Steven on her lap. He tugged at her single string of matched pearls. Olive was surprised. "Oh, do you think so?"

"He has to be. That's why he's so good at his job. The good and the weak shall inherit the earth and God help the rest of us. When are you going to leave him?" Polly had always been direct but now there was an authority which went with her expensive shoes, her air of having come from a committee and leaving imminently for another committee. Dulcie said she had got bossy. Olive saw her as casting herself, for unfathomable reasons of her own, in the role of the embattled British spinster of private means. Polly flung out orders from a tower of loneliness. What about the unmentionable Edward? It was hard to believe that Tim had ever made Polly cry. She had changed; perhaps we all have, Olive thought. We all used to talk about the revolution and now, absorbed in our private climacterics, the group, the vision, whatever we had, seems faintly absurd. The only one who clings to it is Tim, and Tim's mad. Yet we are the same people. Bob said there were only two things that mattered: politics and private life. I have never made sense of politics, which leaves me four months gone, living with the wrong man because I'm too bloody lazy to move.

"I hadn't really thought about it."

"I think you're irresponsible."

"Then I'm irresponsible, aren't I?"

"What about the child? Have you thought of that?"

"What child?"

"Oh come on, love," said Dulcie, "you're spilling out all over. Dennis must be blind if he can't see."

Polly glared over Steven's head. "Whose is it?"

"Mine." Olive shrugged. "Well, Dennis's, but I doubt if he'd notice the difference. I'm the mother, as far as I'm concerned that's all that matters. I didn't want it but I shall. Don't worry, Polly, I'll be a model mother." There was no privacy in this house. Olive thought how odd it was that she, the most secret and fastidious of people should live in a

231

house of echoes, where secrets, even those most deeply locked, were yelled out at the top of the voice from room to room, pillow to pillow. It would be Tim. Tim collected secrets like a tinker.

"How do you know it's Dennis's?" Of course, Polly would know about Bob. Olive was angry.

"Because it was conceived before I went to bed with Bob Wilson."

Polly flushed as if Olive had struck her. "I don't want to know about that, I don't want to know."

"Then why did you ask?"

Dulcie plonked down a pot of tea between them. Polly laughed first.

"Sorry. I don't seem able to stop minding other people's business. I don't know what's the matter with me nowadays. It's rather absurd, isn't it, to think we had all that high-minded fuss and those frightful rows and now the group's finished in any case. It is finished, isn't it?"

"Yes."

"It was hopeless, wasn't it? I mean it was the most awful hypocrisy. None of us really had any idea what it meant to be homeless or starving. I mean, look, there's a biscuit I don't need, I don't even want, but I'll eat it. It's there. Even Tim and his reds wouldn't expect us to pack it up and send it off. I don't see what anyone can do."

Olive reflected. "Oh, I don't know. I think we did do something, we simply weren't properly organised and then once Dennis had the club he couldn't really keep up his interest. Then when it got mixed up with politics... it just fell apart. A few people still come for help."

"What happens to them?"

"Either Tim pounces on them, in which case they run like rabbits. Sometimes I can fix something. Dennis often helps through the club or his contacts. In fact he can do a lot more now he's respectable and in with the right people than he could before. I suppose that's rather funny."

"I miss it all." Polly smiled, the large expensive woman,

232

extravagantly out of place in this chaotic room. "I even miss this room."

"You must be off your head." Dulcie was attempting to darn Tim's socks. The result was striking. She flung it down and looked round the room. The demolition machines at work on the site of Bob and Olive's cellar raised a cloud of dust which travelled for half a mile; it settled everywhere indoors, and in the Connors' room joined with the grease and layers of more ancient dust to produce an interesting surface. Dulcie ran her finger along the table and pulled a face. "We could do with a revolution here for a start." She touched, like charms, a broken wooden toy, a pile of dead socks which she could neither throw away nor mend. "You know Tim's making a bomb. I kept thinking, if it blew up when we were out we'd get rid of all this rubbish."

"Where does he keep it?"

"Under the bed. Until I found it."

"So where is it now?"

Dulcie grinned. "At the Ministry. In the gents' lav I think he said. So if Holborn goes up, you'll know why."

Polly laughed. "This place is marvellous. Nothing changes here. It all seems so ridiculous now, that squabbling."

Olive said, "You should come more often."

"I wish I could." Polly was suddenly serious. Olive thought how precarious was female intimacy. Polly seemed to feel this too for she struggled to explain, "I think you have to make your life. I think unless you're very strong you have to fight to hold on to it."

"Edward?"

"Partly. I'm not very clever really, I can't split up my life." She was fussing in her bag for cigarettes. This was new, she never used to smoke. "I want a child," she said quietly, "that's all."

"Well, love," said Dulcie, "at least you're better off than Olive and me. You know what you want."

"Yes," said Polly, "I suppose I'm lucky."

Some intensity had made them shy. They smoked with regret. Olive thought what a pity it was, how tiring were these female afternoons. She wondered how long they would keep her on at the hospital. Once she had no work to do this would be her world. She shivered although it was hot.

"It's so hot." She flung her cigarette out of the window, it made her feel sick yet she wanted to smoke. In the distance she could hear the engines churning. She wanted a crisp green apple like those in Mr Rawston's orchard. They would be ripe now. "Have you got an apple?" She turned back. The sun, towards the end of this miraculous summer, had thickened to a mythical richness. Sun and dust hung together in the room, touching to gold the heads of the two women while their lower limbs trailed in shadow and the child crawled between them. Looking back from the bright sky, they seemed to be drowning in amber. If life were a picture it would be perfect.

At the end of the month Olive took a week's holiday from the hospital. She planned nothing, but Chris's case was due to come up, she promised to spend a day in the country with her mother, who was staying with Aunt Cat, then there was Catherine, there was so much to do. She lay in bed and watched Dennis dress. He made her coffee. They were very considerate to one another nowadays.

She offered to go down to the club.

Dennis said everything was running so smoothly it was hardly necessary. She should enjoy her holiday, stay in bed, go shopping, get her hair done.

"You've been looking tired lately."

"I'm all right."

In the end she spent most of the week in the cellar, reading and sleeping. She was often asleep when Bob came.

"Tell him. If you won't come to me we'll find somewhere for you to live."

"You're going away, aren't you?"

"No. I don't know. But if I did you'd come with me."

"Why would you go? Where?" She cried, her face turned away from him. "I want to stay."

Mrs Armitage was sitting under a tree, the *Telegraph* spread across her lap. Olive had forgotten her handbag. She came empty-handed across the lawn. Her mother was protected by a hedge of little tables, knitting bags, library books. Olive sat on the grass.

"You'll stay the night?"

"I'm afraid I can't."

Once, there would have been reproaches, rage, now Mrs Armitage began to talk about something she had read in the paper, heard on the radio. She wanted to know all about the cold war, a phrase that appeared now almost daily in the papers. There was something oddly flirtatious in her tone. "You must know all about it. I've never understood politics."

"Neither have I."

"But what about all your revolutionary friends?"

"They're not revolutionaries, mother. They want things to change, but I think they've begun to realise there's not much they can do." Olive thought of the bomb under the Connors' bed. Mrs Armitage would have appreciated that: it would have proved some point or other. They smoked. Aunt Cat had gone shopping. Olive fetched coffee. Walking across the lawn with the tray she saw her mother beneath the tree. Thinking herself unobserved Mrs Armitage sat with thighs spread beneath her ugly flower print dress. Her bare old woman's arms were crossed beneath her breasts. She seemed undisturbed to be caught like this. The women smiled. Olive had always liked this garden. She might even stay the night. Bob would say, this was an old woman, what harm could she do? The illusion of power was her immobility, fixed in the wide garden. Olive lay back and looked up at the tree; the leaves smashed the sun, caught brilliant jewels of light. She was dazzled, even in the shade. She would stay the night and lie in the sun. She would go back to the cellar brown and tell Bob she would go with him anywhere. She could have the child wherever they happened to be; after all, enough people had told her often enough it was perfectly natural. Women, somewhere she had heard of, left the paddy or the plantation or whatever and had their babies and went straight back to work. A friend of Polly's had one in a taxi. Dulcie said it was a piece of cake.

"The rabbit?"

"She means well."

They laughed. Olive thought, this is malicious, Mary Owens is more than her virtues and my mother is so much less than she used to be. If we could get on after all. She stood, brushing the dry grass off her skirt. The lawn had been kept up but the rest of the garden was neglected. Where Aunt Cat had once swooped like a bird between the raspberry canes was a jungle. "I'm leaving Dennis. I'm not sure when, but quite soon."

Mrs Armitage went on about the child. Apparently she had known about it but assumed it was simply the modern way to say nothing. She understood nothing, no one nowadays. Young people had their own way and that was to be expected. Olive's confession had unlocked some gates of hideous obstetrical memories. "Catherine nearly killed me. I nearly died. You were easy, a very easy birth."

"Mother, for heaven's sake."

Olive could not relate her beginning to this woman, and yet she could. If she had not been born there might not have been this thickening, this irreparable loss. Somewhere in this white, frantic body Edith Drury was lost. Who was Edith Drury? Who was Eugene Aram? She was moving closer, through this woman, to understanding Catherine.

"I really ought to get back tonight."

"Presumably you are leaving your husband for a man."

"I'm not sure yet. I haven't decided."

"And this is not Dennis's child?"

"It is, as it happens. But I don't see . . ."

Mrs Armitage had begun to rock herself, an appalling, self-

236

cradling movement, the arms crossed tight again beneath the breasts. Olive had seen orphaned and abandoned children do this. It was more weird and pitiful than tears or screams. She would embrace a child. Before her mother she felt helpless, resentful and yet aching with pity. She was ashamed of her own strong, healthy body, of the fact that she could walk out of this garden and go to Bob. "Mother . . ."

Olive speaking snapped the rhythm. Mrs Armitage spoke in a harsh melodramatic voice, loud and toneless, "Now you're having a child you'll learn what's what. That's an end to your precious freedom."

Olive wondered how it was possible for her mother to hate her so. This must be how she hated Catherine, though more purely, more deeply. What had she done but live her own life? Was that so awful? The garden whirled, the meshed light hurt her eyes and the perfect platitudinous English green of the lawn was so shrill she covered her ears. Aunt Cat flew in the face of the regulations. She crept out at night like a thief to water the lawn. When Olive was a child and first understood the nature of the universe, she dreamed she would fall off the spinning earth and woke crying. What a silly, said her mother, what dreams.

She could understand bitterness and disappointment, but this malice was beyond her. She felt suddenly protective, for the first time, about her child. Apparently, from the stuff she had read with a half-hearted scepticism, the emotions of the mother in pregnancy could influence the child. Would this hate reach its blood, would it know? If Hiroshima bred monsters that was nothing so unusual after all.

Remember, this is an old woman. If you bear in mind that she is only incidentally your mother, you can walk out of this garden, free. Didn't you pride yourself once on your charity?

"I suppose it is," said Olive lightly. The spell which had been thickening in the garden was broken. Mrs Armitage began to talk at once, in a matter-of-fact tone, about the things Olive would need. Was her doctor any good? Doctors were so awful nowadays. Was she eating enough or was that old-fashioned? Perhaps it was the fashion to starve oneself. Olive could see that her mother was already plotting, laying plans for the child. In her own way Mrs Armitage was happy. Olive thought wryly how small were her own ambitions: that it should be born whole and that it should have some chance of happiness. Where it would be born, to what father, seemed a matter of curiosity but no consequence. Lying in the garden, the whole world was spread before her, the possibilities boundless. She left as soon as she could after lunch.

28

OLIVE had been afraid that Chris might break down in court, but his performance was impressive. Mary, sitting beside Olive, was the one who now showed signs of strain; the tension she had suppressed all these weeks caught up with her. Olive was thankful that Mrs Armitage had not come. This was the last place for a confrontation between the two women.

Olive realised, watching him, how unconscious was Chris's charm. She understood now that he was hollow, but hollow like an actor who delivers instinctively the performance that will most please his audience. It is easy, she thought, to despise the need to be liked, but it is a deep urge, the one with which we are born, and most of us overlay it only by cunning. Chris is simply franker about it than the rest of us. What we think of as growth may be a retreat from innocence. Of course, we are right. Innocence is a mixed blessing. It can get away with murder and it can be quite helplessly cut down, it is greedy, vulnerable, heartbreaking and, in a grown man, incompetent. She thought that it was not so long ago since she had felt like Chris: that one should be judged by one's motives. This was a premise which could not be sustained.

"I had no idea what I was carrying. I realise now this was foolish. I blame myself." Chris spoke in a low voice, occasionally almost inaudible. The three women jurors craned forward to hear him. If they could, they would have let him off. Sometimes, when there was a delay—once when the cooling fan broke down—Chris offered them a tight smile. The men on the jury were impressed by his straightforwardness. There had been talk about a missing witness and they were worried that this might be a long affair. Relieved, they un-buttoned their waistcoats. He seemed a decent enough chap, he'd been a bit of a war hero. They'd be home for dinner.

"He's doing well." Olive had a mad urge to applaud. Be-side her Mary held herself deaf and taut in an agony of ten-sion and foreknowledge, trying to catch Chris's eye. He looked down at his hands as the lawyers argued.

Olive felt tired. She could easily have slept. This summer seemed endless, mindless, mythical. Several times it had appeared about to break up, then the sun rose again, each day richer and more melodramatic, giving positively its last performance which was never the last.

A few witnesses were called, a customs officer and a boy from the boatyard. The boy appeared to be on Chris's side but embarrassment at finding himself the centre of attention made him evasive and he gave a bad impression. There were questions about the defendant's partner and an explanation that he could not be traced. At this point Chris winked at Mary and she smiled weakly.

In his summing-up the judge explained that extenuating circumstances which could not be supported by evidence must not be taken into account. Possibly the defendant, clearly a weak character, had been hoodwinked by his part-ner, but the law could not be swayed by surmise. A certain kind of spurious glamour had attached recently to the spivs and parasites who were undermining the moral and econ-omic structure of the country. Smuggling was stealing as much as if these creatures had broken into your own house. Such enemies of society must be judged as harshly as common criminals; the fact that this kind of behaviour had become general practice among a certain section of the population made it even more vital that those who were reprehended should be punished to the utmost severity of the law.

After sentence had been passed Mary was allowed to see Chris. He had smiled vaguely when the jury pronounced its verdict, as if the whole thing were a ridiculous mistake.

240

Olive guessed the shock would hit him later. She waited for Mary outside the court, ashamed that she would have been glad to walk away.

Mary came out and stood for a moment blinking at the sunshine. She held her large handbag like a child.

"How did he seem?"

"I don't think he understands." Mary was suddenly fierce. "I think it is terrible she didn't come. I can't imagine what kind of woman she must be."

"I don't think Chris would have minded one way or the other if my mother came. Will you come back with me? Or would you like me to stay the night?"

Mary shook her head. "I don't know how anyone can live like that. I don't understand. Do you think they'll let me take things into him? It's funny. He seemed to need me so much and now I don't see how I can live without him. You get used to looking after people, don't you? Will he be allowed to smoke?"

"I should think so. Are you sure you won't come back?"

"No. I'll be all right. I might give you a ring in a couple of weeks."

"Do that." Olive watched Mary walk off, a large, pale woman. Other people's lives were a mystery. Mary Owens was either the stupidest or the wisest woman she had met.

Walking to the house from the tram Olive felt the late afternoon sun no longer hot but warm on her back like a consoling hand. There was that odd rich light which comes in England only at the end of summer, and the houses around the bomb site, which only a month before had seemed to shake and threaten, were now in this dying light gilded ruins. Their harshness was softened, the bricks touched by a patina of respectable decline so that there was an hallucinatory effect of antiquity, of memorials preserved from a once noble city. Tomorrow the few left were to be violently demolished; today they looked as if they might

241

stand for a hundred or a thousand years and then crumble quietly to dust.

The soft evening had brought people out into the streets. They stood in silent or murmuring knots. A few scavengers were picking around the houses with the desultory air of men on a beach when the tide is out. They had already been gone over a hundred times by children and dogs. Toni basked in his doorway. Olive waved. She wanted to tell him, he could.go back to Greece. Life was very simple after all, once you had made up your mind.

This was the first time she had found the house empty. Polly, with the air of a ruthless fairy godmother, had snatched up Steven and driven him very fast to Birmingham. Toni's wife, Maria, was looking after the other children. Tim and Dulcie had gone out together.

Olive waited for Dennis. She boiled an egg and lay down on the bed, meaning to read, but fell asleep. When she woke he was standing over her.

"What time is it? Why don't you come to bed? What's the matter?"

"Nothing. Just tired."

She got up quickly. If she were to introduce this monstrous subject it seemed necessary that the context should be as normal as possible. Perhaps she would not mention it tonight, he looked exhausted. She had a pathetically abasing urge to serve and tend him, as if she could say, now I have made you comfortable, now I can leave you. She walked between the table and the stove, bringing him food and coffee. She said, in a voice which sounded artificial in her own ears, "I don't know why you spend so much time down there."

"A couple of clubs in Bermondsey were broken up last week. Someone ought to sleep there."

"Which means you, I suppose."

But there was something else. He shook his head and began to eat the egg and bacon. Tomorrow there would be no eggs, no bacon, he was eating a week's ration. But tomorrow she would not be here. She sat on the bed, lit a cigarette, put it out and leafed through a magazine. She threw it down and waited for him to finish. "I've been wanting to talk to you."

"I know all about it."

So that was it. "Who told you?"

"That doesn't matter." She saw he was going to be as reasonable and sensible as she could have desired. He was going to make it easy. She lit a cigarette and this time she held on to it in spite of the rising nausea. He wouldn't look at her but he said in the same level tone, "We'll have to settle things, won't we. When do you think you'll go?"

"I don't know. There's no hurry. We ought to talk about it."

"There's nothing to talk about, is there?"

She cried suddenly, her head thrown back, "For God's sake, do you have to be so bloody good to me!"

There was a shout from downstairs. The Connors were back with the children. Tim would be talking drunk. There would be a party going on half the night. They braced themselves and faced the door as feet clattered up the stairs. Olive thought, if she ever did leave she would live in a house with locks, secret, in thick pads of silence. This was nonsense, of course, there would be mirrors and telephones. That was the problem. She had had all the company she could swallow, yet she had no desire to be alone with herself.

"You're loyal," said Bob. "You were made to be a faithful wife. There's a lot of it about."

Olive stared out at him, wide-eyed, from a stricken face. Pregnancy had not softened her features but sharpened the cutting bones, deepened and hollowed the eyes. She confessed, "I wanted him to be reasonable about it, but now he is I can't stand it."

"Then you'll have to put up with it, won't you?"

She mumbled, "I thought you'd understand."

"I do." He took her hand. They were sitting on the edge of the rough bed in the cellar. It was a matter of only a day

243

or two before it would be filled with the dust and rubble which occupied her dreams. She smiled, thinking they might be caught at it by the engines, like Mars and Venus in the net, in a golden haze of dust.

"I see what you mean. I feel guilty, so I want him to punish me, so that I can be absolved."

"Something like that."

"Or I want him to be shown at his worst, so that it will be easier to leave him?"

"That's running yourself down again."

"I don't feel so admirable at the moment. You know," Olive said painfully, "he actually offered to move out so that I could stay. He's already got a camp-bed in the club."

"That's not such a bad idea."

"So then you move in and I go on living exactly the same life, only with a different person. You could do that for ever, couldn't you? Musical beds. Is that what we're coming to?"

"Easy."

"That's what everyone says, easy, Olive, take it easy. I'm not ill, I'm simply a bitch. I can't leave and I can't stay and soon we won't even have this. But you never liked the cellar, did you?" She knew she was flaying out, all round, expressing the violence she could not put into words.

"It's not living."

Olive found a room. Toni said she could live above the café till she got somewhere suitable. Suitable to what? The house above the café was full of children. Maria sat at the door of her bedroom planted like a Mediterranean woman on her doorstep. There were always the dark eyes and the bird talk of the children; one ran up to Olive and touched her stomach, as women stroke hunchbacks for luck. Toni was always coming in, soft and anxious for her welfare. Were the curtains thick enough? Did she need another blanket? Were the children a nuisance? No, she said, no, she had everything she wanted, she was grateful. She smiled too

244

much, afraid he would understand that she wanted him to leave, and wanting him to leave. When he had gone, she lay on the bed, sleeping, waking, smoking, wondering how Bob could ever penetrate such a fortress.

Having swallowed her compassion for Dennis she felt, in this time, less than she ever remembered before. Her being was almost entirely physical and self-absorbed, a conspiracy of isolation in which she was joined by the child, which demanded food, sleep, exercise. She had given up her job and wondered vaguely how she would live.

Dennis had moved out to guard the club, so their room would be empty. Bob rang the café, he even wrote, he came downstairs every night in the hope of seeing Olive, but she locked the door and stayed in her room. She hoped and feared that he might burst the locks. Then she heard that Alan had taken off, he had simply vanished in the night, with a loaf of bread and a portable wireless. Bob had gone into the garage business with his brother. This was a signal to which her nerves but not her body responded.

She expected messengers and they came. It was odd to see Dulcie outside the house, without her children. Olive would not be the first to mention Bob, but she ached to hear of him. Dulcie prowled like a cat around the room and began to talk about the children and a Polish family that had moved into the basement. She collapsed in the only chair and closed her eyes. "It's queer, isn't it, being alone. I don't think I could take it now, not for long. Don't you get lonely?"

"There's Toni and Maria . . ."

"No. I mean for . . . Oh well, you were always the bright one, Olive."

"I read a lot."

She had never seen Dulcie embarrassed before. "Don't leave it too long. He won't wait for ever." Dulcie seemed torn. "I don't blame you. I used to think I'd like that, being alone. But when I dreamt of it there was always someone who came, and made the most fantastic love to me, and went

245

away. I suppose I ought to have been a whore, but they go off it, don't they? You've guessed, haven't you, I've not come for tea?"

"Yes."

"Well, it's up to you. I said I'd tell you and I have. He's all right, Olive. You could do much worse."

"I couldn't do any better. I don't know what's the matter with me. I seem to be stuck. I suppose it's this."

Dulcie nodded professionally. "You're going to be big."

"I don't know what I want. Everything I say seems to be something I've learned from someone else. I'm in a sort of funk."

"Aren't we all," said Dulcie. "Is Dennis giving you money?"

"Oh yes. I'm all right. For the time being at least."

"Then what will you do?"

"Go away. I don't know where, but I've got an idea."

"Well, that's something. Look after yourself. Don't forget us. And since you're clearly going to smoke yourself out of house and home here's a present. But don't choke Buster inside there."

Dulcie left forty cigarettes. For some reason this made Olive cry. Dulcie couldn't afford forty cigarettes. Olive could not afford to refuse them, she was so lost. And yet she could not take them if she were to polish and perfect her isolation. She pushed them in a drawer and went downstairs to ask if there was anything she could do to help. Maria clucked and sent her back upstairs. Olive thought she might drown in kindness. What she needed was to see the absurdity of her situation.

Tim came. He dragged her downstairs to eat. He was serious and melodramatic, blowing smoke all over her spaghetti. Toni circled them like a pimp. Tim glared, not eating. "You can't live like this." He made a small speech. Olive thought about the bomb under the Connors' bed, this wild, red man telling her off like a nanny. "You awful Hibernian kangaroo!" She began to laugh, bent double till the child protested. She sat back, panting. Tim looked worried. He thought she had really gone off her head.

Tim was right, she couldn't live like this. At night she went for breathless walks, protected by her hump, down to the river, up to the church, to Lyonesse and back, miles with gritted teeth, conducting in her head imaginary conversations. Sometimes she spoke aloud and thought what a mad, wild woman she must look. She saw a dim light burning in Dennis's club and imagined him lying on his camp-bed, like a knight on his tomb. Once Bob crossed the road in front of her and she ducked into a doorway. He was walking quickly, with his head bent and his hands pushed in his pockets. After these expeditions she slept heavily and woke long after the morning clatter of the café had begun.

From her room she could see the bomb site. The demolition engine swung a ball on a heavy chain, smashing the walls of the houses, baring the intimacy of abandoned rooms and lives. Then whole houses would fall meekly, shuddering like felled trees.

One night she went to the cellar. It had been cleared but not yet filled in. She looked down, half expecting to see the two of them. The engines pounded behind her. A dark figure emerged from the web of arc lights, a workman. The weather had broken, after this week they would work only by day.

The man said, "Someone had been living there, not so long ago either. Tramps I suppose." Something about her attitude struck him, reminded him that in their excavations bodies had been found. "You didn't know them?" She looked as if she were standing by a grave. When she did not answer he shivered and slapped his hands against his arms. She smiled and turned away, a good-looking girl. Queer.

He watched her turn the corner and shrugged. Then on an impulse he bent, picked up a handful of earth and chucked it in the hole.

Part Three

29

"Where are we going?"

"Surprise."

Catherine raised her eyebrows, and sank back in the deeply padded seat. In this car there was no sensation of movement: the scenery slipped past on soundless runners. Sam might have laid it on as he did the car, the plaid rug on her knees, the whole expedition. The label on the rug said Braemar. There was a picture of a worried-looking stag. Sam had been down every weekend this winter, bundled her into the car and driven her round the countryside. Catherine had stopped wondering why. She had become almost entirely passive, disturbed only when it was suggested she was well enough to leave. Then she refused to eat and the whole cycle began again. She was told she was not co-operating. Didn't she want to get well? She had spent a disastrous weekend at Aunt Cat's, in a state of silent panic. Olive didn't come any more. She had written a letter, something about having to go away for a while, which Catherine had not understood; but she tucked it away, along with the chocolates Sam gave her and some beads Rebecca brought. The doctor tutted and clacked at her hoard, apparently it was a bad sign. But Catherine knew she was keeping all these things only until she could make sense of them.

She had only just begun to realise that Sam was coaxing her, leading her farther afield each time. He had cut his hair differently, into a curled fringe. She had a quite impersonal urge to touch the whorls of dark hair. He was the only man she had ever met who could have worn jewellery, the more the better, priceless jewels winking on a deep peacock robe. Any other girl would say you've cut your hair differently.

251

Catherine had learned not to pass casual remarks. They came out too emphatic, too loud.

Bare trees gave way to suburbia, suburb to city.

"London?"

In central London most shops were shut on a Saturday afternoon but not to Sam. A bronze door swung open. It was more like a drawing room than a shop. She hung back. "No."

Sam swept her in. The metamorphosis from silent car to deep-carpeted room was almost painless. She stood.

Sam bought her two dresses and a coat. Shoes later, he said.

"But I can't pay you back. What about the coupons?"

"You can pay me back by having dinner with me."

"No, please . . . I can't. Send them back." She stared at her clenched hands. He took them in his and gently unlaced the fingers. "Is this supposed to be therapy?"

"That's better," he said, smiling as if she had just done something clever, rigid and upright in the car waiting to tear up the darkness. "You're angry."

"I think we should get back," she said primly, and slid her traitorous hands under the Braemar rug. Sam pressed a button and produced a flask. She walked in rather pleased with herself, as if she had languid legs like the Marble Arch mistress, and a small high bosom, with whisky on her breath. There was more tutting. Tears which had been prophesied came and she was in no state for dinner. But she woke up in the night and ate the chocolates. Then she crept between the beds and looked out at the sealed earth, and saw herself looking out.

When Olive first arrived at Highdale she thought she had made a mistake. She had written to Mr Rawston saying that perhaps she could come for a couple of days? The first attempt had been long and explanatory. She tore this up. After several more drafts she was satisfied with a short note: "I should like very much to see you. Perhaps I could come

252

for the weekend." Odd how one stuck to weekends, even when life was no longer ruled by a normal working time-table.

A letter arrived on the Friday saying he would be delighted. If she let him know the time of the train he would meet her at Matlock. There was no comment on her address, no hint as to whether or not he had heard from Dennis. The writing was characteristic: a fluent, rather small copperplate.

There was no time to reply. She waited at Matlock for a connection, feeling how frail was her optimism. One phrase, delivered shyly, formally: "If you should ever need somewhere to go, please remember that this house is here." Had he really meant, if she was eight months pregnant, having left Dennis, bursting out all over, throwing up, with no explanation that could possibly make sense to anyone sane? At Matlock, cut to shreds by the January wind from the Peak, exposed on the empty platform as a large, ungainly aimless woman half out of her mind, Olive almost turned back. One hardly noticed the weather in London. This was a fastness. Trees, land and faces were locked in a deep chill. The rails were iced and the train was late. On an impulse, while she was waiting for a connection, Olive sent Dulcie a postcard of the Matlock wishing well which had the power of almost instant fossilisation, according to the printed message. Well-dressing was apparently common practice in these parts, which must have been irritating for the water board. The few people Olive saw around the station looked much too gloomily respectable for such frivolity. She wrote: "Freezing to death. Send dogs."

Invading Mr Rawston's bachelor seclusion she felt like the whore of Babylon in a monastery. This was unreasonable since he was supposed to have loved his wife extravagantly. Instinct had brought her here yet an overwrought fastidiousness might drive her to leave with her flaunting belly.

She thought of all kinds of ways of putting it and in the end blurted out, "You know we've split up?" They were

253

drinking tea by the fire. Olive guessed that her father-in-law had tea by the fire every evening at nine o'clock. She felt like a thief, enjoying and sharing a tranquillising routine to which she had no right. It reminded her of her childhood, which she had disliked yet still regretted. Mostly she did not think of it at all, and in fact it had been nothing like this. Mr Rawston nodded. "It was my fault."

"Oh, guilt is the most terrible waste of time, don't you think?"

"You were expecting it?"

"Yes." Behind spectacles his eyes were mild and unreadable. "I expected the first world war and the second, and I expect a frost in May which will undoubtedly finish off my Bramleys. And I expect I ought to go to the dentist but they are the most dreadful fellows."

"You are a remarkable person."

"Do you think so? I'm flattered but I had always imagined myself to be exceptionally ordinary. I hope you won't really go back tomorrow?"

She stayed. A routine developed. In the morning she typed his history of the Peak while he prepared the next chapter. At first it was something to occupy her hands. The impact of the industrial revolution on the North Midlands had been till now what Polly would call a fairly yawny subject. Olive became engrossed. "It's good."

Mr Rawston smiled vaguely. "It's subjective. It is easy to become sentimental about engineering on the scale of those first railways. The human cost was appalling, of course."

"I would have thought you were the least sentimental person in the world."

He pondered, then shook his head. "I'll see if Mrs Middleton has made the coffee."

"She doesn't approve of me."

"She has never seen anything like you before. Imagine she is a native in the depths of the Amazon and you won't mind. And now put your feet up." This was his oblique way of acknowledging her pregnancy, which had never been mentioned; as if it needed mentioning, Olive thought wryly, fists clenched in the small of her back as she humped her load from chair to sofa. Dulcie's prediction had been accurate, she was monstrous. She wondered how much her father-in-law was inspired by delicacy and how much by evasion of the only too obvious facts. She liked to give him the benefit of the doubt, for this was the most harmonious relationship she had ever known. She relished it, yet each day was tempted to test it, to break a rule. So far she had failed either to startle him or to draw him. Today, after the ritual of their afternoon walk, she tried again. A parcel had arrived for him from London, more engravings of his everlasting lilies, an eighteenth-century second edition which Olive had to admit was exceptional. The flowers, poised, ecstatic and yet unruffled in their equilibrium, were at once worldly and perfect, and yet spontaneous creations of nature, best shown, as they were here, in the cheerful vague disorder of a cottage garden. Perfect, he said, perfect. He had brought the book to the sofa for Olive to see.

She smiled. "They really are lovely. I wish I could see your garden in summer," she added idly.

He laid down the book but his finger-tips still rested on the leather cover. "But you will."

Olive said gently, "I can't stay here for ever you know." She lay back and looked at the cold racing sky which from the warmth of the room seemed no longer threatening. She felt as if she had never before stood still in her life. She knew that this was a pause, not a permanent state, but there were no frantic undercurrents, as there had been with the summer's hectic lethargy. All the same, she could not live like this for ever because it was not in her nature. She murmured, "Do you think action matters so much?"

"I've managed well enough without it."

She protested, "But your life is so full . . ." then cut herself off. "I'm sorry, I had no right to say that. I can never leave things alone."

"That is because you are an intelligent young woman."

"For an intelligent young woman I am extraordinarily stupid."

"You hide very little, if that's what you mean. This is courageous. Most of us live by stealth. One has the knack of survival. Don't mistake me, I am grateful for it, I have no desire to know the number of my days."

Olive caught the rhythm, rather than the sense, of his words. She thought that Bob could die and she would know nothing about it. The child, which had not stirred the last few days, could be dead inside her. She had wrapped herself in this winter closeness because it was so much simpler than the consequences of action. The excuse was that one had to live. She heard herself say in her sensible charming voice, "I haven't any money, you know. I honestly can't expect you to keep me like this."

"Nor can I afford to keep a typist."

"I mean literally no money." She meant money for the incredible amount of apparatus the books said she would need for the child. She had gone through the list with Maria and crossed out half of it. Polly had sent some coupons through Dulcie who had regarded the fact that Olive was making any preparations at all as a colossal joke. So far Olive had done nothing about it, but she knew she would. Her competence was challenged. She disliked muddle, a distaste she had come to see as a priggish aspect of her nature, but one she could never quite escape. "In fact if I stay any longer I shall have to ask if you can lend me some." Since she had been here Toni had forwarded five pounds from Dennis, then, by the next post, an astonishing letter of hysterical reproach; it was no less, she knew, than she deserved, yet the violence made her physically sick. There had been no money since.

When she thought of the letter even this house seemed insubstantial. She lay awake at night listening to the rattling of casements, she noticed a crack in the ceiling, suspected rats in the cellar, feared Mrs Middleton's heavy hand with the Staffordshire cups. When she found one broken in the

256

kitchen bin it was a tragedy. She sat heavily, in the dark evening kitchen, in a panic. Her father-in-law found her there, biting her hand.

"I can't stay." She followed him meekly to the sitting room and accepted brandy. He tucked the rug round her feet and stirred the fire. They never touched, even on meeting. He looked tired and she wondered how many hours he lay awake in that cell. She curled her fingers around the glass, and grinned. "It's quite normal, you know. Pregnant ladies going off their heads."

"Tell me."

"Well. I never believed it, but it's true. I can't explain. It's like seeing the gaps. I mean, everyone has an idea of their own life, they live in a world they can prove. It's there, you can touch it. In a normal state of mind no one is afraid to look away. The tree in the quad, yours faithfully, God. You believe that, don't you? It *is* there?"

"If I knew that I wouldn't grow lilies. Or perhaps I would. It doesn't seem to me to matter very much." He ordered the objects on the table beside him: a book, an ashtray, a glass. "You young women read too much. Forster's vanishing cow with its sunlit flanks."

"I haven't read Forster."

"Why didn't you stay with him, whoever he was?"

"It's Dennis's child, you know."

"That wasn't my question."

"Oh. Well. It sounds mad but I suppose I didn't stay with him because I'd left Dennis. I mean, in novels there's a terrific showdown scene and whoever it is, the woman or the man, stamps out and runs to their lover's arms. But it doesn't work like that, or it didn't for me. In the first place, there was no showdown. I can't think why I'm talking to you like this, I have absolutely no right."

"But he tried to see you?"

"Bob? Oh yes, he battered at the door. I was the princess in the tower who wouldn't let down her hair. I was very righteous and mean. You see I think it was Bob who told

Dennis what was going on. I can't imagine why I'm telling you all this."

"And why did that matter so much?"

"I wanted to pick the time. I actually thought there would be a right time and I could organise it. This must be extremely boring for you."

"The skirmishes of the world? Oh no, not boring." He stood to damp down the fire with some slack. Without his spectacles he looked like a blind, knowing mole. He wound the clock over the fireplace, opened the curtains and emptied the ashtray; Olive guessed he could have performed this ritual in the dark. "But you should read Forster," he said.

There was no more talk of her leaving. In the morning Olive felt well, better than she should have done after brandy at midnight. She was full of resolves to steer Mrs Middleton out of the kitchen and do the lunch herself. As it was, Mrs Middleton did not turn up. Six inches of snow had fallen in the night. Mr Rawston said, "You wanted to be in control of your life."

"I suppose so. Then I was in a plain cold funk."

He was kneeling by the grate in his shirt-sleeves. The snow was being flung at them from the Peak on an evil wind which made the fire smoke. Olive came in wearing a spotless apron she had been surprised to find behind the kitchen door; because of her hump she had to tie it tight under her breasts. She had scrubbed the floor, put on a casserole and made a list of the supplies they would need if the snow were to continue.

The next day snow had given way to slush and they drove to Matlock through a discoloured spray. A few mad-eyed, long-horned sheep had slithered out of the drifts down to the road. They weaved around, flashing their green eyes and then, startled by the padded silence, set off in a crazed huddle for nowhere. The snow stuck sullenly to the hills. They found a boy, crouched under a haversack by the road. He slanted his thumb in the direction of Matlock and Mr

258

Rawston stopped the car. The boy slid wordless into the back seat bringing with him a gust of icy weeping wind. Olive was reminded of Alan Wilson, wherever he was, stamping the roads of England or escaped perhaps from this locked island. The car would not start again. The boy jerked his head and stepped out, flung up the bonnet and the engine purred. His trousers were as thin as paper, his short donkey coat flew up in the wind, yet he was not a tramp. Mr Rawston remarked on the weather. "Are you going far?"

"North."

"A job? Home?"

The boy shrugged. "Travelling." His accent was flat, non-committal northern, Lancashire perhaps. In town, without a word, he slipped off.

"Where will he go?"

"A driver's café. He'll be in Edinburgh tonight. We get a few like that through here."

"How do they live?"

"Odd jobs. Farms, helping out in a pub, a night's washing-up somewhere." Mr Rawston laughed, remembering something. "I put one up for the night once, a nice boy. He said he was walking round England and when he'd done that he'd go round again, the other way. I gave him the spare room but in the morning I found him on the floor in his sleeping bag. He said if he slept in a bed he'd never walk another step. He was going to stay another night, then he found out I'd been a schoolmaster and he was off in the middle of a thunderstorm."

"I knew someone rather like that. I wonder what happened to him."

"You can't blame them, I suppose. It's not much of a country for the young." Olive wondered how much of her father-in-law's tolerance was compassion, how much it derived from his pleasure in phenomena. Well, she thought, peering down the mound of her stomach, I can give him a phenomenon at least, probably more than he bargained for. Mr Rawston did not refer to the hitch-hiker again, but Olive

259

was haunted by the vision of his skinny form, like a half-starved, questing, sullen dog, dodging the smug shopping women, putting between himself and the car sheets of icy rain.

The town blotted out the melodramatic fastness of the country. The little limp snow that remained was washed into gutters by the rain. Olive did her shopping quickly in bright shops, lit though it was mid-morning. She did not ask for a nursing bra because she had no idea what it was and it sounded obscene. She bought a few baby clothes, a dozen nappies and a shawl. The assistant was sympathetic, which she would not have been if Olive had looked down and out. Most mothers bought far too much and regretted it later: they outgrew so quickly the tiny things. She looked at Olive's stomach, wistfully, blushed and produced a pink rabbit. Olive bought two and sent one to Dulcie, who would get the message.

Mr Rawston was prowling cheerfully among the toys.

"Back?" he said.

"No. I shall take you out for lunch with your own money."

The dining room was as vast and empty as a cathedral. A couple of Scotsmen made goblin talk over shepherd's pie. An extinguished waitress trailed across an acre of pre-war carpet. She looked as if she had been roused from a deep sleep. Roughly where the altar would have been, if this had been a church, the unhappy king stared down nervously from coronation robes upon a heap of dead blancmange. The waitress looked at Olive's stomach and sniffed, "What do you want, then?"

"A glass of sherry and a rump steak."

"Shepherd's pie."

"That would be delicious," said Mr Rawston.

"With or without?"

"What?"

"Veg of the day."

"With."

"It's set," she said, with her first flicker of humanity, "you might as well."

"I really am sorry. It used to be good."

"It doesn't matter, honestly. I don't mind. It's funny. It's odd, but nothing seems to matter much today."

The Scotsmen seemed to be getting drunk on water. They had a rumbling argument, squared up like wild beasts but it came to nothing. They were voluble with one another but softly curt with the waitress like a couple of Celtic kings on a man's spree. The ceiling was extremely high. Olive looked up and was lost. The waitress made her lonely transarctic trek again and said something unintelligible in a thick flat voice Olive could not understand. "What did she say?"

"The pie's off. But the chef is doing a mixed grill from which heaven preserve us and they've found some sherry."

They drank. The Scotsmen began to write furiously on a paper napkin. Olive wondered if they were playing noughts and crosses or concluding an arms deal. The sense of well-being spread ominously through her, a freakish delight in the queer dreariness of the place, its foreignness and the rightness of the goblin men, the somnambulistic waitress. Above an empty fireplace a shelf held two Staffordshire greyhounds, a model of the wishing well and a malevolent pixie. When the waitress approached again Olive said, "Wouldn't you like us to move nearer the door? You wouldn't have so far to walk." The remark struck her as mysteriously funny, a shaft of wit. The waitress was stunned but implacable. She looked at her tray, at her feet and at Olive's stomach but addressed Mr Rawston. She resented Olive's London voice and suspected somewhere in the turgid defeated workings of her mind, a joke at her expense. Without turning, she indicated the field of tables behind her back. "They're done for tea. This is dinner end."

"Then of course we shall stay where we are," said Mr Rawston. One of the goblin men yelled "Lassie!" and the waitress, like a bitch vaguely remembering her name from a world ago, set off to serve them. One of the Scotsmen said something to her in a low teasing voice. He had black hair and violently blue eyes. She giggled.

"She's human, after all." Olive felt triumphant, as if she herself had broken the woman's apathy. She began quite suddenly to talk about her childhood, something funny that had happened on a picnic about Charlie Armitage and a wasp. And something about an awful old mongrel he had brought into the house, all fleas and mange and no bark, but a marvellous smiling dog. "Never laugh at a dog," she told her father-in-law, "they don't like it." There was a point somewhere, but she had lost it. She poked at a bread sausage and heard her own voice from outside her head telling Mr Rawston about Catherine. "She's supposed to be mad, but she isn't, and she's got this stinking rich Jewish beau." Olive was using words that were not in her normal vocabulary. She imagined she was trying to entertain Mr Rawston. She wanted to ask him urgently how he had loved his wife, why he had not gone into the Church, how he could bear his life, why people were their own worst enemies, why Steven was a dwarf, how on earth one could chuck away riches, was everyone's life ruled by fear? Bob was vague and distant in her mind, alone in a house of speechless radios, waiting. But he wasn't like that at all, he was a man who would always find something to do. Dennis was not there at all. Mr Rawston was all spectacles, flashing windows. There was a hoot from the Scotsmen. For reassurance Olive touched with her toe the crinkly parcels under the table. Mr Rawston was talking about the waitress. He had known her father who had been a tenant farmer up at Ambergate. His voice ran on. Olive interrupted, "I'm sorry but I'm feeling rather odd." There were knives in her back and a sensation below the waist of everything converging on a spot of imminent, intolerable pain. This was a matter of the most intense concentration, staying on watch against a beast which visited her through the next twelve hours in various shapes, between patches of frantic rest. Halfway out of the dining room the beast grabbed her again and she stopped, snatching for breath.

262

There was a face very close to hers, goblin eyes. "Steady. Easy. You'll be fine soon, then. It's a bloody liberty, a fucking holy wickedness." She grasped a horny hand and was half carried out to the ambulance between two commercial travellers from Glasgow, whoa-ing and steadying her like a cranky mare, cursing thickly with consoling fluency.

⟶ 30 ⟵

OLIVE woke to a cream and green room on the top of England, having given birth to a female child. The goblins, if they had ever been there, had vanished. White creaked, revealing a nurse. "So we're taking an interest, then."

The child was presented to her, a total stranger, bald, creased and voracious. It was left with her. She was supposed to hold it. All the other women held babies, feeding them, breasts slopping out of nightgowns, talking, several with radio earphones on their heads. A pale wispy girl in the next bed, rather like Dulcie, lay, instead of sitting up, curled around her sucking child. She grinned. "It's against the rules, but I like it. You can go to sleep this way. God, I'm tired. How do you feel?"

"Empty."

The nurse swished back, grabbed Olive's nipple and thrust it into the stranger's mouth. She grunted, "It's not coming through yet." The baby was whipped away howling. Apparently Olive had let it down. The same pointless ceremony was repeated four hours later. Olive thought ruefully of Dulcie and Polly's pig. She slept. When she woke, Mr Rawston was there with daffodils. Their sappy stems creaked like the nurse's white gown and dripped down his trouser leg on to the floor. He looked puzzled, smaller than usual, no longer contained. They could have no dialogue here. The hospital bewildered him, claimed Olive who felt herself helplessly, if wryly, sucked into its powerful world of milk, Dettol and women. He smelled of cold and had snow on his shoulders which melted and joined the flower sap in a weeping pool. The daffodil trumpets were closed tight, secret, they would be cool to touch.

"They're lovely. Where did you get them at this time of year?" Olive asked, not caring, for something to ask. Some madman stoked the boilders here in the entrails of the hospital and flowers opened, blazed and died in a day. The nurses removed them as they did corpses, with a flicker of respect for mortality and a faint disgust.

"I believe they come from the Scillies. How are you? You gave us a fright."

"Us?"

"Dennis. He was at the house when I got back after bringing you in. If you don't want to see him . . ."

"Oh, I don't mind who I see. I should give those flowers to the nurse, she'll put them in water."

"Oh yes." A woman in the far corner had begun to wail like a cat. She clung on to the man by her bed who patted her shoulder uselessly, waiting for the bell. Mr Rawston touched Olive's hand. "Come home soon." Then he was led away by the nurse to look at the child. Once he had gone, Olive was afraid. The sense of confident, bored well-being left her. She shivered in the dry heat and turned away to watch the driving sleet against the window. The daffodils were already opening. The nurses changed shifts. It seemed incredible that people walked freely in and out of this place. Olive's body felt too light, she wanted to replace the child who had been there so long, blankets and eiderdowns, soft, feathery weights upon her stomach. She clenched her teeth. A nice young Irish nurse came on, flat-footed and loud, thumping Olive's pillows with big hands. "It's the milk coming through. Will I sit with you?" Olive was soothed by the presence of the girl, even though she could understand only half she said. She had never cared much for tea, but she took it now in great sweet gulps till she could lie back and listen, almost peacefully, to the girl going on in a voice which sounded as if it had been reared on potatoes and broken by stones then filtered through clear water. It seemed to Olive that there was no one left in the world who

266

spoke the English language, and upon this thought she fell asleep.

"Well, we're the popular one, aren't we." The nurses who had been scandalised by the absence of Olive's husband were now outraged by the attention she was getting.

Olive had sent postcards to Dulcie and to Catherine and a brief note to her mother. Mrs Armitage could do her no harm now, she felt. Letters, flowers and parcels flooded in, from Dulcie and Tim, Toni and Maria. Polly, ever practical, sent a depressing volume: *Child Care, the First Six Months*, by Sister Claire. Olive glanced through it, groaned and pushed it in her locker. It might come in useful some time, she supposed; at the moment she could not imagine being alone with the child, caring for it, being responsible for this insistent life. The connection she had felt before its birth was broken. Her breasts leaked regularly, but this was a symptom no more maternal, she felt, than the spurting bouts of tears which engulfed her without warning. There were times when the whole ward was similarly possessed and there seemed nothing but crying in the world: the howling babies in the nursery, the keening women. Olive could not recognise her own child's cry.

"Is it always like this?" she asked the girl in the bed beside her.

"Oh yes. Every time it happens, and every time I say I'll never do it again. But I do. You forget. Some women go mad."

Most of the nurses were knowing and brisk with the wailing women. The Irish girl stood by Olive's bed as she mopped her eyes, grinning foolishly. "It's a shame, a wicked shame," she said, reminding Olive of the goblin Scot, "what God does to women." She sounded cheerful. She sat down and began to tell Olive about her boy-friend and the film they had seen last night. All she wanted was babies, she loved babies. Olive treasured her. She brought messages from another world.

267

Catherine wrote:

Darling Olive,
   I am happy about the baby. I hope it wasn't too fright-
ful. Are you happy? What will you call her? Does she look
like you, I hope so?
   I am staying for a while at the Davies's. You remember
Rebecca? High living! They have a carpet in the *loo*. I've
got a part-time job in a library, very posh, clean books. I
might marry Sam, he's asked me. Don't worry, I'm better,
I think I'm really *quite* better.
   Chris doesn't seem too unhappy, we went to see him.
He's got fat and he's making cuckoo clocks. Mary Owens
was there.
                     Look after yourself and lots and lots of love,
                                               Cat

One afternoon of brilliant sunlight, cruel to the women
and kind to the flowers, Mrs Armitage swept in on an icy
wind grumbling about trains and hotels, the awfulness of
hospitals and the inadequacies of life north of Watford. She
looked extremely well, demanded a cup of tea, biscuits and
the baby. Olive was determined to be amused. The child was
brought in and crowed disloyally at its grandmother, flirting
with half-focused deep blue eyes.
   Olive sank back in bed and had not the heart to explain
that it was against the rules to pick them up. In any case Mrs
Armitage, quite on her old form, had enchanted and bullied
the nurses into submission, she could do no wrong. She made
it clear to Olive that she thought the whole business was
incredibly hole-in-the-corner if not downright squalid, but
all that mattered now was the baby, which could not be
expected to live in Olive's usual hand-to-mouth fashion.
"Where is Dennis," she demanded, "why isn't he here? I
assume now you have responsibilities you've given up all
that nonsense?" If Olive still had ideas about managing on
her own she could put that right out of her head. Mr Raws-

268

ton must be a very strange man to encourage her in such folly, but, then, men never understood the practicalities of life.

"Oh, mother, honestly." Olive smiled. She was safe here, her mother could not touch her. If she cared to exploit it, Olive guessed, the child had given her the upper hand, she was now in a position to threaten Mrs Armitage: leave me in peace or I'll take your grandchild where you'll never see her. She might do this in any case, she thought. Her mother's voraciousness for the baby alarmed her and gave her, for the first time since its birth, a pang of contact with the child. Possessiveness repeating itself from one generation to the next? Love? Bob's theory that love was inseparable from freedom hadn't worked so well with his own son. She was very tired. The only luxury here, a deep one, was the giving way to sleep. "I'm sorry, mother, but I am rather tired."

"No wonder with the rackety life you lead."

Olive said wryly, eyes closed, "It's not exactly rackety here."

"Well, since I'm not wanted I might as well go." Mrs Armitage began to fiddle in her bag, then snapped it shut. "I had hoped, Olive, that you might see things differently now, that you might understand life is not a matter of self-gratification. I had thought we might talk. I wonder now why I came."

"Mother, for heaven's sake, we've never been able to talk." They were close to breaking, but they never did. Mrs Armitage saw to that. The old woman took a last look at the sleeping child, a disarming picture. There was simplicity as well as threat in this passion, a direct, unspoiled love the thickened beauty had never felt for her own children. Olive was suddenly oppressed by pity for her mother, the defeats and small erosions of life which amounted in the end to a shipwreck. This woman might survive her existence, like a broken hulk on a beach, for ten, twenty years, till a high spring tide took her mercifully.

Dennis came in the evening. Olive woke from a frantic

dream and found him standing over her bed. Afterwards she was not sure if it had all been a dream and her husband part of it. He had seen the baby, she was beautiful, they would make a fresh start, they owed that much to the child, Olive must see. He stood there crying in the dusk, empty-handed.

"I tried to get some flowers, but it was half-day closing."

"I'd like some whisky, but you wouldn't approve of that, would you?"

His fists were clenched. He stooped and pressed his face awkwardly, vaguely in the region of her breasts. She felt a queer, mad sexual urge to drag him into bed and give Sister something to tut about. "It's so dark," he mumbled into the stuff of her nightgown, hospital issue.

"There's a power cut."

"I'm sorry. Sorry, sorry, sorry."

"What for?" Olive felt quite cool, in control.

He was kneeling now by the bed, clutching her hands. The scene would have been absurd anywhere else; in this ward there were many such daily dramas. Olive had only to call a nurse and her husband would be removed: here men were permitted only as penitents or humble acolytes. Stronger than the boredom, the bad temper, the physical degradation and flat-footed nurses was the myth of female power. Olive did not subscribe to this. She felt not fulfilled but robbed, yet she was prepared, if necessary, to call upon her rights. This experience had been a darkness in which she had discovered wells of ruthlessness in herself—the beginning, she supposed, of maternal passion, or simply the struggle to survive, to walk out whole. It was necessary to make a picture of the life she would live with the child. There was a shadow in the corner which she took to be Bob. Dennis did not come into the picture. She was quite surprised when he spoke.

"Can I see her?"

"Why not?"

"No, I mean when you're settled, can I come and see her?" He looked embarrassed. "I saw your mother and we

270

had a talk . . ." He understood he had made a mistake and flushed.

"The plot thickens. What on earth did you find to say to one another? What conclusions did you reach? To have me certified? To kidnap the baby? I'd never thought of you as the paternal type."

"Olive. Love. Come back. I know it will be all right."

She stroked his head and held his face in her hands, pondering, then she fell back on the pillow and began to laugh helplessly, sobbing, at the thought of the two of them together, him and her mother.

He grumbled, "It doesn't seem very funny to me."

"It depends how mad you are," she said, then the protective machinery of the hospital dismissed him, his mouth full of dumb speeches. Power was restored, lights blazed and the baby was brought to her. Olive fed it, humping it with knowledgeable competence from one breast to the other. Its need did not touch her, its good nature did. Doubtless, it would come to hate her. For the moment she was pleased to see a flicker of recognition in its wavering eyes, a tuft of her own dark hair sprouting on the fragile skull.

⊃ *31* ⊂

THE tenderness Bob would have spent on Olive choked him. By day he learned to lavish it, improbably, on clapped-out engines which he nourished and set passionately to rights much as Alan had tended his wirelesses. The new work in the garage pleased him, or he lost himself in it so deep he never stopped to think if it pleased him or not.

"Come and have a bite." His brother Jack was fastidious. Every evening he wiped his hands on a rag, washed them under the only tap, cold, and combed water through his hair. He was younger than Bob, had joined the war later, got his thumb smashed and spent his time in supplies, fiddling with the inspired fervour and charmed life of the true artist. He had emerged with a nest-egg to start the business and a conscience as clear as a cloudless sky. He respected Bob's intelligence and treasured his integrity like a charm, mocking it lovingly, steadily, with a persistence that had led to fights in their earlier years, was now a private game they had, their way of talking, though they didn't talk much. Bob often thought that Jack, settled now comfortably with wife and children, running his business on strictly legal lines, was more of an anarchist than Tim Connor. He believed in nothing, not even anarchy. He was free of guilt, anxiety, free almost of desire, so pure and unattached was his gift for making money. This made it easier for Bob to go in with him. Bob had become not so much a capitalist as a sorcerer's apprentice.

Bob stretched, was pleased to feel his muscles complain. If he worked another hour, then walked, then had four beers, he might sleep tonight. His reply was the same most evenings, "Not tonight, thanks, Jack, I'll stay on a bit."

"Mavis'll say you've given us up."

"Thanks all the same."

"Heard anything of Alan?"

"No."

"Kids are the devil. Janice is out all hours doing God knows what. I tell Mavis not to worry, but she goes up the wall." Jack was off. He had a pre-war flat, controlled rent, above a shop, with radiogram and wall-to-wall, poodle and happy wife. "If anyone wants the Ford, give it away."

"I was going to fix it tomorrow."

"You and God."

Bob worked till nine. Jack, or even the boy who came in half-days, would have gone straight to the heart of the trouble. Bob had soaked up the theoretical knowledge but his hands were still thick as bananas groping in the wombs of cars. At last he had it purring and the feeling was the same as ever: satisfaction in a finished job, regret that it was too late to start another.

The violet evenings were worst, especially since the spring, even in this treeless part of the city, made soft, indecent, westerly suggestions. He walked straight, but everywhere there seemed to be twined couples, burgeoning graveyards, the lap of a warm breeze from the river against his face. At these times, when there was nowhere to go but home, Bob could think of nothing but Olive and his love for her. She had gone into siege against him and he had not the cunning or the simplicity to break it. Since his fighting life with Moira he had abhorred the kind of violence to which many women, even the most intelligent, seemed to respond. Perhaps he'd got too fussy, possibly he had always been squeamish on that score: he had lent his body to the sexual rows with Moira, but had held on with virginal doggedness to his mind. Politics had helped there, so had the war, he had kept intact a vision of the way it should be possible for a man and a woman to live together. As he came to realise the size of his ambition he grew shy of speaking of it, even to Olive.

He had chucked in the job with the council, yet he was

still a Communist and always would be. He disliked Larry Towers, the power-seekers, the ideological donkeys, Party hacks, but Communism was so deeply burned in his mind he could not throw it out. Even though he could no longer produce the required response to the political occasion. After the Prague coup he had spoken once, limply, leaning on the Party line, and had his own doubts thrown back at him by a hostile audience. This was the last time he had been allowed to speak outside meetings of the faithful. Larry Towers and his henchmen had made this clear when they called Bob to account for giving up his work in the union and the council. These betrayals of responsibility seemed to worry them less than what they called his bourgeois objectivism. He had lost them a bridgehead in the council, but he had slipped out quietly, pleading the demands of his new job. His real crime, in their eyes, was lapse from dogma, his doubts as to whether the all or nothing aspect of Marxism was still tenable. He was reminded again of the parallel between those two warring angels, Communism and the Catholic Church. Both demanded an absolute discipline. Neither permitted any kind of reasonable dialogue with the unenlightened. Which brought him back to Moira whom he had sent to hell.

Coming to the river he stepped over barbed wire and slithered down to the foreshore. Water, sea or river, had a way of putting things in perspective, but tonight the broken face of the water was unresponsive, absorbed in its own experience of wind and tide. He kicked a beaten can, remembered the treasures he had found here as a boy, later how he had courted Moira here. That had been a sweet time.

One of their biggest blazing stand-up rows had been when Moira told him what the priest said: that every time Bob used a contraceptive he was putting her in mortal sin. They were to abstain or use the safe time, but too many females in Moira's family had been caught out that way. She came back from Confession and flung this in Bob's face, like a challenge. He did his best not to rise.

"Well, we've been all right so far." This was 1943, he was on leave. For ten years after Alan's birth in 1931 they had used the safe period and got away with it. When the war broke out Bob said they must make sure, Moira couldn't be left saddled with another kid with things as they were. The truth, which he did not admit to himself, was that he sensed the marriage to be already doomed. In the years before the war he had been the one who wanted more children, never mind the fact that for months on end there was no money coming in. He was young then. Now it was Moira who was seized by an hysterical urge to procreation. At first she had pretended not to notice what he was up to, now she called them, with lofty disdain, 'those messy things'. But she had never before brought in the priests.

"Anyway," she slammed marge on bread, still wearing her coat, "I've had to promise we won't use them any more." Alan, now twelve, looked up at them both from his comic with frank appraising eyes, waiting for breakfast. "And you can get out of it," she yelled, "and take your gas mask." He grabbed a chunk of bread and left, snatching up gas mask, satchel and on second thoughts another piece of bread.

Bob said slowly, "You needn't have brought him into it."

"He invited himself. He's all eyes, that boy. And he won't come to Mass."

Bob shrugged. Over breakfast there was a raging truce, then she started again. "I've given my promise. I can't break it."

He relit a half-smoked Woodbine, stretched his legs and thought in twenty-four hours he'd be back in camp, in a week God knew where. It didn't do to think. Leave was marvellous till you got it, still was in patches, Moira's deep whiteness spread before him, sleeping late, tea and books. When she clocked in at church he read in bed and that was good. He was always down and dressed by the time she got back, tea on. "You shouldn't have done that. No one can promise for another person."

This set her clattering dishes, talking to the sink. "Why

276

not? What do you think I did when you went away and I carried on alone? Don't you come back to a decent home? Don't I look after Alan when I could be earning twice as much in munitions? Because I promised for you you'd come back?"

Once this plea, clumsy though it was, would have stirred him to a gesture of love, it still moved him, but he clung like a steady dog to his argument. "I won't be blackmailed by priests."

Now she started on his politics. He shook his head. "It's nothing to do with that." He moved up behind her and laid a hand on her breast, meaning nothing except goodwill. You could argue with someone, surely, but that was no reason for the world to end. She turned and struck him hard on the face so that for the moment he was stunned. "You'll have me in hell will you, you and your books!"

Even Moira seemed startled by the effect of her violence. She watched the red weal grow on his face with something like awe, then she grinned. "You loon, come on upstairs, and I don't care if you wear your boots."

In the pub he set about his nightly task of getting slightly drunk. He had a good head and little taste for too much beer, which made this a difficult job. The door was propped open and though it was now dark there was the same feeling of warm abundance in the air, earth which had long been flattened under tarmac and concrete, stirring and moving. Through the open door stars seemed to race across a windy sky. He wondered what it would be like in Derbyshire, he'd never been there. Colder, he supposed. He walked to the bar. "A pint. Any pies?"

"Sandwiches?" He nodded. "Just like spring." For this nightly ritual he had chosen a pub outside his usual haunts. but they had come to know him, now he was a regular. They had been suspicious at first of his reserve but by now accepted it. One night he would accidentally miscalculate the number of drinks necessary for oblivion, he'd be tired and the beer would work faster, or he'd forget to count, and in drunkenness lay himself open to questions, concern, perhaps abuse. It was time to move on. Just as he was about to turn, balancing precariously the pint and plate of sandwiches, a hand like a bear's paw clapped him on the shoulder.

"Up the revolution!"

Tim Connor was already drunk. He had a weak head but a good way of carrying it; his face grew redder, his ginger hair stood up in wild sprouts, but he was rarely chucked out. Without warning, in the middle of a sentence, he would simply belch and fold up. "So this is where you hide yourself. I don't know how you do it, you lucky sod, but you're driving those women off their heads. Dulcie and Maria have sent me round every pub in England looking for you."

Bob grinned. "Bad luck."

"It's been a pleasure."

They did a little serious drinking. Looking up, Bob caught their reflection in the mirror: Tim professionally sliding another pint down his red throat; Bob, his short hair prematurely greying, sober, contained and inwardly raging, a stranger to himself. Who was this old man? "How's everyone?"

"If you mean Olive, she's had the kid."

"What was it?"

Tim was getting maudlin. "Another little bitch to be mucked about. You know what really worries me? Not the bomb but all these female kids. For one read three or four in thirty years. You see what that would mean? You could get the whole world standing up, or something, on the Isle of Wight, but who wants to die standing up?" He had lost his thread and seemed to have forgotten why he was here.

"How is she?"

"Who? Oh, Olive's fine. She's staying up there for a bit. You've not heard from her, then?"

"No."

Tim wagged his head, slurped back more beer, then

remembered something funny. "She nearly cracked my head open, you know. There was I telling her what was good for her, what a fine upstanding fellow you were and then all of a sudden she begins to cackle like a crazy hen and call me all the names. They're mad, those women, and they'll bury us all." Finally Tim recalled why he was here. "You'll come back with me, then? I'll get no peace till you do."

Bob shook his head. "Thanks, Tim. But give Dulcie my love, tell her I'm all right."

"You won't run into Saint Dennis, you know. He's taken off, I don't know where."

"No thanks, not yet anyway. Maybe in a week or two. You still on nights?"

"Yes, but not till ten." They moved on to another pub and drank more. The drink did nothing for Bob, Tim's nonsense did blur a little the beat of Olive's name in his head. After the sixth pint Tim produced triumphantly a crumpled piece of paper: 'Dg bix 500,000 20,000 crnd bf. Horsham.' He said this was proof that the Ministry were making underground stockpiles of dog biscuits and corned beef in the south-east against the war with Russia. When he was ready he could blow the whole of British security, give it to the Kremlin on a plate. He had defence capabilities, map references, the lot. The only puzzle, as he said to Bob, was what the hell to do with it all.

Outside they snuffed the soft air. Tim walked head sloped, narrow shoulders hunched, suddenly sober. "What's the point? It's all talk, isn't it? It just gets worse. What can we do, anyone like us?"

"What about your revolution?"

Tim stopped and rubbed his hand through his crinkly hair. "Well, that was only an idea, wasn't it? We'll never make it in a thousand million years. In this country we're past that point in our history. Alan's right. He just walked out of it. Good luck to him, poor sod, wherever he is. You're out of it too, in a way."

Bob wondered if he was truly out of it, if he had ever

279

really been in it. He'd never had visions of barricades and London burning, like Tim. Yet he did believe still that things must be changed, that equality was the only way to freedom and that one way or another it would come. His ideas had once been splendid, cosmic; lately, thinking of Alan and Olive, he had pondered on the applications of the revolutionary ideal to private life, which was a grand way of saying having seen everything go up in flames around him, he might now begin to live. When he was honest with himself all that mattered was work and private life. Not even work so much, except that you had to do something. They walked back along the river, pausing at Tim's bus stop. At this part of the Embankment there was little traffic by night. London seemed like an abandoned city until above them a train rattled across the bridge, deafening them. The electric line threw out sparks. Tim yelled something, Bob not hearing shook his head and watched, first baffled, then laughing as Tim turned out his pockets, shredded and flung a bundle of his precious secrets into the river. For a moment it seemed the wind might blow them back into his face, then the flakes of paper were seized and scattered by contrary gusts, spread across the dark water. Three or four gulls screamed, swooped down and veered away in disgust.

"Well, what was all that about?"

Tim shrugged. The manic gesture had sobered him completely and left him bleak. Perhaps he already regretted it. Bob touched him lightly on the arm and made to leave. Tim said, "Why don't you go after her? You're a fool if you don't. Dulcie's got the address, or Toni." Tim's bus arrived and Bob was saved from replying. He walked home. It was quite dark now and ragged clouds were bringing a mild rain. Where was Alan, he wondered? He didn't tell Jack but he'd had one card from him, from the east coast. No point in following up the postmark; if he guessed Alan's purpose rightly, he would have moved on by now. He wasn't worried about his physical well-being, Alan was a survivor in that respect, and Bob was held back from exploring his deeper feelings about his son by the suspicion that he had somehow driven him away.

In the house Bob followed his usual night routine, straight upstairs to Alan's room without turning on the lights; he knew this house like his own body. Normally he simply opened the door, looked in and went straight to his bed, but tonight he sat for a while, smoking, twiddling the knobs of a dead wireless. He turned on the single bare bulb which hung above the bed. The room gave nothing away: apart from the wireless there was a stack of old .nagazines on radio maintenance and repair, a few books and a photograph of the three of them, Bob, Moira and Alan. That would be 'forty-four on leave, a day in the country, Alan thirteen, Moira the big soft woman caught sleeping on Boxhill, nearly dead. He remembered this was a day of smouldering truce, sun and a snappy wind.

The irony was she'd gone to hell for nothing because the rotten thing hadn't worked and she'd got pregnant anyway. She'd said nothing to him nor had she gone to the doctor, so by the time they found it was growing in the wrong place it was too late and they couldn't check the haemorrhage. He'd told Olive he felt no guilt. Was this true? It was a question he had avoided till lately. Meeting Olive, most of all her going away, had opened his mind to the groping tentacles of sorrows and fears he had never before acknowledged plainly. Lying on Alan's bed he realised that he was coming to the end of the time when he could stun himself with work and beer. At this hour of night, unless he fell asleep straight-away, he had grown accustomed like a sick man who knows when the illness will ride him hardest, to the longing for Olive; now added to this, awakened perhaps by Alan's dis-appearance, was the agony of long-atrophied guilt, his shame at having fatally perpetuated a rotten marriage and having refused Moira even the decency of total war. Bob began to see how it must have been for the boy growing in this atmos-phere of ambush, crossfire and sniping. Had he rejected his father's politics so violently because he couldn't bring himself to reject Bob himself outright? How much had Alan suffered when Moira died? Now Bob came to think of it, he had taken it too well, and Bob himself had been so absorbed in his shock he had let the boy go his own way; this had been their relationship ever since.

Well, what could you do about it, what should he have done? What should he do now about Olive? How could you smash your way into someone else's soul unless they asked you in, even your own flesh and blood. It was like breaking into a house. Both Olive and Alan were locked against him, Alan through his fault, Olive for reasons of her own that were as yet mysterious to Bob.

He tried to sleep, failed, lacked the will to go down to his own bed and turn in, dozed, woke sweating from a nightmare to see the dawn come up; first the false lightening, melodramatic and lurid, then dusk, then the true, more hesitant and vulnerable beginning of the day. Lights in the houses opposite were switched on. He saw a family in a small room moving around, laden by sleep, never quite touching, like fish behind glass circling, veering, mouthing.

Bob rubbed limbs aching from a tense sleep. He went downstairs, ate a good breakfast, cleaned the kitchen, then sat down to have a cigarette with his last cup of tea and write a note for Alan in case he came back. He would have liked a map, but failing that pushed an old school atlas of Alan's into the haversack with torch, food and a few clothes. It was hot for March, if the weather held he would be warm enough. He was glad in a way there was no petrol, even if there'd been a car at the garage fit to put on the road. He could have got a train, of course, but the whole point of this journey was that it should be without direction.

He rang Jack from Toni's. "There's nothing much on. I thought I might take a day or two off."

Jack was clearly half asleep. Bob could hear Mavis grumbling behind him, the fancy poodle yapping. "That's all right. Do you good. Where you going?"

"Nowhere special, just walking."

Jack groaned. "Sooner you than me."

It took Bob an hour and a half to get out of London by tram and tube. Then he hitched a lift on a lorry and by midday he was eating bread and cheese on top of the Chilterns. For miles the land was his from the beech wood down to the soft fold of the valley. He could not formulate his feeling about his sudden transposition to this perfect landscape, nor did he wish to. He knew only that the topography answered some deep need in himself, freed a part of himself he had neglected too long.

32

"IF only I could understand!" Dennis paced beside the pram like a policeman. He kept to himself in the mornings, walked alone, read, and in the last couple of days had taken charge of Elizabeth for an hour. Olive, at first appalled to find him there when she returned to Highdale, had come if not to accept him, at least to use him. This was part of her new ruthlessness. He was surprisingly good with the child, and it had never been Olive's intention to keep him from it. If he wanted to help, why not? Most of the time she was insulated by weariness from his aura of self-abasing penitence, his pleading eye. Only at night when she heard him cry was she shocked, driven to tears herself by his weakness, the way he had bared himself to her will, put himself entirely in her power. She thought sometimes that he wanted not so much to get her back as to force her to share his pain. Then she bit the sheet so that her own cries should not disturb Elizabeth who slept in a cot beside her, curled in her own warm, indifferent, vegetable life.

Olive knew there was a temptation, which must be resisted, to use the child as a shield, an excuse for her own irresolution. She knew too that where Elizabeth was concerned, she was vulnerable. The feeling she had for her daughter, even in these impossible circumstances, especially in these circumstances, was the strongest and simplest she had ever known. On the afternoon walks she stepped primly behind the pram, but had fantasies that Dennis might suddenly snatch the baby and run.

"If only I could understand, if you could explain to me, then I might be able to bear it." His tone was breathless, his coherence often on the edge of disintegration. He looked a

wild, mad man, with his jerking walk, face raw in the spring
sunlight, his mood veering more wildly than ever from
pleading to abuse, interspersed with spurts of sentimentality
which she found most difficult to tolerate and which under-
mined all her resolves to be reasonable. How on earth could
she ever have married him? How could she have thought
him strong? He was chaotic. She thought he was going to
strike her, but he grabbed her arm. They stood absurdly
locked on a narrow climbing path which would soon run
out, a stream boiling below them. From the road, she
thought, they might be mistaken for lovers. "It's him, isn't
it? You're just waiting till I've gone to send for him?"

Olive knew if she said yes, this would ease him in some
way, but with the pram rocking between them her pity ran
out. Yet it was still a physical effort, as she struggled against
him, to keep her will intact. The habit of supporting him
was so instinctive, he looked so sick, so wretched. Elizabeth,
woken by the jerking of the pram, opened her dark eyes and
seemed to look at them both with uncritical wonder and no
fear at all. Olive said wearily, "Let me go, Dennis, you're
hurting me."

He released her arm. She turned the pram with difficulty
and he followed her, stumbling down the narrow path, yelling that she had joined with his father against him, her
mother was right, she was cold, heartless, she wasn't fit to
have care of the child. Then he couldn't live without her,
he'd kill himself. At this she began to run, thumping over
the last few stones down on to the road, conscious of his
pounding steps behind her, the tall hedgerow thrumming
with birds, a mesh of green, a flash of yellow and then a
sharp spring rain. Her head was bursting with his voice yet
when she reached the gate and looked back Dennis was no
longer following her. After the sudden shutting off of the sun
the light was venomous and the few early daffodils that were
out looked sickly. Indoors as she moved around, changing
Elizabeth and preparing to feed her, nerves attentive to
the slightest sound, the rooms seemed dark and cramped.

Olive locked the doors and sat by the window, meaning to unlock them as soon as she saw Mr Rawston climbing the hill from the village, but she fell asleep. Her dream was intricate, labyrinthine, exhausting. She woke in a panic convinced that Elizabeth was in danger, to find her father-in-law standing over her.

"Elizabeth . . ." She remembered. "How did you get in?"

"You forgot the French windows."

"Oh." She sank back. "You must think I'm mad."

"I think you could do with a drink."

The sky had cleared and the room was flooded with light. The room was hot and there was a faint scent of honey. Furniture polish? Lily pollen? There seemed a golden dust over everything. A bumble bee flung itself against the window-pane, fell, flung itself again and fell again. There was a clarity, a cruelty to the light at this time of year, you could see too far.

They drank. "It was so melodramatic," she said slowly. "Do you know that shocked me more than if he'd tried to kill me or to hurt Elizabeth? He said he'd kill himself. Why do you let me talk like this about your own son? Shouldn't we look for him? Aren't you worried?"

"No." Mr Rawston smiled. "It's the first sign of life he's shown. He's tougher than you think. He'll survive."

"So I used to believe." Later she said, "I'll have to leave soon."

"Can you go to your mother's?"

"That's the last place on earth I'd go." She brought some ham and bread from the kitchen. Mr Rawston was sitting in the dusk just as she had left him. She thought he was asleep.

"Parents and children," he said. "It seems one of nature's less intelligent arrangements. Such closeness without understanding."

"You were very happily married, weren't you?"

"Oh yes." Olive had always been afraid to ask this question but he seemed not in the least disturbed by it. He said with quiet intensity, "That was quite extraordinary. The

287

most extraordinary thing. I had never expected anything like that in my life. You know, I found it at first difficult to accept."

"Difficult?"

"Well, you see, I was rather a priggish young man, self-contained. I was so full of fine ideas. First the Church, then I had all kinds of revolutionary theories about education. They'd seem very tepid now. It took me a while to understand that I was giving up nothing, nothing of any importance. You see Margaret wanted to live in the country, and in those days village schoolteachers were not expected to be firebrands." He smiled, remembering something. "Margaret used to say no one can understand anyone else's marriage. Love is a private experience, quite mysterious."

"I'm not sure I know anything about it. From what I've seen, it scares me. It seems so devastating, so unscrupulous." She shivered. "I have the feeling Dennis is still around somewhere. You remember those two maniacs in the dining room at Matlock, that boy we picked up? I keep thinking about them, that you're either on your own, or if you try to talk to someone else there's a goblin that garbles everything. Is that ridiculous?"

"No. But it's a limited, selective view. You're frightened. That will pass. It takes some time to get used to vulnerability. You've overrated your strength, that's all."

That night Olive waited until she guessed Mr Rawston was asleep, then she dragged a chest across the door of her bedroom. The chest seemed inadequate, so she piled up chairs and drew Elizabeth's cot over closer to her bed. In the morning she woke early and was astonished by the fortifications heaped up by this madwoman, who must be herself.

It would be a hot day. Her father-in-law was working in the garden and must have been for some time; on the plot where he stood three-quarters of the topsoil had already been forked and raked. He looked up and waved. Turning back into the room Olive caught the end of her smile in the mirror.

It was like a summer morning. By the time Olive had dressed and carried Elizabeth down to the garden the light had thickened, lost the fearful clarity which had disturbed her in the last few weeks. The landscape had been reduced to more domestic proportions and, sitting in a garden chair, drinking coffee, Olive found it impossible to believe that Dennis might still be around prowling the village with thoughts of self-destruction or kidnap. She felt still a faint ache of protectiveness, of regret for them both, but these feelings no longer racked her. Soon, she thought, she would be free of him.

Overnight, it seemed, the single large tree in the garden, an elm, had put on a haze of green. Elizabeth waved her hands at the tangled light.

"Derby?"

Bob heaved himself into the cabin of the lorry and nodded. "Thanks. That'll do."

The driver accepted a cigarette and glanced sideways at Bob, curious. Looked as if he'd slept rough but not a tramp, not your usual hiker either. "Going far?"

Bob shrugged. "Holiday. Nowhere special." He felt disinclined to talk. He closed his eyes as the sun rose and burned straight in at the window. With so little petrol around, lifts had been hard to come by and he had walked about twenty miles a day. Most nights he had found a bed to sleep in but yesterday, stuck in the middle of nowhere when darkness fell, he had made do with his sleeping bag in a barn. He had woken stiff and shaking, and daylight had revealed that he was only half a mile from a substantial village.

He slept and woke around noon, the sun full on his eyes and golden discs swimming like fish beneath his lids, a headache beginning.

"There's char in the flask."

Bob poured some for the driver, then drank himself, gratefully.

"You from the smoke, then?"

Bob nodded. The driver, from Liverpool himself, mentioned a pal in London, as if London were a village. Bob knew him slightly, which knocked the illusion he had enjoyed on this trip of his stride lengthening, taking in areas of unknown country, leaving behind London and the complex mesh of his past, the empty present. England shrank, the point of movement somehow diminished. That must be how Alan felt and many of the young, but while it enraged them, Bob was not oppressed. He smiled at himself. He was getting old enough to relish meaningless coincidence.

He got out north of Derby on the Belper road. The driver was going on to Stoke. Bob was in a village. Women and children and dogs walked about slowly in the astonishing heat. The children looked at Bob, dusty and unshaven, as if he'd come from another planet. The women, not sure what he was, complained to their children and scolded the dogs. There was not a man to be seen, and a strange quiet, as if half an hour ago the men had been driven off to war on garlanded lorries.

Bob had meant to eat and have a shave, if possible a bath, but the shops were shut and in his glass-headed state he was oppressed by the place. It was an illusion, of course, but his arrival seemed to have emptied the street. Doors were slammed against him, hidden lives pursued behind twitching curtains. A single ratty dog snapped at his heels as he eased the haversack on his rubbed shoulders and set off north again. The country improved as he walked and so did his mood. He ate in a driver's café and wasted some time by the river at Cromford. The stream was fast flowing over a clean bed, very clear except where it curled and creamed round a corner or over a rock. He guessed it would be full of fish. He wished he knew about fish.

He had meant to go on, but he fell asleep by the river and in the end spent the night at the pub. Before he went to bed he got out the atlas and the address Toni had given him. By dawn he was off again, cutting across rising country, walking fast.

290

For several days after Dennis's disappearance Olive found herself suddenly but not unpleasantly weary, as if she were in the last stage of recovery from a dangerous illness. In the unseasonably hot weather she lay in the garden, let Mrs Middleton do the cooking and watched her father-in-law work. She dozed and woke to the tinkle of the fork against stone. Mrs Middleton's round face swam in the kitchen window, disapproving. She clucked and sniffed and clattered and looked as if she would like to steal Elizabeth, for decency's sake.

Olive had stopped reading the newspapers. She talked. Her life till now had been hectic, fragmented. She had snatched from ceaseless movement the illusion of control. In this she had been abetted by victims crying to her from so many rooms. She had seen her own life as a house which must, perhaps should, be fired from without since she lacked the courage to kindle it from within. Yet when she came to the point and began to talk to Mr Rawston she understood that there had been no house, only rooms. This was a sobering, rather dreary reflection. She came back to love because it was nagging at her. She and Dennis were supposed to have loved each other and that was now clearly absurd. Because he loved his wife Mr Rawston had driven his son half mad and tried to kill himself. The only love she had experienced which had not been entirely destructive had been with Bob, and it had seemed at the time necessary to end it. Olive got slightly drunk and said, "Perhaps the only way you can love someone is to give them their freedom."

Mr Rawston shuffled the brilliantly coloured seed packets. Elizabeth caught the flash of orange and blue and cried for them. Give me the sun, mother, give me the sun. Charlie Armitage used to sing some terrible music-hall song about having the sun in my pocket and it's coming out today. I liked Charlie but he was a fool. Cry for the moon. There were times when Olive thought the best thing she could do for Elizabeth was to leave her now.

Olive knew she was on the edge of something. "Love . . ."

291

she murmured, sober now and drily apologetic for chasing the same hare round and round Mr Rawston's neat room, "it seems to engender such violence."

"Slightly less than politics I should imagine."

"You see," she said, "I really am stuck. I'll be turning into one of those terrible women who hate men. Perhaps I should go back to good works." She entertained him with stories of the Connors, that room, Tim's bombs. "And yet if he finally blew himself up, it wouldn't be funny, would it?"

Olive felt the relief of having talked a lot, though in fact she had said very little. She became bored with resting and took up typing again, sitting at a table by the open window. From here she had a small but consoling view: in the foreground, directly below the window, Elizabeth in her pram, Mr Rawston mowing the lawn, beyond him, the sloping hill. "When I've finished this I'll really have to go."

A car, exotic as a crocodile sliding up the hill from the village, brought Catherine and her plump beautiful Jew. Very nice, soft hands, eyes like pads of velvet.

"Where on earth did you get the petrol?"

"You wouldn't approve." Catherine answered Olive but smiled at Sam. She looked well, the voluptuousness Olive had sensed in her long ago attentive now, stirring beneath her skin; awakened but still wrapped. Someone had made her stand straight, cut her hair like that. Catherine deferred to Sam, not anxiously but like a beautiful, happy child on a lead. Even separated on the far side of a room, she seemed to lean a little towards him, he to listen for her while absorbed in conversation.

At last Mr Rawston led Sam out to see the garden. Olive and Catherine stood by the window.

"Sam does look funny in an English garden."

Olive knew that Catherine was asking. "I like him." Did she like him? She didn't know him. He towered over Mr Rawston, gave an English laugh, wore his loose coat like a robe. She should be grateful to him. She should like him. He had clearly rescued Catherine.

Catherine held Elizabeth. She looked right, Olive thought, amused, righter than she did herself with her own child. Catherine sat, Elizabeth still in her arms, in a basket chair. Olive brought coffee and regarded them. "Well, you're an aunt."

"What will you do, Olive? Will you stay here? It's marvellous."

"I don't know. I expect I'll go soon. Have you seen mother?"

"Once. Being a grandmother has gone to her head."

"I thought she was going to pinch Elizabeth."

"Maurice Leverett's definitely got a safe seat. He's got married, did you know? That Diana Thing who was there on V.J. day. It's an awful thought, isn't it."

No, this was wrong, they were talking about the wrong things. Olive grinned. "What has he done with Eleanor of Aquitaine? Put her in a zoo?"

"Diana Thing has squashed her. She's gone all batty and meek and mild." Catherine pondered. "That's rather sad, isn't it? People should be themselves."

"If they can stand it."

Catherine humped Elizabeth on to the other shoulder and stirred her coffee. "When I was ill I thought a lot about Harold. I remember once I felt quite sure he was dead."

"It wouldn't have worked, you know, I couldn't have married him."

"I know that now."

"That seems a long time ago, doesn't it."

Sam and Mr Rawston had turned, they were coming back. Over Elizabeth's shoulder Catherine said with her old, direct, apologetic intensity, "I'm so happy, Olive. I don't know how it happened, but I'm happy." Olive was reminded of Mr Rawston: it was extraordinary, the most extraordinary thing.

"I'm glad, Cat, truly." The sisters rarely touched so they rode smiling the moment when they might have kissed. Olive said, "Well. Well, you'll be getting married then, after

293

all. You remember you said you never would?"

"Did I?" Catherine was playing with Elizabeth. The baby had messed Catherine's hair. She was no longer elegant. Olive walked to the window, smoking. The animals go in two by two: Chris and Mary, Polly and Edward, Catherine and Sam. Is that love?

Sam came in, Mr Rawston behind him pausing automatically to nip off a piece of dead wood with his knife.

Olive took Elizabeth who was framing her mouth into a letter-box to yell for food. Catherine turned, smiling, to Sam. He touched her hair and smoothed it back into place much as Mr Rawston would have dealt with a recalcitrant plant. Just for a moment, as Elizabeth was taken from her, Catherine looked lost. Olive thought, however you look at love it seems there must always be an element of need and of power. Every instinct in her rebelled against this conclusion. She caught Sam watching her as if he understood everything she was thinking, a boy with his pockets full of money. He had brought champagne. She flushed, then raised her glass in salute.

Olive thought constantly now of Bob, daily like a prayer at the back of her vague days, so when he walked in it was not so surprising. Her mind had so long prefigured this moment.

"Well."

"You look as if you could do with a bath."

"That's a fine welcome when I've walked half up England."

They smiled at each other. Mr Rawston came in, knowing who it was but expecting, all the same, to be told.

33

THE red haze on the trees was giving way to green. Below them in the valley a horse drew a harrow round a field, exposing the silver edge of the grass. Indoors, in that toy house, Mrs Middleton would be clucking over Elizabeth. A chilly wind lifted the newspaper. Bob crumpled it and pushed it away. "The hell with that."

"Berlin?"

He shrugged, then reached up and pulled Olive down beside him. "You'll come back with me at the end of the week?"

"What for?"

"Life."

She shivered. He held her by the shoulders and thrust her up so that she was forced to look. "Look. What is there to be scared of?"

"I don't know."

"What is the worst thing you can imagine happening?"

"Elizabeth dying."

"You'd have said war once." He smiled. "So that's an improvement."

She wouldn't let him get away with that. "But you'd say war?"

"Yes."

"And that's all right because you're a man and I'm a woman?"

"No. Because we're two people."

Olive turned to look at him. He lay back, propped on his elbow, thinner from his walk, and brown. Yet he didn't look like a countryman, he never would. He had a countryman's ease with natural things, a townsman's nerves and an independence which marked him out as belonging to neither. She took his hand. It was tanned and leathery above, hard but white in the palm. "Perhaps it will come to the same thing," she said, thinking of Berlin.

"Not yet."

"I was once supposed to be an extremely practical person."

"So?"

"So what is a practical person who knows exactly what she wants doing in this state of mind?"

"Recognising the limits of her competence. It's a start."

They walked slowly down the hill, meeting their abandoned newspaper at the bottom. Olive slipped her hand out of Bob's arm. Mrs Middleton would be spying. "You wouldn't like to live in the country?"

"No. We're all past that now, living and dying in one place. We can't expect to spend our lives in one house. Houses don't matter any more. Ideally, if we weren't so cluttered up, we should all live in caravans."

Olive's look was so stricken that he laughed. But she pulled away, stumbling, and cried out, "I'm all right here. Why don't you leave me alone?"

Lacking the opportunity, they had not made love. That afternoon Mr Rawston went to the library in Matlock and Mrs Middleton took Elizabeth for a walk. She had the air of a missionary saving a soul for God. "Poor little scrap," she said. Elizabeth grinned windily. Mrs Middleton sailed off.

The weather seemed to be breaking up. Olive rolled away from Bob and saw flags of cloud in the small window, a spatter of rain. She drew up her knees, warming herself, shutting him out and away.

"You're too thin, you're cold."

"Sorry. It's supposed to be childbirth and all that. It puts you off. The shock."

"I didn't mean that. But life's a shock, one we never get over, I suppose."

"I am better," she said. "I will get over it. I will come back with you."

"It will be all right."

Dennis imagined himself to be part of the intricate mesh of darkness. Threatened, he could freeze to a tree or a bush. By day he rested in an abandoned sheep pen, filled with stores collected in one excursion to Matlock: tins, a primus stove, groundsheet and army surplus sleeping bag.

By night he swept down the hill, as he neared the village skirted outlying houses and avoided pools of moonlight. At first he was startled by animals, a cow coughing behind him and once the jackal scream of a fox. A farm dog barked and a door was opened, catching Dennis in the web of light. "What's that then, Jess? Come in, you soft bitch, it's nothing."

His father's house above the village was a lighthouse, casting its beam wide. By wriggling along the shallow bed of the stream Dennis could creep beneath its watchful brightness and come close enough to see that a few furry moths, roused by the hot weather, batted themselves against the pane. His father seemed to be working, Bob Wilson reading. Olive sat between the two men, sewing in her lap. Someone spoke and she raised her head and smiled. Mr Rawston turned on the wireless, Olive yawned and came to the window, flinging it open only a few yards from where Dennis crouched. Wilson came up behind her and put a hand on her shoulder. Dennis slipped and fell on his knees in the stream. His hands were bleeding, his face scratched by brambles but it was half an hour before he could find the will to move. Back in the pen he ate a dry biscuit, was sick, and at last had the strength to light his small spirit lamp and strip off his wet clothes. His shadow in the dim glow of the lamp was wavering and attenuated, a forked plant climbing the peat walls and folded across the wattle roof.

For the time being Olive was to go back to Toni's room.

She would have to get a job, for a while at least, even Bob agreed; so Maria or her eldest girl, who was working in the café waiting to get married, would care for Elizabeth. Things would look up soon at the garage, the present restrictions couldn't go on for ever, then she and Bob would find somewhere to live together. Bob's brother, Jack, had talked about moving north of the river, Fulham or Hampstead. If they found a business there, Bob and Olive could look for a small house with a garden. Superstitiously, Olive tried not to think too much about this garden, though she could see it quite clearly, as if it had always been in her mind, as if she had lived there once in that house and forgotten it.

Mr Rawston and Bob were talking about war again. Olive understood that her father-in-law saw life as a picture. He seemed to agree with Bob that the cold war would continue and the present Berlin crisis was not as serious as it appeared. There would be no immediate cataclysm. "The Ruskies are trying it on."

Olive intervened mildly but with a touch of malice, "So we'll die in our beds? No one is going to drop the bomb?"

"Oh no, I didn't say that. I believe there is no end to the folly of the human race. Ultimately it will destroy itself."

"And you don't mind," she said, "either of you? I couldn't live like that. It would be futile."

Bob spoke quietly. "But you do live like that, Olive. We all do. Yet you want to live in a house with a garden and an apple tree in a certain place."

"Just like my mother, after all."

"Not in the least like your mother. These things, their permanence, were a faith to her. God help us, we know better than that. Which is why you feel guilty about wanting that house."

"Perhaps Tim is the sane one, after all. Blowing oneself up may be the only decent gesture left, the *only* gesture left."

"We're behind the times, in a way," said Bob. "It always takes a decade or so for the consciousness to catch up with history. It'll be interesting to see how the younger ones get on. I doubt if Alan'll have much use for the priest or the commissar. A politician in a few years will probably be only one up on the lavatory man. Whatever happens, they won't have our guilt. Morally, they'll be starting from scratch."

"But you can't quite give up politics?"

Bob grinned and ran his hand through his short, furry hair. "You can have party politics any day you like, but no, I suppose I can't change now. I'm the worst kind of romantic, the sober one. I'll go on believing people are basically sane, they can be peacefully persuaded to change their society. Only I've lost faith in the machinery, including force, most of all force. Which leaves me a moral eunuch, with the will but not the way."

Through this exchange Mr. Rawston had not spoken. Olive glanced at him. His mild expression gave nothing away. Olive felt a sudden urge to challenge him, not to let him off. "I don't believe in your pessimism."

"So I'm to declare myself?"

"Yes."

"I think that life is meaningless."

"But once . . ."

"No, I have always held to that belief. One can salvage something. On one occasion I considered life important enough to be ended, but having bungled that gesture I never felt the need to make it again. Survival, as interesting as possible, seems to me the only rational point of view."

Olive shivered. Rain beat against the windows, the night creaked, a worn-out tree, a swollen floor-board responding to humidity, signs of decay. She wished now to be in the city in a house supported by other houses. She went upstairs to feed Elizabeth and change her and stayed for a while by the cot, inhaling the milky sweetness. The window was rattling. As she wedged the latch she saw the darkness move and run, a fox perhaps.

He had last eaten with his fingers from a tin not knowing
299

what he ate or when. An hour, a day ago? There had been some sleep, rain. He had slipped from an inner darkness to an outer darkness. He had lain on the stream bed, heard close to his heart the rejecting hardness of stones, felt lapping around his chin the meaningless clarity of water, nibbled at something green and spat it out. He clawed his way up the garden, saw his father's bedroom light go on, then off. Yet there were lights still all over the house: a dim moon in Elizabeth's room, a sun blazing from the kitchen. He had given up carrying a torch the better to learn the darkness, now he was dazzled.

When the kitchen door was flung open and Dennis stood there, dripping and shaking at them like a rag torn from the gale outside, Olive's first reaction was hysterical laughter at the melodrama of the situation. She was holding the big blue teapot and it seemed mysteriously necessary not to put it down, even when she regained her reason.

Dennis kept saying in the same weird, flat theatrical voice, "Go away, Olive, this is nothing to do with you. Go away, I want to talk to Wilson." When he burst in Bob had been sitting at the table, drinking tea, and by some instinct of non-provocation he remained seated, though Olive saw that his knuckles, where he gripped the table, were white.

Olive heard her old nurse voice, "Come on, Dennis, this won't get us anywhere. Sit down and have some tea." He had looked like this when she first met him in the hospital, eyes hollowed and burning. Then she had found his rage attractive, her natural urges, both protective and passionate, had responded; now she was appalled and at a deeper level, frightened; because she was aware that something in her strained to answer Dennis's violence with violence. She had felt the same when it was an effort of will not to share Chris's paranoia, not to agree with Dulcie, in the first shock of Steven's tragedy, that any system which permitted such injustices must be rotten. Rationally she knew, of course, that there was no system and therefore no injustice.

Dennis ignored her, except to repeat, "Shut up, Olive, go away. I'm going to talk to Wilson."

Now Bob spoke. "Go ahead, I'm listening. But for God's sake, sit down before you fall down."

The kettle screamed, bringing Olive to her senses, but the effect on Dennis was alarming. He began to tremble, went a ghastly colour and before either Bob or Olive could reach him he slumped down against the door, his head lolling.

Olive was stricken. "What's wrong with him? Has he passed out?"

Bob pushed back Dennis's head. "He's all right, he's simply chilled through. We'd better get him on his feet, he'll be sick."

In the porch, with Bob's hands under his armpits, Dennis was spoutingly sick. Bob glanced at Olive and gave her a weak smile, but she bit her lip and turned away. In that second, as Dennis momentarily recovered and seemed to recognise his surroundings, he turned and struck Bob across the face with the flat of his hand. It was a woman's gesture but enough to knock Bob off balance. Falling on him, Dennis smashed into his head with both fists, blindly pounding. Except to cover his eyes, Bob made no effort to defend himself. At last Dennis reeled away and staggered into a chair. It seemed to Olive that all the most terrible things, the worst she had ever dreaded, had come to pass.

"You've killed him."

Dennis was gasping too much to speak, but he shook his head. He was right. Bob stirred and heaved himself to a sitting position. He put a hand to his bloody nose and mouth. For a moment Olive thought that her husband might fall on him again, but Dennis was obviously finished. He surveyed the damage he had done with blank eyes, neither gratified nor disappointed.

Olive fetched a sponge and towel from the sink but Bob said painfully, through lips already swelling, "It's all right, I'll manage." Grasping the edge of the bowl, he put his head under the cold tap.

301

Olive made tea. There was a queer, intimate atmosphere in the room, quite without tension, a not entirely hostile connection between the two men from which Olive felt excluded. Bob looked round. He put a cigarette between his lips and Olive lit it. There was still a trickle of blood from the corner of his mouth. "We've made a bit of a mess, haven't we."

She saw now that in the course of the brief struggle—so quickly over, it resembled an hallucination—cups had been swept from the table, a chair smashed against the wall. As far as she could she put the room to rights, then poured tea and took her cup to the draining board, where the broken crockery was stacked. There might be something to save. She was aware of the two men behind her, her resentment of them, and the absurdity of her own competence, calmly sorting the china which could be mended and that which was broken beyond repair.

Dennis said something she did not catch. He seemed tired beyond speech.

Bob answered, "No, we can be gone by the morning. You'd better rest up for a few days."

"Your mouth looks bad."

"It's not much."

Olive wanted to yell and cry. She saw her own strained, panicked, shrunken face reflected in the unyielding darkness of the window. The rain still smashed down. The wind was so high if Elizabeth cried she wouldn't hear her. She cut her hand on the jagged edge of a plate and saw the blood mix thinly with the water. She could stand here, feeling nothing, till she bled to death. She felt a dumbfounded despair which suddenly found voice, then she turned on the men, "You could have killed each other. Go away," she cried, "go away and leave me in peace!"

Olive woke at Reading. They had left at dawn to catch the early train and there had been little sleep before that. Mr Rawston had driven them to the station. He said Dennis was sleeping at last, he could be left for an hour. It was no longer raining but the dawn was queasy. Bob went to get tickets while Mr Rawston helped Olive to lift the carry-cot from the back seat. Then there was nothing to do. They had hardly any luggage.

"I shouldn't wait," said Olive.

Mr Rawston nodded. "I'm sorry it should have ended like this."

"Thank you," she said, "I'll never be able to thank you."

"Well."

"I suppose we'd better go, then."

"You must."

She took his hand and prepared to say something meaningless, the formal words necessary at parting since one could not simply turn one's back, but she asked instead, aware that she was likely to cry, "Do you forgive *everything*?"

"Not at all," he said briskly, then in the same light tone, "There would have been no point in staying, he's beyond help."

"I do hope not." She pressed his fingers and he returned the touch, then stepped into the car. Just before he drove off, when she grasped that it was too late now to explain anything to him—her gratitude, her desolation—he put his head out of the window, "You'll be all right, both of you. I have hopes for you."

"Put your feet up." Bob had seen her cry in her sleep, struggle half awake, then collapse, face slack against the window. He had stayed awake through the long hours, the rocking of the train, hardly able to believe that he had won her back. He knew that pity, an appeal to Olive's strength, was Dennis's only remaining weapon, but a powerful one. All the same her husband had not been able to hold her. His violence had repelled her more than his plight could move her. After that one desperate cry Olive had been quite calm, icily and wearily collected.

Struggling out of sleep she stood to look in the mirror,

bracing herself against the swaying of the train. She had not had her hair cut since she came to Derbyshire and when they left that morning had pushed it under a faded blue scarf. Her skin, its pigment oddly changed since Elizabeth's birth, had yellowed rather than tanned in the sun, and while she had got back her figure well enough she was aware of a feeling of soft slackness still between her thighs, her breasts taut and veined. Once she had forgotten her body for days at a time; now it was a passenger with her always. She supposed this would pass.

She caught Bob's reflection in the mirror: lips swollen, dark contusions matching the bruises of weariness beneath her own eyes. Dragging the comb through her thick hair she grinned. "We look like refugees." And indeed a woman whose arms seemed extravagantly full of flowers but was otherwise just a woman with an angry handbag and a day ticket to London, saw them through the glass and was driven away by their oddness. She panted off down the corridor, startled and spilling flowers. Olive pulled a face. "Well at least we've got it to ourselves." Bob went off and came back with faintly urine-scented coffee in paper cups. "Why did you let Dennis knock you about like that?"

"You'd rather I'd knocked him down?"

"No. Yes, I think I would." Shamefaced, then defensive, "You must admit it was a queer time to start practising your new pacifism. While you were turning the other cheek he might have killed you." Shut up, she told herself, you shrew. "So did it make you feel better?"

"Better," he pondered, then shook his head. "No. Impotent."

Olive was ashamed of herself for pushing him, he looked so weary. She turned her face away, hoping that the demon would leave her. Then he would wake and they would go on as they had intended. But she began to shake and then cry, "I thought he'd kill you."

They clung together, awkwardly. "You're my life," she whispered, but he didn't hear this, he had gone to sleep

304

quite suddenly like a man felled on the field of battle. Olive looked out of the window, Elizabeth curled against her, and recognised, hurtling past, a station where she had once waited though she could not remember why, except that it had been in the war.

34

"Oh well, I suppose they know what they're doing. What the hell, Olive, it was falling down, anyway." Dulcie was stuffing a sack with all the things to be thrown away. She had been at this for only ten minutes when she gave up. "There's some gin somewhere. Present from Polly." She groped under the sink, poured the drink into mugs and topped it with a splash of the children's free orange juice, sticky and sweet. "But it's rough on Dennis."

The house was to be pulled down. A buzz bomb had weakened the foundations, but it had been shored up so long and survived so much devastation they had all assumed it was safe. Apparently they were wrong.

Olive still could not fully grasp that machines would come and smash down this house. In the excitement of her return neither Toni nor Maria had mentioned it, so she had been first baffled, then shocked when on her second evening back she pushed Elizabeth over to see Dulcie.

"But couldn't they repair it? It seems so awful, such a waste."

"It's the foundations, love. Polly made a fuss with some high-up and we had men crawling all over the place for days. They just said it could cave in any time and, anyway, there were too many of us in one room, we wouldn't have been allowed to stay, how long had it been going on, how many lavs had we got, etcetera. They seemed to think we ought to have rabies. Of course Dennis had done his disappearing act, but he couldn't have stopped it anyway. He'll get compensation or war damage or something." Dulcie sat hunched over her drink, cradling it, legs spread. With the back of the hand which held her cigarette she pushed back her pale hair. Her dirty feet swam in a pair of Tim's sandals and her skirt, a cast-off of Polly's, was bunched round her hips and drawn in with a safety-pin, but there was about her a not quite defeated, courageous style of her own. She looked round, a half humorous expression on her face. "You know, Olive, I've complained enough about it, but now it's come to the point I can't bear to go."

Olive was aware that this light confession was more important than it sounded. Everything she might have said rang hollow in her head. Now she was no longer part of this house she felt at once anguished and impotent, disqualified by her own happiness, helpless because she was happy. And ashamed of her disappointment. Once, she had clung to this room like a child. She still counted on it, yet now she would have to manage without them the house, and the room, were already receding; at some time, in a month or a year, they would be history. "Well," she said limply, "at least they'll have to find you somewhere. They can't just chuck you out into the street."

"Oh, they said something about a hostel until they can manage a prefab or a council flat. They were quite nice in a bloody sort of way, thanks to Polly. They wouldn't have Tim, of course, not in a hostel, though it might not come to that."

Olive knew that it was unthinkable that Dulcie should go to a hostel and inevitable that she would. "But that's preposterous! They can't split up families."

"Worse things happen in war. But it would be queer. You know, since he was back we've never been apart, not like that."

"What does Tim say?"

Dulcie got up and refilled their mugs. "You know Tim. One day he'll forget to come home, then he'll suddenly remember us and go off his head. Or not, as the case may be."

"I couldn't live like that."

"You could if you had to."

"I suppose I could."

Elizabeth opened her eyes and Dulcie picked her up and hugged her. "You're a love, aren't you? And you look just like your mum." The question of Dennis hovered in the room, waiting to be explained. Dulcie said to Olive, "You'll be going upstairs? You'll be taking your own things away, won't you? After all, they're mostly yours. Our Dennis could never be bothered with furniture. Seems a shame, you'd made it nice."

Olive walked to the window. Below, Dulcie's older children were playing in the empty evening street, pushing Steven around in a dangerous-looking box-cart. "Well, I expect I'll have to go up some time. But there's nothing I want."

Dulcie was watching her, a grin on her face. "Don't tell me if you don't want to. But they'll have to know where Dennis is some time, so that they can pull down his house. Daft, isn't it."

Olive told her. "So he's with his father at the moment."

"Poor old Dennis."

Olive said slowly, "I can't feel guilty about him, you know. I did for ages and then it just ran out."

"About time too."

"You always thought it was a mistake?"

Dulcie blew ash off her skirt. "For you. Oh, there must be hundreds of females who'd love to carry Dennis around for the rest of their lives, but it made me mad watching you. I suppose it would have been a very good and admirable thing to do, but then we're not particularly good and admirable, you or I, are we? God knows what we are, but we're not that."

Olive thought wryly of Mary Owens, the pale, devoted woman with the large handbag. She had patronised Mary, she knew that, yet she had been stirred to admiration by that last sight of her after the trial. Was there really no such thing as unselfish love? Was Mary a masochist, in it for the pain? What about Sam, as he laid a rug across Catherine's lap in the rich car, did he love? "No, we're not, are we," she agreed, echoing Dulcie.

"So you'll stay with Bob?"

"We're looking for a house. I suppose there'll be a divorce, I haven't really thought about it."

'That's marvellous," said Dulcie. "I'm glad. Honestly, Olive, that's the best thing that could happen. I warned you, I'd kill you if you let him get away." The two women smiled at one another.

"So I couldn't, could I?" said Olive. She looked at her watch. Bob would be round at Toni's at eight o'clock to eat with her. A child yelled from the street, "Mum!" Olive and Dulcie both leant out of the window. "Give us tuppence for chips." Steven was lolling cheerfully in the box-cart, squealing in delight at the bumps. He was still an outstandingly beautiful child. Polly's smart specialist had taken two days and about a hundred tests to tell them what they knew already: nothing could be done. By an irony, Steven's progress, in all respects but growth, was well above the average. Olive still did not regard herself as a woman who cared, in a general way, for children or babies, but Elizabeth's existence had bared in her some unexpectedly female nerves. She found herself looking into prams. She was discovering now that it was better not to think too much about Steven.

Dulcie threw down two pennies. Olive was preparing to leave. "Give Tim my love. Is he still at the Ministry?"

"No. He got sacked. Oh, not what you think. They caught him kipping on the job, but they never found out about the rest."

"You mean they'd no idea about the bombs and so on?"

"Not a clue. That's funny, isn't it."

On an impulse Olive hugged Dulcie. She felt she had failed. Her own happiness and the multiplication of Dulcie's afflictions, however lightly borne, set new bounds to their intimacy. Olive suspected that men did not have this trouble. And if Dulcie had been less courageous, Olive more sentimental, they might have each have found release, Dulcie for her grief, Olive for her pity; but neither was the wailing kind. It seemed sad that the only time women were truly united was in mourning or complaint. "Don't worry too much, I'll do what I can. I'll ring Polly and Bob might know someone on the council."

"I shouldn't waste your time. Honestly, love, there's nothing you can do."

In the street Olive ran into the Connor children. The boys, inconsequential as young dogs, thumped around the pram, hooted and ran off. The oldest girl, ginger like Tim and as skinny as Dulcie, walked a few yards with Olive, admiring Elizabeth.

"Can I take her for a walk some time?"

"Yes, of course."

"Can she talk?"

"She's not old enough yet."

"I don't like kids, I only like babies." This, Olive understood, was a grave, experienced confession, between women.

"Why's that?"

Gravity collapsed. The child was embarrassed to be taken seriously. She began to skip the cracks and giggle. Her brother approached them with the chips from Toni's. The girl was off after him, stick legs flying.

While she waited for Bob, Olive rang Polly from Toni's. She had not expected her to be in, but she was.

"I've caught you between committees."

"Committees?" Polly sounded guarded then she laughed, rather too brightly. "Oh, I don't do much of that now. Though actually, you're right. I've just been to one and my head's splitting. Hold on." Olive imagined Polly in her sister's Chelsea doll's house, kicking off the expensive shoes, reaching for a cigarette, not from a packet but a box. "Women," groaned Polly, "if I go to hell it will be a women's committee."

"But you love it."

She could hear Polly smiling. "Yes, I do. I'm going to miss it. Edward said keep it up, but it wouldn't be fair."

311

"Edward?"

"I'm getting married, Olive, next month." Polly sounded embarrassed. "June bride. But of course you've been away. How's the baby? Can I see her?"

"Any time. Polly . . ."

"Damn! There's someone at the door." Olive waited. The telephone at Toni's was in a closet with the brushes and buckets, a hole off the narrow passage between kitchen and café. Every few minutes someone passed carrying plates of food. There was nowhere to sit, barely space to stand up. Through a murky pane of glass Olive saw Bob enter the café, look round for her and settle at a table with the evening paper. Polly came back. "Olive? You'll come to the wedding, won't you? Olive, are you there?"

"Yes."

"Are you in a box? It was only Harrods for someone else."

"Polly, can't we do something about the Connors?"

"I've pulled all the strings. There's not a hope. Olive, why don't you come over tomorrow, bring Elizabeth? I've got to look at a house in Sussex, we could drive down, have a picnic. Edward would live anywhere you put him down, but I think the country's best for children, don't you? It's frightful about Dulcie, but at least they'll get priority rehousing. Do come, Olive, you know I'm hopeless about houses. I've got to be at the dressmaker at five, but we'd have plenty of time."

Polly ran on. Olive remembered her crying, here in Toni's café, Tim Connor making her blush. Stranded between good works and revolution, Polly settled for a June wedding. Like Olive, she wanted the house with the garden and the apple tree in a certain place, so Olive had no right to reproach her. The instinct, however bad the times, is to the fullest human life. Yet Olive was angry.

"I'm afraid I've got to look for a job."

"Surely one afternoon can't make so much difference?"

"You'd be surprised," said Olive, drily, then was appalled that she could be such a prig. She made a stab at warmth.

"Another time perhaps. And I'd love to come to the wedding, Polly."

"It's awful, I do hate this fuss. Do you think cream would be ambiguous?"

"I'm sorry, I've got to go. I'm at Toni's, someone wants the phone."

"Were you ringing about anything special?"

"Oh no, nothing special."

"What's up?"

"Women."

Bob smiled. "I like them myself."

Olive decided not to tell him about the telephone call to Polly. It sounded so absurd to be angry. It was absurd. Toni came with a cloth and flicked some dust from the red-checked American cloth. The dust rose in the golden evening, reassorted its particles and fell again. Bob said that his brother had made a definite offer for the Fulham garage. Olive told him there was nothing going at the hospital but she might try the local one tomorrow, and if that failed Toni was short of help, and there would be free meals.

"You wouldn't mind that?"

"I'd rather like it."

Inevitably they discussed the Connors.

"I've never know Dulcie defeated before. She seems to have given in."

"Or accepted?"

"Isn't that the same thing?"

"Either way, there's not much else she could do, is there?"

Once Olive would have protested that this was terrible, a shocking attitude. Now she admitted, "No, I suppose there isn't. But you'll look out for a job for Tim, won't you?" Already she was wondering if there was time for them to go back to Bob's house and make love before Elizabeth, now sleeping, needed her ten o'clock feed. If Maria would keep an eye on Elizabeth, and of course, she would. This was a queer camping life but not unpleasant.

313

All the same, she felt sad, a mild, blurred grief. We must be pretty low, she thought, if we have to live by forgetting, that's more like death. No, that's superficial. Death is the only experience which is like nothing.

Maria said don't hurry, she could give Elizabeth her bottle, have a nice walk, it was a good evening.

They walked out into the good evening. "Poor Toni, he'll never get back to Greece now, will he?"

"He'd be lost if he did. He hardly speaks Greek any more."

"Wouldn't he remember?"

Bob took her arm, under the elbow. "I should think you forget even that after a time." Bob told her that there was a house, it was quite small, falling down, but they could do something with it, and there was a garden. He didn't know about the apple tree.

She was so happy and then appalled by herself.

"Aren't you pleased?" He had been saving this up. It was to be the crown of the evening.

"Oh yes!" She smiled, seeing how ridiculous it was to protest that life was so rich, so kind. "But women are disgusting. They are pretty frightful, you must see that?"

35

OLIVE was to help out at Toni's for three pounds a week, one
meal a day free and afternoons off. Once she had moved with
Bob to the Fulham house she might have difficulty working
because of Elizabeth. Besides, there would be so much to
do.

It was odd, assisting at the death of one house while she
breathed life into another. Dennis's house, which seemed so
much more the Connors', appeared for a long time unwilling to give up the ghost. The flat she had shared with Dennis
was easily enough cleared. Maria was to have the furniture;
Olive wrote to Dennis: he could claim it if he wished, otherwise Maria would keep it. Emptying these two rooms was
simply a job to be done. They had never had life so they had
no spirit to lose. Without a past the fact that their future was
numbered by weeks or days was meaningless. Some rooms
grow larger for emptying, most smaller. When, from habit,
Olive finally closed the windows and prepared to lock the
door, she saw that they were not, in fact, as cramped as she
had always imagined. One could have lived here quite well.

Below in the basement the foreigners silently transported
their belongings in small parcels, like mice in a children's
story. They must have left by night, because when Olive and
Dulcie went down one morning there was no sign that this
part of the house had ever been inhabited.

It was the Connors' room which held out. Olive had
always thought of them as self-contained gipsies, always
ready for a moonlight flit, but when it came down to sorting
the necessary, the disposable and the dubious, almost everything seemed at once useless and heartbreakingly precious.
Even when this was done the children pounced on the pack-

ing cases as if they were Christmas boxes, rejoicing in treasures rediscovered, wailing at the loss of household gods.

"I always said this place needed a bomb." Dulcie smiled wanly. "Women are daft, aren't they. I'm almost as silly as the kids about some of these things. Oh well, they've got to go."

Bob's brother had found Tim a job as a long-distance lorry driver. He was to share with Bob until the move to Fulham, then he would take over Olive's room at Toni's. He had discovered some fellow Party members in the union and seemed now quite to have forgotten his night of disillusion by the river with Bob. Not for the first time, Olive wondered about Tim. Was he really mad or did he simply heal more easily, scar tissue covering savage wounds? She guessed he had not yet taken in the implications of the break with Dulcie and the children. However chaotic, this had always been his point of departure and return, a sure place. "Oh me," he would say, "didn't you know? I've got a charmed life," as he ducked from yet another self-inflicted thunderbolt. "I'm the lucky sod." It could be that his luck was running out.

The minimal necessities of life Dulcie was allowed to take to the hostel were pathetic; they filled a single suitcase loaned by Olive. It was hardly a hostel at all, originally a shelter started by the Sally Army in the war and taken over by the local authority who at once closed it down as unfit for human habitation. They then forgot about the whole project until with several thousand homeless families on their hands, they opened it up again as the Saint Mary hostel. A warden was put in, a second-hand madonna donated by a well-wisher and a list of rules stuck up under glass in the hall. There were to be no husbands, no animals or birds, no wirelesses, no cooking except in the communal kitchen, and lights out at nine-thirty. The district nurse checked the children every week for nits and pregnancy was not encouraged. The local teds came, sneered and found it hardly worth breaking up.

Dulcie's fortitude held out until she was told, only a week

before moving in, that she had too many children, some would have to go into care. Through her work for the group and later for Dennis's club, Olive knew the welfare department.

"I'm sorry, Mrs Rawston, but these large families . . ." The children's officer was new, not known to Olive. She was a tired, youngish woman, about thirty, though she looked forty, a very English type. Olive was reminded of Mary Owens, of herself as she might have been: the female with the instinct for causes. They were genuine enough, sincere, unselfish, and to what a shabby cross they were nailed, destined always to do good by halves. It was no one's fault. It was the times.

Olive had come preparing a scene; she was disarmed. "I thought perhaps this once you could make an exception."

"Every case is an exception, you must know that. They have no family? If the children could be sent to a sister or a grandmother . . . ?"

"He comes from Australia and her parents are dead. She has never spoken of them so I suppose they are dead."

The woman nodded. "It is very difficult, you know."

Olive admitted, "I'll be honest, I'm trying to pull strings. These are friends, I know them. If you'll help, I'll be grateful. If not, then I'm sorry I've taken up your time. But wouldn't it cost even more to put them in care than to leave them with their mother?"

The children's officer smiled. She was pretty. A hundred years ago she would have been a country vicar's wife. Olive saw that she wore Air Force wings pinned to her collar: a brother? a fiancé? She was unmarried. "I was sorry to hear that your husband's club had closed down. I met him once, you know. He was doing some very valuable work."

Olive thought, he should have married someone like you. "He's not . . . well."

"I'm sorry." She was sincere. Clearly, Dennis had made a hit. Absently the woman touched the wings on her collar, moved a file from one side of the desk to the other. She looked as if she would like to say more but concluded crisply, "I'll do what I can for this family, Mrs Rawston. The decision isn't mine, of course, but I can recommend strongly that the children should stay with the mother."

"Thank you."

As Olive was leaving the children's officer asked, "By the way, what became of that voluntary group your husband used to run?"

"Oh, it just died a natural death. The usual reasons. Not enough time, not enough energy or money, internal politics. You know, we were only amateurs really."

"That's a pity." But the telephone was ringing and as Olive left the woman's smile was a flicker, merely formal.

Everything Bob had said about the Fulham house was true. It was small, internally collapsing, but the outer walls were solid enough and there was a garden, even an apple tree in a certain place, loaded with blossom. The first afternoon she spent there, Olive found a rusty, savage-looking hand sickle in the outside lavatory and set to work, releasing the small tree from its prison of nettles and cow parsley. A woman looked over the low wall from the next-door garden. "I shouldn't bother with that. If the birds or the wasps don't get it, the fruit's not worth having. I'd chop it down, first thing. They never used to pick it."

"But I mean to pick it," said Olive.

The woman shrugged. "It's pretty, I'll say that."

When Olive had cleared the tree she sank down on the grass by Elizabeth's push-chair. She could not manage the carry-cot alone on the buses. Elizabeth lolled, spineless and cheerful. In the evenings Bob was gutting the interior of the house. Downstairs the two small, poky rooms were to be one. Because of their jobs they were rarely at the house at the same time, so they left messages in pencil on a piece of bare plaster in the hall. As the list lengthened this became a record of their work on the house. Today Olive wrote: *Look*

318

at the apple tree. I love you. O.

Elizabeth would be wanting her bottle soon. "Pretty," said Olive to the baby. "Pretty tree."

Since this house had been empty for so long and the garden neglected there were more birds than was normal in London. The tall grass sang. Olive closed her eyes. Elizabeth grumbled. Olive sighed, humped the child out of her harness, laid her down on her blanket, lifted her legs, pulled off her wet nappy, pushed it in a bag and put on a dry one. The woman next door would be watching, let her watch. Since Elizabeth, Olive had become four-eyes.

Olive looked at Mrs Armitage with four eyes. She saw this as something that had to be done, a task, telling her mother. At the house she had refreshed herself, she carried Elizabeth like a shield.

"So you've come to see Grannie, then."

Mrs Armitage made tea. Olive asked for water for Elizabeth's rose-hip syrup. Her mother was living now in one room, she had let the rest. She insisted that this was all she needed, she managed very well. Look, she seemed to say, how small I can be. World to house to room to bed to coffin. Olive tried to think rationally. We tend to take the miseries of the old as a personal reproach. This is not so. They are diminished, anyway. Mrs Armitage looked well. If this had not been a matter of personal concern Olive might have wryly sympathised with her theatrical instincts. Martyrdom must not only be done, it must also be seen to be done.

Olive had made up her mind to tell her mother quite straightforwardly and unemotionally, and then leave at once, but it seemed matters could never be so simple between these two women. Together, they engendered tension.

Mrs Armitage insisted on boiling the water for Elizabeth's rose-hip syrup. To do this she had to fill the kettle again while her tea went cold.

Then she had to wait for the water to cool. Then she realised that the bottle had not been sterilised so she had to boil the water again. Meanwhile Elizabeth was getting crabby

319

and Olive smoked two cigarettes.

"Honestly, mother, there's no need for that, you know."

Mrs Armitage supposed they didn't bother about hygiene nowadays. Oh well, that was the modern way, but she was too old to learn new tricks. Wasn't Elizabeth rather thin? Elizabeth's wail had swelled to a shout. Normally Olive would have picked her up, but she found it necessary to hide her love for her child from her mother, as she had hidden from Mrs Armitage, always, anything she loved. Yet Mrs Armitage would have liked nothing better, she said, than to see Olive settled and happy with a family, which meant loving her child like a normal woman. Olive's nerves clenched against Elizabeth's shouts.

"She's on solids. She eats very well."

"Isn't she a little young for solids?"

"They start earlier now." If they were to quarrel Olive was determined it should not be over Elizabeth, that would be too trite; grotesque, considering the late development of Mrs Armitage's maternal instincts. It was not as if she had ever performed these servile chores for her own children. Or had she? Perhaps one forgot.

They were having to shout now above Elizabeth's yells. Mrs Armitage held the bottle against the inside of her arm, just below the elbow. All she had was her style, Olive thought, and now she's lost that. She said, in a voice which sounded in her head entirely reasonable, but came out shrill, "Please leave me to bring up my own child."

Her tone of voice startled Elizabeth, who stopped crying. I am the kind of woman who frightens her own child, Olive thought. She had believed that Mrs Armitage could no longer disarm her. She was wrong. Her mother and her child were now four-eyes, against her. "You know," said Mrs Armitage, "I would never interfere."

Since Mrs Armitage had retreated to her one room there was nowhere to go but the lavatory, and that would be ridiculous. Olive took the bottle from her mother and gave it to Elizabeth. Empty-handed, Mrs Armitage was lost, pathetic.

Olive thought, I'm a bully too, tormenting an old woman. I am strong and happy enough to make allowances, yet it is necessary to be ruthless because one concession might finish me. In her loneliness she is more powerful even than she was in her prime.

"Look, mother, I came to tell you I'm moving. I'll be living with Bob Wilson. There will be a divorce and then I shall marry again. I don't expect you to understand." But of course, Olive realised, ashamed of her hypocrisy, she did expect her mother to understand. Her mother was a woman. She knew that these things happened. She had done worse herself, by marrying Charlie Armitage coldly. Now it came to the point she must see.

But she did not see at all. "You're right. I don't understand. When I can no longer understand my own children . . ."

"I'm happy, mother. Doesn't that mean anything to you?"

"You'll kill me, Olive. I've tried to help you. I tried to help Christopher but he turned his back on his own home. This will be the death of me."

Now, Olive thought, she should go, walk out not looking back. But she said quietly and with a deeply ingrained bitterness, "So you'd rather see me unhappy."

"You wouldn't be the first woman to suffer."

"I don't think this is getting us anywhere."

"Oh well," Mrs Armitage had decided to be courageous, the subtlest form of blackmail. "I expect you'll go your own way whatever I say."

"Yes, mother, I will."

"Then why did you bother to tell me?"

"I don't know. I suppose I thought you might be glad, but I was wrong."

"Of course I would be glad to see you leading a normal life." Mrs Armitage's face was stiff. Her hands were still in her lap, but her eyes shone too brightly. She had looked like this the day war was declared.

"And you consider it is only normal to be wretched?"

321

"I don't think you should seek happiness at the expense of your husband and child. I have always put my children first. Since your father died I never lived as I chose. Why do you think I married that man? I do not understand what is going on in the world." Now her hands began to move, stroking the stuff of her skirt, the same spot again and again. Her voice was flat. "I am not well. You don't know. This house is not safe. I am not sleeping at all well. I have not been happy."

Now it was out. Olive knew she should cross the room and take her mother in her arms; however distasteful, this could be done but then she would never be free, this gesture too would be misinterpreted and deformed, there would be no end to it. It is the weak who possess the strong because, as the scorpion said, this is their nature.

"I'm sorry, mother, I'm afraid we'll have to go now. I'll let you know when we move. We won't be so far away." The Etruscans filled their tombs with the birds of life, Olive thought, but no one can die for someone else, simply to keep them company, that cannot be done. She no longer felt any bitterness for her mother, nor at this moment any love, yet she was not free because she was a dutiful daughter however much every fibre in her being rebelled against this duty. So, however we resist it, we are possessed. If I had not pitied her I would have hated her and so that part of me which hated her would have belonged to her until she is dead and after. Bob was right. Happiness did not matter so much, which was just as well since it was unattainable except to the blind and the deaf and the mad. But love? That must be possible, she counted on it.

Catherine was already married to Sam Davies, living in Holland Park. He had a way with Mrs Armitage, which was a load off Olive's mind. Christopher had earned a remission of sentence and would marry Mary Owens in June. They were to live at her flat. The animals go in two by two, thought Olive, except for the Connors.

The house was finished. It had held out until the last moment, but suddenly Olive and Dulcie were standing in the street looking up at the dark cliff.

"It's funny," said Dulcie, "I never thought it would go like this. I thought it might blow up or get burned or fall down on us one night, but whatever I said I never really guessed I'd leave it. You know something? I feel rotten about those people in the basement; those kids, they looked like old men. I reckon Dennis never took any rent from them. It's queer, isn't it. I used to think the best day in my life would be when I left this house."

Olive and Bob were to store the few things worth saving in the cellar of the Fulham house. Bob had tackled a friend on the council and it seemed fairly certain that in six months or so the Connors could have a flat in one of the new blocks. Already, with the building programme well under way, the topography of the district was changing. The eye was drawn now upward. Olive found the new blocks faceless and heartless and was ashamed of her sentimentality. The old buildings, relics of the Victorian conscience, harboured cannibal rats, all the diseases and misery flesh is heir to. The new times would bring their new illnesses, she supposed, but she would not see this, and felt weakly thankful. When she came down to it, she was no better than Polly. Her nerves were bound up with this place, yet she had never been anything more than a tourist and a visitor.

Dulcie was oddly evasive about the idea of a flat. "Oh well, we'll see," she said, "you never know what might turn up."

The house looked solid enough, as if it might stand for ever, though inside, once the rooms had been cleared, they had found signs of decay everywhere: most striking, a jagged hairline crack from guttering to basement.

Olive helped Dulcie move into the hostel and stayed with her for an hour. The children were fretful. On the other side of the dormitory a young priest was talking to a shabby girl with thyroid eyes. It was intensely hot. Washing was draped to form a curtain between family units. A quarrel broke out but the priest went on talking. The girl kept plucking at her sleeve. Olive wondered why they didn't look after each other's children and take it in turns to go out. No one intervened in the quarrel. The warden, if she existed, did not show herself. The priest slid off on invisible castors. Now they were all women.

Dulcie said, "They took her kids away."

"You can't stay here."

The girl who had been talking to the priest was ill. She lay down on her bed, curled her knees up to her chin and began to beat her face against the wall.

36

"IT'S rather fabulous, isn't it." Polly took a tipped cigarette out of a man's silver case, slim as an envelope, and lit it with a gold lighter. This was her fifth cigarette since they had sat down. She wore a dark green suit and her hair was permed a little too tightly. She said she smoked to slim and her face was thinner, but her breasts were still formidable. Tim had admired her breasts. She was to marry next week. Polly and Olive were having tea at Harrods. Olive was ravenous, eating while Polly smoked. "Just like the Connors."

So the Connors were a legend to Polly. Olive felt uncomfortable. She pushed her sandalled feet under the chair. She had worked all afternoon on the house, her fingernails were dirty. The waitress had looked at her feet. The night before Tim had broken into the hostel and taken away Dulcie and the children after a stand-up row with the warden.

"Are you sure you wouldn't like an ice?" Olive shook her head. She felt like a child on an outing. She no longer enjoyed discussing the Connors with Polly.

"No one knows much about it except Bob. Apparently Tim had had a few days off the job, he'd been drinking most of the time. Then he strolled in, stone-cold sober, and said he'd got a van from a chap in a pub and could Bob manage some petrol? He said he was going to blast open that bloody nunnery, as he put it, and drive them all off. That's all we know. Of course there was no need for the theatricals, he could have taken them away any time he liked, but you know Tim. I hope they'll be all right. I think they will and nothing could be worse than that awful place. In a funny way, I think they're survivors."

Polly mused. She poured herself another cup of tea, without milk, and took a saccharine from her bag. She said in the most friendly way, "We all used to be so violent, didn't we? We must be getting old."

Olive laughed. "Not yet."

"We were right, of course." From Polly this was surprising. "It's the only way." Absently, she slid back into her bag the case, the lighter and the saccharine box, and snapped it shut, like someone packing for a journey. She laid her gloves on the table, smoothed them, and twisted her ring. "I suppose there will be some new people now trying to do what we did, and failing for the same reasons." As if there were a connection in her mind between the two ideas, she went on, "You will come to the wedding, won't you?" Her tone was so wistful Olive wanted to touch the large woman, to take her hand, to tell her she would be fruitful as the vine and happy. Then she saw a beautiful girl enter the restaurant. At first she admired without recognising, then told Polly, "There's my sister. Cat!"

"Hello, Olive, I was looking for Sam."

"Catherine's just back from her honeymoon. Polly's getting married next week."

Polly and Catherine talked about houses. Olive smoked and watched them, two young matrons, as she was herself, she supposed. Polly complained about builders. Catherine agreed. A plate of pink cakes arrived. Olive took one; the other two refused, they were slimming.

Sam would be here soon. Sam was to help Catherine choose an evening dress. Sam had bought this dress for Catherine, did Olive and Polly like it? Catherine said Sam said. Catherine was happy and beautiful. Her love, Olive saw was entirely trusting. She was afraid for her. Polly and Catherine exchanged addresses and discussed wallpaper. They were pleased with one another. Sam arrived, flirted briefly with the three women and carried Catherine off. They made a good couple. People smiled at them.

Olive said, of course she would go to Polly's wedding. She wondered what on earth to wear. She thought of Chris and

326

Mary Owens, the meeting at dawn by the prison gate, the shabby wedding, Chris bound by his weakness, his fatal flaw, for the rest of his days to this plain woman, and she knew that life was neither as theatrical nor as simple as this. Other peoples' relationships were unfathomable. No one ever wrote a novel about a happy marriage because no one, even someone inside the experience—least of all someone inside the experience—could anatomise the parts of so mysterious a bond, at once tough and alarmingly fragile. Or perhaps happiness was simply not very interesting. "What a lot of people seem to be getting married. Or did one never notice before?"

Polly could not quite throw off old habits, but she had the delicacy to be embarrassed. "Olive, what about you?'

"Oh, it's all right. We'll be married, if that's what you mean."

"Sorry. I'm being nosey again." The bill arrived, folded on a plate. Polly stared at it, short-sighted, looking but not seeing. Then she remembered that this was a special occasion, a hen party. "We ought to be drinking champagne or something. But what to?"

Right through the brief ceremony at the register office and the slightly strained celebration afterwards in the pub Olive was distracted from the seriousness of the occasion by Chris's appearance. In the last two months of his imprisonment he had been ill and Mary Owens had warned her on the telephone that she would find him changed. Olive had expected that he would be thinner and was prepared for this, but not for the combination of weight and pallor. He was fat almost to the point of grossness and white like those albino grubs you find under stones. Mary whispered to Olive that this often happened, it was the carbohydrate diet and the lack of exercise.

In the pub Olive was the only one who drank.

"Haven't got back into the habit yet," Chris explained, "and now I suppose we can't afford it. Never thought you'd see me on the wagon, did you, Olly?"

"Frankly I didn't."

It was clear that nothing important would be said. Whatever had happened to Chris in prison, whatever the reason for the hand which could not quite connect the cigarette and the match, the blank gaze which refused to meet Olive's, Mary was the only one who could give him ease. They wanted to be alone. They wanted even to be forgotten, though Olive had no intention of doing any such thing. "Will you come and see me in the new house? We're not so far away."

Mary answered for Chris, not for the first time. "We'd love to. Just for the moment, though, Chris isn't going out much."

"Oh yes?" Olive grinned. Mary went to the bar for cigarettes and finally Chris seemed to stir in his sleep. "So you're hitching up with that chap?"

"So it seems."

He said urgently, before Mary could return, as if this were a secret message he was passing, "Be happy." When she was too painfully touched to reply, he went on, "You're right, you know. Never mind what they think, be happy." His voice was blurred as if he were drunk, and it occurred to Olive that he might be drugged.

Mary came back and looked shrewdly at them both. "You've been upsetting yourself again." She was more like a nurse than a wife, or so it seemed from the outside. One never knew. It was as hard to imagine these two in their honeymoon bed tonight as it was to picture the improbable coupling of a tiger and a mouse. Though which was the tiger and which the mouse? Perhaps beneath the skin they were the same species and had recognised one another. Olive hoped not.

She pecked Chris on the cheek, but could not bring herself to kiss Mary Owens who was now Mary Asher. At the door she took a deep breath of the fresh air and then looked back. They were sitting side by side in front of their tomato juices, like a couple who have been married for a hundred years, Mary patting Chris's hand. Olive walked quickly to the bus and was startled by the colour of the streets.

Olive watched the golden liquid gush into the glass. It was almost too beautiful to drink, but she would certainly drink it and probably leave slightly tight. Her heels sank into the turf. Polly and the mysterious Edward stood under the chestnut tree for the photograph, with children. A pageboy picked his nose. There was a small girl who wanted to go to the lavatory and hopped up and down. A summer breeze lifted Polly's off-white veil and dropped it again, shrouding her practical face. Flowered dresses, long-hemmed and tight-waisted, dipped and bellowed, seemed to curtsey. They were inhabited by women with leather faces, who stood, legs slightly apart, as if they might be asked, momentarily, to leap upon a horse. One beauty wavered across the lawn and clutched her cartwheel hat. She seemed to find her legs too elegant to support her. A little yappy dog ran in and out and as the camera clicked a puff of cloud crossed the sun. This was a perfect English wedding.

Catherine and Olive exchanged signals, settled on an iron seat behind the protective curtain of a willow and slipped off their shoes. Olive saw Bob cross the lawn with a plate of food and look around for her. She waved. She was struck again by his containment, how he belonged to himself. He stopped and spoke to a child. She wondered if he had seen her.

Sam Davies was talking to Polly's mother or mother-in-law, Olive wasn't sure which. His head was bent, listening to the woman, but his eyes were on Catherine.

"What's Sam doing?"

"Practising. He collects old ladies."

Olive smiled. She rubbed her toes. "She's not old."

"Oh, she's fifty at least." Catherine touched the single red flower at the V of her white lawn dress. Olive thought, *jeune fille en fleurs*.

"Did Sam choose that dress?"

329

"Oh yes."

"It's nice."

"Look! They've changed and they're coming out."

They were not leaving at once. Polly sat down gingerly in her silk suit. It was like sitting in the audience and being joined by an actress from the stage. Polly was hot and while she had seemed calm and happy enough in the wedding group, she was now nervously talkative, strung up almost to beauty. She sent Edward for water and, pouncing on Bob, began to ask him if it was true Tito had been an American agent in the war and wasn't it too awful about Berlin? The airlift had just begun but in this English garden it seemed extraordinarily difficult to worry too much about it. Though, of course, as Polly said, beginning to sound a little like Mrs Armitage, one did wonder where it all would end. Bob was very patient. He answered as clearly and simply as he could, wryly aware that his answer was light as a feather in this garden. Olive bit her lip. Bob had told her the night before that the Yugoslavia business, and the Party line, had almost decided him to break with the Communists. Knowing that this still meant a lot to him, though how much she could not gauge, Olive had persuaded Bob to wait and see what happened. "It hardly matters," he said, "I'm no use to them now. The truth is, I can't stand any of them."

"But it matters to you."

She wanted to yell at Polly, shut up, you don't understand what you're talking about, but she lit a cigarette and watched the smoke weave up between the willow leaves. Polly had changed the subject. She was talking about Dulcie and Tim, saying what a pity it was they couldn't be here. Olive had a vision of Tim, wild as a boxing kangaroo on all this drink, let loose among a hundred Home County Tories. It might be worth the mess. Then Edward came to claim Polly and they roared off in a cloud of confetti and a sudden gale of late blossom, to live happily ever after, one hoped.

Sam and Catherine were leaving. Catherine promised, truly, she would come and see the new house soon. Honestly, it was just that there had been so much to do. Olive looked at them going away and thought, there are two people who are going to screw. And the best of luck.

"What are you thinking about?"

"My mind is entirely empty. But I'm thirsty." Sam had left a half bottle of champagne. Bob filled Olive's glass.

"Alan's back. He turned up this morning, I forgot to tell you. I told him there'd be room in the new house, if that's all right?"

"Of course." Olive answered rather too quickly. They were both embarrassed. She was ashamed how much she had been counting on being alone with Bob. He said, "He won't be around much. He's been called up."

Now she could be generous. "And he's going?"

"I don't know, I think so. He's an odd boy. He might do anything. I wish you'd talk to him."

"I'll try."

Olive wondered, thinking that after all they would have the house to themselves. "It's rather awful, isn't it, if you live as you want someone always seems to suffer for it."

He propped himself on his elbow and looked up at her. "If you mean Dennis, there's no connection. Whatever we did, it would have been the same for him, you must believe that."

"Perhaps." And her mother, the old woman shipwrecked in the small room? And Harold? And Dulcie, whom surely she could have helped more if she had tried just a little harder? She could not think of Chris, that was too close. "Well, at least Catherine's happy. And it looks as if Polly will be all right."

"Look, everyone's going. We ought to drink to something."

"The bride and groom? It'll be us next I suppose. I've never liked weddings." She was thinking that this was the only whole man she had met in her life and therefore their marriage would not be easy but at least it would be interesting. She felt not at all tight, but saw everything with an hallucinatory clarity. The light had changed and it seemed cold now under the tree. "What if it had been us, not them?"

"We'll be chucked out soon if we don't go."

"It's a terrible risk, isn't it, private life?"

"It depends how much you want from it."

"Everything."

"Well then, here's to private life." So they drank. Then it was raining and they had to run for cover.

A NOTE ON THE TYPE

The text of this book has been set on the Linotype in a type-face called "Baskerville." The face is a facsimile reproduction of types cast from molds made for John Baskerville (Mdccvi—Mdcclxxv) from his designs. The punches for the revived Linotype Baskerville were cut under the supervision of the English printer George W. Jones. John Baskerville's original face was one of the forerunners of the type-style known as "modern face" to printers: a "modern" of the period A.D. Mdccc.